EVIDENCE OF MURDER

Also by Lisa Black

Takeover

EVIDENCE
OF MURDER

LISA BLACK

WILLIAM MORROW
An Imprint of HarperCollins*Publishers*

EVIDENCE OF MURDER. Copyright © 2009 by Lisa Black. All rights reserved. Printed in the United States of America. No part of this book may be used or reproduced in any manner whatsoever without written permission except in the case of brief quotations embodied in critical articles and reviews. For information address HarperCollins Publishers, 10 East 53rd Street, New York, NY 10022.

HarperCollins books may be purchased for educational, business, or sales promotional use. For information please write: Special Markets Department, HarperCollins Publishers, 10 East 53rd Street, New York, NY 10022.

FIRST EDITION

Library of Congress Cataloging-in-Publication Data
Black, Lisa
   Evidence of Murder / Lisa Black.—1st ed.
      p. cm.
   ISBN 978-0-06-154448-4
   1. Women forensic scientists—Fiction. 2. Cleveland (Ohio)—Fiction. I. Title.
PS3602.L296E95 2009
813'.6—dc22   2008025028

09 10 11 12 13   OV/RRD   10 9 8 7 6 5 4 3 2 1

To my mother, Florence, and father, Stanley,
and my siblings, Mary, Susan, Mike, and John,
first in my heart
every minute of every day

CHAPTER 1

WEDNESDAY, MARCH 3

"I have a building full of dead people," Theresa MacLean told the detective. "I don't have time for one who isn't even dead."

Frank Patrick parked the car against the curb and gestured up at the antique brick architecture in front of them. "Not that we know of. But what woman runs out on a rich husband, a cool apartment, and her five-month-old daughter?"

"A stupid one." Theresa pulled her stocking cap more tightly over the red hair she hadn't bothered to curl, and took in the historic structure from a different perspective. "We're in Lakewood."

"So you did pay attention on the drive over from the morgue. I thought you'd slipped back into your coma."

She ignored the coma comment. "I know this place. You can see it from the rapid transit."

"It used to be the National Carbon Company," he told her. The redbrick building in front of her would have looked at home on the Oxford campus; its outbuildings, done in matching brick but with much less style, would not have.

"Why are you involved?" Theresa asked. Frank had been a Cleveland homicide detective for eight years, but the well-to-do suburb of Lakewood had its own force, and besides, the woman was only missing.

"Because of her job."

"At the carbon company?"

"No, this place has been closed for years. Her husband bought the vacant campus six months ago. I meant *her* job." He opened his door and got out, forcing her to follow suit. The March air hung icy and damp around Theresa's face. She pulled the padded jacket with MEDICAL EXAMINER printed on the back around herself more tightly, knowing it wouldn't do any good. She hadn't felt warm in eight months. But the lettering identified her as one of the M.E.'s staff, a forensic scientist, not a cop, so that witnesses and family members greeted her with a shade more warmth than they did police officers.

She waited for Frank to circle the car. Being the middle of a weekday didn't lessen the traffic on 117th and cars whizzed down the narrow pavement; everyone had somewhere to go and wanted to get there fast. Frank darted out of their way; the homicide detective had a long-legged gait and was slender and handsome, with a mustache to go with his light brown hair, but had no more fashion sense than she had, though she wouldn't dare say so. "And her job is?"

"Escort."

"What?"

"Escort. Was, actually—she quit on her wedding day. One of those pretty girls a businessman hires to take to cocktail parties so he can look like a player. The company—and I use the term loosely—is on West Twenty-fifth. I remember her boss from his humble origins and have been wanting to bust him for about fifteen years now. So if she's dead, I'm hoping it's got something to do with him."

"It's good to have a goal."

"Hey, I'm not hoping the woman's dead. I'm just hoping to bust her boss if she is. The Lakewood guys are in this with me, but right now they've got their hands full with that family that got wiped out over on Warren, so they don't mind if I look into it. Let's go in, I'm freezing."

"An escort."

"Which means her boss has an opening, if you're looking to make a switch." He grinned. She didn't. He stopped smiling. She felt guilty because he'd been making her laugh since she was three years old and knew he felt bad that he couldn't do it anymore. But she couldn't help it. Her sense of humor had died with her fiancé, Paul. "So you dragged me out here for a hooker on a bender?"

Humor fled his face as well. "Just take a look at the place, okay? Pick up some things that we can use for DNA testing if her body turns up and then you can go back to the trace evidence lab and hide behind your glass slides and microscopes."

She scowled, but then followed him up the cracked sidewalk and through the unlocked glass door; Frank had also been pushing her around since she was three and she had gotten used to it. Besides, if she argued with him for too long, he'd complain to his mother, who'd complain to her sister—Theresa's mother—who'd give her the concerned *Are you ever going to get your life back together?* looks she'd been giving out for the past eight months. Theresa had gotten used to those too.

Just keep going, she told herself. It's not as if you've got anything else to do.

The lobby smelled coldly musty. "They live in a factory?"

"No, the other buildings are the factory. This building used to be the offices. Apparently he's renovating it as living space for himself and his partner and the programmers. It's high-tech stuff and those types like to work unconventional hours. Sounds like he plans to be the Bill Gates of Cleveland. I got all this from the Lakewood cop who took the report; he was a whole lot more interested in the architecture than in our errant young mom."

The elevator took an inordinate amount of time to rise one floor, and Frank used the trip to tell her more about the missing Jillian Perry. Twenty-four, native of Cleveland, she lived with her husband of three weeks, Evan Kovacic, and her baby girl. Evan Kovacic owned and operated a video-game design firm. He had come home from a downtown meeting on Monday to find the door locked, Jillian gone, and the baby crying in her crib.

"And her husband knew about her former occupation."

"Absolutely. Says Jillian worked as a three-dimensional model."

"Dimensions, right. You keep saying *her* daughter," Theresa said as the claustrophobic elevator shuddered to a halt. "This baby isn't *his* daughter?"

"No. Jillian was pregnant when they met. I guess the father isn't in the picture."

Theresa snorted and nudged the sliding door with her foot to encourage it to open faster. "Great."

"We don't get to pick our victims, Tess."

"Tell me about it." The second-floor lobby had fresh carpeting but a gouge in the plaster outside door number 212. Frank gave her a warning look as he knocked, and she straightened her shoulders. *I'm a professional. Focus on the job. What do I need to do right now?*

I care about every victim. Even if she was a drug-addled slut.

Who doesn't give a crap about her own kid.

She thought that these were the things we say about other people in the shuttered rooms of our own minds, the harsh judgments we would never, ever confess to another living soul.

A man about her age—thirty-nine—opened the door. He had black hair cut fashionably close, and wore jeans and a dress shirt without a tie. The untucked shirt had a hard time staying neat over his medium girth. He seemed more like an overgrown boy than a large man. CNN broadcasters chattered in the background and someone had recently microwaved Italian food.

"Hi, I'm Evan. I'm glad you're on time, I do have to get back to work when we're done. But I let the sitter go home for lunch since I had to be here anyway, so I've got another half hour. Have you found out anything about Jillian? You're Detective Patrick, right?"

Frank introduced Theresa. Never touchy-feely and especially not with distraught family members, she would have been satisfied with a nod, but Evan Kovacic held out his hand, so she had to shake it. His fingers felt soft and too fleshy, and she couldn't picture him building microchips or whatever it was he did. She let him talk at her cousin while she took in the room.

Walking into the home of a stressed stranger no longer felt odd to her. She had done it at least once a week for the past dozen years. But she no longer found it fascinating either.

At least it was clean. The polished wood floors gleamed and the furniture arranged around the leather sofa held just enough of the

5

accoutrements of daily living to look comfortable. Lightweight draperies framed the window with a dramatic swoosh. Video-game designing must pay well.

"Nice place," she said, interrupting Evan Kovacic's questions. Then she cleared her throat and forced herself to enunciate. Somewhere along the line, talking to people had become an effort. "This is a lovely apartment."

"Jillian did the decorating," Evan told her, biting a nail. "She had—has—a real talent for it."

"I need to see her bedroom and bathroom, please." *Let's grab the DNA samples and get back to my routine.*

"In there." Evan Kovacic waved his hand at the hallway, and continued to ask Frank how the police go about looking for a woman who seemed to have disappeared off the face of the earth.

Theresa came to the bathroom first. She had no trouble guessing which toothbrush and razor and hairbrush belonged to the missing woman—Jillian apparently liked pink. Pink hand mirror, pink towels, pink makeup case with pink rhinestones. Theresa donned latex gloves and dropped the items she wanted into three separate manila envelopes. She didn't bother to label them, she could do that back at the lab; as long as the items remained in her custody, they did not have to be sealed immediately. She caught her own face in the mirror for a brief moment, her expression sour and irritated, and left the room.

Stuffing the envelopes into her camera bag, she stepped into the nursery, realized her mistake, and turned to go. But it had been seventeen years since Rachael had been an infant, so she tiptoed up to the gleaming white crib. Mothers never lost their professional curiosity about other people's children.

Jillian's daughter slept soundly on pink sheets printed with the word *Princess*, her little face scrunched, concentrating on some dream or the condition of her diaper or merely the new act of breathing. Light-colored down spread over her skull and both hands made loose fists, the fingernails impossibly small. Her skin was perfect and her bed smelled of baby powder and warmth.

I should feel something right now. Hope, sorrow, empathy. Anything. But I don't.

She left the room, backing away from the sleeping child as if the softest footfall might disturb her, though the men's voices only twenty feet away did not.

The Kovacics' bedroom lacked the immaculate quality of the nursery. The bedclothes had been pulled up in a quick attempt at neatness; satin sheets—what else?—slipped haphazardly from beneath a chocolate velour cover. The matching nightstands had been segregated—a pink ribbon, a book of crossword puzzles, and a jumble of earrings on hers, a handheld video game and a ball cap on his. Jillian's dresser held bottles of perfume and several framed photos, which Theresa glanced at. For a professional model—*and I use the term loosely*—there were no posed shots, just candid snaps of a blond woman, Evan, the baby, and various other people,

Theresa searched for a hamper. The toothbrush, hairbrush, and razor should be able to give them all the DNA they would need to compare to the body, if and when a body turned up, but it never hurt to make sure.

She opened the closet. Jillian's half bulged with low-cut blouses and clingy dresses in every color of the rainbow. Evan's half consisted of sweatshirts, T-shirts, and extreme-cold wear. Quilted nylon pants with FASTER emblazoned in yellow down one leg indicated a skier—no, not a skier, she mentally corrected upon spying a snowboard partially out of its duffel bag on the floor. Next to it sat a plastic laundry basket. Evan had obviously continued to pitch his T-shirts and briefs at it during the three days Jillian had been missing, making the basket only half of the time, because she had to dig down past three sets of men's underclothes and a few dress shirts to find more feminine items. Theresa pulled out a skirt, a V-necked sweater, and the requisite thong underwear, an article of clothing she could never bring herself to try. It looked like sheer torture. She dropped two of these in a fourth manila envelope; vaginal secretions would provide plenty of skin cells—epithelials—for DNA analysis. They might also reveal sperm that didn't belong to Evan, if there were some boyfriends or ex-clients in the picture, but Theresa couldn't see how that would be relevant. If the underwear was here and Jillian wasn't, then any wayward sperm on it probably didn't coincide with the crime. If there had been a crime. If Jillian hadn't simply found marriage and motherhood too confining, and left them behind with her pink towels.

Theresa stood, listening to her knees creak. She couldn't see what else to do. If Evan had killed his wife, he would hardly be letting Theresa poke around unsupervised. She saw no bloodstains or evidence of new paint or carpeting, which might imply a cleanup job. Jillian hadn't left any threatening letters or indiscreet photos lying around, though Theresa hadn't gone through her drawers and didn't intend to. She had come strictly to collect items for future DNA analysis and had no desire to see what ex–professional escorts stored in their bedroom drawers, what people who had a marriage, had a love, had a life kept close at hand. She had no desire to ponder the contrasts between their situation and hers.

Time to get back to the lab, where the cases were no more fascinating but at least the victims were demonstrably dead. No doubt Jillian would come home after an argument with her mother or new boyfriend or whoever she had gone to.

Inertia kept Theresa from moving, long enough to take another look at Jillian's pictures. She had been pretty, certainly, with clear, dewy skin and blond hair falling past her shoulder blades. Even in the hospital delivery room, wet with sweat and exhausted, she glowed as she held her newborn up for the camera. She beamed in her wedding dress, next to the tuxedoed Evan. She either hadn't gained much weight with the baby or had lost it quickly, Theresa thought with a twinge of jealousy. She herself gained and lost the same five pounds every week.

"Is that all you're going to do?" Evan Kovacic asked from the doorway, nodding at her camera bag with its protruding envelopes. "I mean, is there anything else I can give you that would help find her?"

What could she say? *That's it unless a body turns up?* She glanced at Frank, who stood behind Evan, but before Frank could take over the husband's eye fell on the photos. "She's so beautiful. And not just on the outside. I know she would never have left us, not voluntarily. She loved Cara. She loved me."

Theresa followed his line of sight to the photos. *Thanks a lot, Jillian. Thanks for dragging me across town for five minutes of work, thanks for perpetuating men's fantasies of women as nothing but pretty playthings, thanks for leaving your daughter to be raised by a guy who looks as if he can barely take care of himself. Great job.*

Theresa caught her cousin's eye, trying to signal: *Let's get out of here.*

Frank ignored her. "Mr. Kovacic, when you returned on Monday, the door was locked? Everything in place?"

"Yes. Jerry and I—Jerry Graham, he's my partner—we'd been at a software association meeting at Tower City all day. We got back about three in the afternoon."

"Who else would have been on the premises?"

"No one except Jillian and Cara. We're still setting up shop here, Jerry and I. We've got one programmer starting at the beginning of the month and another a week after that, and as soon as we get the manufacturing equipment set up, we'll take on another designer and about four techs—"

"Was the outside door unlocked? The lobby door downstairs?"

"Yeah, probably. We're in and out all day between this building and plants one and two—where we've begun setting up the equipment—so we don't bother locking it. We haven't had any problems with trespassers, and when we renovated we put in a good dead bolt on the apartment door. Though I doubt Jilly would have had it set during the day. I don't know. I guess anyone could have walked right in—"

Frank headed the man off before his mind could travel too far in that ominous direction. "You've searched the entire property?"

"I sure have. Twice. It's not as hard as it sounds, the buildings are empty for the most part, except for where we're stocking all the equipment in number one and setting up the manufacturing process in number two. But Jerry and I searched every inch. We can look again now, if you want."

Theresa frowned at Frank. He said, "The officer taking the report did a walk-through with you, right?"

"Yeah."

"I'm sure he would have noticed anything out of place." Like a dead body.

"I can't see why Jillian would have gone wandering around dusty old buildings anyway. It's been so cold, and she thought the dry air was bad for her skin. She was always so careful about her skin." He picked up his wedding picture. "It was all she had, really, her looks."

That didn't sound very nice. Theresa wondered if he always managed to be so tactful, or only when under stress. Yet his eyes filled with tears as he gazed at the photo.

He added, as the level of desperation in his voice climbed steadily, "I know wherever she is, she'll be worried sick about Cara and me. That's why you have to find her. She knows I can't raise a baby all by myself."

This should have been poignant, but sounded flat and tinny to Theresa's ears. She did not read anything into that reaction; everything sounded flat to her these days. But then he asked, "Are you two going to do the investigation into Jillian's disappearance?"

"We'll be working on it," Frank assured him. "With the Lakewood police."

Evan Kovacic had smooth skin and short, manicured fingernails; he had tucked the shirt in, so that now he looked like a frat boy who'd grown up to be pleasant and reasonably responsible. But his eyes—the color of the irises dark and solid, and hard as marble—swept her from the red hair that hadn't seen a grooming product in months to the scuffed Reeboks she wore to cushion her feet during the eight-hours-without-sitting days. He was assessing her competence, Theresa thought, and finding it lacking. Well, screw him.

But then he managed a smile. "Great."

Taught to be polite. Or a lack of confidence in me somehow reassures him. How much does he really want us to find Jillian?

She let her brain wander on this path for one brief moment. Jillian and her former job had become an embarrassment to the young entrepreneur. Marriage had not changed Jillian's personality or lifestyle and both had worn him down. He had a good idea where she was—holed up with a boyfriend, on a bender, under the Carnegie bridge with a needle in her arm—and didn't need that publicity. Having had a few days to think about it since making the original report, he now knew that he didn't want her back, but as legal husband and nice guy felt obligated to keep up the pretense.

Or perhaps Theresa saw nothing but pain and deceit in her world these days, and this poor guy had made an effort to keep his self-possession while begging them to bring his wife back. Being left with an infant to raise wouldn't make his busy days easier, and surely Jillian's looks helped him tolerate any other foibles.

"Good-bye, Mr. Kovacic." She left the room and the apartment, taking the stairs down.

Outside, the wind cut through her jacket in damp, knifelike slices. They were too close to Lake Erie to avoid the gusting air. Trees were bare, the sky an unrelenting gray. Patrons at the station across the street waited in their cars while gassing up. Unexpected sun in the morning had softened the top of the snow, but now it had frozen to a sheet of new ice once more, the inconsistency harder on living things than a low but steady clime would be. April wasn't the cruelest month in Cleveland, Ohio. March was.

"What do you think?" Frank said, sauntering up to the un-marked police car, pulling his keys from his pocket and jangling them too loudly.

"About what? Whether this bimbo is coming back or not? How should I know?"

He waited for a truck to pass, then walked quickly into the street to the other side of the car. Once the doors had closed, he started the car before saying, "You saw the place. Neat, clean. She wasn't some crack whore. The baby's room is—"

"Immaculate," Theresa said. "That could be the nanny, though. She must have been there all day every day for at least three days, right, if the husband's been at work?"

"He works on the premises, but yeah, the babysitter's been there. I didn't find any trace of drugs," Frank went on, "A little beer in the fridge, that's it."

"How did you get to look around the kitchen?"

"I had a few seconds while he went to see what you were doing. No prescription drugs in the kitchen cabinets or bathroom. Did you find anything in the bedroom?"

"I didn't really look, just collected some underwear."

He opened his mouth to make a comment, apparently remembered that Theresa was his first cousin, and shut it again. "I ran their financials too. Little bit of credit card debt—and who doesn't have that these days?—and a car loan. I didn't have time for more than the basic accounts, but when people run out it's usually because of love or money."

"Same reason they usually murder too." She didn't know why that popped out, since she doubted Jillian had left due to anything other than her own free will.

"Exactly," Frank said.

He spoke as if she had proven some point of his, which irritated her. "Fine. Where is her car?"

"In their garage. The officer who took the original report said it was locked, no signs of damage, no signs of foul play."

"And she's not in the trunk," she said.

"He checked."

"Her purse? Cell phone? Any bank withdrawals?"

"Her purse is still there in the apartment. Phone, money, L'Oreal lipstick in Brilliant Pink still there. How about it, cuz? When was the last time you left home without your purse?"

"The third grade."

"See why I think it's weird? It's as if she went out to get a paper and never came back."

They passed Lakewood Park, and she watched the whitecaps kick up the surface of Lake Erie. At one time this case would have interested her, prompted her to a panoply of theories regarding the fate of Jillian Perry. But that was before watching her fiancé bleed to death. Still, for Frank's sake and to forestall that sympathetic look she had come to dread, she made an effort. "What about the nanny?"

"You've got a nasty, suspicious turn of mind," he said, as if the fact delighted him. "Apparently Evan only hired her three days ago; she's fifty-five and a friend of his mother's. They never needed a babysitter before—they live at his company, and when Jillian worked, her jobs were mostly at night. I'll look into it, though."

They passed the Cleveland city limits, and Theresa grew tired of Jillian Perry and questions with no answers. "Okay. I've got

DNA in case her body turns up. That's all I can do for now, so let's get back to the lab. I have to go over the clothes from that woman they found in the park yesterday, make up some more acid phosphatase reagent, run the FTIR samples, order more evidence tape, and maybe eat lunch before Leo comes up with something else to dump on me."

"I'll take you to lunch."

She gave him a skeptical look. Her cousin could be generous to a fault in large ways, but had never in his life volunteered to pick up a check. "What do you want?"

"At Pier W. It's on the water."

Especially not at expensive restaurants. "I know where it is. We went there for my senior prom. What do you want?"

"The salty wind in your hair—"

"Lake Erie is freshwater, and glaciers give off warmer air at this time of the year. What do you want?"

"Come with me to talk to Georgie, Jillian's boss. The escort-service guy."

"I'm not a freakin' cop, Frank. I'm a scientist. I work with microscopes and fibers. I don't interrogate people, and not even lunch at Pier W is worth chatting with a pimp!"

"He's not a pimp," he corrected her, while pointedly missing the I-90 on-ramp. "He's a businessman. Come on, this guy is never around women he can't intimidate or pay off. He won't know what to do with you sitting there."

"Don't you—"

She had almost said *Don't you have a partner?* Before she remembered that no, he didn't, that his last partner had been shot in a bank robbery, the partner he had resented more than liked, the partner she had been engaged to marry, and since then he had managed to circumvent all efforts of the department to assign him another. And she remembered something else, something that had existed in another time, another life—sympathy for someone other than herself.

"Okay," she said. "But I'm ordering lobster. *And* the Brie plate."

CHAPTER 2

George Panapoulos—aka Georgie Porgie—worked out of a storefront on West Twenty-fifth, just two blocks from the West Side Market, sandwiched in between a bail bondsman and a used-appliance dealer. He had tried to add a splash of color to the grimy street, however, spelling out BEAUTIFUL GIRLZ! in six-inch-high fluorescent pink letters along the window. The inside smelled of bug spray and cigarette smoke, but the receptionist lived up to the advertising, a petite blond in spandex, her eyes a crystal blue and slightly unfocused.

"I'm here to see Georgie," Frank told her in the commanding tone he'd practiced on Theresa since she was four. She'd stopped listening at six, but it still worked on other people.

Heavy footsteps made the thin walls tremble, and Georgie appeared with a cigarette in one hand and a stack of envelopes in the other. Theresa had expected a stereotype, a used-car salesman with lots of gold jewelry, but George Panapoulos looked more like an aging college student. He had neatly trimmed black hair and wore a maroon sweatshirt with jeans. The only concessions to flash were a stylish goatee and a gold band with one fat diamond on his right hand. He only grinned when he saw Frank, and then his eye fell on Theresa. Like her cousin had said earlier, he opened his mouth to make a comment, then apparently thought better of it. "What can I do for you, Detective?"

"I need to ask you about one of your ex-employees. In private."

"I'm a little busy right now—"

Frank waited.

"—but I'll take time for anything that concerns my girls. Come on back." He turned away from them without hesitation and led the way through a narrow hallway with stained wallpaper.

His office continued to work against stereotype. Papers, manila folders, and pictures of girls covered the desk, the bookshelf, and a battered credenza. More pictures covered the walls—girls of every race, size, and hair color, including a few not found in nature; girls in bikinis or less; girls in full-length gowns—pinned up willy-nilly with thumbtacks or even straight pins. It took Theresa a full minute to find Jillian's. Theresa now believed in Georgie's legitimacy—the deluge of young girls seemed no worse than the average magazine or group of billboards, and no way would a pimp keep this much paperwork.

The man no longer in question threw himself into a desk chair covered in 1970s orange vinyl and motioned for them to sit. His guest chairs were the only two uncluttered surfaces in the room. "Now don't tell me one of my girls is in trouble, because I won't believe it. They're all clean. I'm legit now."

"So you told me," Frank said.

"It's worth it, let me tell you. It's worth the taxes and the forms and having to send out those friggin' W-2s every January. I can sleep at night, I don't have to take my gun into the shower with me, and I don't have to call my lawyer every time someone like you shows up at my door."

"I'm happy that you've seen the light."

Georgie glanced at Theresa; again, he seemed on the verge of asking who she was, and then didn't. Her cousin had been right. Georgie Porgie didn't know what to do with her. She perused the photos of girls with lots of makeup and not enough body fat, and ignored him.

"So what are you here about?" he asked again. A phone rang in the lobby, abruptly cut off as the receptionist snatched it up.

"Jillian."

"Which Jillian?"

"How many you got?"

"Three." A dented space heater in the corner kicked on, pushing out puny waves of warm air to do what they could against the heavy dampness, and he raised his voice to be heard over the rattling heater. "Funny, come to think of it. It's not a common name these days."

"Jillian Kovacic."

"You mean Perry."

Frank absently patted the pack of cigarettes in his front shirt pocket; the heavily nicotined smell of the place must have been tempting him. "So you do know which Jillian I mean."

"She was Perry here. She didn't officially quit until she got him up the aisle. Jillian hedges her bets."

"Didn't jump ship until she had the lifeboat in position?" Frank prodded.

"Jillian's not dumb. Besides, she seemed to think her new hubby was going to be a big shot soon and didn't want her job distracting people from his."

"You didn't care that she got married?"

"Why would I care?"

"Maybe Jillian was more than an employee."

"Yeah, so I killed her because I was jealous?" Georgie shook his head and pulled a cigarette from a pack on his desk, looking less like a college student with every minute as both face and voice lost their phony friendliness. "Listen, I've got forty-six girls working for me and Jillian is by no means the hottest one. I expected her to quit once she didn't need the dough no more. I couldn't believe she came back after having the baby. She lost that weight quick, though, I'll say that for her."

Frank let him wind down. "What makes you think she's been killed?"

Georgie didn't hesitate. "Her husband. He's called here twice a day for the past three days asking if I have heard from her, and insisting that she would never just take off and not tell anyone where she went. And he's right about that. Jillian was pretty reliable. That's why I kept her on the payroll even though she couldn't work once the baby began to show."

Frank gave no sign of accepting this explanation, though it sounded reasonable to Theresa. Instead, he asked, "Can you think of anyone who might have wanted to kill her?"

"Sure. Her husband."

"Why would her husband kill her?"

"Spoken like the true bachelor you are, Patrick. Husbands don't need a reason. Neither do wives. Marriage is enough to turn anyone homicidal."

"Speaking from experience? As I recall, that one girl thought you were going to marry her. What was her name? Debbie? Destiny?"

"Diana. I was, too. I still miss her every day," Georgie said with patent innocence. But his body had tensed until the cords in his neck bulged under the skin. He flicked open a silver lighter and thumbed the roller against the flint with more force than necessary.

"She had cigarette burns up and down her right arm," Frank added.

The man took a deep puff, then said, "That's awful," with no inflection whatsoever.

Theresa felt a chill that had nothing to do with the space heater kicking off. What *was* she doing here? Her job was to look at a body or a room or a piece of clothing and discern the relevant facts about those things, to give the investigators what they needed to catch people like Georgie. It wasn't her job to sit there with Georgie. People weren't like inanimate objects. People lied.

On the other hand, she might try to observe something useful. She didn't dare interrupt Frank. She'd started talking in the middle of his guitar playing one day and he'd given her the cold shoulder for a month, which, at thirteen, seemed like a year.

Georgie's hair had thinned a bit on top, revealing a birthmark and an S-shaped scar near the temple. His pupils didn't seem to jump when they traveled from Frank to her and back again, which should mean he had no illegal drugs in his system. Nicotine stained his left-hand fingers, but he held the glowing butt in his right hand. Ambidextrous? Or trained to smoke with any free hand? He had another scar across the right thumb. An oil spot marred the elbow of the maroon sweatshirt, and he didn't rest his back flat against the orange vinyl, which made her think he had a gun tucked into the waistband of his pants. This didn't concern her much; every day found her surrounded by men with guns. Up the hall, the receptionist giggled into the phone.

"Anybody else might mean Jillian harm?" Frank was asking.

"Sure," the man said again. "Her other boyfriend. The one she didn't marry."

"How many boyfriends did Jillian have?"

"Just the two. The one she didn't marry, and the one she did. Those are all I know of, anyway."

Theresa rolled her eyes, then felt embarrassed when the man across the desk noticed. She buried her nose in a brochure. *Beautiful Girlz* seemed to be the official name of the place. *Available for trade shows, corporate excursions, and private parties.* Except that Georgie had misspelled *corporate* as *corporete.*

"His name?"

"Drew, and I only know that because he'd call all the time when Jillian worked here. He'd drive the receptionists nuts trying to leave messages, but we don't take messages for anyone but me here, or else this place would turn into a lonely hearts switchboard."

"Did he know she got married?"

"He must have. The calls stopped when her employment did. But then he started up again the past three days, looking for Jillian."

"This ex-boyfriend's been calling here?"

"Even more than the husband. He's been driving poor Vangie out there crazy. If you talk to him, tell him to stop or I'll charge him with harassment."

"I'll need his last name."

"I don't have it. Vangie might. He'd chat with her and her soft little heart all the time until she got tired of it and learned to cut him short, which made him turn nasty. My other receptionist just hangs up on him. Him, and the thousand other mopes who call here, trying to get private time with my girls." His mouth took on a pouty shape as he seemed to contemplate the nerve of these guys, thinking they could get for free what he had invested in, cultivated. Theresa almost felt a twinge of empathy for him. *It's probably how a Blockbuster manager feels about pirated movies,* she thought.

"How long did Jillian work for you?"

"About a year and a half. Subtracting six months for the baby body, of course. Who're you, anyway?" he apparently now felt comfortable enough to ask Theresa. She introduced herself, and Georgie's heavy eyebrows came together. "M.E.? Like you do autopsies?"

"No, I'm a forensic scientist."

"But that's the morgue, right?"

"Yes."

He puffed for a moment, holding her gaze with either concern or curiosity in his eyes. "So Jillian really is dead?"

Frank cut in. "Only missing. When was the last time you saw Jillian?"

"A week after the wedding. She came in to pick up her last check, from a tech conference last month—three days of holding up a big microchip on a revolving stage, not real classy, but I don't design the shows, just staff them. I told her I had a cocktail party coming up, a real estate developer wanted to entertain some Japanese investors. They love blondes, and Jillian was good at that sort of thing. Smart enough to hold up her end of the conversation but

23

too sweet to do much other than agree with whatever was said. She laughed and said no, she was out for good, and left. That was it."

"She say anything about her husband, her baby? Troubles at home?"

"We didn't chat. Just business."

"She have any repeat customers? Other than Drew?"

"Drew ain't a customer, he's a problem. Besides, Jillian don't have customers. *I* have customers."

"And you get feedback from them, right? Anyone comment on Jillian in particular? Request another performance?"

"Nope."

"Never?"

"No. Look, everyone *liked* Jillian, I'm not saying otherwise, but they like all my girls. Why not? They're quality."

"I see."

"No, you don't." Georgie seemed to be working on a good case of righteous indignation. "You think I'm still a pimp. This is different. These girls are the ones who aren't pretty enough to be models but aren't desperate enough to be hookers. They don't want to be hookers, and they don't have to be. All they have to do is stand up straight and look pretty, laugh at a guy's joke even if it's in another language, and occasionally hold up a product or lean against a car. That's it."

Frank remained impassive. "They never take on side jobs?"

"No. Not like you mean. Do they sometimes date guys they meet through a job? Sure. Doesn't everyone?"

Theresa caught herself nodding, stopped, and coughed. The smoke-scented air had grown oppressive, and the space heater only made it worse. She wanted to leave.

"Did Jillian?" Frank pressed.

"I wouldn't know."

"What did she tell you about her fiancé, when she worked here?"

"You're not listening to me, Detective. I saw Jillian maybe once a week or less. We didn't confide in each other about nothing, not her baby, not the dresses she picked out for the bridesmaids, not nothing."

"If I find out you know more about Jillian than you're telling me, Georgie—"

"What? You'll what? There's nothing you can do. I'm legitimate now."

"Nobody's legit when it comes to murder."

"Jillian's not dead." Georgie stood up, apparently to signal the end of the interview and his patience. But then his expression changed and that look returned, the slight frown and the glittering eyes, worry combined with excited curiosity. "At least I hope not."

Theresa wasted no time in plunging out to the street, sucking in the cold air until her sinuses hurt. Frank had lingered to speak to the receptionist, and he had the car keys, so she stayed close to the storefront door and tried to blend in. She eyed anyone who passed, without making eye contact, then felt slightly ridiculous as two little girls walked by without, apparently, a care in the world. West Twenty-fifth might not be Pepper Pike, but it was hardly a war zone.

Frank emerged but waited until they got in the car, doors shut against the chill and the poverty. "What do you think?"

"That guy was a pimp?"

"You think I'm making that up?" Frank cranked up the heat,

nearly hard enough to break the knob. "Yes, he was a pimp. Don't let that roly-poly friendly-guy act throw you off."

"He just didn't seem that bad to me."

A stop sign gave him a chance to turn and face her. "For five years he worked from a crib in the warehouse district. During that time I fished two of his girls out of the Cuyahoga—and his fiancée, Diana? Found her in a Dumpster behind Tower City. Don't let him fool you. Not for one second."

Her sinuses ached even more. "Then what's your plan here? Did you think you could ask him if he killed Jillian and he'd say yes, here's where you'll find her body?"

"You never know, cuz." The huge stone men holding up the Lorain-Carnegie Bridge looked down upon them as they passed. "You never know."

"His affect when he talked about that other girl, Diana, seemed totally different from when he spoke of Jillian. If the idea that Jillian is dead didn't come as a surprise, then he's a hell of an actor. Plus, Jillian's picture hung on the wall with the others, but another girl's partially overlapped it. That doesn't speak of any elevated status."

"This guy isn't about sentiment, Tess. That's what I'm trying to tell you."

"What did Vangie say?"

"She backs up her boss, says Georgie didn't pay more attention to Jillian than to any of the other girls. And that this Drew's last name is Fleming. He's been calling Jillian for over a year. Vangie thinks they might have met at a 'company function,' as she puts it, but she's not sure. She's never met him. She thought he sounded sweet at first, but now hears his voice in her sleep and is damn sick of it."

"And what did Vangie think of the husband?"

"That Evan is the catch of a lifetime. Not the politest guy on the phone, but his income made him worth it." Frank let her ponder this through downtown Cleveland and out to University Circle. After maneuvering the Crown Vic through the tight parking lot behind the county medical examiner's office, he paused behind the loading dock to let her out. "So where's your money? On the husband or the stalker?"

She stepped into the half-frozen air once more, pulling her camera bag from the passenger-seat floor. "My money is on Jillian getting tired of washing dishes and changing diapers. Girls who work for guys like Georgie don't come from happy backgrounds and they don't lead stable lives. You'll find her crying on the shoulder of the persistent Drew."

"Then why would Drew be calling Georgie?"

"Some other guy, then. Hey." She leaned in and peered at her cousin. "Weren't you going to buy me lunch?"

He turned his watch toward her. "It's already one thirty, cuz. I don't want to get you in trouble with Leo."

She narrowed her eyes with a technique she had worked on until it flustered most men and some women. "I'm going to tell your mother you took me to visit a pimp."

"He's not a pimp," Frank corrected her before driving off. "He's a businessman."

CHAPTER 3

Theresa didn't wait to watch him leave, but merely pulled her coat closed long enough to get through the back door and into the loading dock area. The smell of the building greeted her along with its warmth, but she had long grown used to the mix: the tinny smell of blood, the sharp odor of formalin, and the month-old garbage tang of decomposing flesh. A white-coated deskman blocked her way as he helped two funeral-home transport men to zip the M.E.'s white plastic body bag into a plush burgundy one so that the dead could be dressed for the trip with a little more dignity. The deskman moved to let her pass with a quiet "good afternoon." It occurred to her that it had been eight months and her coworkers still treated her gently. This was an unfair burden on them; M.E. staff members, who spent all day around the dead, were never solemn except in the presence of family members and news reporters, and not even the latter most of the time. Her mother was right. She had to get her life back to normal. Or at least learn to fake it more convincingly.

One of these days.

She took the elevator instead of the stairs and hung her coat up just before the trace department supervisor found her. Leo had two inches of height on her but thirty less pounds, as if his nervous system had taken over and sucked the juices from all other body tissue. He waved a sheaf of papers. "We have a problem."

This didn't impress her coming from a man whose personal-threat assessment level remained permanently stuck on red. "I'm a little busy, Leo. I have to photo and tape the clothing from yesterday's homicide—that woman they found in Rockefeller Park."

"She came in yesterday morning and you're just now getting to her clothing?"

"It was drying."

"Yeah, right. Richard Springer wrote the judge and said you refused to comply with the court order for defense testing."

Theresa headed for the coffeemaker, and not even Leo dared to get in her way when on that path. Of course, since Leo insisted on keeping the machine in his office, this move didn't get rid of him either, and he followed. Springer, a defense-hired expert, had visited the lab weeks before to perform his own examination of fiber evidence.

"He said you were uncooperative." Leo rattled the sheets for emphasis.

"Because I let him make his own slides? How else would he know they were from the real evidence unless he prepared them himself? It's not my problem if he doesn't like to get his fingers in the mounting media."

"He says you created a, let me quote this here, 'unfairly prejudicial work environment.' What the hell does he mean by that?"

"Probably that I told him his client is guilty as hell." She stirred in creamer with a wooden stick; they used to use the sticks for blood enzyme work, now supplanted by DNA. She continued to order the sticks. They made great coffee stirrers.

The secretary strolled in, caught a glimpse of Leo's face, dropped some typed reports on his desk, and sidled right out again, not even risking an empathetic glance in Theresa's direction.

"Terrific. Nothing like demonstrating an inability to be objective." Leo crossed his arms and stared her down. "Is that what he's referring to when he says you were blatantly hostile?"

"Well—" She sipped her coffee as if trying to remember, when of course she remembered perfectly. The human mind seemed perverse in that way; it recalled moments of misery with photographic precision, but pictures of happy times got fuzzy around the edges. Or maybe it was just her.

"Well, what?" Leo demanded.

"I may have wondered aloud how he shaved in the morning, what with the difficulty he must have looking at himself in the mirror."

Leo's mouth twitched, almost in a grin, but he stifled it. "And you thought he'd just let that slide? You think the judge will wink at a charge of interfering in a criminal defense?"

"He got to do the analysis he wanted to do. No court in the world says I have to be friendly."

"Not friendly is a world away from outwardly hostile."

She twirled the loose knob on Leo's barrister's bookcase. The books and papers inside pressed against the glass as if pleading for escape. "This was after he started asking where I went to school, how long I'd been in forensics, why I hadn't poured a cast of the shoe print found under the window, crap like that."

"Well?"

"Well what?"

"Why didn't you pour a cast of the shoe print?"

"Because it was two o'clock in the morning, because the budget wouldn't allow us to order more dental stone, because it wasn't a homicide so we had a live witness."

"And maybe you just didn't care."

She stirred her coffee.

"Not caring is a dangerous condition in this line of work."

"I care." Now. In the middle of the night, when you hadn't slept well for months, when dying sounded like the only reward for living, caring had proved much more difficult. But she couldn't confess that to herself, much less to Leo. "He was fishing for weaknesses so he could report back to his client and collect his fee."

"That's his job."

"No, his job is to report facts and form an expert opinion. It's the lawyer's job to impeach me, and it's not even *his* job, it's his job to present his client's case in the best possible light, not to use the most underhanded tactics he can think of to shred an impartial fact finder just so he can get a rapist out on the street again. Do any of these guys ever wonder how they'd feel if one of their former clients moved in next door? Would they still let their kids play in the backyard?"

"Theresa—"

"So he was hostile first," she finished.

"Is that what you're going to tell the judge? He started it? Sure, the school-yard defense never fails to impress the court."

"His client raped a teenager at knife point. And I should guard the feelings of some hired whore trying to get him off?"

"That's what jury trials are for. What *you're* for is to maintain the reputation of this lab."

"No, I'm here for the teenager, and to make sure the guy who did that to her goes away and never comes back."

Then you should have cast the damn shoe print, shouldn't you?

Leo's elongated, sallow face exhibited several tics at once. One jumped at the outer edge of his left eyelid. A second prompted the muscles to bunch around the vein in his right temple. A third caused his mouth to open and say, "All the bad guys will come back if the work of this lab is not completely above reproach."

Leo spoke the truth, even if the trace evidence department provided his only *raison d'être*, until he could not distinguish between the prestige and reputation of the lab and himself, and vice versa, though she would not say so, because if she did, she would surely be fired. Leo could weather any disaster except a blow to his ego. She wondered if it would be worth it but knew it wouldn't, not with Rachael's college tuition looming on the horizon. Her exhaled breath sent the surface of her coffee into ripples and she thought of student loans and the young female victim: "I know. Sorry."

"Sorry? He's coming back here on Friday with the friggin' defense team *and* the judge and you're sorry?"

"He's dragging a judge here? Who the hell is this guy?"

"I expect we'll find out." A good supervisor would have let her stew for a while, think it over, but while Leo had his talents, supervising had never been one of them. So the man who spent at least one day each week red-faced and screaming added, "You didn't used to have control issues."

Again, he spoke the truth. Strict self-control had gotten her over the speed bumps of life, from her father dying a few days after her fourteenth birthday, to her husband racking up more girl-friends after their wedding than before, to raising a teenager. But it couldn't get her past watching, via security cameras, her fiancé bleed to death on the marble floor of a bank building.

Don't think. Just keep going.

"Maybe it's age," she told Leo. "I'm getting cranky as I push forty."

His tone softened. "Maybe you've got that posttraumatic stress stuff from someone putting a gun to your head during that bank robbery. Just be ready to be nice to this guy when he comes back here on Friday. No comments on anything but the weather, got it?"

Nothing could be quite as deconstructing as unexpected empathy. "Sure."

"And go take care of that homicide clothing."

She took her coffee with her, down three flights of steps to the amphitheater, and retrieved the dead woman's clothing from the locked trap room. Her name had been Sarah Taylor—the killer had emptied her wallet of money but not ID. A movie-star name but not a movie-star life. The thirty-year-old had supplemented her welfare checks with sporadic work as a prostitute. The killer had left her body propped up against the statue of Goethe and Schiller in the German section. The Cleveland Cultural Gardens in Rockefeller Park, begun in 1916, had areas dedicated to twenty-four different nationalities. Despite the park's beauty, hers had not been the first body to appear there. Theresa wondered what the two poet-philosophers would have had to say about that.

Sarah Taylor had been strangled with her bra, and had shred-ded her own neck with acrylic nails as she fought for air. Theresa needed to tape the clothing for hairs, fibers, and other trace evidence the killer might have deposited during the brutal attack. The snow-soaked articles had needed to dry first—she hadn't entirely fabricated that—but they had hung around long enough, and besides, it gave her something to do until her brain forgot all about defense experts, irritated bosses, and Jillian Perry.

Until her body turned up at Edgewater Park, two days later.

CHAPTER 4

"I hope you weren't planning on going home anytime soon," the DNA analyst, Don Delgado, said to her at four o'clock that same Wednesday.

"It's always a bad sign when you begin conversations that way."

"You ain't kidding. We got a dead kid."

Everyone in law enforcement cringed at those words, perhaps because it made them think of their own children, perhaps because even bad kids were still kids, perhaps because they saw too many of them. Like most of her responses, Theresa had learned to stifle this one. "Sure, I can use the overtime. Rachael will be picking out a college soon. When will the kid get here?"

"They want us to go there. Apparently the circumstances are unusual."

She folded up the last of the murdered prostitute's clothing and sealed the bag with red tape, adding her initials and the date. "Unusual how?"

"He's fifteen and he's in the woods behind the zoo. That's all I know."

"The woods, as in outside?"

"It's kind of hard to have a woods inside."

"And the temperature is?"

"Five. Fahrenheit. And I didn't wear my parka today either," he added with deep gloom.

She gathered up the sealed paper bags into one larger one, to store on the shelves of the trap room, puzzling over this statement. Usually only one person from the lab went to a crime scene—they lacked the manpower to work in teams. "Are you joining me? Who is this boy? Somebody . . . ?" She hesitated at the word *important*. Every human was important. Unfortunately, some people would always be considered more important than others, and this remained as true in death as in life.

"All I know is, he lived in the area."

Hardly rich, then. So why—the morning's conversation with Leo came back to her. "It's not the kid, it's me, isn't it? Leo is sending you along to make sure I don't screw up."

Don rubbed his eyes, stood up, and said nothing, which probably meant that those had been Leo's exact words. Don would never lie to her.

"I can be ready in ten minutes," she told him.

Don parked the county station wagon on the side of Park Road, behind Frank's worn Crown Vic, and Theresa pulled her crime scene kit from the backseat. The snowy expanse between the asphalt and the tree line had been reduced to a fractured mess of shoe prints and crime scene tape. One uniformed officer kept watch while the others huddled at the trees. Theresa wore a scarf, earmuffs, and two pairs of gloves, but the air wove through those items as if they were made of mesh. She complained as much to Don as they fought their way through the thick white blanket of frozen raindrops.

"Yeah," he said, panting, "but it's a dry cold."

"All the DNA analysts in this country, and I get Henny Youngman."

"Who?"

"You're too young. Hey, cuz," she greeted Frank, who waited for them under the boughs of a huge oak. "Do you know what my mother will say to you if I get frostbite?"

"She'll say you should have dressed warmer. Hi, Don. Okay, here it is: we got a fifteen-year-old white male, frozen pretty stiff, no signs of OD or violence. He lives right behind here on West Thirty-eighth"—Theresa turned to glance at the street of close-packed homes; even a coating of snow could not disguise the general untidiness—"and there's sort of a path through here to the baseball park."

"Where's the zoo?" Theresa asked, and realized she'd been hoping for a glimpse of the animals.

"That way, on the other side of Fulton." He gestured to his left. "So maybe this kid was heading for the baseball diamond, a popular hangout even in winter, or taking a walk. Either way, he's pretty dead."

"Who found him?" Don asked.

"His mother."

So many questions occurred to Theresa that she didn't know which to ask first. "Wh—"

Frank nodded at a woman standing thirty feet away, farther

in the woods. Her face had reddened from tears or the cold and she held a handkerchief to her nose, but cried only in occasional gasps. The collar on her quilted jacket had been turned up to meet her short graying curls. She spoke to two officers, one of whom jotted notes in a small book. "The kid, Jacob Wheeler, argued with her after school yesterday and stalked off, then didn't come home last night. She didn't call the police because it had happened before. The kid's not major trouble—he has one arrest for petty theft from the Home Depot at the Steelyard shopping center, charges dropped—but he has flopped with friends when he's ticked off at her. No drug history, at least according to Mom, but I get the impression he's definitely not on the honor roll. Anyway, when he didn't come home from school, his mother called and found out he hadn't gone at all, and got worried enough to go looking for him."

"Out here?"

"He spends a lot of time out here, she says, especially in the summer. Again, I get the impression he's enough of a snot to alienate the other kids on the street, so he'd kick around in here by himself. Mom only knows two of his friends and called both last night and this afternoon, but they gave the usual know-nothing answers."

"So he comes out here to sulk and winds up freezing to death?" Rachael often left the house to walk off a snit, but had better sense than to die of exposure. At least Theresa hoped so. Sense did not seem to be hardwired into the teenage brain.

"That, we're not so sure of. Come on, follow me."

The trees should have protected them from the icy wind, but somehow it didn't feel like that. Snow had slipped into Theresa's shoes and melted. The air smelled of cold, and trees, even without their leaves, muffled the hum of traffic on I-71. Slush and dead twigs snapped under their feet. "Sort of a path" described it pretty well, since it left room for single-file movement only. A lone officer guarded the body. He stamped his feet, and Theresa hoped he wouldn't stamp them on anything important.

At his feet sat a dead, frozen boy.

Jacob Wheeler wore a heavy Timberland jacket but, like many stubborn teenage boys, no hat or scarf. His arms were crossed over his chest with his hands under his armpits, his knees drawn up almost to his chin, his feet in scuffed work boots. Unkempt brown hair covered his ears and part of his face, but Theresa noted thin lips and high cheekbones, plus a few assorted body piercings. His eyes were closed. The pockets of his coat had been turned out and the contents set on a blank sheet of notebook paper.

Theresa sighed, her exhaled breath briefly but clearly visible. "Too mad to go home, he stays out here to get good and miserable first so he could think of himself as a victim."

"Take a look at his head," Frank told her.

She stepped closer, keeping her feet on the path of already-trampled prints. The boy had his chin down, tucked into the shelter of his chest and knees, the top of his head exposed. A drop of blood had dried at the hairline of his right temple.

Theresa retreated, found a safe spot for her crime scene kit, and turned the camera on. Then she approached the body again, Don close behind her.

After she photographed the body, she sacrificed her two pairs of warm gloves for latex ones and parted the boy's hair with her fingers. The blood had trickled from a cut to his scalp, about an inch long but not terribly deep. The area had begun to bruise. "It hardly seems enough to kill him."

"Victims don't usually sit meekly by and let someone slug them either," Don said. "I'll bet he got in a fight and then came here to think it over. Perhaps it disoriented him enough that he sat down to rest and never got up again."

Frank added, "There are two shoe prints up the trail and more around the back of this tree that the cops swear aren't theirs, so the scuffle could have occurred here. It's not a convenient place to dump a body, and he's one-forty if he's a pound, so I can't see someone lugging him all the way in here just to get rid of him. But the guy must have walked back toward Park Road and not the ballpark, unless he could fly. Then Mom and the cops and you and I obliterated his prints. We haven't looked at the boy's shoes yet. We were waiting for you."

Theresa crouched next to Don and poked at the meager belongings removed from the boy's pockets. Jacob had carried his wallet with two dollars and fifty-three cents in it, an iPod, and a spring-loaded knife in excellent condition. "So he met someone out here?"

"His dealer, I'll bet," Frank said. "No matter what Mom says, no doubt this kid had some connections. He tries to stiff the guy—no pun intended—or they disagree on terms."

Don suggested, "A girlfriend? She took her purse to his head when he tried to get friskier than she was in the mood for?"

Theresa shook her head. "Not unless she carries a brick in her purse. What about his two friends? I assume you've sent a car to their homes?"

Frank nodded. "It's kind of weird if you think about it."

"What is? I mean, aside from a teenager freezing to death five hundred feet from his house?"

"This is the second frozen body we've found in as many weeks, and both sitting up against something. Usually our frozen people are in cars or apartments where the heat was turned off or something, not usually completely *outside*." No one in Cleveland took the weather that casually, not even murderers.

"She was a black thirty-year-old hooker, and she was strangled. This is a white high school student with a bump on his head. Not too many similarities there. Speaking of his bump, any sign of a weapon?"

"We're surrounded by them," Frank said.

She looked around. The open spaces between tree trunks bulged with fallen limbs, twigs, and dirt, all melting into the same shade of white-topped brown. Snow penetrated the canopy in inconsistent patches, making it impossible to tell what might have been recently disturbed, whether a piece of wood had been flung in from the path or had been lying there since the previous fall. They would canvass, but a needle in a haystack would be a breeze by comparison. She got on the other side of the boy and motioned to Don. "Let's turn him. I want to get a look at his shoes."

The boy wore Nikes with a standard waffle pattern. Stepping gingerly, Theresa noted that the prints farther up the trail matched his down to a worn spot on the right toe, as if he had continued along the path for a few feet and then stopped. Had his attacker called out to him? Then he'd turned back, because he knew who it was.

The print to the right of the tree, however, consisted of plain tread lines crossing the foot, almost like Keds or some other light-weight wear. It certainly didn't belong to the victim or any of the large men surrounding her now. "What did the mother do when she found the body?"

Frank said, "Screamed, touched his face, and checked his neck for a pulse—as if his subzero temperature didn't tip her off—and ran back to her house to call 911."

"That's all?"

"I asked her three times."

The print looked too large for the mother, anyway. "We're going to have to cast that."

"In snow?" Don asked. "I thought that was, like, nearly impossible."

"Just about. But after my last experience with shoe prints I didn't lift, I'm not taking any chances." Casting compound generated heat as it hardened, which, obviously, had a deleterious effect on prints in snow. Some precasting sprays provided limited help. But forensic scientists didn't get to create their scenes; they could only work with what they were given. "I'll get the tripod and the shutter remote for the camera."

Theresa and Don examined Jacob's bedroom with its worn orange carpeting but found only a few Ecstasy tablets and one well-smoked marijuana roach. A few violent drawings accompanied his sporadic note taking during classes, but no letters or journals turned up and only a few phone numbers, which Frank would run down. Jacob had apparently spent his days playing video games, reading comic books, and not listening to his mother.

"His father left for good two years ago, but he never had been around much," his mother, Ellen, had wearily described from the doorway as she watched them work. A tough life had leached away muscles and fat and left a bit of padded skin over bones. Theresa had at least six inches and more pounds than she wanted to think about on the poor woman. "I just never *got* Jacob. I tried tough love, but as hard as I could be on him, he could say much harsher things to me. I tried talking about his feelings—he ignored me. When I tried restricting his video games, he broke into my room as soon as I went to work and got them back. I got tired of—when he *did* speak, which wasn't often, he just wouldn't give me a kind word. Ever."

One of the advantages of cases involving teenagers had to be that Rachael suddenly became an angel by comparison. Theresa decided to tell her so that evening.

Her phone beeped. A text message, a form of communication she had not yet grown accustomed to—typing on a teeny number pad required too much patience and she couldn't bring herself to use the shorthand devised by the young and hip. Chris Cavanaugh, the hostage negotiator who had handled the armed-robbery standoff that had killed Paul and nearly herself, had sent a message: *Can you meet me for lunch?*

As if on cue, her stomach grumbled. With one thumbnail, she punched out: *No.*

She tucked the phone neatly back into its clip on her belt. Then she picked up a baseball glove, nearly hidden under a pile of black T-shirts. "Did he play at the diamond there, the one the path led to?"

Ellen shook her head. "Not since he was little. His father liked baseball. Never played with him, of course, but liked it."

Theresa looked around. "I don't see a bat."

"He lost that years ago." The words caught in her throat and came out as a mangled sob. "He lost everything, years ago."

CHAPTER 5

FRIDAY, MARCH 5

Jillian Perry's body was found at approximately 8:00 on Friday morning.

Don came down to the amphitheater to tell her, and also to help with Jacob Wheeler. The kid had now thawed out enough for her to remove the clothing and unclench his fists, one of which held a piece of colored paper. As with the dead woman from the Cultural Gardens, Theresa hung his clothes to dry thoroughly before taping. His wallet contained a credit card with his neighbor's name on it, apparently stolen from his mail earlier that month. That, along with the iPod in his pocket, ruled out robbery. The scrap in his fist, about an inch square, had been ripped from the corner of a sheet of paper with colored graphics on both sides, but without any handy notations like a phone number. Jacob did not have a cell phone—couldn't afford one, and neither could his mother, hence her return to the house to call 911.

It wouldn't have mattered anyway. Not every problem could be helped by instant communication.

Theresa took the county station wagon to Edgewater Park. This time Leo did not insist on sending Don as well, so Theresa arrived, alone, just before nine.

"I hate to say I told you so," Frank began.

"Good." She carried her camera bag and two heavy equipment cases, stepping carefully over the ice-slick walkway. "Don't."

"But I told you so."

"No you didn't." A young patrolman took one of the cases from her and she smiled her surprised thanks. "You said *if* she was dead, then the pimp killed her."

Frank waved one hand and led the way along the paved walkway, which continued up a steady incline. Trees lined one side, the white and frozen lake on the other. "Let's not quibble in front of the help."

"You can shoot him," Theresa told the patrolman, "if you want to."

They followed her cousin, a parka clutched over his suit coat, as the path wound past the Conrad Mizer memorial and along the cliffs leading down to the beach. The temperature had warmed to thirty over the past few days, so the lake breeze didn't instantly numb exposed skin; it took its time about it. Even without the sun, the hazy gray light on the ice forced Theresa to squint. She didn't know how far out the ice extended, but at a glance it seemed like forever.

Frank stopped at a curve in the walk, where the land jutted out slightly, and turned his back to the water. "There she is."

Theresa saw the shirt first, a flash of brilliant aqua not found in the northeastern woods, just visible through a mesh of pine boughs and saplings. Only after staring a while could she distinguish the head, the face nearly as white as the snow, and the dark pants. "Who found her?"

"Jogger. Who else? Joggers and hikers find more bodies than anyone . . . it would put me right off that activity, if I were them. Lucky for me I never exercise. This trail had iced over, kept most people off it all week except for a few crazy people like you who run in subfreezing temps."

"But they wouldn't have their heads turned toward the woods. They'd be concentrating on the icy path, or looking at the lake." Theresa turned again to the water; too bright or not, she had trouble keeping her eyes off it for any length of time. The brisk, slightly fishy air meant that her family was on vacation in the years before her father died, that they were up at Catawba Island for a whole week, and she and Frank and a passel of other cousins had nothing to do but swim, suntan, and roller-skate.

If summer ever came, perhaps she'd get out her scuba gear and dive on the wreck of the *Dundee*, sunk off the coast. Maybe. "Do we have a path we're taking to the body?"

"I don't know where the jogger stepped. Or the jogger's jogging partner."

Theresa breathed out, a *pfff* of irritation.

"Sparky here picked the right side of this growth to walk around, and I stuck with him. That's all I can tell you."

"I didn't see any footprints," the young CPD officer told her. The tip of his nose had turned red, catching up to the hue in his ears. Half of her wanted to tell him to wear a scarf, and the other half wondered, absently, if he was single. "I just went in, established death, checked for ID, came out, and called it in."

"EMS?"

"I didn't call them. An EKG wouldn't have helped."

"Good for you." The fewer people in the crime scene, the better. She set her cases on the paved walking trail, selecting only her camera and a plastic ruler. "Did you find any ID on her?"

"No."

She asked her cousin, "Then what makes you think that's her?"

Frank looked grimmer than he had a moment before; the excitement of the find, of having his suspicions confirmed, had worn off. "You'll see."

She began to approach what was left of Jillian Perry.

Thin branches, stiffened by the cold, brushed against her legs and snapped under her feet, covering the ground thickly enough to prevent footprints. At least three men had traveled this area, but the growth had not meshed that thoroughly and only an occasional branch hung awry. Four feet from the body she stopped, since her ankles snagged on a wild blackberry bush. She shook off its embrace and aimed her camera.

The dead woman sat at the base of an oak tree, its trunk supporting her back, her skull nestled into a slight hollow created by the undulating bark. The aqua color belonged to a sweatshirt with BAHAMAS embroidered in white across the chest; a pink collar poked out from underneath it. Her legs, in dark blue jeans, stretched straight out, and the toes of the white tennis shoes pointed neatly upward. Her hands were empty and lay loose at her sides. No gloves, no coat, no hat. Either she had already been dead before arriving in the woods, or didn't much care that she soon would be.

Why didn't you care? Theresa wondered. Did you even think about your daughter?

In summer, by now, her flesh would be purplish, bloated, beginning to slip and smell very bad, but the winter cold had slowed decomposition to a crawl. The body began to break down from the inside out, causing a darkening under the bluish-white skin, but the outer shell remained intact. The kinds of animals who wouldn't mind gnawing on dead flesh were all hibernating or staying deeper in the woods, away from the icy winds, near easier sources of food such as garbage cans. Jillian Perry didn't exactly resemble Sleeping Beauty, but she could have looked a lot worse.

And it was Jillian. If the color and the length of the hair didn't convince Theresa, the necklace spelling out JILLIAN in gold wire would have. It rested on the sweatshirt's neckband; the short chain had been pulled free of the pink collar and the sweatshirt. Jillian had been left there like a piece of luggage, the tag turned outward for easy identification.

A faint smell made its way to Theresa's nostrils as she grew closer, the unmistakable sign that organic cells had succumbed to entropy.

Why did she assume that someone had left Jillian there? The aqua sweatshirt and jeans had no blemish, no sign that she had been shot or stabbed. No blood stained the blond hair. Theresa pulled at the collar. The neck, with its telltale necklace, had not been throttled or even bruised. There was no reason to think that Jillian hadn't walked out into the woods under her own power, to purposely end her life. Freezing to death was supposedly painless and, perhaps important to a model, not disfiguring. Shooting or stabbing would tear the flesh, hanging would distort it to grotesque shapes. Even overdoses produced messy vomiting. But this left the victim looking, aside from the skin color, serene.

Jillian had probably killed herself. Case closed. At least the body had been recovered, so her family wouldn't have to spend the rest of their lives wondering. All Theresa had to do now was finish her photos, call the body snatchers to collect the remains, get a cup of hot coffee, and call it a day.

Except she didn't believe it. Not because Jillian, a beautiful, married mother of a baby girl, had everything to live for. That hadn't stopped others before and wouldn't again. They were only a three-mile walk from Jillian's apartment and the girl was in good shape. She could easily have done that—but not without a coat or hat, not without getting frostbite, and her ears and nose showed no sign of it. Theresa's cheeks were already tingling.

It also seemed odd that Jillian would leave her necklace in view but not carry any ID—if she wanted to be identified, why not keep her driver's license in her pocket? And freezing might not immediately disfigure her, but if her body remained undiscovered, a thaw or two would reduce it to soup. But mostly, Theresa didn't believe it because she had felt the effects of overexposure at too many northern Ohio bus stops, football games, and sled rides. The last few minutes of freezing to death might be painless, but the hour or so leading up to it would be sheer agony. Jillian would have really wanted to die, which didn't quite jibe with the image of some flighty, selfish, pretty girl.

Either there was much more to Jillian than Theresa knew, or

someone else had helped the woman to die, to abandon both her own life and that of her infant daughter's.

After the first battery of photographs, Theresa donned gloves and turned Jillian Perry's right wrist outward. The nails were unbroken, perfectly manicured, without blood or even dirt underneath them. The left hand matched the right, an impressive diamond solitaire winking from the fourth finger. Theresa sheathed each in a brown paper bag, pulling it tight around the wrist with red evidence tape. Her toes had gone numb.

Twigs snapped behind her as Frank approached along their set route. "What do you think? The setup has some similarities to the other hooker, but I didn't see a mark on this one. You find anything?"

"No. Of course she could have a syringe sticking out of her arm, for all I know, but we'll have to wait until she's undressed. I doubt it, though. I've seen a lot of overdoses, and she hasn't got the look." She pulled up the bottom of the sweatshirt, just enough for a peek at the pink pullover beneath it. Sections had begun to darken as decomposition fluid seeped from the body, but she saw no defects from bullets or knives. At least in the front.

"So you think pretty Jillian decided to end it all?" Frank asked. He sounded disappointed, either in Jillian's abandonment of her family or the loss of a reason to arrest George Panapoulos.

"I think I'm going to treat her as a homicide until I decide she's not."

Frank digested this as Theresa taped the front surfaces of Jillian's sweatshirt and jeans. The cold lessened the adhesive qualities of the tape and, in light of the fact that the body had been exposed to the elements for days, made it enormously unlikely that any useful trace evidence would be found, but the process was quick, cheap, and nondestructive. Without a table or work area handy, she didn't bother pasting the pieces of tape to sheets of clear acetate paper, merely folded the pieces back on themselves and dropped each into a hastily labeled manila envelope.

"She hasn't got a mark on her," Frank repeated. "Unlike Sarah Taylor. But one was a prostitute and one's an escort."

"Sarah was malnourished and poor. Jillian had found her way to a different world." She combed her fingers through the detritus around the body, lumbering around in short hops, like a short sumo wrestler; ungraceful in the extreme, but she could not kneel or she'd have wet pants as well as cold feet. She had even clipped a few branches from the blackberry bush—if it had caught on her clothes, it might have snatched at someone else's. She found only a crushed Coke can that appeared to have been there since the last millennium, a gray plastic ring about an inch in diameter, and a broken piece of red rubber, the same width as a heavy-duty rubber band. She bagged and tagged these items, doubting that they would relate to Jillian's death. They were not on a remote mountaintop; over two and a half million people called Cleveland home, and the Edgewater beach and park were popular, even in the winter months. She could probably find debris from human beings in every square inch of the wooded area if she looked long enough.

When she had searched the ground with reasonable thoroughness—reasonable defined as longer than she wanted to but not so long that she shrieked with boredom—she turned Jillian Perry onto her side. Frank helped her, but it was not difficult given Jillian's slender frame and the assistance of gravity. Theresa quickly taped the back surface of the clothing as well. Another peek under the clothes—not difficult since the pink polo-type shirt had not been tucked into the jeans—confirmed their suspicions: Jillian Perry had not been shot, stabbed, or bludgeoned.

Frank stood up, rubbing his arms, his mustache framed by red cheeks. "Damn, it's cold."

"I'd still rather be here. A brilliant forensic scientist hired by the defense for their poor railroaded client is visiting our lab as we speak."

"I take it he's not a buddy of yours. She could have gotten here on foot from her place," Frank thought aloud. "It's not even three miles by car. Less if she walked along the train tracks."

"I know."

"She disappeared Monday afternoon. The high that day was six degrees. How long does it take someone to freeze to death?"

"A long time. Overnight would be enough. But if she came here in the afternoon, why didn't she go farther into the woods? She's visible from the path. Someone could have found her, even on a cold day. You said yourself there's always some crazy hiker around."

"She *is* visible from the path, and still it took five days for someone to notice her."

"But it's a risk."

"Maybe she wasn't very good at thinking things through. Maybe she was too drunk or high to think clearly."

Theresa looked around, and decided that she had done all that could be done at the scene. She pulled out her Nextel to call for the ambulance crew—i.e., the body snatchers. "We'll just have to wait on tox for that. No drugs or alcohol at the apartment, you said?"

"A little Michelob Lite. Of course he had time to clean up for our visit."

"Or throw the stuff out, if he knew she wasn't coming back."

Frank considered this, then shook his head. "Nah. The husband's got no record past a speeding ticket or two. If she's got drugs in her system, then my money is on Georgie. She was lighting up for old time's sake with her boss and OD'd. He needed to get rid of the body and dumped it here."

"Then it's not murder, exactly."

"I know."

"And there are a lot more convenient places for someone on West Twenty-fifth to dump a body, starting with the Dumpsters at the West Side Market and moving about a thousand feet to the river."

"So what are we looking at here?" He stood next to the oak, his face turned to the silent woman at his feet. Frustration tinged his voice; they both knew that without more information, they could ask questions of each other from then until the next fall and not be able to answer a single one.

"A little girl who's never going to know her mommy," Theresa told him.

CHAPTER 6

The autopsy suite in the sixty-year-old medical examiner's office, scrubbed every afternoon, was the cleanest room in the building. Or at least it appeared to be—the staff took general precautions against cross-contamination but beyond that placed no particular emphasis on sterility. The patients opened up on these tables did not have to worry about infection.

The room held three stainless-steel tables, two sinks, a central floor drain; small red ceramic tiles covered the floor and half of the walls. Unless a victim's organs were currently open, it did not smell bad, more like the humid odor of a seedy bar during the day. Autopsies were performed one after the other until the doctors ran out of candidates; sometimes this would be early in the day and sometimes late. The dieners, or autopsy assistants, would then clean the room and go home, a system that provided every incentive to work quickly and efficiently.

Any new deceased who arrived after cleanup joined the queue for the following morning's work. Jillian Perry made it in under the wire.

"Could have been an early day." Jesse, a skinny black man

who didn't look old enough to have a driver's license, absently hosed the body as he grumbled. He did not seem at all enamored of the beautiful model; a hot dead girl was no match for paid time off.

Undressed, Jillian's body continued to show no signs of violence. No needle marks, no injuries, not so much as a bruise. Lividity, of course, on the buttocks and backs of the legs, but Theresa expected that. She and the pathologist, Dr. Christine Johnson, had already collected fingernail scrapings, a rape kit, and a few hairs and fibers from the skin. Now the ebony-hued doctor held a small but brilliant flashlight up to the mouth.

"Her throat's clear. I don't see any of the foaming you usually get with an OD."

Jesse offered his opinion. "She froze to death."

Theresa peered down the throat as well. "That would take a long time. It wasn't *that* cold out."

"Just long enough to screw up my day. If she'd been here this morning, I'd be going home by now."

Theresa had often proposed a law restricting all crimes to only daylight hours to keep from being dragged from bed, and didn't blame him. "It sucks to be you."

"Not as bad as it sucks to be this chick today," Christine said, clicking off the flashlight with a brisk snap, similar to the way she discouraged potential suitors. The young, black, brilliant pathologist was too interested in studying for her board exams to be distracted by romance. "It seems we have a rash of people freezing to death in the woods all of a sudden."

Theresa said, "Not really. We have a thirty-year-old, half-clothed, throttled prostitute, a warmly dressed fifteen-year-old boy

56

with a single blow to the head, and now a lightly but fully dressed twenty-four-year-old mother dead of—what?"

"Good question. I'll let you know what I find."

Theresa relinquished control of the body and went next door to the old teaching amphitheater which, by virtue of its size, availability, and the fact that it had a table in the middle, doubled as the trace evidence department's examination room. She covered the table with fresh brown paper and spread out the aqua sweatshirt, noting its size, color, and brand. It smelled faintly of perfume, a light and undoubtedly expensive floral scent. Would a woman intending suicide wear perfume? Sure, why not? No need to save the good stuff for a special occasion, as Theresa did. She still had perfume from high school.

Aside from a little dirt and some dead leaves, almost certainly picked up when they rolled the body, the shirt was clean. Theresa turned it inside out—more of the same, except for a smear above the right cuff, on the inside of the forearm. It could have been a minuscule amount of oil. Perhaps Jillian had had something in her hand when she pulled the shirt on? But the victim's hands were clean, and no spots appeared on the shirt's waistband, where she would have had to tug downward.

The pink polo shirt under the sweatshirt had become discolored from the seepage of the decomposing tissues. Theresa hung it on a wheeled rack; when it dried she could tape its surface to pick up any loose hairs or fibers. Odd that it hadn't been tucked into the jeans underneath the sweatshirt, which would have kept her warmer, but perhaps the victim had dressed in a hurry, or it had something to do with the current fashion.

The jeans were a designer brand, size four, making Theresa

think there might be something to the rumor that clothing manufacturers had downgraded all women's clothing sizes to make customers feel better about their bodies, and, by extension, better about parting with the cash to clothe them. Jillian seemed slender, but by no means undernourished for her height. A close look at the back pockets yielded a tiny dusting of white powder, which Theresa dutifully scraped into a paper fold to be tested for the presence of cocaine. The left front pocket contained some lint. The right front pocket held a single stud earring—a small cubic zirconium, as near as Theresa could figure—and a phone number with a Cleveland exchange scribbled on a piece of paper.

Don Delgado poked his head in. "What's that?"

"This is what we, in law enforcement circles, call a clue."

He dropped his six foot three frame into an amphitheater seat too small for him and ran two hands over his shiny olive skin. "Clue to what?"

"Maybe nothing. Maybe to whoever left Jillian Perry to freeze to death at the base of an oak tree."

"I thought she did that herself."

"She probably did. I'm just not so sure."

"Why not?"

She did not own up to any guilt over her first harsh assessment of Jillian Perry; Theresa's ex-husband had taught her the folly of exposing any personal weakness. So she told Don merely this: "I have a hunch."

"You don't get hunches."

"I thought I'd start. It will help me keep up with all those TV detectives."

"You'll have to start wearing high heels and low-cut sweaters too."

"Forget it."

"That's a pity. You'd look good in them." He clasped his hands behind his head and watched her work. He did not offer to help, no more than she would have offered to help him. The lab tried to maintain one forensic scientist per case—it cut down on staff time spent in court when the defendant came to trial.

Jillian had worn white Keds with socks. Not the sort of thing Theresa would have picked to walk three miles in, especially in very cold weather. The treads seemed clean for having traveled through the woods, but then it had been much colder on Monday than today and even mud or slush would have been frozen to an icy solid. "Are you hiding from Leo?"

"Yep. He has to meet with the companies bidding to handle the move to the new building, doesn't want to leave his office or the coffee machine, and is looking for a handy substitute."

"That doesn't sound that bad, really. At least you could get away from test tubes for a while."

"I like DNA. It don't talk, just stays in its little incubator and multiplies. Besides, he wants you to take the moving companies— least you could do after bailing on that defense expert. He wants *me* to search the deep freeze for a piece of bone from a 1994 case."

Theresa cringed. The deep freeze, a walk-in subzero room used for long-term storage, smelled bad enough to sicken strong men, and anything placed there before she was hired could not be located without hours of work. Organization, like supervision, had never been Leo's strong point. She turned on the alternative light source and a blue beam of light at 420 nanometers flowed out of the flexible head. She donned a pair of orange plastic goggles and said, "Hit the light switch, would you?"

Jillian's underwear did not glow, indicating an absence of semen. One errant fiber lit up on the sweatshirt, but the taping had removed most of them. The embroidered words stood out as the optical properties of the threads reacted with the ultraviolet light. Then Theresa turned it over.

She heard Don approaching in the darkness. "What's that?"

The smudge on the right cuff glowed brightly under the light. "I think that's the smear of oil I saw. Why the heck is it glowing?"

"It's not just glowing. It's signaling the mother ship."

She marked the area with a Sharpie in case it became difficult to see in regular light. "Sounds like a job for the FTIR, Robin."

"Don't call me Robin. You can be Batgirl if you want, but I ain't going to be Robin. Stupidest name for a superhero ever."

A knock sounded at the door. The building's receptionist, an older woman with the physique of a wren but not the sweet voice, cracked it open, turned on the lights, and gave them both a suspicious look, as if wondering just what the two had been up to in the pitch black. "That suicide you just brought in, name of Perry?"

"Yeah?" Theresa asked.

"There's a guy here wanting to claim the body, and giving me the impression he's going to stage a sit-down strike until he gets it."

"He's working fast. She's still on the table. Has he made an arrangement with a funeral home yet?"

"No, and I doubt he'll be able to. He's not next of kin."

"Is his name Evan Kovacic?"

The receptionist wrung her hands, though from daily contact Theresa knew that this action came as naturally to the woman as blinking. "No, Drew something. He told me he's not the husband, but he wants the body, which of course he can't have, but every time I tell him that, he asks more questions about her death, which of course I wouldn't answer even if I could. Can you talk to him?"

"Me? I can't tell him anything either. The autopsy isn't even—"

"But the phones are ringing off their hooks and this guy just stands there, sniffling, half giving me the creeps, if you know what I mean. I need some help up there. I've got too much to do." She cocked her head as if she could hear the switchboard buzzing, though of course she couldn't, not without some sort of psychic ability.

"But I—" *avoid grieving people*, Theresa wanted to say. Though she wondered if the man could shed some light on why Jillian would have left her daughter and sat down in the middle of a frozen forest. She'd feel more comfortable with a finding of suicide if there were some history to back it up.

"Please?" the receptionist added, then piled on more hand-wringing until Theresa relented.

"Good luck," Don said. "I'm going to stay here and hide some more."

Theresa folded the jeans over their hanger and shoved the whole clothes rack into the storage room, locking the door. The receptionist waited, bobbing her head in gratitude, and then led the way back to the front lobby. Theresa had to trot to keep up.

The man waiting there could have used another ten pounds and a J.Crew catalog. And a box of Kleenex. Straight brown hair hung past his shoulders. He paced the worn linoleum with fists plunged into the pockets of a jersey jacket, the outline of each finger visible beneath the taut cloth.

"Mr.——?" Theresa prompted.

"Drew Fleming. I'm here to claim Jillian's body." He made no move to shake hands and neither did she.

"Jillian's not ready to be released yet." She did not tell him that Jillian currently lay on a table in the autopsy suite with her torso flayed open for all to see. "If you don't mind my asking, Mr. Fleming, are you here on behalf of Evan Kovacic?"

"I wouldn't cross the street on behalf of Evan Kovacic." The man shifted from side to side and had difficulty meeting her eyes for more than a glance. She would assume the influence of some drugs, but his words were clear and his pupils weren't dilated or jumpy. He was not under the influence but crying, lightly and without pause.

"He *is* Jillian's husband."

"The guy she married, yeah, I know that."

"Then I'm afraid——"

"Because I loved her! Not him! He never loved her. He probably won't even claim her body." His eyes welled up, making the blue irises even bluer, and a shudder ran through his body. "*I* loved her."

Theresa considered him, balancing the discomfort of conversing with a distraught bereaved with a sudden and intense curiosity about the circumstances of Jillian Perry's life, as well as her death. It was not Theresa's job to talk to witnesses, but on the other hand, no rules prohibited same. "If you'd like to come upstairs, Mr. Fleming, there's a conference room where we can talk."

He followed her without a word.

Once they were settled in the central conference room, a musty-smelling area furnished in dingy 1950s decor, she asked, "How did you know Jillian was dead?"

"I think I've known for four days. Everyone said she was nowhere to be found—"

"Who's everyone?"

"Her work, Evan—"

"You spoke to her husband?"

"Yeah. He's in the apartment in the evenings, though I used his cell too."

"He didn't mind you calling?"

Drew Fleming seemed surprised by the question. "Why should he? She married him, not me. Anyway, no one knew where Jillian had gone and I knew she'd never just walk off and leave Cara. She was an excellent mother. Even if she'd had some kind of total freak-out and run away, she'd have told me."

"But how did you find out that we'd found her body?" Theresa persisted.

"I checked in with Vangie at the agency, to see if they'd heard from Jillian, and she told me."

"How did she know?"

"Evan called them."

"He called Jillian's boss? Ex-boss?" In the first few hours after learning his wife was dead? Most people would be too busy with family members and funeral arrangements. But then perhaps they didn't have much family.

He snorted and gave a hopeless chuckle. "Yeah, but did he call *me*? No."

Legal complications could no doubt ensue from questioning a witness without his lawyer or a reading of his rights, except that Theresa was not questioning a witness, she was gathering information about a victim's history and possible state of mind. Therefore she asked without hesitation, "When did you last see Jillian?"

"Last Friday. I went to visit, she made lunch."

"Was Evan there?"

"At work. Out in the barns, I guess."

She left that for a moment, shuffling topics as she'd seen her cousin do. "How did Jillian seem that day?"

A burst of laughter floated up the hallway from the busy records department. Theresa's stomach rumbled. Fleming seemed to be thinking back, and his eyes grew wet with each memory. "Fine. Cara had been spitting up a lot, Jillian worried about that, but she'd gained another pound and she had just had a checkup. Cara's perfectly healthy, her doctor said so. She got a new pair of shoes— Jillian did—at DSW and she loved the color, but they rubbed on the back of her ankles, so she planned to take them back. She complained about not having any sunlight for so long, not that she gets that seasonal affective disorder or anything, but the gray skies get to everybody by this time of the year. Does it always smell like that in here?"

"Yes, it does. She didn't seem upset or worried about anything in particular, then?"

"Just being married to Evan."

"Why would that upset her?"

"Because he didn't love her! He just wanted a piece of eye candy to show off to his clients and his friends, none of whom have matured past the age of thirteen. They play games all day, for Pete's sake."

"I wouldn't think a woman with a newborn would be ideal eye candy."

The man gave her a pitying look, as if sorry for anyone who could be that clueless. "Jillian would be eye candy if she had five newborns, if she were ninety, if she had leprosy."

Theresa had seen Jillian's picture, and felt he overstated the case. "You dated Jillian before she met Evan?"

His gaze dropped. His finger traced the fake wood grain on the table. "Not really, no. We were friends. We've been friends for four years, since we met at Tri-C."

The local community college. His occasional lapse into the present tense when referring to Jillian didn't surprise Theresa. Most people had trouble adjusting immediately after a death.

"Did Evan know you came by to visit his wife?"

"Sure." Again the surprised tone.

"Jillian told him? And he didn't mind?"

"Like I said, why should he? She married him, not me."

Drew Fleming and Evan Kovacic, Theresa thought, were either very, very modern or very, very old-fashioned.

"You're sure Jillian told him?"

"Yeah, always. Besides, I ran into him on my way out of the building that day."

Drew showed up for lunch and was still there when Evan came in from work? Or did Evan pop in and out all day? "What happened?"

"Nothing. We said a few words."

"About Jillian?"

"No, about Polizei." At her blank look, he added, "His video game. The one that made all the money. He's coming out with version two in a few weeks."

"Polizei?"

"That's Russian for 'police,' I guess. The character is a cop in the future and he takes his team to infiltrate this castle—I think it's in Romania because there are vampires, and there's a magic sword . . . it's pretty cool."

"*Polizei* is a German word."

"Oh. Whatever. Evan can do games, I'll say that for him."

"I understand Evan is not Cara's father?"

Drew blinked, apparently still lost in Romanian castles. "What? Oh, no, he isn't."

She waited for him to answer the obvious question. He didn't. "Who is?"

"What? I don't know. She never talked about him."

"Uh-huh." The desire to do right by the woman Theresa had initially dismissed began to seem a little silly. Jillian Perry had had one man's baby, had a less-than-perfect marriage to another, and had a third coming by to let her cry on his shoulder. People had opted out of much less screwed-up lives than hers. Every year more people killed themselves than were killed by others. She started to push off the conference table with both hands. "I'm very sorry, Mr. Fleming, but you will not be able to claim the body, unless Mr. Kovacic decides not to—"

"You're not listening," Drew Fleming said flatly. Coldly. The weepiness evaporated from his eyes and they turned to ice in less time than it took her to notice. He enunciated his words, as if for someone not very bright. "I have a pretty plot in Riverside, under a tree, that she can have. Evan will just cremate her—and that will destroy all the evidence."

Theresa had stopped halfway through the act of rising, her body obeying the instinct to retreat from the odd man, knees half bent in a way that worked her thighs. "Evidence of what?"

He couldn't maintain the icy control, and the timbre of his voice climbed upward. "Murder! Evan murdered her, of course!"

"What makes you say—"

"Why else would she be here? That's what you investigate, right? Murders?"

"The medical examiner's office investigates all deaths, Mr. Fleming, natural deaths, homicides, suicides—"

His hands, on the table, clenched into fists. "He murdered her."

She tried to speak gently. Fleming seemed to be more tightly wound than could be considered healthy, both for himself and others. "We will know more when all the tests are completed, Mr. Fleming, but it appears that Jillian died of exposure. No one harmed her."

This did not convince him. In fact, her words did not even seem to penetrate. Fine, straight hair fell in his face as he shook his head. His skin had been white from the cold when he first arrived and hadn't grown any rosier during his visit, only emphasizing the deep blue irises and red veins in his eyes. "I don't know how he did it, but he did. Don't let him fool you. He fooled her too, at first."

She worked to hold on to her patience. "Why would Evan Kovacic want to kill his wife, Mr. Fleming?"

Again the stare, the aura of surprise at how little she knew about the life of Jillian Perry, at her seeming incuriosity about a woman who had apparently been the most fascinating woman to ever walk the planet. "You mean you don't know about the money?"

"What money?"

A touch of color finally pricked his skin, a pinkish hue almost like a faint glow of triumph. "Sit down."

She sat.

CHAPTER 7

"So get this," Theresa told Frank while shifting her niece's one-year-old to her other hip. She had driven directly from work to her cousin's middle child's tenth birthday party in Parma, and now stood in an overwarm, overcrowded house with a marauding horde of sugar-crazed children, a passel of widowed aunts, and the harried generation—her generation—caught in between. As long as she ignored the claustrophobic air, the warmth felt good, and her mother beamed to see her at a family function. She had avoided far too many of them in the past nine months, and family was everything to her mother. Everything.

"Jillian's grandparents left a huge amount of money to her baby, Cara. Like a million and a half huge."

Frank shoveled another spoonful of potato salad into his mouth despite having made the comment earlier that potato salad was a summer dish and there was something weird about eating it in March. "So Jillian was rich? Then she didn't marry for the money."

Theresa's niece reappeared and collected her son. He took a handful of Theresa's hair with him, but at least the danger of a spit-up had passed. Theresa began to rethink the glories of a large family gathering. "According to Drew, she's never drawn on the money. It's sitting in an account, waiting for Cara. Jillian paid her bills with her salary from Beautiful Girlz. Her parents disowned her, more or less. They didn't care for her choice of careers, and they certainly didn't care for her having a baby and not only not marrying the father, but not even telling them who he was."

Theresa's daughter, Rachael, chose that moment to dart in for another piece of her grandmother's cheesecake, and Theresa took the opportunity to add, "As any parent wouldn't. Something all daughters should keep in mind."

Rachael just laughed in response and carried her prize off to a corner of the living room, rejoining the daughters of Theresa's cousins. The girls burst back into conversation. Theresa's heart gave a contented sigh to see her daughter laughing; perhaps she had managed to keep up enough of a show at home that Rachael's life, at least, had gotten back to normal. She *did* wish the kid would eat something other than dessert, like potato salad, though the cheesecake actually had more nutritional value. "But Jillian's grandparents felt sorry for her and slipped her money now and then. They died, three days apart, two months ago. They left all their assets to Cara."

"Hmm. Lucky kid."

"She's now an orphan."

"Okay. Poor kid. Very rich poor kid."

With some difficulty, Theresa turned her back on a plate of brownies. "And now it will be Evan's. Or will it? He's not Cara's father."

"A man married to the mother is considered the father unless a court rules otherwise," Frank recited around the potatoes.

"Unless the biological father shows up and sues for custody."

"Obviously that mystery man hasn't heard about Cara's nest egg. Though isn't it all tied up in trusts or whatever?"

"No. Her grandparents thought Jillian would need the money now, so that Cara wouldn't starve to death before she reached her majority. They didn't have much faith in either Jillian's job or her fiancé, according to Drew. No trusts or mutual funds for them, just a big ole pile of money with no strings attached." She watched Frank chew thoughtfully, no doubt deciding what he could do with a million and a half.

One of their aunts nudged him out of his daydream before Theresa could, placing a birthday cake festooned with pink-frosting roses among the other dishes. Theresa moved bowls out of the way to make room while the aunt grilled Frank about his latest girlfriend and when they could expect to hear some news. She did not give Theresa the same treatment. The nice thing about being a divorcée in a large Catholic family was that no one encouraged you to remarry. Oh, they had supported her engagement to Paul and planned to attend the wedding. They would be happy for her again if the same situation occurred, but they didn't actively encourage the idea, an attitude for which she felt only gratitude. She had enough thoughtless coworkers encouraging her to "start dating again." The thought made her want to gasp for air.

As a bachelor, however, Frank remained fair game.

"What about the phone number in her pocket?" Theresa asked him.

"The main line for some place called Delta Dynamics. They do data processing for trade shows. Don't ask me what that means, but neither the receptionist nor the manager had ever heard of Jillian Perry."

"Trade shows. She could have worked one of theirs."

Frank said, "Yeah, and one of their employees slipped her his number. Maybe Jillian did take on side jobs."

"Why? She obviously didn't need the money. It could have been for a number of reasons, for that matter—a future contact for Georgie, or even Evan. He's sponsoring a tech show at the factory tomorrow. I got that off his Web site." As her aunt lit tiny pastel candles, Theresa asked, "What if Drew tried to get custody of Cara?"

"Applied for guardianship? Why would he do that? Does he want the baby?"

"Probably not. He seemed more interested in Jillian than her child."

"He'd have to prove that Evan is unfit, or at least that he'd be a better guardian than Evan would." He sneaked a finger into the frosting before his aunt could slap it away.

"You haven't heard him discourse on the many ways in which he truly loved Jillian and Evan truly didn't."

"He'll need more than that. This guy sounds like a loony tune."

"He's harmless," Theresa said, but without conviction.

"Jeesh, Tess, how do you figure that? What you've described sounds exactly like your classic call-twenty-times-a-day, leave-notes-on-your-car stalker."

She knew this to be correct, but still felt oddly protective of the weepy man. "Because I *dated* guys like him. Nerdy, sweet, too shy for their own good. The biggest mistake I made was marrying the one who *wasn't* nerdy and shy. I don't think Drew's dangerous."

Frank considered this, since he had met every boy she had ever dated, but still shook his head. "You don't know that. Obsession can be a very dangerous thing."

They paused to sing "Happy Birthday," a chorus of happy and only slightly off-key voices. Theresa stammered through the third line; she had forgotten whose birthday it was, but consoled herself with the thought that the lack of oxygen in the room had starved her brain cells.

The birthday girl ripped into the wrapping paper like a human chain saw. Theresa's aunt returned to cut the cake. Theresa didn't envy her the job of dividing the swirls of colored frosting among close to fifteen panting children with strong views on the particular decoration to which they were entitled. She turned again to Frank. "Yes, obsession can turn violent. But so can greed, and the idea of that much money makes me look at Jillian's marriage in a new light. What happened when you told Evan?"

"I said we found her body, he started crying, that was about it. I offered victim-assistance services, he declined. He asked all the standard questions, where, when, how did she get there. The usual."

"And he said she disappeared while he was at work on Monday?"

"Yeah. She was doing the breakfast dishes when he left at nine thirty, gone when he got home about three."

"What had she been wearing?"

"He couldn't remember. At least not when I spoke to him today—it might be mentioned in the initial missing-person report."

"Strange."

"Not really. Do you remember what Rachael wore to school today?"

Theresa handed a slice of cake to a redheaded boy. "The same shirt she has on now, but her black jeans, which are way too tight and I hate them."

"Yeah, but you're female. I wouldn't be able to recall what my date wore the last time I went out even if you promised me Indians tickets to do it."

"But you're not married to her," Theresa argued.

"Married?" the aunt asked.

"Indians tickets?" the redheaded boy asked. Theresa stuck a fork in his cake for him to use and ushered the next child forward.

She said again, "It just seems weird. This guy marries an escort who's had someone else's child, someone else's very wealthy child, and three weeks after the wedding the wife is dead?"

Frank snagged a piece for himself, earning a glare from the next child in line. "Am I missing something here? Jillian wasn't murdered."

"We don't know that yet."

"You said yourself there wasn't a mark on her. She committed—" A sharp glance from their aunt stopped him. Children's birthday parties were not the place to discuss suicide. "She did it herself."

Theresa persisted, disinclined to stifle herself for a traditional family gathering. The last traditional family gathering she had attended had been Paul's funeral, and memories of the warmth, the crowd, the discomfort filtered back to her. "I won't be positive until the toxicology results come back. What if she had too much stuff in her bloodstream to walk, much less walk two miles?"

"If she did, I'll look into it. Until then, there's nothing I can do. You really think the husband murdered her?"

"He said 'had.'"

"Beg pardon?"

"When I complimented the decorating. He said Jillian *had* talent, not *has* talent. We didn't even know she was dead and he's already using the past tense?"

"Some people always mix up their tenses."

"True. And I'm not discounting that this Drew guy worshipped a woman who just married another man. But a million and a half is one heck of a motive."

"Evan Kovacic seems to have plenty of money, and according to the tech geeks at work, he will soon have so much of it he could buy IBM."

"Yeah, I figured that out from his Web site too. Apparently Cleveland has become the Silicon Valley of the East, lots of companies I've never heard of and can't figure out what they do. Hence the career day tomorrow."

"A million and a half is probably a drop in the bucket compared to what investors have given him. I'd still bet on Georgie—he always gets my radar pinging. But I can't do anything for the next day or two. The chief put me on the Cultural Gardens homicide because Sanchez and O'Malley are swamped, so I've got fifteen witnesses to interview tomorrow."

The last child stepped up, a look of disappointment on her face to see that all the pink roses had already been claimed. "I know it's unlikely for all those reasons, but just suppose for one minute that somehow Evan killed his wife for Cara's bank account. What now? If he's automatically Cara's next of kin and he's willing to kill for money, where does that leave this kid's life expectancy?"

"That's quite a leap." Nevertheless, he wore an unhappy expression as he folded up his paper plate. He didn't like coincidences any more than Theresa did, and a strange death occurring in conjunction with an overwhelming motive was one hell of a coincidence.

"I mean, do you know how easy it is to kill an infant? You just put a pillow over its face. You don't even have to press down."

A ripple of silence moved outward from the aunt and the girl with the last piece of cake, to the children playing cards nearby, to Theresa's mother and two cousins seated on the couch. If suicide did not seem an appropriate topic for a child's birthday party, infanticide ranked somewhere off the charts.

Theresa gulped, grateful she had grown too old to be sent to her room.

The snow drifted down in small but constant flakes, bursting into brilliant white under the streetlights but fading to a hazy gray as it receded into the dark. It would have been pretty if Theresa hadn't been trying to drive in it. She hit the brakes a little too hard for a red light and slid the last three feet to the stop line.

"Your aunt Claire asked me about that boy you found in the woods," her mother, Agnes, said.

"Mmm." Sometimes Theresa told her mother and daughter more

than she should about open cases. Sometimes she said nothing and hoped they wouldn't catch the news that day. Child deaths always fell into the latter group.

"She wanted to know if it had anything to do with the girl in the Cultural Gardens."

"Huh? No, of course not—that wasn't a girl but a grown woman, and she was strangled. The boy wasn't."

"But they were both outside, propped up against something. And now you've got this third woman. Claire thinks it might be a serial killer."

"Claire's imagination is running away with her."

Rachael chimed in from the backseat. "No, they said that on the news too."

The approached another red light. This time Theresa gave herself plenty of stopping distance. "The news media likes serial killers. They sell papers and increase ratings."

"So it's your testimony, Ms. MacLean, that we do not have a ravenous murderer on the loose in Cleveland, Ohio?" Rachael asked with the cadence she had picked up from one semester of Business Law.

"I deny it categorically."

"He was near the zoo?" her mother asked. "I used to go swimming there when I was little."

"They had a swimming pool at the zoo?" Rachael asked. Theresa merely nodded, having heard the tales of her mother's childhood, tales from a time when children could roam the city without cell phones or worried parents.

"The only place *to* go swimming was Brookside Park. They had a round cement pool, and you had to pay a dime or something to get in. My brothers and sisters would take me along. We'd walk all the way from Natchez Avenue."

"Even Aunt Claire?"

"Aunt Claire turned all the boys' heads."

Rachael was silent for a while, no doubt trying to picture a hot summer in 1935, and her grandmother as a little girl. "That was a fun party."

Theresa agreed while becoming deeply suspicious. Whenever her teenager expressed such an old-fashioned sentiment, it meant she wanted either to borrow the car or go on a ski trip with her numerous first cousins once removed.

Rachael continued, "Dora's going to come to the talent show next week, even. I need to hang with her more often. We haven't been to her mom's in, like, forever."

"We stopped by at Thanksgiving."

"Mom, that was four months ago."

"Oh." Had it really been that long?

"We need to get out more."

How diplomatic. The *we* instead of *you*. "I know."

Theresa's mother, in the passenger seat, said absolutely nothing. Theresa, no doubt, had often been a topic of conversation between Rachael and her grandmother; this struck Theresa as both heart-warming and deeply humbling.

Into the silence, Theresa asked, "Are you still thinking about electrical engineering?"

"Huh? As a major?" Rachael caught up to the leap in topics. "Yeah. Those guys make bucks. Why, do you have another college to check out?"

Theresa explained about the high-tech career expo at Kovacic

Industries. Rachael could not be defined as a video-game junkie, but she would be majoring in science, and any sort of career-development exposure could not hurt for a high school senior currently working on picking a college.

"Oh." Rachael slumped a bit into the gloom of the backseat, only her eyes visible in the rearview mirror. "You want to use me as cover to investigate a guy in one of your cases."

Was that what she was doing? If so, Frank would kill her . . . though attending a public career fair could hardly be considered either an official investigation or bad parenting . . . "I thought of it as killing two birds—more like multitasking. You've been debating about engineering instead of the natural sciences."

"Yeah. It's just that you haven't voluntarily left the house, except for work, church, and the grocery store, for months. And now, all of a sudden—"

Nine months, to be exact. Theresa concentrated mightily on a red light, avoiding her daughter's all-too-knowing and compassionate stare. "I'm sorry. I know I've been out of it. . . ." Her tongue stumbled over the useless euphemism for grief, for the selfish desire to make the world go away by ignoring its occupants, including the one she had brought into it.

Agnes said, "That sounds like fun. I have the afternoon shift at the restaurant tomorrow anyway. You two could eat out."

That decided Rachael, her eyes in the rearview mirror regarding her mother as carefully and without judgment as a doctor, a therapist—or a parent. As if she were the mother and Theresa the child, to be guarded and cared for until strong enough to take care of herself. "Sure. I think that's a good idea."

To help the case? Theresa thought. *Or me?*

CHAPTER 8

SATURDAY, MARCH 6

"Mrs. MacLean."

Evan Kovacic didn't seem overjoyed to see her, but then he didn't seem dismayed, either. More like confused, and she could well understand that. She stood out in the crowd of people inside one of the cavernous National Carbon Company buildings. Almost all the other attendees were younger, had at least one body piercing in addition to earlobes, and had never in their lives tucked in a shirt.

"Your Web site said the event was open, and my daughter is considering an engineering degree. I hope you don't mind."

"No, not at all. This is your daughter? Wow." He shook Rachael's hand, and the way he looked her up and down made it clear that his "wow" was not for the fact that Theresa had a daughter Rachael's age. It seemed to be for Rachael's bra size, all too apparent in the tight, strategically torn T-shirt Rachael had insisted on wearing under the pretense of "dressing the part."

Rachael smiled, even blushed, and Theresa questioned her own game plan. Involving her daughter in an investigation might not be the smartest thing she'd ever done. In fact, it was a *horrible* idea, and what kind of mother—and he was still checking her out, the—*do something!* "I also never had a chance to express my condolences. I'm so sorry for your loss."

Did it take him a split second too long to tear himself from her daughter's form and snap back to the reality of a dead wife? Or did it just seem that way to a protective mother?

"Yes, of course. Thank you. I appreciate that. And I'm glad you came." He turned to Rachael again, but this time with a professional tone in his voice. "We have over twenty-five technology and digital-media firms represented here, with demonstrations every half hour on the main dais—over there, under the lights. It's cool you're here, we need more girls in the field. It's still very male dominated."

"Math doesn't bother me," Rachael boasted.

He raised his voice to be heard over the cacophony. "It's not that so much, it's that the technology has always lent itself, first and foremost, to shoot-'em-up scenarios. The very first video game was called Spacewar, and was something like Asteroids. The first one for home use was Pong. The industry's goal became to do the same actions over and over, only faster, and girls get bored with that a whole lot more quickly than boys do. So most games are still designed by boys, for boys."

"You need more complications," Rachael surmised.

He smiled, looking cynical and amused and remarkably more attractive than he had yet so far. For the first time, Theresa had a glimpse of what his wife must have seen in him besides a steady income. He was not stupid, this Evan. "Exactly. Complications are what make life interesting."

"Did Jillian help you with the design? Give you a female perspective?" Theresa asked.

This question seemed to confuse him as much as her presence. "Jillian?"

"Evan!" A slim black man held to the back of a display board for Beachwood IT Solutions, snaking multicolored cables over the front of it. He gestured for Evan's assistance.

Evan excused himself and trotted over, darting between the milling young people.

"You think he killed his wife?" Rachael's tone, and the way she followed the man's large form, made it clear she thought her mother way off the mark on this one.

Theresa felt ready to agree. "I didn't say that. She may not have been killed at all. But I have a lot of questions without answers and wanted to see this place. Come on, let's look at the exhibits."

A banner reading NEOSA—NORTHEAST OHIO SOFTWARE ASSOCIATION was hung along the far wall. At least fifteen booths lined all sides of the hall, each decked out with colorful displays and plenty of video and stereo equipment. A cacophony of sight and sound, letting everyone know that things were happening, and they were happening in Cleveland.

Theresa followed her daughter around the booths, knowing that Rachael would not have to feign interest in the career options presented. Only some of the firms present dealt with video games; they also met a woman from the fastest-growing bioscience firm in the country and watched a man demonstrate how to turn lake water into drinking water almost instantly. Theresa's mind wandered through a Web-development display, but she forgot why she had come when they found a compendium of items useful to law enforcement, including a wireless camera shaped like an egg that could be tossed through windows to provide a 360-degree video of the room.

Halfway through the room they found Kovacic's own booth. Rachael tried out a demo version of Polizei while Theresa read the display board. A photo of Evan and the slim black man, shorter than Evan and wearing a New Mexico sweatshirt, had been affixed to the center top. The caption identified the other man as Jerry Graham, Evan's business partner. The brief bio said the two were both originally from Cleveland, but had met in class at MIT. Jerry concentrated more on hardware and had a patent pending on a virtual-reality helmet. Neither bio mentioned wives or other family. Perhaps they figured personal details would not be of interest to their young and largely male clientele. They did mention their favorite foods (fresh perch, beer, edamame, and more beer), hobbies (snowboarding, spelunking, and miniature golf), and favorite place to pick up girls (the E3 Summit).

"It's the most popular PC game in the world right now." This information came from an older man wearing a tie, the first such item she'd seen that day. He also wore his short hair neatly combed, which set him apart from most of the other males in the room, even more so than the tie.

"PC game?"

He leaned toward her slightly, as if to protect her secret from the crowd. "You're not a game player, are you?"

"Not since I finished Riven."

When he stopped laughing, he explained, "PC games come on CDs and are played on the computer. As opposed to console games, which are put in cartridges that get plugged into a home system and are played on your television."

"Oh."

"Polizei is available in either format. But I keep telling Evan to design an MMO version—a massively multiplayer online game. That's where the real money is these days. You don't just have millions of people buying one cartridge. You have millions of people paying to play it, the same people, month after month."

"You know Evan Kovacic?"

"I finance him. Cannon, Jennings, and Chang." He pulled a card from his shirt pocket and handed it to her. "Venture capital."

His business card repeated this information, and identified him as the first of the three names. "You lent Evan the money to buy this factory?"

"Mostly we lent Evan money to produce the next version of Polizei. He could have done that in his living room and then outsourced the hardware, but apparently he has bigger plans."

Over his cologne, Theresa caught a whiff of motive in the air. "You're worried about your investment?"

"I always worry about our investments. That's my job. But I don't think this one can lose."

Rachael looked up from the demo monitor long enough to swat her mother's arm. "This is cool, Mom!"

The man tilted his head toward the girl. "See what I mean? We'll get our money back in spades once Evan's up and running. But I still think he could do an MMO at the same time."

The man in question interrupted them. From the dais at the end of the room, he announced into a microphone, "The time has come for me and Jerry, your humble hosts, to demonstrate our wares. But to do that, we're going to have to take a quick walking tour of the currently underutilized Kovacic Industries campus. Zip up your coats and follow me."

Theresa turned to the financier. "What *are* his bigger plans?"

"You're about to see."

"Did you come here to find out?"

He chuckled. "No, I already know. I'm here to remind Evan that he's missed two release dates. Your daughter might want to see this. I don't want to leave out any potential customers."

"Tear yourself away, Rachael. We're moving on."

The vendors at the other booths watched in resignation as the customers filed out, though a few used the break to put their feet up and open Styrofoam containers of lunch. Theresa and Rachael followed the crowd through a set of double doors at the rear of the building and past a crowd of smokers braving the below-freezing temperatures to satisfy the nicotine craving. The scent of tobacco followed her, tempting and taunting. But if Paul's death hadn't pushed her back into the comforting arms of burning tobacco, nothing would. It wouldn't get worse, right?

"I want to buy that game, Mom. They're having a sale."

"Good idea." Perhaps she could deduct it as a business expense.

"The main character is Captain Alastair, and first he has to lead his team around these really cool cliffs to get to this castle, and there's these branches that come off the side from the trees above you and form sort of a tunnel, and you think they're just roots, but then when you're about halfway through—well, after you kill the troll—they come to life and you have to figure out how to get them to stop—"

Theresa's mind wandered back to the idea of venture capital as she took in deep breaths of frigid air, noting the architecture surrounding them. Eight rectangular, barnlike buildings, including the one they had just left but not including the fancy offices/apartment building near the street, lined the fenced property. The sounds of traffic and the rapid transit rolling past faded quickly, dampened by the thick snow. A brass plaque, turned green with age, hung on the wall of the next structure; it told her the National Carbon Company had been established in 1886. That sounded terribly old, though beyond the peeling paint and rusting metal fixtures, the walls seemed sturdy enough.

She didn't interrupt her daughter to tell her that the carbon company had been instrumental in creating Lakewood. They needed a workforce and encouraged the influx of Slavic immigrants, saturating the area around the turn of the century. The company provided homes within walking distance, and the surrounding streets, with names like Thrush and Quail, became known as Birdtown. It had been a time of great opportunity. Of hope.

The walking tour skipped the closest building, and moved through heavy steel doors into the one beyond it. It smelled like dust and metal, the air turned to a shade of gray by the combination of overcast outdoor light and high windows that hadn't been cleaned since, perhaps, its original construction. The entire building existed as a single open space with catwalks running the two-hundred-foot length on either side. Whatever carbon-processing equipment it had once housed had been removed, leaving only pits and discolorations in the concrete floor and three vast metal silos in the southeast corner, but the two cameras mounted above them, in opposite corners, appeared quite new. Closed in by a metal-mesh cage, the silos bore faded labels in red paint: NCC, N2, and even a haphazardly drawn smiley face. Remnants of the past. In the center of the building, however, stood the future.

A gray gyroscope, at least nine feet in diameter, stood balanced on black rubber supports. The beams crisscrossed each other, interrupted here and there by protrusions or short cables. On either side of this sphere computer monitors balanced on stands, displaying the Polizei logo.

The crowd gathered around this centerpiece, talking rapidly but not with the reverence Theresa expected to hear. "It's a virtual-reality sphere," a waif of a girl declared to her companion. "I saw one at the tech show in Columbus last month."

"Cool but way too pricey," a boy to Theresa's left intoned.

"I did this at the carnival last year," Rachael told her mother. "That was just a ride, though. I think this one is meant to be used with a video helmet."

"A what?"

As the last of the crowd drifted in, Jerry Graham stepped into the sphere, moving gingerly until he strapped his feet into two of the protrusions on the inner frames. Then he plucked a set of goggles from a bracket at the top and a gun from another at the side. The gun—or plasma rifle or phaser or whatever futuristic weaponry it represented—and the goggles remained attached to the frame by flexible spiral cables, long enough to let him move in all directions but not long enough to tangle as he ran, twisted, turned, and jumped. The rings of the gyroscope rotated with him, but the entire sphere itself remained in place, resting on its rubber chocks without a quiver.

Evan took his place next to the object, speaking into a wireless microphone so that his voice seemed to boom from all four corners of the building. "This is a virtual-reality sphere. You've seen them before. Doppler ultrasound tracks your moves, and instantly translates them into the game. The haptic interface lets you interact with the objects around your character. With this you don't just see what Captain Alastair sees, you feel it. You feel the snow crunching underneath your boots. You feel your thighs aching as you climb the winding staircase. You have to duck low to avoid the spiders. You live the game."

The monitors behind him changed to a scene in motion, an underground stone tunnel. The view advanced, lit only by the flicker of an occasional torch, with every step Jerry Graham took within the gyroscope. The rocks glistened with subterranean sweat. Theresa could almost smell the mold, and had to remind herself that, given the age of the building, she probably *did* smell mold.

Some sort of humanoid appeared from the dimness ahead, did a double take at the approach of the captain/Jerry/the crowd, and began to lift a sword. As Jerry held the weapon out in front of him, the tip of it appeared at the bottom of the monitors, and a burst of fire felled the unlucky henchman. The people around Theresa gasped and applauded. The venture capitalist had not exaggerated the game's popularity.

From there the action moved into a treasure-filled cavern, where gold and diamonds glowed with such real color that Theresa felt a twinge of jealousy toward the captain's team.

"Cool, Mom. Can we get one?"

"No."

Rachael laughed.

"I'm glad you're not a video-game junkie, by the way. I'm getting the feeling my bank account couldn't handle it."

"That's what credit is for," Cannon said.

"You all know what happens next," Evan said, with such a boyish grin that the crowd giggled and even Theresa couldn't help but smile.

"What happens next," Evan went on, "is, you decide you have to have one of these. Every serious gamer does. But there are two problems. What's number one?"

"Affordability!" shouted a man in a Harley-Davidson T-shirt. Several other attendees echoed this sentiment.

"Good point. We're working on the price—more on that in a minute. But what's your second obstacle?"

"Availability?"

"Software support?"

"Size?" suggested the waif in front of Theresa.

Evan pointed at her. "Exactly. The problem is Mom."

Confused silence. Theresa noticed the venture capitalist standing on the other side of Rachael, waiting. He did not seem the least bit confused.

"Really," Evan went on. "Would your mom let you install this thing in the middle of her family room? Or even your bedroom? Mrs. MacLean, you're a mom. Would you want a gray sphere this size next to your coffee table?"

The heads around her swiveled in her direction. "No," she admitted, with the trepidation of the outnumbered.

"Whose mom would? Or whose spouse? Or you yourself—would you want this blocking your big screen during playoffs?"

Murmured dissent.

"Of course not. So let me show you something new. Jerry, if you would tear yourself away from the treasures of the keep there. . . ."

His partner hung up his gun and goggles, unstrapped his Nikes, and stepped out of the gyroscope.

"Jerry Graham, everybody, the inventor—no, not the inventor of the virtual-reality gyroscope, let's say the perfector. Because Jerry has patented a way around both these obstacles. Jerry, show them what they *haven't* seen before."

The man touched no more than three spots on the frame, flipping small latches, and then pushed. The rings rotated to nest within each other, almost completely flat save for the various protrusions. In less time than it took to pick up a remote and change the channel, the sphere's width went from nine feet to less than a foot.

The crowd sucked in its collective breath.

Jerry Graham demonstrated the movement again, expanding the gyroscope, locking the frame and climbing inside to show its stability, before hopping out and collapsing it into itself. It remained a nine-foot-in-diameter object, but the reduction in depth made it seem downright svelte.

Evan continued to delineate the sphere's attributes. "Unlock the casters and you can wheel the sphere anywhere you want, up against the wall or into a hallway. It's made of recycled plastics, so it's environmentally sound as well as lightweight and durable. You, come here and try to move it."

The tiny girl in front of Theresa placed both hands on the collapsed frame and gave a shove. It rolled easily. She asked if they were going to manufacture the spheres on-site.

"Exactly," Evan told the crowd. "It will keep costs down since we'll be doing both the software and the hardware. But it's not just for Polizei—although it is the coolest game in existence, not that I'm biased or anything. No, you can play any PC or console game that lends itself to virtual reality in this sphere. I'm not going to make something that only takes my games— we've all been down that road before. You buy some cool piece of equipment and in two years you can't get games for it, or you have to buy a new game for both your console and PC. Uh-uh. If you buy Polizei for your Nintendo, it will come with a version for the Graham sphere *and* a PC version. If you buy the version for Xbox, same deal."

This seemed to impress the crowd even more than the collapsible aspect had.

Theresa leaned around her daughter. "This is his bigger idea, Mr. Cannon?"

The financier nodded. "It's the next logical step for home entertainment. But it has to be affordable and convenient, the two most important things to an American household. In most families the second is becoming more vital than the first. It wasn't only lower prices and more versatility that made people start buying home computers—it was that they didn't take up half the room anymore. Once they fit on a desktop and had rounded edges, they became a necessity. Same with video games. Once consoles got small and light enough to be tossed in a cubbyhole when the kid went to school, sales shot up."

A black woman with her hair twisted into spiky clumps and cheekbones to die for approached Jerry Graham and greeted him with a kiss. They exchanged a few words and parted with another kiss, and not a professional-colleagues one. A girlfriend or wife. She must have seen quite a lot of Jillian, since the two men were so close. She might be an interesting person to talk with.

"Say," the financier went on, "are you single, by any chance?"

She still wore the engagement ring Paul had given her. "No."

"How about you starting us off?" Evan said from beside the gyroscope, and Rachael moved forward without a glance at her mother. Theresa followed, watched her daughter step inside a globe with moving parts that resembled the inside of a blender, and tried to tamp down the nerves tightening around her throat. It's a toy, she told herself. Just a toy. It couldn't hurt anyone. They must have checked the design for every possible danger, certainly, before demonstrating it in front of a hundred or more potential customers.

Theresa took another step forward, and felt a tiny lump under the worn sole of her Reebok. At first she thought someone had dropped a coin, but it turned out to be a flat ring of gray plastic, similar to the one found with Jillian's body, but not exactly the same diameter. Theresa picked it up.

Rachael slipped on the goggles. According to the monitor, she now faced a slowly advancing army of pale but sexily clad vampires. Using the weapon, she gleefully dispatched the front line. The crowd drew in closer to call out advice and encouragement.

Theresa felt Evan watching her, and caught his eye. Two

young men had begun to ask questions as quickly as he could answer, and yet he seemed interested in Theresa's reaction. Why?

If he thought he had a sure sale, he had another thought coming. Rachael would have to use her car fund if she wanted the circular monstrosity; hardly likely—games were fun, but wheels were a teen's holy grail. "I thought vampires couldn't die," she said to Evan.

"The bullets are silver."

"Must get expensive."

"It's only virtual silver," he said, laughing.

She held out the piece of gray plastic. "What's this?"

"Garbage." He took it out of her palm and tossed it into a nearby can with one arc of his right arm, then appeared surprised by her surprise. "They're just punch-outs from the sphere arms. We swept this room, but there's still a ton scattered around, I'm sure."

"What's the holdup with Polizei Two?" one of the boys asked.

Evan bounced on his toes, his gaze darting between Rachael, Theresa, the boys in front of him, and the rest of the crowd. "Trying to get the fuzzy wings on the vultures just right. The graphics are killing me."

"Seriously, dude. It was supposed to be out for Christmas."

Evan bounced harder. "There are a lot of factors at play here. I wanted the sphere to be ready for preorder with the game."

"You could have embedded an ad and order form in the higher levels. Why hold up the game?"

Theresa wondered if the boy, with his Chinese-symbol tattoo and peach-fuzz beard, felt the same urgency about his geometry homework.

His friend, thinner and pastier, came to Evan's rescue. "Don't hassle the guy, dude. His wife died, and all."

The first young man remembered his manners. "Oh, yeah. That really sucked, didn't it?"

"Yeah," Evan agreed, watching Rachael. The bouncing subsided.

But then the sympathetic one revealed his own area of curiosity. "But wasn't it weird, like, being married to an escort?"

The first one perked up again. "Yeah, was that cool? Did she do all sorts of—stuff?"

"But didn't it bug you what she was doing with, you know, other guys?" the second one ventured, cautious but persistent. "I would think that would be kind of—"

Say something, Theresa urged Evan with her mind. *Tell them to shut up.*

The first one ran with the idea. "Well, yeah, I bet it'd be like being with a porn star, every guy looking at you and wondering what she'd do that he can't get his chick to do."

Evan let his gaze wander over the crowd; he didn't respond to the boys' questions, but neither did he seem bothered by them. In fact, his earlier grin surfaced again at the corners of his mouth.

Well, it bothered Theresa. *"Boys."*

The second one blushed. The mouthy one seemed pleased to have regained her attention, like a little boy who just belched in front of his mother. Evan simply watched her, as if the conversation had nothing to do with him. Shock? Or indifference? Or just happy to get off the subject of his overdue video game?

"I'm sorry about your wife," she repeated.

"Thanks."

"I'm afraid the pathologist hasn't ruled yet. Her case is still open." She didn't know why she said that, perhaps just to keep him talking about Jillian. Perhaps to prompt some solemnity in the two brats standing there.

It didn't work, or maybe having other boys around to posture for made him reckless. Maybe he truly didn't know how to express his feelings. Maybe anything, but he said, "I can always go back to Georgie and hire another one."

The boys tittered.

The crowd cheered as Rachael triumphed over another vampire. Evan watched Theresa, as if there were no one else in the building. She wondered if he could see the rage spreading from her brain through the rest of her body, until her fingers tingled and her toes went numb and her stomach clenched into a fist.

"Good luck with the guardianship," she said.

He blinked, as if perplexed by the change of topic, but that tiny upturn to his lips remained. Maybe he, not much more mature than these boys, enjoyed baiting her just as they did. "What?"

"You'll have to go to court to get guardianship of Cara. I just wanted to wish you luck. I've heard that can be a long process."

He began to bounce again, just a slight up-and-down lift to his body. "I already have Cara. She's my daughter."

"Not legally."

"I was married to her mother. That makes me her father since she doesn't have one." A furrow appeared between his eyes, his mind forced away from the video-game world. The boys shifted, bored by talk of babies and courts.

"No, see, I spoke to one of my cousins at a birthday party last night—she's a lawyer. Since you weren't married to Jillian at the time of Cara's birth, you're not her legal father. Of course, you'll almost certainly be granted guardianship, given the absence of any biological father or other applicants."

He came to rest. "Exactly. Jillian's parents have never even come to see the kid."

She nodded, forcing her face into an expression of empathy she didn't feel. First he spoke of his dead wife with a stunning lack of emotion, now he didn't even give his stepdaughter a name. "Nevertheless, they're her legal next of kin. If anything happened to Cara."

His body went preternaturally still as, she felt sure, the implications of this filtered through the matrix of his brain, assessing the threats and forming a plan, just as Rachael now did in the center of the sphere.

Then he shrugged. "I'll get my lawyer on it; he loves easy and billable hours. Jillian's parents never showed the slightest interest in them."

Them, not us. "That's too bad. Though they might change their minds if they thought Jillian's death wasn't an accident. Or suicide."

"So," the tattooed boy asked, "does Polizei Two take place at the same cas—"

Evan brushed past the kid and came closer to Theresa, so close she could feel the heat from his torso. She had taken a step back before she could stop herself, even with a hundred witnesses surrounding them. The posture felt threatening, but his voice sounded merely curious.

"Do you have any proof?"

She blurted out, without thought, "That's an odd question. Not *what makes you think that* or *what are you talking about?* Do I have any *proof?*"

"Exactly. Proof."

She said nothing, and that became answer enough.

He straightened, still close, a large fleshy wall that seemed quite adult now. "I thought so. You don't want to start a pissing contest, Mrs. MacLean. You'll need an umbrella. I have some"— he looked her up and down, obviously unimpressed by something, her stature, her gender, or her taste in shoes—"natural advantages."

"So do I," she told him, though she could not for the life of her have listed a single one at that moment. Rachael emerged from the gyroscope, and Theresa took her arm and guided her out of the building. While shutting the door behind them, she saw Evan install another participant in the sphere, this time choosing the man in the Harley shirt while proclaiming that the sphere could support much more body weight than the typical undernourished teenager. He did not look in their direction.

Rachael didn't argue at their exit, still in the throes of an adrenaline rush. "I'd like to try that again. You know what that would be great for? Exercise. You could be, like, snowboarding in the Himalayas, or walking on a beach in Hawaii."

"Uh-huh." They headed back along the snowy sidewalk. Theresa probed her memory of the past two minutes. What the hell was Evan Kovacic? A cold-blooded killer? Or a somewhat immature young man more adept with computer software than people?

"They could hook up little fans and things that could blow air on you so it feels like you're moving, and maybe put some scents in there like pine trees or saltwater—"

"Uh-huh."

Theresa bypassed the first building, continuing on the snowy sidewalk. "Are we leaving?" Rachael asked.

"Yes."

"Why? We haven't gone through all the booths yet—"

"We have to go." They headed for the red Tempo, Theresa still holding her daughter's coat sleeve. Jerry Graham's girlfriend had just pulled out of her space and headed for the street. She drove a dark green Camaro with DELTA DYNAMICS printed on the door.

"But why are we leaving now? I thought you wanted me to think about career development. I wanted to ask that guy about an internship. If he's just starting up here, it will take him a while to fill all the positions. I could co-op—"

She finally released Rachael's coat long enough to let her get around the car to the passenger door. She didn't turn to look up at the second floor of the renovated offices, where Cara Perry slept in her crib, Jillian's princess, now left without a champion. "I'm sorry, honey, but I don't want you near Evan Kovacic."

"Why?"

"Because he may have killed his wife."

CHAPTER 9

SUNDAY, MARCH 7

Not even a tattered wisp of crime scene tape remained to mark the spot where Jillian Perry's body had lain. Tree limbs lined with optimistic buds waved gently in the breeze off the lake, and a light dusting of snow made the wooded area innocuous, peaceful. Theresa studied the oak tree, waiting for inspiration. None came. The tree and its clearing had given up everything they had, the body, the few items with it. But nature couldn't tell her what it had seen that day as the life faded from Jillian Perry. She would have to figure that out on her own.

She turned to go. After a few steps she could see a man on the path, watching her, the sky and lake one solid mass of light gray behind him. With a start she realized it was Drew Fleming.

He said, "Hi. I thought that was you."

Somehow it didn't surprise her to find him haunting the site, but it sure as hell startled her. "Good morning, Mr. Fleming."

"Have you found out any more about Jillian's death?"

"No." She emerged from the trees and stepped onto the concrete path. Drew Fleming slouched in the same jersey jacket, not warm enough for the weather, and wiped his nose with one knit-gloved hand. He looked even worse than he had two days before. Pale as the snow around them, with eyes so reddened the insides of the lids resembled raw steak. Here lived the grief so conspicuously absent from Evan Kovacic. Or could it be guilt? She kept a healthy distance between them, and turned as he moved so that she always faced him straight on.

"Are you out here to collect more clues?"

Exactly why *was* she there on a Sunday afternoon, on her own time, a forty-minute ride from her home in Strongsville when she had laundry to do and groceries to shop for, to look at the scene of what might have been a suicide? Because Evan Kovacic had irritated her? Because someone needed to care about Jillian Perry? Because it beat doing laundry? "Nooo . . . not exactly. What are you doing here?"

"I've stood on this spot about ten times already since they found Jillian. I keep coming back, wondering what happened, asking her to tell me what happened. I don't know why she won't talk to me. Jillian always told me everything. I know she's dead," he added with a sudden, sharp anger. "Believe me, I know that. But my mother used to say that the dead would communicate with you if you really loved them."

Theresa could not guess how to respond to that, and tried to tell herself that the wind off the lake had caused the prickling at the back of her neck.

"Besides," he went on, "I live here."

She gave that time to sink in and it still didn't make sense. "I'm sorry, what?"

"I live here. At the marina." He waved his hand down the slope to the north to a largely empty maze of wooden docks. In the summer months they would house a flotilla of sailboats and cruisers. "I have a houseboat. If I had looked out my window, I might have seen her, and that's what's killing me. I keep wondering if she had been coming to me and sat down for a rest. They say people get disoriented before they freeze to death."

Several things occurred to Theresa at once. Drew, the spurned lover, lived a two-minute walk from the crime scene. Also, he seemed to have gotten on board with the suicide theory . . . though if he wanted to murder someone, why not drag the body out to the edge of the ice and dump it into the lake? Why leave it on his own doorstep?

Unless he needed the body found. Getting hold of the funds would be difficult if Jillian were only missing and not dead. But how could he expect to get custody of Cara? Perhaps Theresa should be concerned about Evan's safety. More likely, Drew didn't care about the money. He cared about losing Jillian, with the finality of a marriage vow, to another man.

But if he killed Jillian, how?

While the wheels in her head smoked, she realized Drew had spoken. "What?"

"Would you like to see it? My houseboat?"

"Yes," she said without hesitation. Drew Fleming could, of course, be a murderous psychopath. But he also knew a lot about Jillian Perry, and she now had an invitation to question him further. She couldn't pass it up. She clutched her coat more tightly around herself to shelter her body from the wind rushing in from the lake, and walked with him down the paved path to the boats.

Constant exposure to the elements had worn the marina's veneer to a look of mild neglect, and a coating of frozen slush did not neaten it up, though the few boats remaining appeared large and expensive. Nylon straps and pulleys kept them above the frozen water. Theresa's ex-husband had once kept a boat at the Edgewater marina and she had cringed over the price of the rent. It was simply not possible to keep a waterfront location tidy; of course, this was part of the charm.

Drew lived near the end of one of the long wooden docks, and used a warped, loose two-by-four to board his home. Theresa put one foot in the middle of it and didn't look down. The Edgewater marina used the Mediterranean system of docking; instead of fingers of walkway extended between the vessels, ropes and pulleys connected to freestanding posts kept the boats in place. The only way to get on and off a boat was from the rear. Theresa remembered that detail from her ex-husband's boat as well. Returning to shore had been a panicky and bruising nightmare, dashing from stern to bow with a hook in hand, trying to get ropes and spring clips where they needed to be before one hit the dock or, worse, another boat. She loved the lake as much as the next Clevelander, but didn't miss that part of it. Or the boat payments.

She landed on a teak deck lightly dusted with snow; the finish had darkened, but it felt solid enough. The straps swayed a bit with the vibration. The open area at the rear of the ship held a wooden folding chair and a plastic recycling bin. Anything else would have frozen or blown away.

Drew unlocked the door and slid it to one side. "Come on in."

If Jillian Perry had been murdered, Drew had the best motive and the best opportunity. And Theresa stood poised to lock herself in with him, without anyone knowing where she had gone, without a soul near enough to hear her if she screamed.

But Drew had existed for Jillian, and if anyone could tell Theresa more about the woman, he could. In a worst-case scenario, Cara's future could depend on what Theresa could learn about Jillian Perry.

She pulled out her cell phone. "Hang on a sec. I'm just going to call my daughter and tell her where I am."

He nodded without apparent interest and slid the door shut. Trying to keep the houseboat heated must be a constant struggle against wind and water.

Theresa did, indeed, call Rachael and told her precisely where her mother had gotten to, including the number of the dock and a description of the houseboat. She could only hope her daughter retained some detail over the siren song of satellite TV.

The warmth flowed over her skin as she stepped into Drew's living area. The inside felt as cluttered as the outside was bare; a worn but fashionable leather couch took up one wall and faced a small entertainment center and a slender wine rack. The tiny kitchen had a teak dining set wedged into one corner and stainless-steel accessories on the counter—blender, food processor, and cof-feemaker, now perking with a low grumble. Instead of dead fish, gasoline, or just that musty-unused-boat odor, the smell of hazelnut filled her sinuses.

Drew offered her a cup and she took off her gloves to wrap her fingers around the hot porcelain, then sat on the couch. A space heater on the floor added a separate burst of warmth. Every inch of wall space had been devoted to shelves, stereo equipment, posters, and photographs.

"I didn't know anyone lived on houseboats year-round in Cleveland. I would have thought it would be too cold."

"Most people only use them as second homes, but there's a small and dedicated contingent of us who can't afford a first one."

Comic book heroes adorned the posters, and comic books covered the coffee table. The cover closest to her featured a tall man in spandex holding what looked like an M60.

Drew dropped into an armchair across from her and gave his nose a discreet wipe with his sleeve. The change in air temperature made noses run. "That's one of my more popular series."

"You write comic books?"

He shouted a laugh. "I wish! No, I sell them. At a store on Madison."

"A bookstore?"

"No, comics. And graphic novels. Some collectibles."

The dead boy had been a comic book fan. "I have a piece of evidence in a case, a corner ripped from a page that has colored graphics on both sides. I assumed it came from a magazine but the paper seemed thinner. Now that I look at these, it could be a comic book. The colors look different."

"They're inked drawings, not photos. It's different."

"But it's glossy."

"Deluxe edition." He pulled a slim booklet titled "Batman #663" from the bottom of the pile on the coffee table and handed it to her. "They have glossy pages. It makes the colors more vivid. They use it for special storylines, like the whole Kingdom Come series. Or any time they want to charge more. Have they figured out what actually killed Jillian yet? Did she freeze to death?"

"It's looking that way, but toxicology results will take a while." She had no intention of discussing confidential details with a man who was not Jillian's next of kin, but that much had been printed in the *Plain Dealer*. "Does Jillian have other family in town? Now that her grandparents have died?"

"Her parents live somewhere in Parma, but they haven't spoken to her since they found out she's an—she became an escort. She told them she was a model, but her father took her business card and called George, pretending to be a customer, and got an earful. He screeched at Jillian and they haven't spoken since. Not even when Cara was born."

"What about her mother?" She didn't know why her cousin described interviewing as difficult. Drew could happily have spoken of Jillian Perry for the next three days, pausing only to sip coffee. He told her that Jillian had one sibling, a brother in New Mexico, but he never left the sunshine to come visit. Jillian's mother would take her call every few months, but only if the father wasn't home. Cara had been born without any significant problems, and Jillian did not seem unhappy at the absence of the baby's father. Anyway, Evan had entered her life.

Theresa, obviously free to pry to her heart's content, asked, "And she never told you who Cara's father is?"

"No. I told you that before." He shifted with apparent discomfort, as if more hurt by Jillian's refusal to share her secret than by her refusal to share her body.

Theresa tried to think of a kinder way to say it but couldn't. "I thought she told you everything," she said.

"Some things I didn't want to know," he snapped. "Wouldn't you, if you were me?"

The other men in her life seemed to be the only thing about Jillian that Drew didn't want to dwell on. Theresa tried another route. "Why *did* Jillian work as an escort?"

"It paid enough to cover her rent and had flexible hours. That way she could keep going to Tri-C."

"What did she major in?"

"She started in biology, but switched to education. She dropped out to have Cara. I enrolled to get an MBA to help me run the store, but I got too busy once the place developed a steady clientele."

"How did she get the job at Beautiful Girlz?"

Drew shrugged. "I think she answered an ad. I know it seems a little sleazy, but it wasn't, really. That job is sort of what you make it. There are sleazy girls there, sure, but Jillian just did the straight-pay, modeling-type things. Trade shows, business parties. Occasionally a date, when the guy wanted to impress his friends. But she wouldn't even let them kiss her."

As he went on about Jillian's healthy beauty and sweet nature, Theresa stopped listening and looked around. She had found pink cotton fibers on Jillian's sweatshirt, fibers that hadn't belonged to the polo shirt. They didn't appear to match anything in Drew's living area and most likely had come from Jillian's own towels. That smear of oil on the sleeve, though . . . there would be lots of things needing oil on a boat, right? He wouldn't be running the engines in the middle of winter, but plumbing and electricity still had to work.

". . . worried about Cara."

She tore her gaze from a *Star Wars* action figure from the original movie, its packaging intact. "What was that?"

"I said, Evan doesn't care about her. He only wanted Jillian's body, not her baby. It worried Jillian, how little interest he showed in Cara. What kind of life is Cara going to have, growing up with Evan?"

Theresa sipped her coffee, taking a moment to think. She had never interfered with a victim's family in any way, but for once considered making an exception. When she had suggested—well, threatened—the idea to Evan yesterday, she had had Jillian's parents in mind. But any applicant would do. As long as Evan thought Cara's million and a half wouldn't go to him upon the baby's death, the little girl would be safe. Even better than safe. If Evan needed to win a custody hearing, he'd keep the baby's well-being demonstrably perfect. Assuming, of course, that Cara had anything to fear from Evan.

But that had been before she learned of Drew's proximity to the crime scene. Now, though her gut wanted to trust the sweet comic-book salesman, her mind waved a few bright red flags. She perched on the fence, trying to remain in neutral territory. "Perhaps Jillian's parents will take Cara."

Drew's neck slumped into his shoulders. "They've never even seen Cara. I was the only friend Jillian had. She said so—look at what she sent me for my birthday."

He handed her an envelope, postmarked a month before, holding a funny American Greetings card. Under the punch line, Jillian had inscribed: *Thanks for always being there for me. Love you always, Jillian.* The friendship hadn't been all in Drew's head.

Theresa tried some gentle probing, a technique at which she'd never been particularly adept. "Cara appears to have been well cared for since Jillian disappeared, and lots of men aren't fascinated by babies, not until they grow old enough to show some personality. What makes you think Evan would be a bad father?"

"He treated Jillian like a princess until after they were married. Then she became just a pretty body, without a mind, without feelings. Look at that apartment, how it's decorated."

"It's very nice. He said Jillian did it."

"He ripped a picture out of a magazine and told her to copy it. The colors, everything. She added a wardrobe that she found at an antiques shop and he made her take it back. It wasn't in the picture."

Theresa leaned forward and opened her coat. The air had felt cozy at first, but now the warmth grew too heavy. "People often have different ideas about decorating. It took my ex-husband and me three months to find a coffee table we could agree on."

"He talked about his new video game constantly, but never listened or asked about her work. Think about that—you're a guy with a beautiful fiancée whose *job* it is to meet other men, and you don't ever ask where she's going or who she's going to be with?"

"Maybe he trusted her."

Drew straightened, and gave her a look so knowing that she decided to stop writing him off as a slightly warped dweeb. "No man trusts like that."

"That still doesn't make him a bad father."

Drew got to his feet with an agitated twitch. "The way I see it, there are two possibilities. One, Evan murdered Jillian to get Cara's money. Two, Evan drove Jillian to—" He stopped, gulped, went on. "Suicide. So how can we stand back and let someone like that raise her child?"

We? Again Theresa felt as if she tottered on a precipice, balancing between the safety of not getting involved and the possibility that Cara could be in danger. Instead of jumping, she tried to calm Drew—and herself—with reason. "But they'd only been married a few weeks."

"I can show you." He dove for the table in front of her, rummaged around in the slippery piles of comics, and came up with a pink vinyl photo album. He plopped it on Theresa's knees, startling her into spilling the coffee on her jeans.

She set the mug down after Drew cleared a spot among the comic books for the wet bottom. The photo album had a Hello Kitty emblem in one corner but no other markings. It had one subject: Jillian Perry.

Photos of Jillian on the houseboat, at the beach (in a maternity bathing suit), the grocery store, a few with endless racks of comic books behind her, obviously Drew's shop. At the hospital, a scrunched-up, red-faced Cara in her arms. Aside from the baby, no one else. In a few shots, other people stood near Jillian but Drew had cropped them out, cutting people off to just a sliver of human. Only Jillian remained.

"See?" Drew seated himself next to her on the couch, too close, reaching over to turn the pages faster to point out photos in which Jillian appeared as especially lovely. "See how happy she was? She glowed when Cara was born. Just glowed. Here's her old apartment, before she moved in with Evan. She made the curtains in that nursery by hand. They matched Cara's eyes, see?"

"Uh-huh." She really wished he'd move over.

He flipped another page. "Now this is after the wedding."

He missed a photo op like Jillian in a veil? "Did you go?"

"To the wedding? Yeah."

"But you didn't take any pictures?"

The muscles in his cheek tightened to cords. "Nah. Look at her face. This is a week after the wedding." He pointed out a photo of Jillian on the deck of the boat, a comely Eskimo in a pink parka, the baby a bundle of swaddling against her chest. Jillian smiled, but only smiled. No glow, and even a tiny line of worry above her eyebrows.

"Perhaps she was uncomfortable. It had to be freezing out."

"And here." Jillian by her car, obviously the same day, inserting her key into the door lock, only the barest of smiles and a discomfited one at that.

Jillian in her apartment, scrubbing a pan in the sink. Jillian holding Cara, with a smile, yes, but a tired one, apprehensive around the corners. The carefree grin of the earlier photographs had been erased. If Jillian hadn't been afraid of something, she'd at least been very, very concerned.

Still, Theresa thought it might not be wise to encourage Drew to blame Evan. That might invite further disaster. "Having an infant is exhausting, Drew. I can attest to that."

"She could have given perky lessons to Disney employees two months after Cara's birth. All of a sudden, at five months, she's tired? The only thing that changed was Evan."

"And her apartment. Maybe she wasn't sleeping well in a new place. Maybe Cara wasn't. That's the way it is with babies, Drew, one month isn't necessarily like the next. And marriage is a big change."

He sat close enough for her to notice the ink stains on his fingertips, and that perhaps he should launder his clothing more often. "She went from smiling to not in just a few days. Maybe I haven't walked down the aisle myself, but I know that's not how it's supposed to work."

She studied the photographs, the creepily plentiful photographs. The change in Jillian's mood did seem apparent . . . but there could be many reasons for that. Perhaps Jillian didn't like living on the old factory grounds, or couldn't sleep with the noise of the train tracks nearby. Perhaps Cara had developed a health problem, even something mild, that Jillian worried about but did not discuss with the childless Drew. And the first few months, the first year, of marriage were the hardest. She might have had a habit of calling her old friend after a good blowout with her husband. And perhaps Drew had kept only pictures that proved his theory, that Jillian had married the wrong man.

Or perhaps Jillian thought marriage would finally dampen Drew's obsession with her, and that had not happened. After all, Evan did not appear in the photographs to prompt that touch of fear in Jillian's eyes. Only Drew had been present.

"You've known Jillian for four years, you said?"

"Yeah, four years and a couple of months."

"Did you only recently get a camera? This album begins, what, five months ago?"

He spoke without hesitation. "This is the current one. I have others, um, at least seven. Would you like to see them?"

Eight photo albums of nothing but Jillian Perry. How had she walked that precipice of her own with this man for four years? Maintained a friendship without anger or despair? Kept him from falling into the abyss? Even marrying hadn't helped. No wonder she had trouble smiling for the camera.

All at once Theresa's skin crawled. She had done enough investigating for one day. The album slid from her lap as she stood; Drew Fleming caught it, cushioned it from harm. "Sorry, no, I have to get going."

He grabbed her arm just above the wrist. "But I have some really good ones."

"I'm sure you do."

"You have to understand, Theresa." His fingers tightened. "I'm trying to show you what happened to Jillian. I knew her better than anybody else."

Her thighs gave a twinge as she struggled to rise, her arm beginning to feel pinched. Afraid she didn't want to know the answer, she asked, "What happened to Jillian?"

His eyes were shiny, the blue glacier hard. "Evan did."

She breathed out in relief. For a moment she had expected a confession. Then she slid her arm from his fingers, stammered something about her daughter needing help on a school project, and thanked him for telling her about Jillian. She crossed the floor in four steps and pulled at the sliding door, her fingertips slipping from the shallow handle.

"No problem." He slid the door open for her and she escaped the cabin. Frigid air slapped her cheeks, woke her up. The deck swayed under her feet.

Still think he's harmless? Theresa asked herself.

Now Drew looked up at the gray haze that represented the sky. "You'll let me know what the doctors say, right?"

"I'll ask them to call you." This didn't guarantee that they would—normally medical information would be released only to the next of kin—but there was nothing she could do about that. From the rear deck she could see the copse of woods where the body had been found, and again felt that frisson of worry. Jillian Perry had practically died on her stalker's stoop. "You said you thought that Jillian might have been coming to visit you?"

Drew had already followed her line of sight. "Yeah. I mean, it's right there. I could have seen her from here."

"Were you home all day on Monday?" A nice way of asking if he had an alibi for the time of the alleged crime.

"No, I was at the shop. I'm open nine to seven."

"Did Jillian often walk here to visit you?"

He thought about this, holding his body tighter in his too-thin coat. "No, she always drove."

"Always?"

"Yeah. Jillian wasn't into exercise, believe it or not, despite her figure. She always told me, 'I'll jog only if someone's chasing me with a gun.' " The laugh faded from his lips as quickly as it had appeared; obviously he thought someone *had* chased Jillian, right into an icy death.

She climbed onto the back of the boat. "Does this . . . craft . . . have a name? I don't see one."

"It's on the front."

She waited.

"What else? It's *Jillian*." He shrugged as he said it, with a wry smile that seemed so reasonable, so normal, that her anxiety dissipated like a wisp of hot air on an icy day. Drew Fleming was not the only man who had ever carried a torch for an unattainable woman. And if Drew Fleming had killed Jillian, why wouldn't he sit back and let her be written off as a suicide? Why show up at the lab insisting on murder? Obsession could turn every bit as murderous as greed, but not as often. Greed remained the far more common motive.

"Thanks for talking to me," he added. "I'm just glad that someone else cares about her besides me and Cara."

Theresa placed one foot on the two-by-four, preparing to make the leap to solid ground. "Maybe we'll get lucky and Jillian's parents will win custody."

"I told you—they're not going to ask for it. They may not even know Jillian is dead, unless Evan told them. I certainly didn't."

"They'll be told. They're the official next of kin, so they'll have to at least be informed of Cara's guardianship."

Drew frowned. "But Evan is already the guardian. Isn't he?"

The two-by-four bent under Theresa's weight. It would hold her for a quick leap, but if she tried to balance on it for any length of time, it would bow too deeply, and she would fall to the frozen ice below.

"Not exactly," she admitted.

CHAPTER 10

MONDAY, MARCH 8

Theresa picked at the red tape stuck to her fingertips. She had sealed up no less than fourteen bags from the victim of an early-morning shooting, including two pairs of pants and four shirts of varying thicknesses. This by no means represented the record. Layering remained the best way to stay warm through a Cleveland winter, and those who spent many hours out of doors, like drug dealers, had to dress for the weather.

She tossed the last of the tape into the wastebasket, exited the amphitheater without watching where she was going, and bumped into the corner of a gurney parked in the hallway, sending it, with its occupant, sliding into Chris Cavanaugh. The Cleveland police department's star hostage negotiator and all-around great guy, if you read his book jackets.

"That's a hell of a greeting," he told her. Even the dim light in the hallway couldn't mitigate the dimples, the twinkling eyes, the gloss of each dark hair receding from his forehead.

"What are you doing here?"

"That's a hell of greeting too. I'm sorry you couldn't make lunch on Wednesday. Maybe another time."

She didn't respond, but he had already turned his head, watching through the open autopsy room door as two dieners swung a heavyset man onto a stainless-steel table in one well-practiced heave. The man appeared to be about forty, with a tattoo on one arm and a round, seeping hole in his chest.

"What are you doing here?" she asked again, but gently this time, guessing that she didn't want to hear the answer any more than he wanted to say it.

He continued to watch the activity around the dead man. "We had a domestic standoff this morning. It didn't end well."

A snotty comment about his formerly perfect no-bloodshed record would probably put an end to the sporadic lunch invitations, but she couldn't bring herself to do it. She thought about asking why he had come to attend the autopsy, but he would probably point out that detectives attended the autopsies of the cases they worked, so why not?

Besides, she thought she knew why he had come. "That's going to happen, you know," was all she could think of to say. "Things going bad."

"I know." He smiled and for a moment she could fool herself into thinking that she had cheered him up. The fact that she hadn't was made apparent by his brisk tone when he said he supposed he shouldn't keep her from her work and strode into the brightly lit autopsy suite as if counting on momentum to get him over the threshold.

Pride or guilt? She couldn't tell.

And she didn't care, right? The next door along the hallway led to the stairwell, and she climbed one flight to Christine Johnson's office.

The young pathologist had inherited the cubbyhole from a predecessor and wasted no time in filling its walls with medical texts and photos of her younger siblings. Theresa would have leaned on the writing counter—the office had room for only one chair—but it already swayed from the collection of knives, guns, and blunt instruments spilling over from a cardboard box. She leaned on the doorjamb instead. "I love what you've done with the place."

The doctor sat back in her chair and ran long fingers through her raven hair. "It has twenty-year-old carpeting and no window, but at least I don't have to share it. I don't share well."

"Really? You seem so sweet to me."

"You haven't ticked me off yet." Christine didn't smile when she said this, either.

"I'll keep that in mind. I need to ask you about a case."

"The kid? I have something for you, by the way—here are the wood flakes I pulled out of his head wound."

Theresa took the tiny envelope, feeling the fold of glassine paper inside it. "So the killer hit him with a wood object? Like a baseball bat?"

"I doubt it, the wound had some irregularities. But all I can really say is that it's wood, and you'll have to figure out the rest. Sign here and it's yours."

Theresa signed the evidence form. "Actually I wanted to know about Jillian Perry. White female, came in late Friday?"

For such a pretty face, Christine's could produce a scowl that would have stopped an army of advancing Huns. Perhaps Theresa had finally ticked her off.

"Her," the pathologist seethed.

"What about her?"

"She's driving me crazy, that's what. Insane. I sped up the tox results, looked at everything, histology sections, skin samples, history. Everything."

"Okaaay . . . and?"

"And I can't figure out why she's dead."

"She didn't freeze to death?"

"She might have."

"Or OD?"

"She might have. You can have a seat on my ammo locker, there."

Theresa sat on a small khaki-colored box next to the wall. With a handle on the top, it didn't make for the most comfortable seating, but she'd been on her feet all morning. "I don't think I've ever worked a freezing death before. Though I could have—if it's not a homicide, I don't pay much attention."

"I've seen a few, usually the homeless or drug addicts who tried to stay outside too long. Jillian Perry shows some of the signs of it, the bluish-white skin, slightly reduced lividity. It would have taken only a few hours—right next to the lake, which would put moisture and wind in the air and speed it up. She was slender and not warmly dressed; that would speed it up too. Were the branches around her broken as if she was stumbling around?"

"Not really. I think she took the same path into the woods that we did. I noticed two broken branches that had ice on the broken parts, so it wasn't the cop or Frank who broke them. Nothing else within sight."

"She didn't have bruises, scratches, or tears in her clothes either, so she probably sat down before the disorientation set in. After that her heart would have stopped. Was she frozen to the ground when you found her?"

"She was pretty stiff. It's not like we had to chip her away or anything, but then several days had passed. The temperature rose and fell a few degrees."

"True."

The doctor drummed her fingernails, coated in a chocolate color that nearly matched her skin, on a copy of *Medicolegal Investigation of Death* for so long that Theresa finally interrupted, "So did she freeze to death?"

The drumming stopped. "A few things bother me."

Theresa leaned forward, pressing her shoulders toward her knees. The handle of the ammo box deepened its impression into her buttocks.

"Freezing is, by nature, not an obvious diagnosis. You don't have any hard-core proof of it as a cause of death. Kind of like drowning—if you find someone in the water and no other signs, you assume they drowned. You might find water in the lungs, or you might not. In freezing, you might find cherry-red lividity, petechiae in the peripheral muscles, abrasions of the skin, or you might not."

"And in Jillian?"

"Nothing. The only unusual thing about her body was a kind of weird smell to the organs. But I could have been imagining that for all I know, so unremarkable was her autopsy. Meanwhile, I'm having tox check for amylase in the vitreous humor and elevated levels of catecholamines. That might tell us something."

"It might tell *you* something. *I* have no idea what you just said."

"Those are chemical indications of hypothermia. Sometimes. Did she have a white residue around her nose and mouth when you found her? Maybe it looked like she'd eaten a mouthful of snow?"

"No. Though the temperature had warmed up some."

"But it never went above freezing all week. I checked. Most victims will have a white rime on their faces; their respiration freezes once outside the body."

The significance of that flooded Theresa's brain, expanding the set of possibilities. "So she wasn't breathing as she sat in the cold? She didn't freeze to death?"

"I don't know. All these indications might be present, might not be. They don't prove or disprove either way. Human bodies vary a lot in their responses; no matter how science advances, there's still so much that we don't know. That's why if you're going to bring me victims, give me a good shooting or stabbing any day. I know what to do with that." She stroked the twelve-inch blade of a large knife serving as a paperweight.

"I'll keep that in mind."

"Supposedly she walked to this spot by the lake?"

"We found her car in the garage."

"Two or three miles away?"

All this talk of cold made Theresa feel overwarm. "Depending on the route she took. That's not very far, really, I jog two miles every day."

"Ever try it in six-degree weather with no hat or gloves?"

"No."

"Want to know what your extremities would look like if you did?"

"Something tells me I don't."

"I did my residency at Metro. I had a rotation on Christmas Eve—"

"Bummer," Theresa interjected without thinking, knowing how important holidays were to someone from a big, close-knit family.

"Christmas Eve and Christmas Day. You can't get much lower on the department totem pole than that. Anyway, this mother and her teenage daughter came in with frostbite to their hands and the tips of their noses. They had decided to make an after-dinner convenience store run in nearly zero-degree weather without gloves. Now their situation was worse—the walk was nearly two miles each way, and the freezing, then thawing when they reached the store, then freezing again on the way back, then thawing when they got home and tried to help themselves by putting their hands in warm water, definitely aggravated the situation. But their hands were blackened and the skin shrunk against the fingers. It looked as if they'd held their hands in a campfire."

"Ew."

"I'd been working on accident victims and homicides for three months, and it still made me want to throw up. Now here we have Jillian Perry. Perhaps she had five or six more degrees of temperature in her favor, but still. They lost fingers and toes. Her skin is unblemished."

Theresa agreed. She had examined Jillian's hands and face thoroughly, and seen nothing like the damage Christine described. "So you're thinking she was already dead, and someone placed her body in the woods?"

Christine picked up the knife, wiggling it toward Theresa in a vague gesture. "Same problem. What did she die of? There are no obvious signs of hypothermia, but there are no obvious signs of anything else either. No violence. No needle marks. No pulmonary emboli or even congestion. I even looked for birefringent crystals. I had to drag the polarizing microscope out from behind Banachek's filing cabinet."

"You could have used mine."

"I'll remember that next time."

"So she didn't OD."

"I don't know yet. I'm having tox run the blood and gastric again for lower levels of narcotics, something that might have gently slowed her down until she simply stopped breathing. Was she taking anything?"

"I don't know."

"You went to her house, right?"

"To collect for DNA comparison only." Theresa tried to stamp the defensive tone out of her voice. "Frank checked the kitchen and I checked the bathroom medicine cabinet. Nothing but the usual household stuff."

"The bedroom was clear?"

"I don't know," Theresa said again, kicking herself. Searching a victim's, or potential victim's, area for drugs was standard procedure. Even if the items were perfectly legal, the information would be needed for a clear picture of the death. And a cursory search did not always suffice. Theresa had once found a twenty-one-year-old's heroin kit neatly packed into an innocent-looking sewing kit and left in plain sight on her closet shelf. She had stumbled on it only because she had grown bored waiting for the body snatchers and had nothing else to do but poke around. Jillian Perry could have had a pharmacy in her nightstand for all Theresa knew.

"Well," Christine comforted, "it's hard to take enough narcotics to kill yourself without it showing."

"What if it were a combination of the two? She took enough narcotic, say sleeping pills or something, to depress her bodily functions, but then the cold finished her off? There wouldn't be any white residue because her breathing became shallow, with no signs of OD because she didn't take enough drugs."

"That leaves us in the same boat. There are no definite indications of either hypothermia or overdose, and even working together they'd leave some trace. *Something* had to have killed her." She emphasized this last point with the tip of the large knife.

"Would you mind not pointing that thing at me?"

Christine glanced at the knife in her hands as if she didn't recognize it, then tossed it into the box with a clatter. "So that's what bothers me. What bothers you?"

Theresa collected her thoughts, and summarized: "This woman had a really weird life. Lived in a factory, worked as an escort, still best friends with a wannabe boyfriend, never touched her daughter's huge trust fund. The new husband has a motive and an attitude. I can't help feeling there's more to the story even though there's plenty to the story already. Call it a hunch."

"You don't get hunches."

"Maybe it's time to start."

The doctor smiled for the first time since Theresa entered the room. "I'll admit, it's nice to see something pique your interest. That hasn't happened in a while."

Not since Paul died. Theresa knew the other woman spoke the absolute truth, but still resented it. "I've been negligent?"

"You've been depressed."

"No, I haven't." Theresa stood, smoothing her lab coat down. "I know depressed, and this isn't it."

"Grieving, then."

"Let me know if you find anything further in the Perry case." She turned to go.

"Theresa."

She stopped. Ridiculous, since Christine was a good dozen years younger than she was, but doctors were taught that voice-of-authority trick in med school. They were also taught that look, the one that could tell you hadn't slept a night through, truly enjoyed a meal, been able to concentrate on a movie, or exfoliated your skin in nine months and still cried at every stupid, sentimental thing you saw, from greeting card commercials to a perfect autumn day.

"How are you doing?"

She'd come to dread that question during the past months. Every time, it felt as if she'd never been asked such a question before, one so strange and difficult. She gave the answer she always gave, also strange and difficult because it was a lie and lying didn't come easily to her. "I'm fine."

"I saw that hostage-negotiator guy here earlier. Is he still calling you?"

The question surprised her into facing Christine again. "Now and then."

"Asking you out?"

Theresa cut the topic off without heat. "That would be problematic. I met him the day my fiancé died."

"Yeah, but . . . he seems nice. I saw him on TV yesterday, explaining how they tossed a camera into this domestic standoff. Nice dimples. I'm just saying, perhaps you should let him buy you dinner, put him out of his misery."

Happy to discuss anyone but herself, Theresa pointed out, "A guy who's seen with as many different women as he is is hardly miserable."

"But he's gorgeous," the young woman persisted, teasing.

No one had dared to tease her for eight months, and it felt kind of good. "Think this through, Christine. This is a man whose entire job is to manipulate people, to get them to do what he wants them to do. Why would I want to date someone like that?"

"Ahem. Did you miss the gorgeous part?"

"I didn't miss it. I'm just ignoring it. Besides, Rachael keeps me busy enough. She's got a concert tonight, a school talent show this Wednesday, and she's working on a ski trip. Doubling as her chauffeur eats up all my spare time."

Theresa stepped out of the way as another pathologist shuffled in, his nose buried in a thick autopsy report. He began to ask Christine about a victim's spleen, but she interrupted him. "How about Dr. Banachek, then? He's cute."

Theresa couldn't help but laugh as Dr. Banachek, rotund, bespectacled, and old enough to be her grandfather, blinked at them in confusion. "I can't go out with Phil. He's married."

"But," he said, "I *am* cute."

CHAPTER 11

The lightening of her mood didn't last one flight of stairs, and by the time she reached the trace evidence lab, she could feel the wrinkle forming between her eyebrows. Don spotted it too. "What are you looking so glum about?"

She perched on a task chair, hoping the hard rubber seat would massage out the imprint on her butt left by the ammo box handle, and rolled a few feet closer to him. "Jillian Perry."

"The suicide-by-freezing?"

"Alleged suicide. Maybe accidental. Maybe homicide. I don't know."

He unwrapped a sterile, disposable scalpel and used it to cut a tiny square from a swab. The white cotton had barely been stained. "You know, you give me swabs for DNA analysis, you could at least make sure they have some DNA on them first."

"That's from the straps of the bra used to strangle Sarah Taylor. No blood, sorry. I'm hoping for some skin cells from the killer's hands."

"This was her bra," he stated.

"Yep."

126

"Which she wore right up against her skin."

"Hey, I don't make the circumstances, I just react to them. Sure, you'll probably find a mixture, but the other half of it will most likely be male and then you can do Y-STRs." She rested her chin on one hand.

"Which we don't have a database of yet." Y-STRs were the target strands on the Y chromosome used for DNA testing. They were useful for separating male-female mixtures of the same type of cells, but the results hadn't been compiled into a database for years and years, as with the older PCR and STR analyses. They would need a suspect to compare to any Y-STRs found, and so far the cops didn't have one.

"It can't be that hard. They do it on TV all the time."

He dropped the tuft of cotton into a microtube, squeezed the flip cap shut, and wrote a number on it with a thin Sharpie marker. "Did your Jillian Perry have any signs of violence?"

"Not a one."

"Well then."

Theresa sat up and buttoned her lab coat. "Yeah. I should probably just write it up and forget about it."

"You probably should."

"Yeah."

"But you're not going to."

"No one can figure out what she died of. How often does that happen?"

"Lots of times. Heart attacks, SIDS . . . often there's no obvious pathology."

"It's bugging Christine too."

He folded the shirt back into its original packaging and pulled out the red evidence tape. "Oh, boy. You and Christine together. Jillian Perry's case will remain open for the next hundred years."

She watched him fill his row of microtubes, using a repeater pipette to dispense a reagent to break down the cells and release the DNA. "Don, do you like video games?"

He looked askance at her, but, as always, rolled with her shifts of mind. "They kept me sane during board exams. Why?"

"Jillian Perry's husband has a game called Polizei. I mean, he created it, owns it, sells it, whatever you call it."

"The guy who made that lives in Cleveland? I didn't know that."

"You've played it?"

"I never got all the way through. I get stuck at the banquet hall every time. At first you think these army-guard-looking guys are there to protect you, but once you close the doors they turn on you because they're actually vampires, and—"

"Whoa. I'm not going to be playing it, thanks."

"—it's pretty cool," he finished after gesturing with the pipette.

"Could I borrow it?"

"I thought you weren't going to be playing it."

"I'll have Rachael handle the shooting and finding the secret passageways. How popular is this game?"

"It's big. And getting bigger every day. If you're a teenager and you've never heard of it, you'll probably get beat up at school."

"What a lovely analogy. So the guy who makes it must be pretty rich."

"And getting richer." He finished placing microtubes, one by one, into the incubator. "Why?"

"It kind of knocks out money as a motive."

"Motive for what?"

"The perfect murder, apparently. One that doesn't seem to be a murder, and probably isn't."

"You're not making a lot of sense."

"I know. Tell me more about this game. I promise not to interrupt you this time."

"I'd love to, but it's time for lunch and I'm supposed to meet Janelle for a pizza. Want to join us?"

"No, thanks. I've got some samples from the clothing that I want to run through the FTIR."

He slipped a timer into the pocket of his lab coat to remind him of when the DNA samples would be ready to come out of the incubator and stood up. Then he added, without looking at her, "It's nice to see you semi-obsessing over a case again. But I wouldn't let Leo catch you after you stuck him with that defense expert's visit on Friday."

"Catch me doing what?"

"Breathing."

She watched him leave. His current girlfriend worked at the Rainbow and Babies & Children's Hospital next door, and the attached medical school had a food court. Theresa felt a twinge of guilt at not being able to recall the last time she'd accompanied him to lunch; she usually liked to meet his girlfriends. Not one had yet lived up to her standards, any more than had Rachael's boyfriends. She wanted perfection for the people she cared about, and she cared about Don.

She sat in front of the stereomicroscope and opened the envelope of the tapings she'd collected at the scene from Jillian Perry's clothing. A second envelope held the tapings she'd collected from the clothing after it had been removed. The stereomicroscope functioned as a very powerful magnifying glass, and the squiggles of color caught in the adhesive turned into hairs and fibers, pieces of leaves, and even one tiny metallic sphere.

The surface of the acrylic aqua sweatshirt had given up, naturally enough, a number of aqua fibers, and also some pink ones, most likely from the polo shirt. Dark blue cotton fibers probably belonged to the jeans, but one dark, smooth fiber lacked the irregular convolutions of cotton. Theresa removed it, cleaned any residue of tape adhesive with xylene, and mounted it on a glass slide. Then she took the housekeeping step of mounting fibers from every item of clothing Jillian Perry had worn on her body. All this took some time, but it had to be done. Evidence meant nothing without a standard to compare it to.

Using the comparison microscope, which transmitted light through an item instead of shining a light onto an item the way the stereomicroscope did, Theresa could magnify the fibers up to forty times. She could even cheat and put the tapings directly on the stage to observe the fibers in transmitted light without mounting them on glass slides first—the quality lacked, but it was good enough for a quick elimination. She took the sphere over to the toxicology department and gave it to Oliver. He had gone into his usual charade of refusing to waste the mass spectrometer's time on it, as if the large machine had a busy social calendar, but after five minute of goading he relented and said he would get to it when he had time. Oliver also gave her the distinct impression that this condition would not occur in any sort of timely manner.

Over the next hour or so, between the microscope and the infrared spectrometer, she learned that the aqua fibers belonged to the aqua sweatshirt—or rather, in the correct parlance, were consistent with having originated from the aqua sweatshirt. She could never *prove* they did, since there could easily be two aqua sweatshirts floating around Cleveland's west side. Some of the pink cotton fibers on the aqua sweatshirt belonged to the polo shirt but some did not, though with Jillian's penchant for pink there must be plenty of sources at the apartment. The blue cotton had come from her jeans. There were a few other fibers, a purple trilobal nylon, a black round nylon, and two black fibers that confused her at first. Their composition seemed to vary along the length, which eliminated synthetic fibers, but the shaft appeared too regular to be natural. A third strand of the same type of fiber had been snagged by the blackberry bush.

Could Jillian have had a blanket with her, which someone— perhaps a homeless person who figured she wouldn't need it anymore—later removed? Theresa moved to her computer and clicked on the folder with the photos from the scene, but saw no signs of her temporary theory. The snow had settled on Jillian's body and the surrounding area evenly. If she had originally been covered, the cover must have been removed promptly after her death.

Theresa took a minute to separate out the photos from Jacob Wheeler's scene and place them in a new folder. Before moving them to the hard drive, though, she took another look at the shots of his bedroom, zooming in on the stacked cases in front of his TV stand. Sure enough, Polizei sat right on top. Don hadn't been wrong when he said the game had become insidiously popular.

She closed that folder and took another look at the pictures of Jillian's apartment. She had taken only a few, and only to document from where she had collected the items for possible DNA analysis. All her towels, bedding, and other textiles seemed to be pink or brown. No black. The rest of Jillian's bedroom appeared as innocuous in the photos as it had in real life. Theresa hit the magnifying glass icon and zoomed in.

Perfume bottles, a bra, the book of crossword puzzles. Pillows in disarray. A few pieces of paper, half folded and tucked behind the baseball cap on one of the end tables. Theresa zoomed in further. The resolution did not allow her to read the paper, but since the information had been arranged in columns she took it to be a financial statement, particularly since the tidy letterhead featured a green-and-yellow circle with a dollar sign. It didn't seem a bit familiar or like any local bank's logo. Theresa hit the printer icon, lost in a happy fantasy that she would both find the Kovacics' accountant and that he would be an extremely garrulous one.

"What are you doing?" Leo asked, his face next to her shoulder. She shot a few inches straight up, bumping his chin and sending her heart rate off the charts.

"Just looking something up . . . I was working on Jillian Perry's fibers. I've got kind of a strange one here—"

"That hooker who froze to death? You're still working on that?"

"She wasn't a hooker, and Christine can't find a cause of death."

"She also isn't a homicide. We have people here who are. Plus your old friend Richard Springer is going to be here any minute, with entourage."

"I thought he came Friday."

"Oh no, my dear. I put him off. I wasn't going to endure a visit from that weasel all by my lonesome. Besides, I'm not paying you to work closed cases."

"Odd. I thought the taxpayers of Cuyahoga County were paying me."

"They're not paying you to work closed cases either."

"It's not closed. It's still very, very open," she insisted, but to empty air. Leo had darted off again.

She took advantage of the quiet to place the tapings back into their envelopes and remove the piece of aqua sweatshirt with the oil stain on it. She carefully smeared the stain onto a round, flat circle made of potassium bromide and dropped this into a slot on the stage of the FTIR. The Fourier transform infrared spectrometer pitched a beam of light through her sample and provided a single colored line on the results graph. The peaks identified the functional groups present in the molecules of the sample. She stared, consulted her library of spectra, stared again.

It wasn't oil. It wasn't paint, adhesive, dirt, or lip gloss. So what the hell *was* it?

The only familiar compound seemed to be phenol, a corrosive often used in the DNA process. It hadn't been strong enough to damage the sweatshirt, but had left just a spot.

She repackaged the piece of sweatshirt, still puzzled. Now only the envelope Christine had given her remained on the counter, so she examined the tiny pieces of wood left in Jacob Wheeler's scalp. The particles appeared, under strong magnification, as irregular chunks of dark and bloodstained matter, with sharp edges. Theresa did not consider herself an expert on wood, but she had seen particles over the years—baseball bats and two-by-fours remained popular murder weapons—and though she would not swear to it in court, this did not appear to be treated wood. It seemed too porous, with no trace of an adhering varnish or other polishes.

Well, Christine had said the wound had been irregular, which would not indicate a smooth surface like a baseball bat. More likely, the killer had picked up a handy, hefty tree branch and brained young Jacob with it. It knocked out premeditation. It also made recovery of the weapon nearly impossible, for where does a wise man hide a stick? In a forest. Preferably a forest where it has snowed all night, so that the murder weapon, if tossed away, would be covered with a layer of white by the time the body was found, and would be impossible to distinguish from all the other fallen branches and leaves and twigs and underbrush around. It probably didn't have any blood on it either, since the first blow usually doesn't bleed quickly enough to transfer to the weapon, though it might have hairs or skin snatched up by its rough surface—

"You remember our trace analyst, Theresa MacLean."

She looked up to see Leo guiding three men to her workstation. The defense expert and the defense attorney both glowed in smug victory, while the judge looked irritated. Theresa focused on his shirt, a light blue designer job with minuscule burgundy stripes.

"Tencel," she said.

The attorney stepped back, as if she were raving and possibly dangerous.

"I beg your pardon?" the judge asked.

"Tencel. It's a cellulosic fiber, made of wood pulp but very strong. Retains dye better than rayon and drapes nicely when combined with wool or silk. Good afternoon, Mr. Springer. Awful weather we're having, isn't it?"

CHAPTER 12

The Internet made everyone more independent. Instead of having to pick up the phone and perhaps speak to another human, Theresa had typed what little she knew into Yahoo! Maps and printed out directions to Delta Dynamics, arriving there in less than ten minutes without a single wrong turn.

The company occupied a second-floor suite in the Hanna Building at the corner of East Fourteenth and Euclid. At this time of day, just before the rush-hour race officially commenced, more people were leaving downtown Cleveland than approaching and Theresa found a vacant metered space. She dropped in a quarter, which might not suffice if the person she had come to see proved as talkative as Drew Fleming.

A revolving door took her through a little convenience store and out to the elevator banks, where she stared at the ornate ceiling before entering the car. The hundred-year-old building had been well maintained.

Except for the Delta Dynamics suite. No decor hid the chipped paint and the air smelled like plastic, but the heavy black girl at the counter beamed with welcome.

Theresa could have called Jerry Graham and asked for his girl-friend's name, but Evan Kovacic had become her suspect, without doubt, without mitigation, and she saw no reason to announce her intentions to his camp. And so she stumbled through an explanation of who she needed to see, and why. "She's a black woman, about my height, slender, very pretty."

The receptionist nodded her encouragement, but did not fill in a name.

"I think she's friends with, or is dating or something, Jerry Graham from Kov—"

"Shelly Peters." The receptionist picked up her handset, dialed some numbers.

"Oh. You know Jerry Gr—"

"Everyone knows Jerry Graham. The guy's brilliant. Shelly? Yeah, someone here to see you? Theresa MacLean. I don't know. Okay." She hung up, looked up, and went on. "Everyone who's into video games, I mean, which is about seventy-five percent of the people here. Crazy, I say. We all work on computers all day long and then go home and play on them all night long. I swear I weighed one-twenty before I discovered Ultima Online. Now look at me. Way too big."

She didn't seem bothered by it, however, so Theresa did not comment. "What's Ultima Online?"

"It's an MMO—massive multiplayer online. Totally addictive. You never know what's going to happen in there. It's like its own world. Characters have businesses, merge, betray. Last month a bunch of people sent their characters to the castle at the same time and had a sit-down strike until the company gave them a release date for the upgrade."

Theresa tried to picture this, and couldn't. "You mean players went to the factory, or something?"

"No, in the game."

"Revolt is written into the game?"

"No, the game just defines the world. After that, what happens depends on what the players do."

"The players can do things the manufacturers didn't design?"

The receptionist laughed. "Yeah, of course! The manufacturer is like God. Once he makes the world and lets people in, the people will do things he didn't plan on. Just like human beings," she added, her face growing serious as she pondered this philosophical insight. "They do all sorts of things He didn't plan on. Sometimes bad things."

The woman Theresa had seen kissing Jerry Graham appeared. She wore a formfitting pantsuit and her hair had come loose from its spikes, framing her face. She extended her hand and smiled. "I'm Shelly Peters. What can I do for you?"

Theresa introduced herself as a medical examiner's office investigator, which was a lie and not a lie at the same time. Investigators had a specific position, different from hers, but on the other hand all forensic staff were to consider themselves investigators, not robots simply collecting and analyzing and doing only what they were told, according to Leo, so she felt safe with the statement. "We're still working on Jillian Perry's death certificate, and I'm trying to determine her state of mind prior to her death."

Shelly Peters immediately stopped smiling. "It's such a tragedy about Jillian. I can't believe that would happen—it's so weird. Why on earth would she—why don't you come back to my office and we can talk there? I have some questions for you too."

Theresa thanked the receptionist before following Shelly down a narrow hallway, dodging cardboard boxes. "Please excuse our mess," the woman explained as they went. "We moved before the painters could get in here, and so we're trying to unpack only what we absolutely have to have so that we don't have to move it all again to get at the walls. But we're so busy, that's proving impossible, so there's just stuff everywhere."

The walls of her nine-by-nine office remained blank, but apparently Shelly could not resist installing a few items on her worn metal desk—a teddy bear, a bundle of silk flowers, and three framed photographs, one of herself and Jerry Graham. The rest of the office space had been given over to paper, keyboards, hard drives, two file cabinets, three loose monitors, and more paper.

"I don't even have a place for you to sit," she apologized. "You can try that stack of Office Depot boxes."

"I'm so sorry for your loss," Theresa began, finding the cases of copy paper to be more comfortable than Christine's ammo box. She had heard about Jillian from men; high time to get a woman's perspective. "Were you close?"

Shelly seemed to think that over before answering. "We were friends. I saw quite a bit of her, with our men always being together. But we weren't *best* friends or anything. I've only known her for, oh, two years or so. Maybe a little less."

"Where did you meet?"

"At a trade show." She gestured at their surroundings. "Delta handles all the data-management needs for trade shows. A lot of business gets done there, and the attendees need networking, Internet access, printers, et cetera, beyond what the hotels can provide and beyond what the vendor's representatives are familiar with. They're salesmen, not IT guys. So we come in, and not just in Cleveland. I travel all over the country. Anyway, I met Jillian at the Outdoors Expo. She was leaning on a Hummer and we got to talking."

"We found the phone number for these offices on a piece of paper in her pocket. I assume you gave it to her?"

"Yeah, we had the phones installed only last week, so I wrote the number down when we were at dinner last Saturday, I think it was. I didn't have a direct line. Still don't, as a matter of fact," she said, chuckling. "I wanted her to have it in case . . ."

"In case what?"

"I don't know," she said, and from the look on her face, she really didn't. "I just figured, all alone in that big place, with a baby, Evan and Jerry gone all the time either setting up those other buildings on the campus or downtown at meetings. You had to know Jillian, really. She always struck me as too sweet. Vulnerable, you know? Not dumb—she was smart enough to handle her own life and take good care of Cara—just too . . . sweet."

"Did she seem depressed? Maybe have the baby blues?"

The woman smiled at the idea. "No, not at all. Cara enchanted her, totally. She thrilled at every single thing about that baby. She said she couldn't wait for Cara to wake up from her naps because she missed her. That is why I can't really believe Jillian killed herself."

"I'm having a hard time explaining that too, how she could have frozen to death. Did she drink at all? Do any drugs?"

Shelly scowled, and Theresa held up her hands. "We're not

looking to prosecute anybody. I'm trying to find out why Jillian walked three miles from home in six degrees without a coat or hat."

"I understand, and you must hear this a lot, but no, Jillian didn't do anything like that. She'd have a glass of wine once in a while, after Cara was born, but nothing stronger than that. She didn't even smoke. That was one of the reasons I introduced her to Evan, to get him away from all those nerdy little VG groupie girls. At least Jillian lived in the *real* world."

"You're not into video games?"

"Sure, I like them. But I've been to conventions with Jerry, and let me tell you, you get the feeling some of those people have lost the ability to distinguish between fantasy and reality. Of course you could probably say the same thing about Trekkies."

"So Jillian wasn't into video games either?"

"Nah. She tried Polizei, since Evan talked about it all the time, but she didn't see the attraction. Besides, Cara kept her pretty busy."

So Jillian wouldn't have frozen to death trying to re-create a scene from the game, the way Dungeons & Dragons had been blamed for a few accidents over the years. "You introduced her to Evan?"

"Yeah. I didn't know she was pregnant. She told him right away, but he didn't care. That's quite a guy who will take on someone else's child. I spent a few years raising my sister's kids, and in my heart of hearts I hold it against her. Can't help it. But Evan, as far as he was concerned, Cara was his. He's a good guy." She held Theresa's gaze when she said that, as if defying her to argue. "Jerry wouldn't be his friend if he wasn't."

"And they were married only three weeks ago?"

"Four, now, yeah." Her eyes grew damp at the recollection. "One of the prettiest weddings I've ever seen. Small, but perfect."

"Any honeymoon?"

"No, not with Polezei Two still not done. All leaves canceled, that sort of thing. Besides, Jillian didn't want to either leave Cara or travel with her; she's still too little."

A young man in a fuzzy sweatshirt zoomed in, dropped a thick file on Shelly's desk, said, "Bath and cosmetic products, Atlanta, April twenty-second," and zoomed out again.

"Goody." Shelly opened a Day-Timer, made a note. "I love those free samples—one of the perks of the job."

Theresa tried to think of her own job perks. Only the prodigious supply of latex gloves and an appreciation of anything that smelled nice came to mind. "Were Jillian and Evan having any problems?"

"That would make her suicidal? I doubt it. At least I don't think so . . ."

Theresa waited.

"Not with Evan, I mean. But Jillian said once that she was the only family Cara had. I think she felt bad that her parents wouldn't even come to see her."

Theresa, not for the first time, gave silent thanks for having a mother who would have supported her if she had borne Adolf Hitler's baby. "What's up with them, anyway?"

"You ask me, it's a control thing. Daddy controls the universe and his wife has to do what she's told. Then baby girl has the nerve to not only *not* marry the football hero Daddy had picked out for her, but she leaves the house, works at a job he doesn't want to explain to his friends, and gets knocked up by some mystery man she won't even name."

"Who *is* Cara's father?"

"No idea." Shelly shook her head. "I asked once or twice, encouraged her to get child support, and she said, 'That knight's armor has tarnished.' That's all, subject closed. When I said Jillian was sweet, I didn't mean she made herself an open book. She hardly talked about herself at all. I liked her, but I can't say I really *knew* her. I'd like to ask you, though, what about that woman found in the Cultural Gardens? Channel Fifteen says there may be a connection between her and Jillian and that teenager."

"Channel Fifteen is wrong."

"But this black woman was murdered?"

"Definitely."

"And you're investigating Jillian?" Who probably wasn't, Shelly's expression said. Because a white girl always got more action than a black chick, even if they were in a similar line of work.

"We're investigating both of them, of course, but I don't believe they're connected. Sarah's crime scene was quite different from Jillian's."

"Sarah?"

"Sarah Taylor. I'm sorry, but I can't say more than that about an open investigation." Shelly's shoulders relaxed a bit, apparently reassured that Theresa at least knew the dead prostitute's name. Theresa moved on. "Are you acquainted with her friend Drew Fleming?"

Shelly wrinkled a pert nose. "The comic-book guy? Yeah, I've met him."

"You don't like him?"

"I guess he's okay. Seems like a nice guy." Shelly pressed her lips together, cutting off any further comment.

So Theresa pressed. "Seems?"

Now Shelly nibbled on the bottom lip. "Weird. Way too obsessed with Jillian. He came to the wedding, standing in this room full of people, and he never stopped staring at her. I tried to talk to him, he answered in monosyllables, never looked me in the eye. She made a beautiful bride, but come *on*. It seemed creepy to me."

"Did Evan resent this?"

"Another man worshipping his woman from afar? Why would he?"

That fit, in more genteel language, with what Evan had let the boys at the tech show assume. "Because Drew didn't stay afar. He kept seeing Jillian, even after the wedding."

"Look at Drew and look at Evan. No contest. Nothing to worry about there." The idea made her smile, but then the grin faded, changed to something worried. "You don't think Drew could have done something to her, do you? Picked her up, had an argument, dropped her off at the beach and told her to walk, and she couldn't make it?"

It didn't sound as if Shelly knew where Drew lived, and Theresa didn't see the need to enlighten her—yet she had to stop feeling protective of Drew just because he reminded her of a few geeky cousins and uncles of her own. His proximity to the scene, his moodiness, hung in her mind, a faint but persistent fog of doubt. "Even from the beach it's a short walk to the street. She could have gotten to a warm store or a gas station, used the phone."

Another young man, this one wearing a dress shirt and too much facial hair, stopped in the doorway. "Shelly, we need—"

"I'll be there in a sec."

"I'm sorry," Theresa said. "You're busy."

"That's all right. Anything I can do . . . I really want to know what happened. Jillian was my friend."

Theresa pulled out the picture of the letterhead on Evan's nightstand. "Just one more thing—do you recognize this logo?"

"Yes. It's one of the company's investors—Evan and Jerry's, I mean, not Delta. Why?"

"What's their name, this investment group?"

Shelly's parents had obviously taught her to tell the truth, but right now Theresa wondered if the girl wished they hadn't. "Griffin Investments."

Theresa looked again at her own photo with genuine surprise. "And they don't use a griffin as their logo?"

This non sequitur must have reassured Shelly, who laughed and added, "They're out of Detroit, I think. Why?"

"Just curious, really." Theresa stood. "I'd like to talk to Jerry too. Do you think he'd mind?"

Shelly put out a hand to shake. "I'm sure he wouldn't. He'd like an answer as much as me, or Evan."

I wonder, Theresa thought as she waited by the expired meter for a chance to dart onto East Fourteenth and enter her car. Shelly would like to know the truth about Jillian's demise, but Theresa wondered if Evan would be more than content to write off his wife as a suicide. Assuming Jerry Graham had nothing to do with Jillian or her death, whose wishes would he side with? His girlfriend's or his partner's?

Only one way to find out.

CHAPTER 13

Problem was, she didn't know where to find Jerry Graham, and knew only one place to look. Theresa pulled out of the parking spot and headed for the freeway instead of the lab. Leo might wonder what had happened to her, but she would think of something to tell him. Quitting time grew nigh anyway.

She crossed over the Cuyahoga River. A Coast Guard tug, black and white with touches of red, thrust itself through the frozen water below. It chopped up the ice to give the ore ships access to the river and begin the year's shipping season. The wind moaned across her windshield and she wondered how long it would take nature to undo the ship's work.

The cold had been insidious for the past month. If Evan—or Drew—had taken Jillian, either alive, unconscious, or dead, to the edge of the water, he must have used a car. Carrying a 110-pound weight for a three-mile walk might have been possible, but would have been enormously risky and physically excruciating in such cold weather. Thus a car, one with no outstanding warrants—and he would have been careful to avoid breaking even the most minor traffic rule during the three-mile drive. He should have had Jillian in the trunk, though, just in case he did slide through a stop sign or commit some other faux pas. If a patrol car noticed him, if he got to Edgewater and there were people around, he could always go home or circle around until the coast, literally, cleared.

The risk could be minimized on the trip to and from, then. The real risk came with getting Jillian out of the car and into Edgewater Park.

If Drew had taken Jillian, he would have had to do all this in broad daylight, on Monday morning, after Evan left the apartment. It seemed more likely to have been Evan, who could have brought his wife to Edgewater in the wee hours, then simply lied about the last time he'd seen her. For this exercise, then, Theresa would picture Evan as the killer.

Could Jillian still move under her own power at that point? *Oh, good evening, Officer, my wife is a little intoxicated and I thought we'd walk it off* . . . sure, it was the middle of a frigid night, but it probably wouldn't have been the strangest thing the average patrol officer had ever seen. But if Jillian were already dead or unconscious?

Rush hour had begun to gather on Route 2, and she hit the pedal as brake lights lit up in a chain reaction ahead of her. The car gave a sickening lurch as the tires slid against the icy pavement, but then the truckloads of salt that Ohio routinely dumps on its roadways did their job and she came to a stop with two feet to spare.

Dead, she decided. Jillian would have been dead. Evan would never have left her there unconscious and simply hoped she would freeze to death. That would have been too big a risk.

Theresa pulled into the Edgewater parking lot, completely deserted on the cold afternoon. The wind shoved her hard enough to make her stumble.

A paved walkway extended into the lawn and it crunched under her feet. Old shoe prints in the snow had frozen solid, but a fresh coating of flakes covered them, giving the pavement a lumpy appearance. Would Evan have stayed on the path? She wondered if the park plowed or at least salted the walkways. Even if not, snow on concrete melted faster than snow on grass, so it would have been an easier way to go than striking out over the lawn.

However, by parking in the far corner and cutting over to the small forest, he would have shortened his path considerably. She returned to the parking lot and walked over to the rear of the forested area, chin sunk into her upturned collar, double-gloved hands stuck deep in her pockets.

The expanse of snow-covered earth between the lot and the trees appeared pristine. She took a few steps, marring the surface. Her legs disappeared to more than midcalf. Evan wouldn't have come this way carrying the 110-pound Jillian. Too easy to fall, and the indentations left by his feet would have lasted too long. The snow might have covered them by now, but he could not count on her body lying undiscovered for five days. It might have been found the next morning, with the tracks still visible. Tracks on the sidewalk would be easier to explain, and might be obliterated by other walkers. She passed two such hearty souls after returning to the sidewalk, young boys bundled to the eye-teeth, their noses red.

She continued toward the water, wondering how dark the wee hours could get there. One light stood where the path from the parking lot intersected with the path along the water. More lights circled the parking lot. She found none near the trees. The white snow would have reflected every photon, but there had been no moon—she'd already checked.

Evan would have been plainly visible to anyone present to see him. This clearly represented the riskiest part of his plan. How could he move Jillian's body without detection? Was he strong enough to grasp her around the shoulders and carry her along beside him, hoping that no one would get close enough to notice that her feet were dragging on the ground? Or did he have a partner? Had Jerry been on the other side, helping to support Jillian between them?

But her shoes had been awfully clean. Unlike Theresa's, where lumps of snow picked up from her foray onto the lawn had slid down and melted into her socks.

Had Jillian's socks had wet spots, where they had frozen to the shoe? How would she be able to tell after they thawed out at the M.E.'s office, and surely snow could have gotten into them while moving the body. Still . . . *why didn't I pay more attention to this stuff at the time?*

Because I didn't know it would be important.

Surely he didn't heft her over his shoulder. That would have looked more than suspicious, though it would also have allowed him to move as quickly as possible.

No one appeared to stir on Drew's houseboat, though she had to squint to see that far. He probably hadn't come home from work yet. Drew could have killed her on his houseboat, carried her here. Even in daylight there wouldn't be many visitors to the frozen park, and the trees would hide most of his route from the road. Then he'd have to drive Cara home, for Jillian wouldn't have left the apartment without her daughter. But Drew seemed barely capable of carting around his own weight, much less a full-grown, unconscious woman.

She reached the spot where Jillian had been and faced, as before, the lake instead of the trees. The breeze slapped her with the smell of dead but frozen fish, and her nostrils stuck together when she breathed in. Damn, she loved the water.

When her cheeks began to tingle from the icy onslaught, she turned into the woods. An obvious dumping ground for Drew, but how would Evan decide on this spot? Had he been here often? Even with all the trooping in and out she had done with Frank and the M.E. staff, no path seemed apparent in the close-knit brush. The blackberry bush caught her ankles once more. Snow covered the ground only sparsely in here, filtered by the thick evergreens above her.

What could tie Evan to this spot? Nothing would be significant regarding Drew, since he lived nearby and had already admitted to having visited the spot several times. But Evan . . . the fiber from the bush's thorny branch? Evergreen needles . . . no, there were evergreens on the carbon company grounds . . . hell, there were evergreens all over Cleveland. On the other hand, plants had their own DNA, which could be individualized just as in humans or animals. She had no idea how to do it, but surely they could find someone in the United States who could. Pulling out a packet of manila coin envelopes she had thought to stuff into her pocket before leaving the car, she broke tips off the boughs around the crime scene, labeling the envelopes as best she could.

She collected a few dead oak leaves from the base of the tree where Jillian's body had sat as well. Why not? If she were grasping at straws, might as well grasp at all of them.

Okay, what else? Dirt. Dirt could be individualized to a particular place, depending on its composition. Theresa had once attended a seminar given by a cute Canadian Mountie about soil analysis. Unfortunately for her, the old, simple ways to analyze soil, such as gradient density, had been largely discredited, and the lab lacked a scanning electron microscope or an energy dispersive X-ray to use for more sophisticated tests. She still liked to collect soil, however, to check to see if there were anything in it that could be useful— fibers, paint flakes, etc. If that didn't pan out, and if she got desperate enough, at least she would have an excuse to call the cute Canadian Mountie.

The frozen earth did not want to give up its surface. She had to kick at it for a while to dislodge a relatively snow-free clump of dirt. She doubled-wrapped that, since surely the moisture within it would start to seep through the envelope once it thawed.

Moisture. Water. Diatoms.

Diatoms were a type of plankton, usually one-celled, with intricate and beautiful cell walls made of silica. They were found in both fresh and salt water, and Lake Erie, microscopically speaking, was choked with them. If she could find diatoms on Evan, his clothes, shoes, maybe even his car tires, it would prove . . . that he'd been near the water lately, which, in Cleveland, was not hard to accomplish. The man lived in freakin' Lakewood.

Still . . . she collected a sample from the parking lot as well. The asphalt, as nearly as she could tell underneath the snow, had been there for years, with several dirt-encrusted areas of cracks and potholes.

Out of ideas, she dove into her car and turned the key. As the engine warmed, she called her cousin and asked if he could get Evan's and/or Jillian's financial information from Griffin Investments.

Silence on the other end of the line, or the digital satellite transmission, or whatever. "Why don't we just bug his apartment while we're at it?"

"Okay."

"I was kidding, Tess."

"I wasn't."

"Okay, then. No. With what little you've got so far, I will not be able to get a subpoena for financials."

"What about his car? Can I get a search warrant for Evan's car? He had to use it to transport the body."

"And you have probable cause to support that?"

She threw the car into gear and backed up, sliding across several unoccupied parking spaces.

"Do you even have probable cause yet to show she was murdered?" he pressed.

"Okay, what about the outside of the car? If it's parked in a public place, and I collect something off the tires, say . . . would that be admissible?"

"No."

"No?"

"I don't think so." She let him mull it over for a moment. "Actually, I'm not one hundred percent positive about that, but I'm pretty sure it won't be. What would you be looking for, anyway?"

"Diatoms. They're microscopic algae found in—"

"I know what diatoms are. You think he might have picked them up at Edgewater Park? Okay, I'll check, but unless you hear from me you stay away from him, his car, his factory, everything, got it?"

She approached the intersection of Madison and West 117th. Lights shone in the windows of the second-floor apartment. "Um, good idea. Thanks, Frank."

Her nonchalant tone never had fooled him. "Tess—"

"Have to go." She flipped the phone shut and pulled past the iron gates.

A lone car sat in the parking lot at the old carbon company, slowly collecting flakes of snow across its roof and windshield—a Dodge K car that she would have thought couldn't travel another ten feet, and not the sort of thing two breaking-out young designers would drive.

The door to the lobby of the ornate office/apartment building opened easily. Evan either did not worry about crime or heating bills or found security too cumbersome. She headed for the stairs, feeling no enthusiasm for the shuddering elevator in a building this empty. The door to the lobby clanged shut behind her. The stairway, however, stretched upward, with only the dusky light from unclean windows and oppressive silence.

It did release her into the second-floor hallway, where someone had repaired the gouge in the plaster next to the door of apartment 212. She knocked. Still quiet, then a shuffling sound as if something large were approaching on the other side. The speck of light through the peephole darkened as the something checked her out.

The door swung open, and the woman inside, though portly,

was not half as large as her tread made her sound. She had accumulated enough years to be considered middle-aged and, to judge from the perfection of each burnished curl, seemed to have spent half of them doing her hair. She held an oval of baby blanket in her arms, from which protruded two tiny fists. "Hello. Looking for Evan?"

"Jerry, actually."

"Doesn't matter, honey, they're both out in the barns. Can you find them, or do you want me to call and have him come here?"

Over her shoulder, Theresa scanned the living room, now as tidy as the baby's room had been. "I'll find them. How is Cara doing?"

The woman smiled all the wider and turned her bundle outward so that Theresa could see the round face and impossibly huge blue eyes. "She's great, poor little tyke. Eats like a linebacker."

Theresa did not let the opportunity go by. "Did you work for the Kovacics' before Jillian's death?"

"No. I sat for them a couple of times, but that was it. I don't think they had anyone on a regular basis."

"How did Jillian seem to you, just before she died?"

The woman began to rock Cara with an agitated motion, yet her answer promptly tumbled out. "She seemed fine to me, but you can never tell, can you? Though I only knew her to say hello and good-bye to. It's Evan I've known since he was a little boy. I lived next door and his mother and I would get to talking."

"It's kind of him to adopt Cara now, since he's not her real father." She had to make herself say it, accompanying her words with as close to a genuine smile as she could muster, aware that Evan's friends and family might not be privy to that detail. But the nanny merely agreed, saying that Evan had always tried to help others, even as a child.

"Did he play video games back then?"

The rocking slowed to a smoother pace. "I don't think they had too much in the way of games, but he had plenty of fun taking things apart—alarm clocks, the blender—I remember that. His mother couldn't keep any mechanical device intact, so she'd give him jobs. A device to keep squirrels out of the bird feeder. He made me a little puller thing to help me start my push mower. When he was twelve years old he installed an electric eye to let his mother know when his baby sister got out of her crib. Then there was the gate closer."

"Gate—?"

A low whine sounded from within the apartment. "That's my tea. Could you hold her a second?"

Theresa found the baby thrust into her arms, the pink blanket swathing a tiny human in pink flannel pajamas, with miniature hands feeling the air. Cara did not protest at the change in her view, merely studied this new face with solemn detachment. Did she have any inkling at all of how much of her world had changed this week, and what it would mean for the rest of her life? Of course not, and yet . . . her eyes, so resigned . . .

The sitter fixed her cup while Theresa proffered a finger for Cara to grasp, feeling that inevitable melting sensation when the baby did. "He and his brother were always forgetting to latch the gate that led out of their backyard and their dachshund would get out, so, a typical male, instead of remembering to stop and latch the gate, he tried to invent a mechanism that would shut it automatically."

She sipped tea and continued, "Problem was, it worked too well. It snapped shut with such force that it cut the poor dog in half."

"What?" Theresa straightened so suddenly that she ripped her finger from the baby's grip and Cara frowned.

"Well, crushed it anyway. Poor Evan. He must have felt awful. His brother started screaming, and I remember rushing outside to see what on earth was the matter. There was Evan, wiping the blood off the mechanism so he could adjust it. I made him bury the dog first. His brother finally calmed down some then."

Cara let out a small cry as Theresa's arms tightened around her.

"Oh, there she goes. Probably filled her diaper again."

"Did they move after that?"

"Oh, heavens no. They lived there until the kids were long gone and then they retired to Florida. Never got another dog, though, even though he nagged his mother for one something awful. At first I thought he wanted to make his brother feel better—it was sort of the older boy's dog, see—but he told me he wanted to make sure his machinery worked right. He couldn't test it right without a dog, he said, and I told him that's ridiculous, just push on the stupid thing, but you know boys, once they get something in their heads . . . here, I'll take her back, she's deciding to be fussy. There, there, baby. Nothing to cry about here. Would you like a cup, dear? It's so cold out."

"No, thank you, I'd better be going. I—I hope everything goes well with Cara."

"Oh, sure. There's nothing wrong with this little tyke." She rocked the infant with a swooping motion as she closed the door behind Theresa with a quick good-bye.

The hallway had grown darker in the meantime, or perhaps it only seemed so, to keep pace with her thoughts.

Every child loses a pet more or less tragically. It didn't mean anything.

But why did she say Evan *must* have felt terrible? She came upon the incident seconds after it had occurred. Wouldn't you say "Evan felt terrible"?

Unless he clearly hadn't, more focused on perfecting his invention than on the death of the dog. Just as now he was more focused on marketing his virtual-reality sphere than on the death of his young wife.

It didn't mean anything.

She corrected herself. It didn't *prove* anything.

She made her way down the staircase in the darkening hall and headed for the outbuildings. The sun, still on winter time, had half set already, so that now she could wander through very large and increasingly dark buildings alone, seeking a man she believed had murdered his wife. The man's partner, actually, but according to the nanny, Evan would be there as well. She pulled out her cell phone and called Frank, just so he would know where to look for her body.

"You're where?" he demanded, and then cautioned her not to collect any evidence unless Evan gave her permission to, otherwise it would not be admissible, and he had to go, he had three more houses to canvass for Sanchez's Cultural Gardens murder, and that he hoped she—Theresa—knew what the hell she was doing.

That I can answer, she thought. *And the answer is no.*

Maybe I'm saving an innocent child from her impending murder.

Maybe I'm just ready to think about something besides Paul.

She yanked on the door handle of the closest building, the one where the tech show had been held. It did not open. Apparently Evan did think about security now and then.

Rounding the corner, she saw lights in the windows of the next two buildings farther down the line. A shadow moved behind her, on the sidewalk, but it proved to be a hulking orange tabby that paused to fix her with that look cats have, the one that says plainly, *Who exactly do you think you are?*

"Good question," she told it, and walked past. It watched her go.

CHAPTER 14

She approached the door of the second building slowly, her Reebok-clad feet silent on the thin cushion of snow. A small chock of wood maintained a quarter-inch opening between the door and the jamb. Steady but not heated conversation wafted out to her ears. The cat watched from a safe distance.

Was she legally permitted to eavesdrop? Since she was not a sworn officer, she was not bound by Miranda warnings or any other rules of interrogation. She put her face up to the door. Evan and Jerry worked on either side of a central row of machinery. Jerry threaded a bolt through a curved plastic hood as Evan sprayed the underside of a conveyor belt with a can of silicone spray. The machinery span appeared to be only four feet wide but at least forty feet long. Gas tanks lined one side of the building, and two reality spheres sprawled open on the other side.

Evan, unsurprisingly, did most of the talking. He stopped to gesture with the can of silicone.

But could she be considered, as a defense expert had recently charged, an agent for the prosecution? Would her testimony be admissible?

No matter. Eavesdropping might be legally permissible, but she could not feel comfortable with it. Besides, she didn't feel like standing in the snow for an hour listening to Evan debate the relative merits of letting the vampires use axes instead of crossbows once in the Sanctum of Sacrifices. She pushed the door open and stepped inside.

Both men noticed her instantly and straightened from their work.

"Hello." She patted her pockets with her fingertips, searching for the pack of cigarettes that hadn't been there for over ten years, a residual habit she could not break.

"What are you doing here?" Evan asked, sounding considerably less than friendly.

She forced her hands still and moved to the end of the line of machinery. "We're still trying to complete your wife's report, Mr. Kovacic. I had a few more questions about Jillian's habits and state of mind. I also need to speak with Mr. Graham."

She had hoped Evan would be courteous, wanting to keep up the pretense of a really nice guy who had suffered a tragedy. He did not seem so inclined. "I've got nothing to say to you, and neither does Jerry."

"I know you're stressed, Mr. Kovacic, but I'm trying to determine exactly how Jillian came to die."

He dropped the can of silicone on the conveyor belt and came closer. She resisted the urge to back up, but he stopped on the other side of a low workbench fitted with magnifying lamps, exactly like the ones she used at the lab. "Jillian killed herself, and you and your pack of ghouls won't let her rest in peace."

She noticed the two wireless cameras mounted at opposite corners of the building. At least if Evan attacked her, she would have it on tape. *If* the cameras weren't just dummies, if they recorded as well as monitored, and if she could figure out where the hell the recorder would be and could get to it before Evan. He would be good at that sort of thing, rewriting the story, making every detail fit his vision.

Jerry Graham had not moved. He spoke in a sympathetic tone, saying, "Evan just wants to bury his wife and raise his child, Mrs. MacLean."

"I understand that, and we're doing the best we can, but Jillian didn't leave a lot of clues as to her state of mind."

Evan knocked one of the lamps aside, so that it seemed to freeze in the air like a wounded crane. "Jillian didn't have a state of mind! She was blond hair and implants!"

The words hung in the air, unfortunate and infuriating. Theresa had worked hard to maintain some doubt of Evan's guilt and now watched it crumble into dust. She no longer considered retreat. In fact, she felt ready to rip his head off and spray the silicone down his neck. "That seems like a rather cold way to describe your late wife."

He did not become more circumspect at this rebuke. "You cut people open and you think *I'm* cold? You're trying to take Cara from her home and you have the nerve to look down on *me*?"

She didn't bother to explain that she did not perform autopsies, distracted by the latter charge. "What?"

"Drew Fleming has applied for guardianship of Cara," Jerry Graham told her, and let his mien do the rebuking. "Evan will have to go to court and ask for custody of his own daughter."

Oh, boy. "He would have had to go to court anyway, but—I

mean—that's got nothing to do with me. This is the first I've heard of it."

Evan moved beyond the magnifying lamps to within two feet of her. Her fingers slipped around the edge of the table, an anchor to keep her traitorous body from giving in to the flight instinct. "Come on. You and I have that little conversation about Cara on Saturday and first thing Monday morning Drew goes to the courthouse? You think I'm stupid?"

"Mr. Kovacic, I have absolutely nothing to do with Drew Fleming's legal plans. I certainly didn't advise him to do anything regarding Cara—"

The truth. Technically, and, she hoped, accurately. Even if Drew hadn't murdered Jillian, he remained an unstable obsessive not to be aimed toward a vulnerable infant. But then you can't toss a snowball onto a slope, even without thinking, and then deny responsibility for the avalanche.

Apparently Evan agreed. "Yeah, yeah. Get out!"

Jerry Graham moved closer to her as well, but he seemed more of a comfort than a threat. At least until he said, "Evan is very upset about even the idea of losing Cara, Mrs. MacLean. I'm sure you understand, as a mother."

She looked at his face, smooth with calm, even the expression in his eyes nothing but gentle.

"Perhaps you should leave now," he added.

Oddly enough, this more subtle deflection made her stubborner than Evan's leashed violence. "When was the last time you saw Jillian, Mr. Graham?"

"The Saturday before she died," he answered promptly.

"When you went out to dinner with Shelly and Evan and Jillian."

"Yes."

"No." The color flushing Evan's pale skin receded only slightly. "You saw her on Sunday when we were putting together the booth for the tech show."

His partner thought, without any change of expression. "That's right. She brought out some hot coffee."

"And then Monday morning, when you picked me up for the downtown meeting."

"Yeah, you said good-bye to her. But I thought Mrs. MacLean meant the last time we really *spoke*, and that would have been Saturday night."

"What did she say?"

"You're not getting this." Evan reached her before she could turn her face from Graham. He sank both hands into her forearms, but instead of pulling her closer he pushed her back, cracking a few vertebrae against the edge of the worktable. His breath smelled of curry and beer and, she thought, hate. "We're through answering your questions. You can hold my wife's body hostage until she starts to smell, you ghoulish bitch, but I'm still done talking to you. Get out."

"Evan, calm down." Jerry Graham came to her side, one hand held out as if trying to restrain his partner by force of will, and gestured to her with motions that shepherded without touching. "Come on, Mrs. MacLean. I'll walk you out."

She stepped carefully to the side to remove herself from Evan's range. His hands shuffled as if they itched to strike her and her feet shuffled as if itching to run. She did not turn her back on him. Her mind might not be convinced that Evan was a killer, but her body certainly was.

With this unsteady gait she made it to the door and reentered the snowy night, aware that Evan did not seem to fear her tête-à-tête with his partner, and aware that the controlled Jerry Graham could be an even more formidable foe, should he choose to be. But they were in an open area and the glimmer of light left in the sky reassured her. Besides, if Jerry Graham had anything to hide, he deserved an Oscar for his acting talents.

"I'm sorry if Evan seemed irate, but he's just lost his wife."

"The one who had blond hair and implants," she couldn't resist pointing out, even though she wanted Graham to talk to her.

"Evan has a lot more finesse with superconductors than he has with people, I'm afraid, but don't take that to mean he didn't love Jillian. He won't talk about it, but he's having a real hard time with the idea that she was unhappy enough to die."

The snow made a creaking sound as it compressed beneath their feet, and flakes turned to water as they touched her flushed face. "Do you think she did this purposely? Committed suicide?"

"I can't believe that, though I suppose people always say that after something like this happens."

"What did she say, when you were at dinner on Saturday?"

He stopped as they reached Theresa's car. "I hate to admit that I don't even remember. Just small talk—Cara was starting to crawl, the locks on her car doors had frozen shut, wasn't it great that Polizei had won the year's top slot from *Gamer* magazine. That kind of stuff."

"What kind of mood was she in?"

"Typical Jillian. Sweet, upbeat, otherwise quiet. If she harbored bad thoughts, she kept them to herself. But Jillian kept a lot to her-

self, so—" He shook his head, the few lines he had on his face settling into sadness. "I just can't believe it."

Her heartbeat slowed to nearly normal. "I'm sorry to have to
ask you these questions, but as I said, I'm trying to find out what
happened to Jillian. I—I didn't have anything to do with Drew
Fleming's guardianship petition and I didn't even know we still
had Jillian's body."

"That's Fleming too. He's petitioning the court to get custody."

"Of Jillian's *body*?"

"The guy's nuts."

Theresa secretly agreed. Drew might have a slight legal
chance with Cara's custody, but Jillian's body would be released
to her legal next of kin—her husband, period. The idea of
what Drew might want to *do* with Jillian's body made Theresa
shudder. Poor Cara—lost among a possibly murderous stepfather, an obsessed stalker, and grandparents who refused to
acknowledge her existence. For the first time, Theresa felt a
sense of urgency. This case needed to be resolved, and fast. It
wasn't just about her feeling a little guilty anymore. Cara could
be in real danger.

"I'm sorry to hear that. No wonder Evan isn't pleased to see me."
She waved her hand at the beat-up Dodge. "I didn't even think he
was here, but I'd already stopped, so I came in anyway. I assume
that's not Evan's car."

As she had hoped, he seemed relieved to discuss anything besides Evan and Jillian. "My girlfriend dropped me off. Evan's
car is having its bath at the SuperWash. We usually park in the
garage around back anyway. It keeps us from having to scrape the
windshield."

"The joys of Cleveland in the winter," she said, and climbed into the driver's seat. "Thank you for your time, Mr. Graham."

"No problem. Just—if you can help it—"

"Yes?"

"Don't come back."

Every item of clothing the kid at the SuperWash wore had a stripe running down the side. Shirt, pants, jacket, in an attempt to be either fashionable or too unfashionable to pilfer.

She had no idea what Evan drove, but Jerry had mentioned SuperWash, and when she reached the corner of 117th, lo and behold, there sat a SuperWash facility, WHERE YOUR CAR IS TREATED LIKE A HERO, and if one had to leave one's car, it would certainly make sense to leave it somewhere within walking distance. She approached the kid. "Excuse me."

His black skin shone with effort. Either he really liked waxing cars or he had to finish this one before leaving for the day, because he didn't seem to care for the interruption. "What?"

"Do you have Evan Kovacic's car here?"

"Yeah. That one." He waggled the chamois in his hand toward a jet black Escalade slated to be next in line through the indoor pit of hoses and sprayers.

She studied the setup, an idea forming in her mind. Evan Kovacic had killed his wife. Theresa didn't know how or when or precisely why, but he had, and she was going to catch the bastard. He had used Jillian and then dismissed her. He would not find Theresa so easy to get rid of.

The rest of the small building had been abandoned, the lights in the glassed-in office turned off. The work bay, however, remained bright enough to hurt the eyes. "What are you going to do to the car?"

He stood up with an irritated leap, having finished one side of a vintage Mustang and moved to start on the other. "*Wash* it, lady, what you think?"

"Just wash the outside?"

He attacked the hazy wax covering the paint with the limitless energy of youth. "Full detail. And before I leave tonight too. You see anyone else still stuck here? No, they're home with their dinners. Lucky for him I need the overtime—"

"What does that mean, full detail?"

"Why you want to know? You thinking of bringing your car here?"

"It's kind of a long story. Do you vacuum the inside?"

"Inside, cargo area, Armor All the dash, scrub the tires. At least he ain't got no whitewalls. Anything else you want to know?"

"Then you throw out the vacuum bag?"

"No vacuum bag. There's sort of a filter in that big thing there that gets replaced every so often. Don't know, it ain't my job."

"You scrub the tires?"

"Get the treads clean as a whistle. Mr. Kovacic insists. That's us. Service above and beyond. Anything else you want to know, lady?"

"How many people ask for their tires to be scrubbed?"

"You takin' a survey?"

"Sort of."

His biceps tightened and relaxed in sequence as he finished up the passenger door. His entire body language spoke of his annoyance, and yet he remained either too polite or too incurious not to respond. "Only him, that I know of."

"Is this the first time he's brought his car here?"

"Hardly. Every week. He thinks a lot of that car, I guess."

"But this is the first time he's asked for the tires to be scrubbed." That sounded like circumstantial evidence to her.

"Nope. Insists on that every time."

Maybe not.

"Says the salt ruins the rubber. It don't, you know."

"Would you mind if I removed some of the dirt for you? Just the stuff in the tires, and the lint on the upholstery."

He drew himself up to his full height, a good head taller than hers. "You some clean car fairy or something?"

"Not exactly."

"Then *what* . . . exactly?"

"I work for the medical examiner's office. I want to collect any loose hairs, fibers, soil from Mr. Kovacic's car. It will be less for you to vacuum up, look at it that way."

His shoulders fell a bit, and the lines in his forehead smoothed out. "You mean, like clues? You looking for clues?"

"Yes."

"You a detective?"

"No, I'm a forensic scientist."

He nearly broke into a smile. "Like you work with all those test tubes and stuff. Like you get DNA out of a bloodstain. Right?"

"Yes, sometimes."

"Let me get the keys."

She retrieved her crime scene kit from her car and met him at the Escalade. The young man held up a key fob shaped like the triangular *Star Trek* logo and jangled its four keys in triumph.

"Thanks." She smiled and introduced herself.

"My name's Antwan. You know if you put a scratch on this thing, it's my ass, right?"

"I won't get anything scratchy anywhere near it, I promise. I'll tape the trunk and the seats and then vacuum, and then I'll clean the treads. But I'll use a plastic scraper for that. It won't damage the rubber."

He unlocked the doors and opened the rear hatch for her. "What are you looking for?"

"I've been asking myself that all week," she muttered as she placed a strip of clear tape on the carpeting in the empty cargo area. Evan either kept an obsessively clean car or else he removed his personal items prior to dropping it at the car wash.

"You think he killed somebody?"

She moved the piece of tape up and down, from left to right, getting a fresh piece when the adhesive became clogged with detritus. If she said yes, was that slander? If she didn't say he *did* kill someone, only that she *thought* so . . . really, she needed her own attorney just to help her with these issues. "I don't know. I'm only trying to reconstruct what happened over the last week."

"I saw on TV, they used a light. This light attached to a box with a hose."

"An alternate light source. We use that mostly to find semen."

He snickered at her matter-of-fact use of the term. "And you're not looking for that here?"

"Nope."

"So you don't think he raped nobody."

"No, I don't. Really, this is quite routine—"

"Doing your job in a car wash?"

She moved on to the backseat, repeating the taping action, not relishing the thought of examining all those strips of tape, now stuck to sheets of clear acetate. Long hours at the stereomicroscope could get hard on the eyes. Long hours at *any* microscope could get hard on the eyes.

Antwan followed her. "Are you going to spray that stuff that makes blood glow? What's that called?"

"Luminol?"

"That won't ruin the leather, will it?"

"It wouldn't hurt it, but I'm not going to use luminol anyway. Just tape and a vacuum, as I said."

"So you don't think he murdered anybody either? What *are* you doing here?"

This was why she tried not to converse with people on the job. "I'm not looking for any blood."

"So he offed someone without blood?" The young man put a hand to his chin. "Hmm. That's cool. Are you looking for hairs? I saw hairs on the Discovery channel. They have that special DNA in them, right?"

"Mitochondrial." She finished the taping and hooked up the vacuum. At least the noise put a stop to the kid's questions, for a while.

Nothing about Evan's car stood out as suspicious, but then, why would it? If involved at all, it had only been as a cargo transport, moving Jillian's body from the apartment to Edgewater Park. The best she could hope for would be some hairs of Jillian's where they shouldn't normally be, like in the cargo area. But even that wouldn't prove anything, not really.

And diatoms in the tires. She folded the nylon netting from the vacuum's filter and sealed it in a manila envelope, taking care not to lose any of the trapped fibers and dirt. Then she turned to the tires. The sky grew darker than pitch and Antwan's overtime meter continued to click, but he had stopped complaining.

It took a while, but she cleaned out every valley of every inch of each tire's circumference accessible to her with a plastic probe, trying not to leave even a scratch in the rubber that Kovacic could complain about.

"Did he run her over?" Antwan guessed. He did not seem upset that Theresa refused to confirm or deny any one scenario; instead he seemed to enjoy brainstorming as to what her little foray implied. "Like a hit-and-run? Left the scene of an accident?"

"No. Look, I'm sorry I can't tell you anything about an open investigation—mostly because I'm not even sure it *is* an investigation. It's more of a fact-finding mission. I'm trying to—"

"Reconstruct the events, yeah, you said. But let me ax you this. You're going to want to keep your little project between us, right? As in don't mention nothing to Mr. Kovacic, right?"

Was he going to blackmail her? "I can't ask or tell you what to say or not say. I have no authority to do so."

"Neat answer, but you'd rather I didn't, right?"

She honestly didn't know. Perhaps if Evan felt pressured, he'd make a mistake. In any event, she could not hide her actions. In forensics, mistakes could be dealt with, but covering up, even appearing to cover up, even covering up *nothing*, would kill your career faster than being found with kiddie porn. It was the Point Beyond Which One Could Not Go. "I'm not going to ask you to tell him or not tell him or not tell your boss or anyone else. I'm not hiding anything here, Antwan. I can't."

He kept nodding with a knowing smile, and it worried her. "Yeah, yeah, I got that. But let me ax you this—this place you work, the M.E.'s office, what would I need to work there? A college degree?"

"At least a bachelor's in the natural sciences, biology, chemistry, or general forensic sciences, yeah. That would be good."

"So if I got one—I'm going to Cleveland State in the fall—I could apply for a job like yours?"

She couldn't help but smile. Forensic junkies. They were everywhere. "Certainly."

"And you'd remember this little favor, if I did?"

She pulled out her card and handed it to him. "There's no guarantee. Lab staffs are a lot smaller than you'd expect from watching TV, and everything depends on the budget, but if there's anything I can do to help, a tour of the lab, explain the application process, don't hesitate to call me."

He studied the card carefully before storing it in his back pocket. "Thanks."

"No, Antwan. Thank *you*."

On her way home, she stopped at Don's house and borrowed his copy of Polizei. The time had come for her to enter Evan's game.

CHAPTER 15

Theresa hadn't dated since Paul's death, to say the least, hadn't thought about dating, refused to even consider thinking about dating. And yet when she entered her home that night, her daughter waiting for her at the kitchen table, drumming her seventeen-year-old fingers, Theresa felt as if she'd been out on a date, had returned past curfew, and was now in very big trouble.

"Hi," she chanced, trying to remind herself that she was the mommy and Rachael was the little girl, not vice versa. She failed. "I forgot about your concert, didn't I? How did it go?"

"Super," Rachael deadpanned. "Working late?"

"Yeah." Theresa removed her coat and hung it on the hook next to the door, and, talking too fast, said, "I questioned Evan's business partner's girlfriend and then the business partner. Did you play that Mozart piece after all?"

"You don't question people." Her daughter repeated what Theresa had said herself during numerous forensic-themed TV dramas. "You work with evidence. Cops question people."

"Well, I was questioning them about the evidence, I suppose, the evidence being Jillian. Look." She held up a plastic case containing the borrowed Polizei disc. "I brought you something."

Rachael's expression did not change as she stood up. "I don't play video games."

"Please."

Her daughter stopped, halfway out of her chair.

"I need your help."

She had been through so much, her daughter, during what should have been her carefree high school years—her parents divorced, her grandmother gone back to work, she'd endured a constant stream of cocktail waitress potential stepmothers, gotten used to a stepfather only to lose him before the title became official, and then watched her mother drift through an eight-month depr— funk, present in body only, the mind out of reach. Theresa didn't have to be Freud to know that everyone has a breaking point and she was pushing her daughter toward hers.

Rachael held out her hand. "Hand it over."

The girl opened the lower doors on the entertainment unit and dragged out a passel of wires. The game cartridge fit into the designated slot on a console Theresa had paid a lot of money for but very little attention to, until now. Rachael changed the TV channel and a blue screen appeared, with START GAME written in blood-drenched letters.

Theresa's stomach grumbled but she didn't dare leave her neglected daughter's side; at least Rachael would have eaten—interests and talents often skip a generation and Rachael had inherited her grandmother's respect for food. Theresa perused the game case instead. The background summary, which repeated what Don had already told her, spoke of a castle, a treasure, murderous vampire guards. The hero, a brawny young man with spiky blond hair and a gleaming plate of armor on his chest and back, had only his trusty sword and a glowing amulet that glowed more brightly when he took the right path. He could, however, pick up other trinkets along the way—a crossbow with flaming arrows; ropes; lock picks; a drinking/fighting buddy or two; and even a bull mastiff, as both a pet and a formidable weapon. By the third paragraph, even Theresa wanted to play the game.

Two things she found particularly interesting. The hero had not come to the castle to find the treasure. He had no interest in the treasure; he had arrived to rescue his brother from the castle's innermost keep before the evil overlord of the vampires could absorb his life energy.

She also found the location of the castle intriguing. Evan described it as "on the banks of a frigid blue lake, enveloped by dead trees and pelting winds of doom." It echoed the location of Jillian Perry's body, except that Lake Erie always appeared more green than blue. And the "winds of doom" part. Gusts from the lake could be wicked, particularly when walking on East Ninth, but *dooming* seemed a bit strong.

She watched as Rachael made her way from the boat up the steep mountain pass, dispatched a band of heavily armed—well, bad guys, for want of a better descriptor—and entered the castle. The vast hall shone with golden candelabra and stained glass, and Theresa could have spent some time merely sightseeing, but Rachael and her horde pressed on.

After dying for the fourteenth time, however, the teenager grew tired and threw the joystick aside. "There's no way over this chasm without falling. You'll have to take over, Mom. I'm going to bed."

"Already?"

"It's eleven twenty, and I have school in the morning. At least that's what you always tell me when I'm watching Letterman."

"You're right." Theresa yawned. "Turn in. And Rachael?"

"Yeah?" Her daughter paused, one foot on the bottom step.

"I'm sorry I missed your concert."

"Don't worry about it. We didn't play any good songs anyway."

"That doesn't matter. I should have been there."

Rachael smiled. "I'll let it go this time." Then she went up to bed, and Theresa gave silent thanks that if her ex-husband had to pass one characteristic on to their progeny, it had been the ability to let anger go as quickly as it had come. Theresa, on the other hand, could nurse a grudge until it graduated from college, got a job, and bought a house.

She lowered her aging knees to the carpet and reached for the joystick.

The bones in her spinal column began to protest shortly after finding the portrait gallery and its hidden door, from which stairs wound up to the east tower, and her shoulder blades had begun to chime in when Rachael materialized at her elbow.

"Are you still playing?"

"You weren't supposed to go over the chasm, you had to go under it. There's a passageway—what are you doing up? Did I wake you?"

"Mom—I'm going to school. It's seven A.M. Have you been playing *all night*?"

No wonder her back hurt.

TUESDAY, MARCH 9

"And then the wall opens up and there are three hallways. Two have steps going up or down, respectively, and the third seems to go straight ahead."

"Did you get any sleep at all?" Don asked, peering at her over the edge of his coffee cup. They faced each other over the chipped Formica-covered table in the staff lunchroom, each trying to ignore the campfire odors that had seeped into their lab coats after wrestling all morning with the victims of a house fire.

She shook her head. Then her female instincts woke, prodded by the caffeine-infused steam and the sympathetic look in her co-worker's eyes. "Why? Do I look like crap?"

"Of course not. But you look tired."

"Tired equals disheveled. Isaac Asimov said so. Never tell a woman she looks tired. Evan killed his wife, Don, I'm sure of it. He plans everything. He planned this whole *world*. It tells a story, you know—it's not Asteroids, where you shoot at anything that moves and you can go in only two directions. This is a house, and you can choose which room you want to enter, and what's in there might be there every time and it might not. You decide what to do—take the ax or leave it there, kill the guard or ask him to let you by. Do you see what that means?"

"No," he admitted, with more of that concerned tone, the one she'd heard almost every day since Paul died. At least now it had a different edge, as if he'd gone from worrying about her emotions to worrying about her mind.

"To design a game like this, you have to anticipate every

single move a player can make, then design a response. You can limit responses so that no matter what decisions the player makes and in what order, he will eventually progress into the next room or figure out he has to pick up the magic shield or whatever, but there's still a great deal of flexibility. The player can stop, go back, try to blast a hole in the wall instead of using the stairs, kill his own teammates. It's like those TV shows that let the audience call in and vote on how the show should end, whether a character should live or die, but the game gives the player a choice like that every minute or so."

"So he's a planner."

"He's a planner extraordinaire. Anticipating a response and figuring out what happens as a result of it has been this guy's life for the past ten years. I found out more about him on the Internet this morning. He was a chemistry major in college, but started hanging out in the computer lab and designed his first game before he even graduated."

"How many cups of coffee have you had?"

"I lost count at six. Are you listening?"

"Attentively."

"He worked for a subsidiary of Microsoft and then used Polizei to start his own company. He wants to expand into hardware, with Jerry Graham's inventions, hoping that they can keep everything proprietary long enough to bankroll what he calls the third wave, a gaming empire to rival Xbox, Wii, and PlayStation."

"He said that?"

"To *Modern Science*. He's quite forthcoming about his ambitions, to judge from a few other articles I ran across, but that seems to be normal in that field. They're mostly young men and they produce aggressive, kick-ass games, so a certain amount of verbal assertiveness is expected. Kind of like professional wrestling."

"I see. And you're taking this as evidence of—"

"Planning. Not just his games, but his own life, the course it's going to take over the next twenty years."

Don set his porcelain cup on the Formica with a gentle thud. "And you think he planned to kill his wife."

"Just run with me for a minute. Jillian was tailor-made for him. He needed her money. Why, I don't know exactly, since he's got financing, but he's behind schedule with the game sequel and that may have something to do with it. He found Jillian, abandoned by everyone in her life except for an obsessed fan and a very rich baby. I think he planned every last detail, anticipated that her death would look like an accident, or if not, a postpartum or parent-problem induced suicide. If that didn't work, if by some strange twist we did start thinking homicide, he had Jillian's former job to fall back on, that Drew or some ex-client stalked her. He even has these other two deaths that have the city thinking 'serial killer.' That will be his first suggestion if we rule anything other than accidental death."

"Now you're anticipating him."

Some of her weariness got past the caffeine and she rubbed her eyebrows—not her eyes, of course, that caused wrinkles. "I'm trying. It's not going to be easy. At least he couldn't have counted on Drew contesting him for custody of Cara. As long as her inheritance is in question, she's safe. But that won't last. No judge is going to give custody to strange, unstable Drew. If Cara's going to live to see kindergarten, I have to prove that Evan murdered her mother."

"And you're sure about this." Don's face made it clear he wasn't. "You don't just have a bug up your bu—have it in for this Evan guy?"

"Have I ever done that before?"

You've never been mourning a dead fiancé before, his face said now, but aloud he said, "That leaves you with one big problem."

"I know." She lowered her face to her hands, flat on the Formica, and felt the comforting pat of Don's palm on the back of her head. "How did he do it?"

"It's not going to be an open casket," the deskman told Theresa as he helped her wheel Jillian's gurney into the hall. "She's already marbled."

The long wait for her ride to the funeral home had not been kind to Jillian. Aside from the scruffily sewn-up gashes from her shoulders to her navel and the one along the back of her head, the skin had mottled with uneven dark patches as the flesh underneath decomposed. "She's headed for cremation?"

"Soon as they pick her up. We got the court form this morning."

As expected, Drew had been found to have no legal claim on the body, and disposal of Jillian fell to her lawfully wedded spouse. Theresa had only a few more minutes with her biggest piece of evidence, and she didn't even know what to look for.

"Shove her back in when you're done," the deskman told her, and left her to it.

Theresa could have examined the body inside the cooler room—it wasn't that uncomfortably cold—but she hated the idea of that steel door slamming shut behind her. Being shut in with dead bodies did not bother her. But being shut in at all, that was intolerable. Besides, she needed better lighting.

If she couldn't prove Evan killed Jillian, perhaps she could prove he moved the body.

Though it still seemed precarious to her, driving your murder victim to a dump site. One thing she had learned from living in a college dorm: whatever ungodly hour of the night you might be awake and about, someone else would be up too. Evan might have conceived of an untraceable poison or undetectable manner of death, but all it would take to unravel his plan would be one bored night-shift clerk watching the factory from the window of the 7-Eleven or one homeless park dweller with a sturdy parka and insomnia.

But Theresa had also learned from reading every tale of true crime she could get her hands on that if the perfect crime existed, it had not yet been discovered. Every murder involved some risk. And in Polizei the young captain had no choice but to jump over the river at the end of the tunnel from the dining room. It had taken her two solid hours of play to give up the hope of finding a way around it. She had to leap into the abyss. The alternative was to stop playing.

And Evan would not stop playing. Not now, with world domination within his grasp.

So he would take that risk, that one, unavoidable risk, and drive to Edgewater Park in the middle of the night. With Jillian in the passenger seat? The backseat? The cargo area? The answer might lie upstairs, in the material she had collected from Evan's vehicle. But would he take his car? Why not Jillian's? If the bored 7-Eleven clerk saw her car in the area, then that would support the theory of suicide . . . except, how did the car get back to the carbon company, idiot?

Besides, Jerry had said that Jillian told him the locks on her car had frozen shut. Her car might have been unavailable or too risky to use.

His car, then. Was there anything left on the body to show it had been transported?

The body had been washed, autopsied, and washed again, so the odds of finding any trace evidence had gone from slim to none. Theresa had already collected samples of the not entirely natural blond hair to compare to hairs found on the clothing. She wasn't sure what else to do. Other than berate herself for not having gotten on board with the homicide theory earlier . . . maybe there would have been something to find, at the scene, at the apartment, maybe Evan had made some slip that she would have noticed, had she been paying attention.

"Sorry, Jillian," Theresa said aloud, startling herself. She didn't usually talk to her victims. It didn't pay to get on a first-name basis with people who could not respond. Still, she persisted. "I won't let Cara go the same way. I won't."

Jillian's blue eyes had clouded. As before, her perfect nails showed no signs of a struggle; however, bluish circles had developed on the forearms, which had not been there before. It could have been decomposition artifact, but the color didn't seem consistent with the other patches on the body.

She left the body in the hallway, with a piece of paper reading DON'T TOUCH on top of the body bag.

* * *

"*Her* again." Christine stood up from the microscope, the movement releasing a light wave of perfume through the tiny office. "I'll be happy to take a look if it will help you figure out what killed her."

"That's your job, missy," Theresa told her as they pounded down the back staircase like unruly schoolgirls.

"I gave up."

They reached the ground floor and Theresa held up Jillian's left arm. "Is this a bruise?"

Christine examined the dead woman's skin. Then she pushed the gurney into the autopsy room—crowded, but the most brightly lit room in the building. Three other doctors, three dieners, and three dead people paid no attention to them. Once more Christine examined the skin.

Theresa couldn't wait. "Is it decomp?"

"No, I don't think so. But there's only one way to be sure." The young pathologist donned latex gloves, unwrapped a fresh scalpel, and plunged the blade into Jillian Perry's flesh.

"Eew!"

"You can't say 'eew.' You work at a freakin' morgue."

"That doesn't mean I can't say 'eew' when it's warranted." Nevertheless, Theresa leaned closer to the exposed muscle.

Christine pointed out the tiny blood clots, visible—with difficulty—against the darkened tissues. "There are some abrasions here. I'd say this is a bruise."

"But it didn't show up at autopsy?"

"Sometimes they do that." She picked up Jillian's other arm.

"What do you think it means?"

"By itself, probably nothing. It's vague and nonacute . . . unlikely to have occurred in some life-and-death struggle. There's a bit forming on this arm as well—see here? Almost sort of a streak, a pattern about an inch wide. See it?"

"No."

"Along here."

The strip of discolored flesh ran at a slight angle across the undersurface of Jillian's right arm, the differences in color so difficult to distinguish that they could have been a trick of the light. Theresa would never have noticed it without the pathologist's more discerning eye.

"Someone tied her arms. Left over right, the binding against the outer surface of the left arm and the undersurface of the right. Not very tight. Not very tight at all."

Christine positioned the dead woman's arms over her stomach, then abandoned them to slide back onto the steel gurney with gentle thuds. She unzipped the body bag the rest of the way and examined the feet.

"Now what are you doing?"

"When someone's arms are tied, their legs usually are as well. Doesn't make much sense to do one without the other."

"We need to get a gurney in here," a diener interrupted. One of the autopsies had been completed, and the finished corpse had to be removed from the steel table. Jillian's gurney partially blocked the door.

"Yeah, yeah," Christine muttered.

Theresa pushed the wheeled contraption. "Anything there? Do you have to—aw. Now I have to say 'eew' again, and I know how that annoys you."

"I'm going to have to amend my report. Evidence of binding

of both hands and feet. Here, just above the ankles. But why such light bruising? She didn't struggle at all."

"It could have been some sex thing," Theresa brainstormed.

"It would have been difficult to have sex with her ankles crossed, and we found no sign of sexual activity, forcible or nonforcible. No state of undress, no bruising or tears, no semen. Yet someone tied her very gently."

"Maybe she was unconscious? That's why she didn't struggle against the bonds."

"Then why tie her?"

"In case she woke up?"

"Then why not tie her tighter?"

Every question made Jillian's death seem more bizarre. "Because he knew she wasn't going to wake up. Could she have been dead already?"

Christine said no, but without certainty. "These shouldn't form after death. Bruises are weird, though. You can never be sure. Besides, if she was already dead, why tie her up?"

The room suddenly seemed too bright, and overcrowded with death. "He didn't tie her limbs together to keep her from escaping. He tied them together to make her body easier to transport."

The two women stared at each other over Jillian Perry's body, ignoring the talk, movement, and slicing scalpels around them. "So she didn't walk into those woods on her own."

"It explains a lot," Theresa said. "Why her shoes were clean—"

"Why no frostbite on the extremities, or rime around her mouth."

"Why she showed no signs of depression . . . because she wasn't depressed. Because she wanted to live."

Another deskman entered the autopsy suite, glancing at the busy tables with distaste before asking Christine, "Are you two guys finished? The guy from the crematorium is here for her."

"In a sec. Help me turn her over."

The two women examined Jillian's dorsal surface, but found no more bruising. They had to release the body. Theresa could only hope they hadn't missed anything else. Surely all bruising would show by now. It had been over a week . . .

Christine began to zip up the bag. "Uh, Theresa? She has to go now."

"Yeah, I know."

"You're holding her hand."

With a start, Theresa released the cold fingers, and watched the dead woman disappear under a layer of clean white plastic.

CHAPTER 16

"I need a search warrant," Theresa told her cousin. She could hear other voices in the background, and the city sounds of cars and wind.

"What for?"

"For the carbon company grounds. All the buildings, not just the apartments."

"What are you looking for? Just some mustard, thanks."

"You're not eating a hot dog out of an aluminum cart parked on the sidewalk, are you?"

"Sure, why not?"

"Mystery meat and botulism—it's quite a combination."

"This poor guy's standing outside in subfreezing temperatures, trying to eke out a living, and you're criticizing his wares? He's giving the radio a dirty look right now, and so am I."

"I had to get up in the middle of the night and bring you ginger ale the last time you had food poisoning."

"Well, I couldn't call my mother—you know she needs her sleep. What do you want a warrant for, and how do you know that whatever you're searching for is there?"

She outlined the conclusions of the morning. "I need to find evidence that Evan transported Jillian's body to the woods. He must have carried her in something, something that wouldn't attract attention. Even wrapping her in a blanket would have looked completely suspicious."

"I thought she disappeared during the day."

"Supposedly."

"You think he had someone else move the body from the apartment while he was at the meeting? It would have been a perfect alibi."

"Maybe. But this guy is used to creating his own world. He's a control freak. I can't believe he would trust an accomplice. He doesn't seem to have any close friends other than Jerry Graham, who was at the meeting with him."

"So you think it was Drew?"

"Swallow before you talk. Why would I suspect Drew?"

"Because he *wasn't* at this meeting on Monday. He had all day long to move Jillian around before Evan came home, and he might have liked the idea of Jillian in his woods. He could sit on his boat and know she was there."

The words gave her a shiver, and yet she protested, "Drew is no bigger than I am. Jillian weighed a hundred and ten pounds, and someone moved her three miles without dragging or damaging the body, without even getting her clothes dirty."

"Maybe Drew had an accomplice."

She hadn't considered that idea. "I suppose it's possible. I just don't think so."

"Because Drew's one of those harmless stalkers."

The sarcasm in his voice made her stubborn. "Yes."

"And because you think Evan did it."

"Two-hundred-and-fifty-pounds-if-he's-an-ounce Evan, yeah. The one who stands to inherit all Cara's money."

"But you're not sure."

"I'm *pretty* sure."

"Great. I've got to go assist with some interrogations, kiddo. I might lose this call in the elevator, so one more time, what do you want a search warrant for?"

"For fibers that match those found on Jillian's clothing, fibers from some item used to transport her body. Ones that match what I found in his car, as soon as I have time to go through what I found in his car. I'll have that done before you get the warrant, and then I'll know what to look for."

"Back up. Car?"

She explained her activities of the previous evening. From the sounds Frank made into the phone, her activities had caused him to choke on his hot dog.

"You're asking me for a search warrant, Theresa, so I assume that means you understand the concept of one."

"Yeah."

"You searched Evan's car without a warrant."

"I didn't search it. I removed detritus."

"So what? It's still inadmissible evidence."

"No. It's abandoned property."

A slight pause. "Come again?"

"The car wash attendant would have vacuumed and scrubbed away all the items I collected, and disposed of them. He had Evan's permission to do so—in fact, his instructions to do so. It's exactly the same as when you see the suspect drinking from a cup and toss it in the trash can, and then you pick it up and have us swab it for DNA. You can take abandoned property. The hairs and fibers from his upholstery and the dirt from his tire treads were abandoned property."

"They hadn't been abandoned yet," he protested, but weakly.

"He had left them there for disposal. Therefore, abandoned."

Her cousin remained silent long enough that she wondered if the Nextel connection, always tenuous, had been broken. "Interesting, cuz. I'm not sure it will work, but it's interesting."

"I'm also looking for narcotics or poisons or anything that would have made her unconscious or dead. We should probably grab the bank statements showing Cara's account, as well. That's his motive."

"Question—what about Georgie? He's also two-fifty if he's an ounce, could carry a one-ten body without straining, and Jillian would have opened the door to him. She would have even hopped in his car and driven off to Edgewater Marina without a care."

"And without her baby? Not likely. And does Georgie strike you as clever enough to murder someone without leaving a trace?"

"How did Evan kill her without leaving a trace? What did she die of? I thought she froze to death . . . I'm not hearing an answer. You still don't know why she died?"

"No, and that's just it. Do you know how difficult it is to kill someone without leaving any trace? It could only be done by a control freak who's trained himself to plan every last detail. A former chemistry major who needs that million and a half for his new company."

"Absence of proof is not proof of absence."

"That's cute."

"It's also true. Can you prove Jillian didn't walk out into those woods and freeze to death? Yes or no, Tess."

She could hear the *schtick* of the revolving doors as he walked into the police department side of the Justice Center, the sudden deadening of the outdoor sounds, the frustration in his voice.

"No," she said, hating the word.

"What you want to do is go fishing, and a judge isn't going to let you. You have to have probable cause to show that A, a crime occurred; B, this person is likely to have committed that crime; and C, evidence is likely present on the property that would help you prove same. You don't even have A, much less B or C."

She sat at her desk with the phone pressed to her ear, her forehead held up by the palm of her hand. Frank was right, and she knew it. "So he's going to get away with it."

"A search warrant is definitely out unless you can get me some probable cause. Now consider an alternative theory for me, just for a minute. Have you found any trace in common between Jillian and Sarah Taylor?"

"None. Sarah favored jewel tones over Jillian's pastels. Pieces of vegetation were consistent with the location of the body. No diatoms. Sarah smoked, and ash and tobacco particles were consistent with her own brand. No mysterious smears of phenol," she added.

"What?"

"Long story. Did she own a dog? A good-size black thing, maybe a Doberman?"

"Honey, Sarah Taylor barely had a place to live. She flopped in a one-room no-tell motel off of East 117th without a toothbrush and about ten articles of clothing, all told. No pets allowed."

"Then I'll bet your killer does. The press is still connecting these murders, the two women and the boy."

"I'm wondering myself. Word on the street is, Sarah Taylor used to work for Georgie. In his less reputable days."

"How long ago was that?"

"Years. But now Sarah Taylor finds she's down to her last dime. If she knew where a body or two were buried, she might have tried to shake down her former pimp. I know exactly how Georgie would react to that."

"Possibly. But she was a hooker, Frank. Their daily work is to get in a car with some stranger and drive off without telling anyone where they're going. They're tailor-made for sick and violent men. And if Georgie killed her, then why did he kill Jillian? She certainly wasn't down to her last dime."

"Yeah. I know. But you're getting yourself stuck on Evan, and you're not usually so . . . inflexible. Do you have any results on Sarah Taylor?"

"The rape kit came up positive for semen. So say your prayers tonight for a CODIS hit. We should know in a few days. But it's not a serial killer, Frank—the MOs are different, and then there's the kid—the boy didn't have any connection to the women, right?"

"Nope. He stuck to his own neighborhood, and if he could have afforded Georgie's rates, then he could have afforded a damn cell phone. I'm getting into the elevator, in case we get cut off. Hang in there, Tess. It's nice to see you—" The rest of his sentence disappeared into a cloud of static and broken syllables. Theresa hung up the phone.

She prodded her chin with the top of a retractable pen. She did not put it in her mouth. One learned very quickly at a medical examiner's office never to put a writing implement in one's mouth. You never knew where it had been.

The rules of Sarah Taylor's life also applied to Jillian Perry. Her clients might have been more nicely dressed and had better table manners, but they were still a group of strangers often with less-than-laudable purposes. She could have met her killer through the same channels as Sarah Taylor, and Evan could be merely unlikable, but innocent.

But she didn't believe it.

Don dropped himself into the chair at the opposite desk and eyed her over a short bookshelf littered with texts, family photos, her Beanie Babies, and a box of disposable pipettes. "What's the matter, babe?"

"I got nothing."

"I wouldn't say that. You're beautiful, intelligent, relatively young—"

"I'll 'relatively' you, you supercilious—"

"Did I mention beautiful?"

"I need proof, and I don't even know what it is I'm trying to prove."

"Jillian Perry?"

"Yep."

"So what's your plan?"

She moved a bean-stuffed tiger to see him better. "What?"

"Don't you have a plan?"

She stared at him for a few more moments before speaking. "I don't. That's been my whole problem." She dug through a desk drawer and pulled out a legal pad. At the top she wrote, in block letters, MEANS, OPPORTUNITY, MOTIVE. Then she added a fourth column, PROOF.

"What are you doing?"

"I'm going to show Evan Kovacic that he's not the only detail-oriented control freak in this city."

"What do you want?" Oliver discouraged visitors to his corner of the toxicology lab. He kept all the spare gas tanks clustered in a fencelike barrier. He had removed all task chairs except his own, which he rarely left, his extra flesh overflowing the seat and his ponytail brushing the armrests. He displayed printed epigraphs such as I'LL TRY BEING NICER IF YOU'LL TRY BEING SMARTER and IT MAY BE THAT YOUR ONLY PURPOSE IS TO SERVE AS A WARNING TO OTHERS. He varied neither wardrobe nor hygiene. But he seemed to know everything in the world, particularly the chemical world. "I suppose you're here about that piece of solder."

"What?"

She'd seen Halloween masks with less of a scowl.

"That tiny sphere you gave me, the one you just *had* to have analyzed. I suppose you're going to tell me, after I've done all this work, that it isn't important and I can forget about it."

"Not at all. It's very important. It's solder wire, the stuff you melt to hold metal things together?"

"Solder paste, actually. Tin, silver, a touch of bismuth. No lead. Water soluble."

He did not continue. She strove to look properly awed by his abilities in inorganic analyses. "What does that mean?"

"Probably used in electronics."

Suspicious, but not conclusive. Jillian Perry had been surrounded by electronics. "Thanks, that's very helpful. Regarding that same case, I need to know about Jillian Perry's blood work. Did she have anything in her system?"

"Normally we put such information into reports. You might have seen them, pieces of paper with words and multicolored graphs. These reports are given to the pathologist, who in this case is Christine Johnson, and since you two seem to be best friends, I'm sure she would share it with you if you asked nicely, or maybe took her some candy."

"You did, and she did. The problem is—"

"Because otherwise I can't release tox results, even to trace evidence staff, even though you passed biology, which I'm sure is an admirable achievement in some circles. Tox results are confidential. I'd have to kill you."

"I'm trying to solve a murder here, and it's not my own. Christine said you found a small amount of barbiturate?"

Oliver nodded. "I can confirm that, partly because you have already obtained the official results but mostly because I don't give a shit about confidentiality. Diphenhydramine, forty nanograms."

"Not enough to kill her?"

"Definitely not."

"Enough to knock her out?"

"No."

Theresa leaned against a gas tank. It shifted, and she jumped away. Explosions were *so* not her favorite thing. "Are you sure? She wasn't a big person."

"Doesn't matter. She'd need at least thirty nanograms per milliliter to even feel drowsy."

"Is there any way to tell what medication it was?"

"Other than clairvoyance? Unlikely. It could be anything that contains diphenhydramine hydrochloride—Sominex, NyQuil, a hundred other formulas. Did she have any such items in her medicine cabinet or nightstand? Prescription or over the counter?"

"I don't know."

Oliver raised one eyebrow. It gave her the distinct impression of a caterpillar trying to escape. "I beg your pardon, I thought you went to the scene."

"I did. Nothing in the medicine cabinet except Tums and aspirin P.M."

"Nightstand? Purse? Engraved wooden box on the coffee table?"

Theresa occupied herself with scraping loose paint from the compressed gas tank with her thumbnail. "I didn't look."

The overweight toxicologist gazed at her. Examining a victim's home for drugs and medications would be done in all cases, from heart attack to homicide, by rote. The pathologist always needed the information, whether the drugs had caused the death or not. "You didn—"

"No. You can beat me later, but right now I need to get this straight. She *didn't* have enough narcotics in her to put her to sleep?"

"Enough to make her sleepy, certainly, but not enough to make her sleep through her own killing."

"And/or abduction?"

"And/or abduction."

"What about the powder in her back pockets? Was that cocaine?"

"No, young woman, it was not cocaine. It wasn't heroin or even aspirin. That powder you so thoughtfully threw on my pile of work to do contained various calciums—sulfate and hydroxide—and lime."

"Plaster?"

"Got it in one. And with just a biology degree, no less."

She thought about this long enough to forget about her previous experience and lean on the gas tank again. She grabbed the top valve to keep it from tipping over. "Don't drugs, like, metabolize?"

"They've, like, been known to." Oliver worked in sarcasm with the flair of a toddler in finger paints. All drugs metabolized, meaning they broke down into their components during the digestion process. In testing, some of those components might appear as normal by-products of the body and some might not. "And these did, to nordiphenhydramine, DM—never mind. I extrapolated from those to calculate the original dose."

"So she might have had more in her system originally? Maybe enough to make her unconscious, but then her body absorbed part of the dose before she actually died?"

"Someone doped her, and then let her sleep most of it off before they killed her? Doesn't sound very smart."

"No. And he's pretty smart. But he did have to transport the body. How long would that take?"

"Let me understand your question. You think Jillian Perry consumed enough narcotic to pass out, but then her killer left her alive long enough to metabolize some of the drug?"

"Exactly."

"Why?"

"Because he didn't want it to look like an overdose. Because he used the time to transport her. Because he was busy, I don't know. How long would he have?"

Oliver frowned, but she ignored it since he almost constantly frowned anyway. "I'm not some kind of idiot savant who can break Vegas, you know. Those kinds of numbers would have to be worked out carefully, depending on her weight, activity level . . . a lot of work to establish a—what, guess?"

"Timeline. It's important, Oliver. It might be the key to the whole case. Now, what about her gastrics?"

"What about them? No drugs, no undigested capsules."

"So it had already passed out of her stomach? The narcotic?"

"Affirmative."

"Did she have anything else in her stomach?"

"How should I know?" He shuddered in distaste. "That's your job."

Now Theresa shuddered. "I know. And I hate it."

CHAPTER 17

Forensics involved getting up close and personal with a great deal of icky, smelly, completely gross substances, but Theresa's least favorite, by far, was gastric contents. The examination of same also lacked any great scientific certainty. The trace evidence department did not use a gas chromatograph or a mass spectrometer to detect chemical compounds like toxicology did. The trace evidence department used a plastic kitchen strainer, some running water, and, occasionally, nose plugs.

Jillian Perry had not had much in her stomach when she died, and the tox department had already consumed some of it. Theresa placed a cloth mask over her face, started the water running, and swirled the goop at the bottom of a quart-size Nalgene jar. She had to work quickly, to minimize the amount of time the contents were exposed to the air. Otherwise the whole lab would retain the sour odor for the rest of the afternoon.

She poured half the contents of the jar into the strainer, and immediately rinsed the liquid with a gentle stream of tap water. When the strainer and the odds and ends caught in its mesh were clean, she turned off the water, placed a paper towel under the strainer, and layered an open petri dish under the towel.

"Hey!" the secretary protested. The smell had traveled to her workstation.

"Sorry. S'got to be done." Theresa moved to the stereomicroscope and placed the strainer and its accompaniments under the lens. A stereomicroscope used incidental light—light shining on the object from above—instead of light transmitted through the item from below. It viewed larger, opaque items that could not be mounted on a tiny glass slide, essentially a powerful magnifying glass. Plus, it left her hands free to poke at the strainer's contents with a thin metal prod.

This was the other part she didn't like about gastrics. The lab had scientific means for identifying bodily fluids and select inorganics, like gunshot residue and paint. Not food. To draw any conclusions from a gastric-contents examination they were reduced to poking at a bit of it and asking each other, "Do you think that could be a piece of tomato? It looks like a piece of tomato."

Theresa dutifully poked. Jillian's stomach had contained, indeed, a piece of translucent red skin that could be tomato, surely an odd food considering that the last meal she consumed would have been breakfast. Unless she liked southwestern omelets. Or the skin could be from a dried cranberry or strawberry, common breakfast food additives for the health conscious. Or, Jillian had lived past lunch.

Leo materialized at her elbow. "What did you stink up the lab for? Are you doing a gastric? Who do we have where time of death is in question?"

While toxicology examined gastrics for undigested drugs or

drug capsules, the trace evidence department usually looked at gastrics with only one purpose in mind—establishing time of death. Bodily processes more or less stopped when a person died.

Leo got a look on his face that she guessed had nothing to do with the smell. "Tell me this isn't Jillian Perry."

"I did Jacob Wheeler too," she informed him, hoping to sound virtuous. "The fifteen-year-old?"

He paused. Nothing brought pressure on the office like a child murder, and the press, when they hadn't been expounding serial killer theories, had been demanding to know who had killed one of the city's youth in his own backyard. "Find anything?"

"Tortilla chips and pickles. Consistent with what his mother said he snacked on when he came home from school. He probably died shortly after leaving the house."

"And now you're working on—?"

"Uh—can you take a look at this red thing? What do you think it is?"

Normally, asking Leo's opinion stroked his ego enough to deflect any criticism. Not now. "We have to talk about Jillian Perry, Theresa."

"Okay. But can you take a look first? I always have a hard time with gastrics. Everything looks like it could be anything to me."

He couldn't resist this, and she really did need the help. After a two-minute consultation they decided that the dark green flecks were pepper, the light green fleshy bits were apple, and one piece of brown matter could be hamburger. The red skin could be a number of things.

"Okay," Leo said after Theresa had washed the contents of the strainer down the sink and flushed the sink well to dispose of any remaining odorous substances. "Now let's have a chat about Jillian Perry. Or actually, let's not bother. The M.E. wants to see you."

"Stone?"

"We have only one M.E., Theresa."

"When does he want—"

"Now."

This was out of the ordinary, to say the least. Stone had long been an expert in delegation, and appeared in the trace evidence lab only once or twice a year. He had spoken to Theresa privately to tell her she had been hired, and that, ten years previously, had been their last one-on-one chat. Her heart began to thud against her rib cage, gently but persistently. "Why?"

"You might as well ask him that since you'll be in his office in thirty seconds. Won't you?"

"But—"

"Now."

"Not even a hint?"

"I told you. Jillian Perry. Now go."

She stopped in the ladies' room to check her hair and the crevices between her teeth, and traveled the one flight of stairs down to the second floor. Carefully, as if any misstep could result in the breaking of bones.

The M.E.'s secretary showed her in without the slightest trace of sympathy, but there had long been lingering resentments between the trace lab and the administrative staff. The secretaries had been instructed to treat the doctors like demigods, and chafed at the scientists' easy familiarity with same. So this didn't mean her head had been placed on the chopping block. But it didn't mean it hadn't.

Elliot Stone waved her to a seat. He seemed much friendlier than his secretary, though this also meant nothing. The office upholstery smelled faintly of leather. The shelves around her held a few books and many pictures of the man behind the desk with other people, the memorabilia of rubbed elbows. Stone excelled at rubbing elbows.

Like now. Evan Kovacic and a young man in a sharp suit occupied the two other chairs.

Evan nodded at her. "Mrs. MacLean."

To his credit, Stone could be succinct when he wanted and apparently he wanted. "We have a problem. Mr. Kovacic is planning to file a lawsuit against this office for abuse of authority. He intends to name you as the agent."

Her lower jaw slackened. "What?"

Evan's attorney grinned like a lion upon spotting a legless gazelle. Evan didn't grin, but he had the same sheen to his eyes.

The M.E. held up a stack of legal-size papers. There must have been twenty sheets, stapled together. Why were attorneys always so long winded? "I have the complaint here. He says you advised another man to sue for custody of not only his wife's body, but their baby daughter? Mrs. MacLean—Theresa—I hope you have a good explanation for this"

"It's completely untrue, Yo—" She almost said *Your Honor* from force of habit. "Dr. Stone. Drew Fleming came here and asked me about Jillian's case. I never told him to sue for custody of the body, and frankly, it's downstairs waiting to be picked up as we speak."

Stone continued the interrogation, and Evan's attorney seemed content to let him. Why not? The job of decimating her career was getting done regardless. "Apparently this other man is not a family member or legal kin. And you discussed the victim's case with him?"

"No, of course not. I asked for information about the deceased. I didn't tell him anything he didn't already know."

Stone did not appear convinced. He fixed her with a look so shrewd that for the first time she did not wonder how he had risen to the position in which he now found himself. She went on, "Drew is suing to be awarded guardianship of the man's stepdaughter, but that has nothing to do with me. I certainly never advised him to do so."

Technically. She swallowed hard, ducking her head to keep the motion from the men present.

"So you admit Drew Fleming would be a completely unfit parent?" the attorney asked.

"I wouldn't have any idea what kind of parent Drew Fleming would be. All I know is that it is not my decision."

"That hasn't stopped you from interfering so far," Evan said. He had not glanced away from her since the moment she'd entered the office.

The best defense is a good offense. "I'm surprised you aren't more curious about your wife's death. I would think you'd want me to do my job."

"Trying to get the court to take my stepdaughter away? Questioning my friends and business associates about me? That's your job?"

"Yes."

That brought all three men up short, but only for a moment. Then the lawyer said, "Dr. Stone, I'm afraid we'll have no choice but to go through with this lawsuit if Ms. MacLean persists in interfering in Mr. Kovacic's domestic situation—"

"There will be no further interference," the M.E. assured the man.

"I never interfered in the first place!" Theresa protested.

"She thinks Mr. Kovacic is guilty of something. What that could be, I don't know, since his wife clearly committed suicide."

Theresa said, "There's nothing clear about it. And as a matter of fact, it's a good thing her body was not immediately released, because we found more evidence this morning."

Evan's attorney ignored her, continuing to pour out subtle and not-so-subtle threats to the medical examiner, but Evan himself lowered his head and his skin flushed, as if he were morphing into one of the undead soldiers of Polizei's nether regions. "What evidence?"

"Bruises on her arms."

The lawyer said, "So you think she was murdered by that serial killer?"

She ignored him and spoke to Evan. "Do you have any idea how they might have gotten there?"

He responded with only a muscle flexing at the back of his jaw.

"Did Jillian have any trouble sleeping?" she persisted.

The lawyer switched tacks once again. "Apparently Mrs. MacLean makes a habit of this behavior. Aren't you currently under investigation for harassing a defense witness?"

"No." A reprimand from a judge did not constitute an investigation. "What about Griffin Investments?"

Evan turned away to stare out the window. But winter days in Cleveland often grew so dark that the window became a mirror, and she watched his nostrils flare with a sharp intake of breath.

"Dr. Stone, do you tolerate unlawful acts from all your employees?"

Stone, she figured, would happily toss her into the arena if it would get the lawyer out of his office, but not if the smear might extend to him. "Investigating a death is hardly unlawful. To the contrary, it is the very act we are compelled, by law, to do. Mrs. Kovacic's case will be closed very soon and the body is ready for release right now. I don't know what to say about your custody troubles, but they cannot be helped or hurt by anyone in this office. Good day, gentlemen."

The attorney left with the smug look his type used to make everything appear to be a victory, and Evan followed with a heavy tread. Stone had nothing to say to her, so Theresa left as well. Reaching the door at the end of Stone's large office, however, Evan turned and lowered his head to hers, too far from either Stone or his lawyer to be overheard.

"I don't know where you're going, but you're not going to get there. Jillian killed herself and you can't prove otherwise."

"How would you know?"

If she had any remaining doubts about his guilt, he now dispelled them by the way he did not answer this question—couldn't, without confessing that he knew every detail of Jillian's death. That and the venom in his voice as he blotted out the crowded, busy office around them with his body and spat out, "I warned you—"

Sweat pricked through her skin, and her heart threatened to pound itself into pulp. She locked her knees and pushed her heels into the floor, refusing to let weakness get a toehold. "Yeah, I know, a pissing contest and I should bring an umbrella. Well, let me tell you something, Mr. Kovacic. You might want to invest in one yourself, because I'm about to rain on your parade."

Jerry Graham answered his phone on the second ring, his voice impatient and distracted. After she identified herself he grew less distracted but no less impatient. "I'm really not interested in speaking with you, Mrs. MacLean. Evan has been my friend for many years."

"I have no interest in paining Mr. Kovacic. I'm simply trying to find out what happened to Jillian, and why."

"We'll probably never know why."

"That may be true. Anyway, I didn't want to ask you anything about Evan at all. I just need to know what Jillian had for breakfast Monday morning."

"What?"

"We're trying to narrow down time of death. Once we have that, then I'm sure we'll be ready to issue the certificate." This being, more or less, a blatant lie, but it sounded reasonable enough. Jerry Graham had spoken as if he hadn't actually *seen* Jillian on Monday morning, and Theresa needed to confirm that.

"Breakfast?"

"It has to do with gastric contents, which is, well, I'm sure you don't really want to hear about that—"

"No."

"But I had the impression that Jillian had been eating breakfast when you and Evan left for your meeting on Monday morning. Do you remember what she was eating?"

"No, I—I don't know. I didn't see."

She would have liked to see the expression on Jerry Graham's face as he evaded her questions, but didn't dare set foot on the Kovacic grounds again. Did he simply not notice the breakfast table, was he lying, or was he simply grossed out by the thought of someone looking at the contents of Jillian's stomach? "What was on the table? Do you remember that?"

"I never went inside. I knocked on the door and Evan came out. We were cutting it a little close and had to get going."

"Oh. You didn't step inside the apartment?"

"No. I was juggling a couple of files I wanted to review on the way downtown. I don't think I even glanced up. If I did, I don't remember."

"Did Jillian say anything to you? Call good-bye, or anything?"

"No. I don't know if she knew I was there, or maybe she was in the bedroom or something."

So he hadn't seen Jillian. "Did you hear her say good-bye to Evan? What did she say?"

"I don't know. He shouted, 'Bye, Jilly,' or something like that before he shut the door, but I don't know what she said. We needed to hurry."

"Did you hear anything from Jillian at all? Even if you couldn't understand the words?"

His speech had gradually slowed, and now it stopped entirely. She pressed the receiver to her head firmly enough to cut off the supply of blood to her ear, trying to interpret his silence. Did he stop talking to rack his brain, to reconstruct every detail of that morning? Or was he examining every answer to determine if it might harm Evan?

Or had he begun to have some very uncomfortable suspicions about his best friend? A million tiny details might be suddenly falling into place in Jerry Graham's mind, and she wished she could be privy to each one of them.

Or had Evan thought of each detail and worked every one out with his friend Graham, who now wondered if they had done so thoroughly enough? But if they had collaborated in Jillian's death, these two very intelligent men, Jerry would know the right answers and repeat them without hesitation.

Ultimately, Jerry Graham hedged his bets, giving her the worst possible answer. "I don't remember."

"Do you remember the tone of her voice?"

"No, sorry. I might have heard her say something, I might not have. I just can't be sure."

A completely reasonable, and completely unprovable, statement. She added some follow-up, just to keep him from getting too nervous about their conversation. "Did Evan mention what *he* had for breakfast? Maybe they ate the same thing."

"I doubt it—I mean, I doubt he mentioned it. We had a lot of other things to talk about, and he doesn't eat breakfast half the time anyway."

"Okay. Well, it was worth a try. Thanks for your time, Mr. Graham."

She hung up. Leo dropped into Don's desk chair across from her, letting the air escape his lungs as if he'd been on his feet all day and might collapse. "Well?"

"Jillian Perry never made it to Monday breakfast. I bet dinner on Sunday became her last meal."

"I meant the meeting with Stone. Do you still have a job?"

"Far as I know. That's how Evan got Jillian's body to Edgewater without being seen—in the middle of a bitterly cold night when not even the drug dealers would have been risking frostbite. I can check opportunity off my list. He had it."

"Bully for you." Her boss remained, clearly, unimpressed.

"This guy's trying to make a fool of us, Leo."

"He's going to succeed if he sues the office."

"He thinks he's smarter than us," she goaded further. If she could get Leo's ego on her side, she'd be unstoppable, lawyer or no lawyer.

"If he makes you lose your job over a whore like Jillian Perry, he's right."

"How can you *say* something like—"

"On my fifth birthday," he began, settling back in the chair with his hands clasped around the back of his neck, "my daddy got elected head of the school board in Larchmere, Ohio. The first issue on his agenda centered around a young teacher who felt that children should be taught about the birds and the bees early on so that they'd know what mistakes to avoid later. Standard practice today, but not then. My daddy agreed wholeheartedly, since he hadn't really planned on my sister and me, talked to the board, talked to the parents, and then fired the teacher. Without severance and without a recommendation."

Theresa frowned.

"Because if he hadn't, he wouldn't have lasted out his term. You have to pick your battles. It don't matter how smart or good looking or even right you are. If you ain't going to win, then you're only going to bloody yourself."

Theresa considered this unquestionably wise statement, and rejected it. She had bled before. "It's not just the dead woman, it's her daughter. If this guy could kill a grown woman without leaving a trace, how much easier will it be for him to murder the baby?"

"That doesn't change a thing. If you can't prove Jillian Perry was murdered, then you're going to have to move on."

This would have sounded kindly, almost paternal, were it not for the warning edge to his voice. Any battles she picked had better damn well not spill onto his field.

And she had better be sure she could win.

CHAPTER 18

The comic-book shop on Madison, where Drew worked, surprised her. Venetian blinds covered the windows, the shelves had been hewn from solid cherry, and the air seemed remarkably free of dust. Every last inch of space had been utilized, but neatly. Classical music tinkled from hidden speakers.

It could not be wise to show up there so soon after Evan's accusation of collusion, but Theresa lacked sufficient paranoia to think he would have her followed, and felt a face-to-face with Drew would be more productive. He could hang up a phone too easily.

Drew was conversing with a customer at the counter, too engrossed in his topic to notice her approach. "Do you have number 437? That one was really cool because he finally really talks to Marina about her father. And he beats up Doctor Sin too. But he gets away—"

"Drew," she interrupted, refusing to be distracted by the history of Doctor Sin.

Drew turned, saw her, gulped. "Excuse me a minute," he said to the customer, who hitched his computer case strap higher onto his shoulder and shuffled off toward a glass display case labeled FIRST EDITIONS. "Hi, Mrs. MacLean."

The polished wooden counter dug into her waist as she leaned toward him. "Did you tell Evan Kovacic that I told you to apply for guardianship of Cara?"

"Um." The red had faded, mostly, from the whites of his eyes. Perhaps he had finally ceased the relentless sobbing. "No."

"Are you sure? Because I just met with him and his attorney and they have that distinct impression."

He pulled his knit zip-up cardigan more tightly around his thin frame, and his eyebrows crept up in an imitation of innocence. Today he seemed no more dangerous than a stray kitten.

"He's threatening to sue me and my employer," she added.

"I'm sorry! I didn't mean to! His attorney called me after I filed the papers and asked who my attorney was and when I said I was representing myself he said then I have a fool for a client and who the hell—though he said more than hell, which I didn't think was very professional of him—did I think I was, trying to take a man's daughter away from him?"

"Okay. And where did I come into this?"

"He said Evan had the resources to give Cara a decent life, and a loser like me had nothing."

This situation had disastrous potential for her and she needed to stay on track, but still, she couldn't let that go by. "Attorneys aren't known for their tact, especially when they're trying to get you to drop a case, Drew. Don't pay any attention to his insults. But as for me—"

"I might have said something like, well, that you didn't think it was such a bad idea. If I got custody of Cara."

Oh, hell.

"You don't, do you?"

"Drew, I never advised you to—"

"But you don't, right? Wouldn't it be better for Cara to have a father who really loved her, and not just her bank account? And let's look at the facts—Evan didn't do such a good job of taking care of Jillian."

"Jillian was a grown woman, Drew."

"But—"

She fiddled with the items near the cash register to take a break from his gaze, a collectible Batmobile, light sticks in a variety of colors, the "take a penny" bowl, and tiny plastic Legolases. "Look, despite the fact that your emotions seem to—fluctuate—I'm sure you would be a perfectly good father . . ."

"Thank you," he said and beamed.

"But whether you would, or whether Evan wouldn't, none of that is up to me. Your court case over Cara has nothing to do with me. I can't help you with that—"

"Sure you can. Prove Evan killed Jillian."

"Drew, I don't know that he did." Didn't she? Then what had she been doing for days, neglecting her job and the rest of her life to retrace a dead woman's steps? Okay, she knew it. But she couldn't prove it.

"Sure you do."

"You're not listen—"

"You got in trouble at work, I get that. I promise I won't mention your name to anyone from now on, I'll say it was entirely my idea to ask for Cara. I'll pretend I don't even know you. Just put him in jail, and Cara won't have to be raised by the man who killed her mother. I know you can do it, because you understand."

"Understand what?" she asked, fairly certain she did not want to hear the answer.

"What it's like to lose someone. I looked you up, in the library newspaper archives. I—I read about your fiancé dying. That was so awful."

As always, she didn't know what to say.

"But that's why you understand about Jillian, why I have to know what happened to her and punish Evan for doing it. I have to." He patted her hand and she tried not to jerk it away. "You'll figure it out. You're like Wonder Woman. Just pull out your lasso of truth, all your lights and test tubes and microscopes, and justice will prevail."

"Wonder Woman," Theresa said. "Sure."

Jillian's mother, Barbara Perry, managed an antiques store in Cuyahoga Falls—not a storefront affair, but a vast box perched on the edge of a forested valley. Parked cars clustered near the door, filling one-third of the lot in the middle of a weekday. Theresa sat in hers and stared. What was she doing here? Frank had contacted Anthony and Barbara Perry, been told that they hadn't spoken to their daughter in months, and that they could shed no light on her life or activities. "Quote," Frank had told her. "That's exactly what her dad said, 'no light.' "

That was why it had taken Theresa four days to pay Jillian's mother a visit.

Who was she kidding? She simply hadn't wanted to converse

with a woman who had just lost her daughter. Too easy for parallels to pop up and linger.

And, truthfully, if they hadn't seen Jillian in a year or two, they would be unlikely to illuminate Jillian's state of mind or her relationship with her husband. So why was she here, taking over for the investigators like some sort of deranged Nancy Drew?

Because she had a right to ask what they knew about Jillian's state of mind. That *was* the job of the medical examiner's office. Maybe not *her* job, specifically, but close enough. She opened the car door and stepped onto the asphalt.

And because she wasn't going to turn her back on Jillian Perry again.

The frigid air filtered out of the valley with the smells of evergreens and frozen earth. Cuyahoga Falls tried to live in harmony with the nature surrounding the town, and for the most part had the funds to do so. Apparently the antiques business had not suffered along with the rest of the economy. The shopgirl who had answered the phone earlier said that Barbara Perry would be in all morning and could pick up the line as soon as she finished with a couple and their butler's table. Theresa hadn't waited. Barbara Perry had at least seen her newborn granddaughter, and with luck might know more about her daughter than anyone suspected.

There was only one way to find out.

Still, the walk to the lettered glass door seemed to take many more steps than it should have. The air felt especially bitter, and one lone starling gazed at her as he perched on the luggage rack of a silver Audi. The starling squawked.

"You shouldn't be here either, my little feathered friend. Aren't the smart birds still in Florida?"

Its marble eyes did not waver. She reached the door.

What are you hoping this woman will do? Tell you that Jillian said Evan threatened to kill her and also said, by the way this is how I'll do it? Tell you that Jillian had been contemplating suicide, so she walked into that woods of her own accord and Evan is simply a tactless, shallow, but innocent man? Decide that perhaps she should sue for custody of Cara, since Evan is all by himself and not even a blood relation to the little girl?

Maybe.

Then he'd sue you for sure.

But Cara would be safe.

She pushed the door open and stepped through. Not even the smell of wood polish and old upholstery could unclench her stomach.

She saw Barbara Perry immediately, her hair and eye color too identical to her daughter's to miss. The woman held a glass bowl out to an older man in a heavy parka, not removing her own hands until his had firmly clasped the beveled edges. She wore a simple pantsuit in light pink and a heavy cardigan sweater that seemed to pull her shoulders down. The blond hair was set in precise curls. The blue eyes never left the bowl.

Blowing a sale would not get their relationship off to a good start. Theresa browsed through lamps and then a few shelves of knickknacks until the man decided to pony up for the bowl. As soon as he left with his carefully wrapped package, she approached the woman.

"Mrs. Perry?"

"Yes," she said and viewed Theresa without apparent interest.

Theresa introduced herself without specifying her position at the medical examiner's office. "I realize this is a difficult time for you, but could I please have a few minutes?"

"We couldn't do this on the phone?" She sounded more surprised than upset. Only plumbers made house calls these days. "I'm working."

I thought you might be more forthcoming without your husband. "I was in the area anyway," Theresa lied blatantly. She'd lived in northern Ohio all her life and only visited the suburb east of her perhaps three times.

"I don't think I can help you. My daughter and I haven't seen much of each other these past few years."

"Anything you could tell me would help. We're trying to complete her case file, but I wanted to be sure that I spoke with all her next of kin first."

With the carrot of closure dangled before her, Barbara Perry agreed to take a break. She said as much to a skinny teenager with CARLOTTA on her name tag and led Theresa to an area next to the office that showed almost as much sophistication as the showroom. The coffeepot had deep stains and the microwave needed cleaning, but the sofa had been upholstered in crimson jacquard and an orange carnival-glass teacup held the Splenda packets.

Theresa's heart beat a little desperately as she planted her bottom on the red cushions.

Pretend she's Rachael's teacher, she coaxed herself. She's given Rachael a C instead of an A on a recent test that Rachael insists she aced, and you're not leaving until you find out why. "Thank you for your time, Mrs. Perry. I'm sorry for your loss."

The woman did not speak until after she'd craned her neck to get her coworkers in her line of sight. The teenager on the floor moved to greet a pair of young women crossing the threshold, and a man of indeterminate age spoke, low and without pause, on the phone in the adjacent office. Apparently reassured, Barbara Perry stated, "I loved Jillian."

"I'm sure you—"

"No." She looked at Theresa, pressed her trembling lips together. "I loved Jillian. I think she made some mistakes, and perhaps I did too, but I loved her. You don't know how many times I've wished I could say it's all right, it doesn't matter. But it wasn't right, bringing that baby into the world without a father, using her body instead of her mind to make a living, and how could I say it was? What's the point of being a parent if you don't try to influence your child to take the healthiest path?" She turned her palms up. "What am I here for if not that?"

Theresa stammered, "I see your point."

"I could say to myself, Jillian's an adult now, she has to make her own decisions, and of course that's true. But I'd be saying it to absolve myself of responsibility. I see others doing the same thing, with kids younger and younger."

It took this woman thirty seconds to confess to a parent's thorniest worry, Theresa thought. She wants to talk. She particularly wants to talk about Jillian. "What was Jillian like as a girl?"

An awfully broad question for a medical examiner's investigation, but Barbara couldn't be expected to know typical queries from the atypical. Nor did she seem to care. "Sweet. They were both so easy, she and her brother. That's why it jolted us so when she dropped out of school to be a model. She had always planned to be a teacher, and all of a sudden, after two years of college . . . at first I thought she'd gotten lazy, even though she never had been before. She had always worked hard for her grades. She'd had a job at the Dairy Queen since the tenth grade. Jillian was never lazy. She *wanted* to be a model."

"It sounds like a fun job," Theresa put in when the woman's voice faded.

"For how long, though? She needed to be able to make a living, be independent. I always thought it had to do with breaking off her engagement to Jeremy."

"Jeremy?"

"They dated through high school and into college. A nice boy. Even Andrew liked him, felt he would take sufficiently good care of his little princess."

"Is that what your husband called Jillian?"

"Always." A gentle smile showed, in no uncertain terms, the origin of Jillian's looks. "Both our kids, the prince and princess. Just a family joke—it's not that they were spoiled. Our son wasn't interested in being royalty, only in running and playing ball and getting a car. But Jillian, she would play dress-up in my old clothes and fashion tiaras for herself out of pipe cleaners and costume jewelry. Every day in the summer she'd be in the backyard with a court of stuffed animals and dolls."

She seemed in danger of getting lost in the memory, so Theresa said, "My daughter did the same thing after I brought home a tape of Disney's *Sleeping Beauty*." She didn't add that Rachael had tired of the pomp and circumstance in a week, after figuring out you couldn't ride a bike in a ball gown.

"My husband finally built her a castle. It was basically just a plywood crate and she was nearly ten, barely enough room to turn around in, but Andrew put a little turret at the top and painted it as best he could. She'd spend hours in there, winter and summer. I'd go out and check on her, make sure she didn't faint from heatstroke or freeze to—" She stopped.

Theresa didn't press the image. "Jillian and her father were close?"

"We both were," the woman said firmly, nipping that idea in the bud. Problem girls often had daddy issues, and sexually precocious behavior often sprang from molestation at a young age. But so many years with her steady, the "nice boy" Jeremy, did not mesh with that profile.

"What about her brother?"

"The typical bickering when they were kids, but otherwise fine."

"What about as adults? I understand he lives out of state?"

"New Mexico. I don't know if they spoke much, but I doubt it. He's busy with his own family now . . . and he and his father have too much conflict. They love each other, but they're too alike."

So you've lost both your children because of your husband. Theresa tried to think of a tactful way to ask for her reaction to that. "Did Jillian say why she broke up with Jeremy?"

"She felt disappointed in him. She didn't get more specific than that, so I don't know what she meant, but I assume the relationship went on too long. He began to take her for granted; she began to think she had settled down too soon and was probably right. I wasn't concerned about Jeremy. If she wanted to broaden her horizons, I thought that was a good idea. Dropping out of college to become a model, that wasn't."

"Was she living at home?"

"No, she had her own place by then. That's why it took us almost a year to figure out that modeling wasn't paying her bills. She didn't get jobs—she had a pretty face but her personality . . . Jillian glowed in person, but the camera couldn't catch that."

Theresa nodded. She realized her thighs were aching from pressing her knees together, trying not to fidget or do anything to break Barbara's train of words. The man in the office had hung up the phone and Theresa hoped he would not come out and interrupt them. "Being beautiful and being photogenic are two different things."

"I think that's how she got into the live modeling. I don't know how she wound up with that—*man*—downtown. Then one of our friends saw her out with a group of businessmen and told Andrew. He called that *man* . . . I don't know what he said, but it nearly killed Andrew. One day I had a daughter." She sighed. "The next, I didn't."

"Your husband disowned her?"

The woman waved her hand at the idea. "We're not the Hiltons. There wasn't much to disown her from except us. He stopped speaking to her, which was a million times worse. Jillian thought the world rose and set on her father."

"But she wouldn't quit the agency?"

"No." Barbara crossed her arms over the pink knit top, as if protecting her midsection against a new onslaught of pain. "I don't understand. I never understood."

"Perhaps she wanted to, er, enjoy her youth after being in a steady relationship all those years."

"My daughter wasn't a slut, Mrs.—I'm sorry, I've forgotten your name."

"MacLean."

"My daughter was a romantic. That was the problem all along. She had no realistic sense of how the world worked. She expected a man to come along and build her a castle."

"Evan."

This made Barbara look at her, the blue eyes startling in their clarity. "Was my daughter happy?"

She should have been. She'd found a man to replace her father, in charge, controlling, a man who designed castles and took her to live in one with her very own little princess at her side. She should have been very happy. "I don't know, Mrs. Perry. She might have been."

"Then why is she dead?"

"I don't know that either."

"Barbara." The office man had materialized next to them and Theresa gave a little start. "Here's the order for that wardrobe. They'll be in this afternoon."

She took the folder he held out. Her hand trembled.

He did not appear to notice the wet eyes or quavering voice. Perhaps he had poor eyesight or an utter lack of empathy. "Be sure it's wrapped properly. We don't want another disaster like the Bennings' china cabinet."

"No, of course."

When he had returned to his desk, Theresa asked, "Did Jillian have any health problems?"

Barbara seemed a bit relieved to have a specific, answerable question to tackle. "She was born with a hole in her heart, where the wall didn't close up."

"A septal defect? Between the two ventricles?"

"Yes. It had healed by the time she started school. It didn't hold her back from any activities, but Jillian didn't care for sports anyway. She had chicken pox at ten, and mono her first year in college. Other than that she was hardly ever sick."

"Any allergies?"

She shuddered. "Shellfish. I let her try my crab at a restaurant once, on her first day of second grade. She turned blue and we had to go to the emergency room. She scared me to death, and completely terrified her father."

There had been no sign of anaphylactic shock in the dead woman. "Anything else you can think of, something that might have affected her physical condition?"

"I thought Jillian froze to death. Do you think it could have been natural causes?" The stillness in her face eased, and her spine straightened just a millimeter in cautious hope. "Do you think some physical ailment could have affected her mind? Is that why she walked into the woods and froze to death?"

"I'm just gathering information, Mrs. Perry—"

"Maybe she didn't know what she was doing. Because I don't believe she would kill herself, I really don't. Only if she had taken a lot of drugs, but Jillian hardly took aspirin, and you didn't find any drugs in her system, did you, or you wouldn't be asking all these questions. Maybe it was a brain tumor?"

"We would have found that during the autopsy." It pained Theresa to dampen Barbara Perry's hope that her daughter had not chosen to end her own life. Some bizarre biochemical reaction would be preferable. A brain tumor would be preferable.

Murder, even, would be preferable.

"I don't know exactly how Jillian died, Mrs. Perry. That's why I'm trying to find out."

"I know there's some explanation. You don't know how frustrating it is, to know that there must be an answer out there but without any means of finding it." For the first time her fingers unclenched. "I have to wait for someone like you to find out for me."

Great. First Drew and now Jillian's mother, both counting on her to uncover the truth. But only their specified truths. Drew wanted to know that Evan murdered Jillian and Barbara wanted to know that her daughter had found happiness before dying of an unexpected and unpreventable physical disorder.

Theresa wanted to ensure Cara a long and healthy childhood.

Tall orders. Tall, and perhaps mutually exclusive. Even for Wonder Woman.

"Your granddaughter Cara—do you know who her father is?"

The brief reprieve for Barbara Perry's emotional health had come to an end. Her shoulders sank so, she could be accused of bad posture. "A soldier, apparently. He died in Iraq."

Theresa had been waiting for an "I don't know." "Really?"

The woman shrugged. "She said so after I asked for the fifteenth time. I expect she planned to tell Cara that someday."

The salesgirl, Carlotta, approached the sitting area. "Barbara?"

"I'll be done here in a minute."

"That couple I have are interested in a canopy bed. Do you want to show them that one from the estate sale—"

"Herd them over to it, slowly. Be sure to show them the lamps. I'll be there in a minute."

The girl trotted away. Barbara smoothed her skirt as if preparing to stand, but Theresa pressed on. "You don't think it was the truth? Because whoever he is, he either doesn't know or doesn't care about Cara's money, or you'd think he would have reappeared in a hurry."

"Andrew said if the soldier story was true, Jillian wouldn't have kept it a secret. She would have been able to tell us something about him, what he did, where he was from. A name, at least."

"Jillian invented him to make everyone around her feel better?"

"She never could lie. She was terrible at it."

"She didn't say anything else about him?"

"It's hard—" Barbara took a deep breath. "But I have to conclude that she didn't tell us anything about him because she didn't know anything about him. He was a one-night stand. Or a client."

Or a pimp.

Or what she *did* know was so bad that Jillian gave up child support in order to stay away from him. Could that have gotten her killed? Some secret from her past that had nothing to do with Evan, or Cara's money?

In any event . . . Theresa chose her words carefully. "Evan has had to apply to the courts for guardianship of Cara since he was not married to Jillian at the time of Cara's birth and makes no claim to be her parent."

Barbara responded with what seemed to be equal caution. "Yes?"

She was probably going to get sued anyway, so she might as

well do what she had been accused of. "You and Mr. Perry are the baby's next of kin."

"We can't take her."

"Of course that would be a huge decision—"

Barbara didn't ask why she'd brought it up, or seem to take any offense at the topic. "I know she's our granddaughter, and no matter what, I'll love her. But we can't go back to raising a child. My husband wants to take early retirement next year and the income will be fixed." Now she did stand, dismissing the idea with a stilted wave. "I know what you're going to say, that Cara comes with her own funding, but it's not the money."

"About Cara's account . . . was your husband angry when Jillian's grandparents left the money to her?"

The implications of this question went right over Barbara's head. "No, that's what I mean—it's not the money, it's the *time*. When my husband retires we'll finally have time for ourselves, maybe travel while we're still young enough to keep up with a group. I know that sounds horribly selfish."

"It doesn't."

"But I did my job. I just can't do it over again. Even with all the money and help in the world—" Her eyes grew wet. "I just can't. I'm too old, and I'm too tired."

"I understand perfectly. Thank you for your time, and again, I'm sorry for your loss."

Out in the parking lot, Theresa waited for the engine to warm up. A couple strolled on the sidewalk in front of her, a young man and woman, each carrying a matching Tiffany glass lamp. They must have been happy with the purchase; they stopped to congratulate each other with a kiss.

She hadn't thought of Paul all morning, and, as if the feelings had accumulated in the meantime, like held mail, longing and abject pain rushed through her now. Her stomach had begun to sink with her visit to Stone's office and continued through the up-close-and-personal visit with Barbara Perry and her loss. Now it did its best to shrink into her spine, while her lungs froze up in that limbo that comes before a sob.

Oh, Paul.

Was life ever going to seem good again?

Stop. Focus. Concentrate on the work. Did I learn anything from the interview? Only that Jillian had been healthy, and her princess Cara would not be rescued from the castle's turret by her grandparents.

Not that Theresa found that difficult to understand. Would I want to raise Rachael's kids? Hell, no.

Though it would be different if Rachael's child lay beneath a suspended sword, ready to fall from its thread the moment Evan became her official next of kin. But of course she couldn't tell Barbara Perry that, because she couldn't prove it.

Yet.

CHAPTER 19

"Thank you for seeing me." Theresa gathered her purse and her coat and stood up with as much grace as she could muster carrying these heavy accoutrements. Normally grace did not register on her list of priorities, but something about the muted colors and pristine leather of the firm's waiting room prompted her to awaken her inner Emily Post. The offices of the venture capital firm Cannon, Jennings, and Chang made Barbara's antiques shop look like a garage sale.

Mr. Cannon led her through the well-appointed hallways to his office, which bulged with enough expensive good taste to cap off the tour. She had stopped noticing, however, and slid into a suede armchair with barely a glance around. "If you remember from the tech show, Mr. Cannon—"

"Nick."

"Um, Nick. I work for the medical examiner's office—"

"Our local *CSI*. Yes, I remember. I hope you're here to take me up on my lunch invitation, though I can't do it today. I have a noontime meeting at John Q's with my two partners and a guy who's going to revolutionize the data services field. Or so he says. I would much rather have lunch with y—"

"No." Her stomach had had a bad day so far, and the idea of eating out with a man who was not Paul finished it off. "Thank you, but I will need only a few minutes of your time. We're still looking into Jillian Kovacic's death, trying to figure out why it happened."

If disappointed by her lack of enthusiasm for his company, he hid it well. He also wore a wedding ring on his left hand, which made her go *hmm*. But he nodded with no change of expression and she went on. "Everyone who knows Jillian is at a loss to explain how she wound up in those woods. I'd like to know if there were any financial worries in her life. I'm sure your arrangements with Kovacic Industries are confidential—"

"Not necessarily. We keep fairly open books here, once a deal is made. Secrecy produces things like the Enron disaster. Cannon, Jennings, and Chang does not believe in secrecy."

She stifled the urge to smile at this prim announcement. "At the tech show you told me that you finance Evan's work. I understand he's been quite successful."

"Enormously."

"So he and Jillian should have plenty of money."

The man chuckled and leaned back. "Successful doesn't always mean plenty of money. His games are selling like hotcakes. We expect part two to sell equally as well, which is why we lent him the start-up money to produce it. We're sort of the meantime people."

She lifted her eyebrows, and that gave him all the encouragement he needed to go on. "In the meantime, between selling game one and when game two will be on the shelves and generating income, Evan needed extra cash flow to buy equipment, hire more staff, and support himself while he's writing the game. We provide that cash flow. We became limited-term partners with Kovacic Industries."

"So both sides are betting that the new game, part two, will be successful enough to pay everyone back."

"With a healthy profit, yes."

"But there's a risk."

"There is no profit without risk, Mrs. MacLean. We study it, do our best to minimize it, of course, but there is always risk. The biggest risk here would be a competitor releasing a similar, or worse, better product shortly before we do. That would be about the worst that could happen. Other than that, Kovacic Industries is a sure thing."

He beamed, delivering this reassuring news. Problem was, it did not reassure her about her theory. If Evan had no money woes, why would he kill his wife?

Perhaps she *was* wrong, biased, overreacting in her grief. "At the tech show, you said something about a release date."

He stopped beaming. "Yes. Polizei Two was supposed to be out five months ago. Evan has been too distracted with his factory and his virtual-reality tie-in to finish it. Not that it isn't all going to make money eventually—I'm not as enamored of the virtual-reality hardware as I am of Polizei Two since it doesn't have a proven track record, but I do recognize the potential."

"That's why you agreed to finance it. Does—"

"Not the hardware. Just the game, Polizei Two. Say, I'm stuck at an awards banquet this weekend for the city business council—it would be a lot less boring if you'd come along."

"You've only financed the game? Then where did he get the money for that reality ball or whatever it is?"

"The virtual-reality sphere? I assume he used his profits from Polizei One. And what does all this have to do with his Jillian killing herself? Not that I believe she'd do that."

Theresa had opened her mouth to make one response, and now made another. "You knew Jillian well?"

Did that half-a-heartbeat moment of hesitation spring from a disinclination to speak ill of a client, or something else? "We loaned Evan Kovacic a great deal of money, Mrs. MacLean. Even though all went well, I still spent a lot of time with him and his concerns in the past few months. And frankly, I still don't see what it all has to do with his wife."

Theresa kept her voice calm. "When people are unhappy with their lives, it's usually because of love or money. She seemed happy with her husband, so that leaves money. This must be an interesting job, trying to figure out what's a good investment and what's not. You must have to consider every factor that could affect the outcome, just like Evan designing his game."

"Sure. Except that in my case, it's real. No vampires or zombies, only interest rates and stock market dips. Which are a lot scarier."

Theresa worked on a smile. "So you investigated Evan's finances before you agreed to take him on, of course."

"Sure. Sterling, absolutely. Yet another reason we felt confident investing in Polizei Two."

"And he had the money for the factory and the hardware line?"

Cannon paused. "Some, yes. But he formulated those plans after our agreement had been reached. I believe he has separate financing for the factory."

"Not with you?"

"No. As I said, Polizei Two is a sure thing. Virtual reality, well, that's like gasohol. People keep trying to get it off the ground, but the runway is littered with aborted flights."

"Who did finance the factory?"

"I'm not sure anyone did. He probably used the profits from Polizei, as I said. It would have been tight, but apparently he's doing it."

"Did he ask you for funds to purchase the factory?"

"I don't recall, really. He might have run it up the flagpole, but we wouldn't have saluted, so that would have been that."

"You don't know if he has arrangements with any other venture capital firm?"

"He doesn't. That's a detail we make sure of, to avoid scams where a fake entrepreneur gets financing from several sources, then the next thing you know the money has been transferred to the Caymans and there's no sign of your guy. We wouldn't automatically nix the deal, but we'd definitely be aware of any such arrangement with another firm." He pulled at his lip, apparently toying with the interesting question. "Unless he had an angel."

"What's an angel?"

"The corporate world's version of a loan shark."

"Like Griffin Investments?"

The name did not produce a reaction. "I'm not familiar with them."

"Never mind. What does an angel do?"

"Exactly what we do—provides the start-up capital for a growing firm, but is an individual person instead of a group of investors like we are."

"Is that legal?"

"It's perfectly *legal*," he said. "In theory. In execution, of course
. . . the arrangements can be whatever the two parties agree on, and
depending on how desperate and/or optimistic one party is, well,
you can get into loan shark territory. Outrageous interest rates,
percentages of the gross—"

"Murder?"

"I doubt it . . . well, the CFO of a start-up pharmaceutical turned
up dead in California last year, but I think that's a story brokers tell
each other around the campfire with flashlights under their faces.
Besides, if Evan had some angel he had to pay off, he would have
been asking me for a capital increase, and he never mentioned it.
They have plenty of money. At least they will once Polizei Two hits
the shelves. This banquet I mentioned is on Saturday night—"

"Except that Polizei Two is late. Is he worried that you'll pull
the plug on his cash flow?"

She expected him to pooh-pooh the idea, but in a somber tone
he admitted, "There's always a danger. If the delay goes on for
too long, we could decide to cut our losses and leave him with big
bills and a game he doesn't have the means to finish. Kind of like
a Hollywood producer making a movie and having the studio bail
out before he's finished shooting. Everyone loses in that situation.
Happily, there's no need for anything that drastic. Evan will be finished with the game soon, the money will start pouring in, and all
will be right in our world."

"Even though it's five months overdue."

"That's part of the business. No one's too concerned about it."
He tapped the blotter again, compressing his lips in a way that
made her think he overstated his sangfroid. He and his partners

had been shelling out money five months longer than they had expected to, without a definite end in sight. But if they were still supporting Evan, why would he need Jillian's money?

She needed to know how much Evan had profited from Polizei the first, and what he had done with the money. And she doubted this man could, or would, tell her that. She got to her feet. "Thank you so much for your time, Mr. Cannon."

He guided her back down the sumptuous hallways. "Not at all. Anytime you'd like to hear about the oh-so-glamorous world of venture capital, please call on me. And I do hope we can do lunch sometime."

She paused at the exterior door. "And would your wife be joining us?"

The question apparently surprised him. No doubt most women didn't ask, played along with—

"My wife died two years ago. Cancer." He glanced down at the ring on his hand, for a moment with the same empty, desolate face she saw in her own mirror every day. "I just can't stop wearing this."

"I'm sorry." The words left her throat in a choking rush, and she fled to the elevator bank without waiting for absolution. Gulping in huge, deep breaths, she made it to the lobby before the tears came.

"But it's just his finances," she protested to her cousin. The Justice Center sat only two blocks from the venture capital firm and she had walked it, putting her hands over her ears for the last half block to protect the thin flesh from the lake air that whipped past the old courthouse in arctic bursts. Now she sat at the desk across from Frank's, the desk that had been Paul's. The cracked Formica top held nothing but dust, a stapler, and a bit of overflow from Frank's work files. Oddly enough this did not affect her. She had rarely visited the plain, brightly lit, and largely impersonal homicide unit and did not look for traces of Paul there. "Can't you subpoena Griffin Investments to find out if they gave him the money to pay for the factory?"

"No."

"You can't just call them and ask, then?"

"I'm surprised you haven't already."

"I did."

"Tess!"

"I'm establishing Jillian's frame of mind, and she may have been acquainted with Evan's financial manager at Griffin. He may even have been her financial manager, for all I knew. The receptionist didn't find it that bizarre."

"Unless the receptionist doubles as the firm's legal counsel—"

"It doesn't matter, because I didn't get anywhere. You know why? Because Evan's financial manager at Griffin is on a second honeymoon in Asia and refused to take his cell phone with him. The receptionist—she found this very romantic—said it was a dream of the guy's wife but they'd never wanted to spring for it until a generous client gave them the trip as a thank-you. Want to guess who the generous client was?"

Frank pulled at his lower lip. "Evan?"

"That's my guess too, but I can't be sure. The receptionist either didn't know or wouldn't tell. They left Detroit *yesterday*, Frank. I had to open my mouth when Evan complained to the coroner about me. He wasted no time in getting this guy out of the country for a few weeks. If I had called Griffin the minute I learned their name—"

"They wouldn't have told you anything anyway," Frank stated.

"I know, they probably wouldn't have . . . you can't find out that information somehow?"

"I'm sorry, Tess, but no. This isn't communist China or something. We have a little thing called civil rights here. Not that I'm always fond of them myself, but if I want to keep my job I have to get something like a *warrant*. Which, as I believe I've explained, no judge is going to give me based on your—what, hunch?"

She had warmed in the interior temperature and now removed her coat. "Means, opportunity, motive. He had opportunity. I want to find out if he had motive."

"What about means?"

"I'm still working on that."

"Work harder. We don't even need motive. Besides, they were married, that's motive enough." She gave him the look she had learned from their aunts and he added, "Sorry, but it's true. Husbands and wives always have motive, anything from a million-dollar insurance policy to a piece on the side to leaving the cap off the toothpaste tube. You don't need motive, you need concrete facts. The kind that will convince a judge that Evan Kovacic murdered his wife."

"Like what?"

"How about some evidence? Isn't that your stock in trade?"

"Anything he left on Jillian, hairs, fibers, bodily fluids, is not significant. They lived together. You would expect to find his trace on her and vice versa. That's the problem with family killings. If he used some kind of weapon, poison, pills, I don't know what it is and I won't know if it's on his property without getting a search warrant to search it, and you say I can't get the warrant unless I have reason to believe the weapon is there."

"Welcome to my world." Frank sipped from a porcelain mug, then made a face as if the coffee had gone cold. "So the body isn't going to help you."

"Except for the fact that it was moved. He somehow got Jillian from her apartment to Edgewater Park. Maybe in the middle of a freezing-cold night, so no one saw him. Maybe she was somehow still conscious, so he might not have had to carry her."

"Then why would she agree to go to the lake in the middle of the night? Especially if it meant taking the baby out in the cold or leaving her alone in the apartment?"

"She wasn't thinking clearly, perhaps. Even if she had been . . . Jillian was too sweet for her own good. Evan could have convinced her to go there. He probably could have convinced her to jump in."

"So that brings us to his car. What did you find on the stuff you stole from it?"

"Two of her hairs and one pink cotton fiber in the cargo area." Frank saluted her with his mug.

"But that doesn't mean anything, as I said. She could have gotten stuff in and out of his car a million times. The only really interesting item is the diatoms in the tire treads. That proves he drove to a location near the lake."

"Even better."

"Except that the whole city is on the lake."

He scowled. "So you stole this stuff and now you're telling me it's worthless?"

"I don't know yet. I'm going to get samples of other lakeside parking lots, anyplace he frequents near the water, and see if there's any difference in the diatoms. I never had marine biology, so I don't know if diatoms are homogeneous throughout the lake or if different types flourish in different areas. And I didn't steal it."

"Yeah, yeah, abandoned property."

"If I could tie him to Edgewater Park specifically, he'd have no explanation for that."

"Unless he went there for a walk, before her death or since."

"He doesn't strike me as the outdoorsy type."

"He snowboards."

"That's true." Their sentences had overlapped as the words spilled out; now she slowed. "That's true. And he's got a huge bag in his closet for the snowboard. Slender Jillian would easily fit in it."

"He could have used the board to transport her."

She tried to picture this. "Only if she were still in the bag; otherwise her arms and legs would overlap it, and they showed no signs of dragging. But it would leave a distinctive track in the snow."

"We got four inches on Sunday night. It would have covered the tracks."

"Hefting it over his shoulder would still look less suspicious, I think, but either way I need a search warrant for his house and car."

"A series of guesses does not constitute sufficient probable cause. Look, I'm glad you're trying to get back in the game—"

"I'm just doing my job. It's not a game, and even if it is, I never left it." This sounded pale and unconvincing even to her, and she avoided his gaze by opening and closing Paul's desk drawers. Not even a paper clip remained.

"You don't think you're overcompensating a little bit for your, um, lack of job enthusiasm during the past few months?"

"*Enthusiasm?* I work with dead bodies. Exactly how enthusiastic am I expected to be?"

"Okay, forget that. But are you maintaining some sort of objectivity here? At least the possibility that Evan might not have done it?"

"Like you and Georgie?"

"I can admit that nothing is turning up to implicate my Georgie. Can you admit that you are, perhaps, overly sympathetic to this Drew character?"

This stumped her. "Drew?"

"He lives at the edge of the crime scene, he's squirrelly, and he has a better motive for murder than Evan does. Yet you immediately eliminated him. That's not like you."

"I know there's a remote possibility—"

Frank rubbed his face before going on, uncomfortable but determined. He leaned over the stacks of folders, notes, and encrusted coffee cups to keep his voice low. "He lost his beloved. So did you. You haven't noticed that you and he have a lot in common?"

"Like insanity?"

"Like intensity. Hell, your cat died three years ago and you never got another one."

"I got tired of fur coating every surface of my house."

"You don't love easily, Tess. That's my point. This situation is affecting your judgment. You're gunning for Evan Kovacic to take your mind off—" He stopped.

"I'm trying to put a man in jail because I need a hobby, is that what you're saying? I believe Evan Kovacic killed his wife and that he's going to kill her daughter. That isn't grief talking, it's logic. And I'm not going to let him get away with it!"

She slammed a drawer shut and stood up, nearly knocking down a dark-haired woman holding an overstuffed carton, a bulging briefcase dangling from one shoulder. "Oh! Sorry."

"That's okay." Detective Sanchez, normally the picture of confidence, shuffled her feet. Theresa assumed she had overheard their conversation until she noticed that Sanchez kept glancing at the desk. Nor did she leave, but stood there staring into her box as if it could help.

Theresa glanced at Frank, who had the same concerned, waiting expression he'd worn around her for months.

"Are you moving in here?" she asked Angela Sanchez.

The woman's eyes were full of sympathy. "Yep. I've been assigned to work with Frank."

Theresa instantly smiled. The smart, attractive Sanchez would keep her cousin on his toes, and they would work well together. . . . "Good. I'm so glad."

The woman's olive skin seemed to melt in relief.

Theresa got out of her way. "Put that down, it looks heavy. Did you think I'd get hyper over Paul's desk? Please! It's just a desk, and frankly, I can't believe they left it empty this long, space being at such a premium around here." She watched Sanchez unpack her belongings, noting with approval the neatly labeled files and the framed family photos, knowing that she was talking too much but made verbose by the opportunity to put someone at ease instead of making them uncomfortable. Was Sanchez divorced or never married? Not that workplace romances were ideal, but the female detective would be a huge improvement over Frank's usual choice of date . . . Theresa moved behind Frank and patted her cousin's shoulder. "If he gives you any trouble, just call him Francis. That slows him down. If that doesn't work, you can add the middle name, L—"

"Hey!"

"Okay, okay. I'll save that tidbit to blackmail you with later." Glad to see a genuine smile on her cousin's face and vaguely aware that it might have something to do with her own, she donned her coat and prepared to leave. "I'll be calling later."

"Should that worry me?"

"Not at all. I just meant I'll give you a ring when I figure out how Evan Kovacic murdered his wife."

CHAPTER 20

Soft notes tinkled from the baby grand in the corner, over the crystal and china set at the tables; the place settings and their linen napkins were ignored, however, in favor of the bar at the other end of the room. At least ten couples mingled there, some by the floor-to-ceiling windows that looked out on downtown Cleveland and the lake from twenty-five stories up. The women—girls, really—were slender, well built, and uniformly coiffed in long hair of varying colors. The men all wore suits and had gone gray years previously, whether they let their hair show it or not. The restaurant's name, Macy's, decorated each pane of interior glass that closed off this private room from the rest of the facility. Theresa had never been there before. From the prices on the menu she had perused while waiting, she never would be again.

She watched as a waiter whispered a message to George Panapoulos, who promptly glanced behind him to where she stood behind the lettering on the glass. He frowned, said something to the redhead next to him, and left the room.

"What the hell are you doing here?"

"I wanted to ask you a few questions. I also wanted to see how this works. Those are your girls?"

"Yes. They look like cheap little sluts, don't they?"

The women wore dresses of clingy, swishy fabrics, but none were exceptionally short; low cut, but not obnoxiously so. Stiletto heels, but nary a fishnet in sight. "They really are beautiful."

Her tone must have sounded wistful to him because he softened enough to ask, "So what can I do for you?"

"I'm still working on Jillian Perry."

"I told you—"

"Mr. Panapoulos, I don't believe you killed her. I don't believe you had anything to do with her death. But she had a very limited circle of friends and acquaintances and I have run through all of them except for you."

"And what do you think I can tell you?"

"Who she was. What she was. What went on in her mind—"

"Sheesh, like I'm gonna know. Kid, stop a minute." He held his hand out to slow down a smooth-faced young man with a black jacket and a tray of champagne, and snatched one of the delicate glasses. "You want one—sure, yeah, you do, have one. Okay, that's it, you can go now." He handed the glass to Theresa and let the boy get the door for himself.

She sipped it immediately. She was thirsty, and she liked champagne.

He watched her. "None of that line about not drinking on duty?"

"I'm not a cop. Besides, I never turn down free food or free booze."

"Good philosophy. Now, Jillian. I wouldn't have the slightest idea what went on in her head, Ms. MacLean, and I wouldn't waste a lot of time on it if I were you. Jillian wasn't some deep, troubled soul, she was a pretty, nice, few-lights-short-of-a-marquee-sign girl. That's it. What you saw was what you got." He leaned against the glass and polished wood and focused on his sparkling wine for a moment before looking directly into her eyes. "I know what you're thinking, that I'm one step out of the cave and should be wearing a fur pelt. But I've spent most of my day, every day, for more years than I care to count now with women, looking at women, talking to women, telling women what to do. I dress them. I undress them. So maybe you should consider that I know my subject."

Theresa considered herself lucky that he didn't sell used cars, or she'd have been signing on the line for a used Audi sportster right then and there.

"Jillian Perry didn't have a dark side, or a flip side, or any side but the outside. She had no secrets."

"Then who is Cara's father?"

"Except that one." He sipped the champagne, frowning. "Okay, that's the exception in her life that proves the rule. I just know it ain't me. Beyond that, I don't care."

"What if it were a client?"

"That's his lookout, not mine. Though I'd be a little peeved—I go through all the trouble of hiring these girls, coaching them a bit, and then some idiot knocks her up and she's out of work for months? Yeah, I'd be peeved. But that's the great circle of life and all that crap."

"Did Jillian have a relationship with any of your clients?"

He drained his glass. "Nope."

"You seem sure of that."

He leaned back a bit, away from her, as if he no longer cared if she bought the Audi or not. "I am. The girls don't freelance, it's a rule. Sure, some break it and I fire them, but not Jillian. She didn't seem all that enamored of my clientele. It was just a job to her."

"No one she liked . . . in particular?"

"Not that I know of. Tell you what, you can talk to Vangie if you want. I'll tell her it's okay. I know women, yes, but I also know that they talk more to each other than to me sometimes."

"Thank you."

"You're welcome. You ought to do that more often."

"What?"

"Smile."

"Any clients that Jillian particularly *disliked*?"

"Whoops, there it went. Okay, Jillian, disliked . . . she got along better with Hispanics than Asians, and hated it when old guys would pinch her, but aside from that, nothing sticks out."

"Her mother says her father called the agency once."

"Oh, yeah. Daddy dearest thought he'd be clever and check up on his little girl. He requested Jillian, then kept asking for details, would she do *this*, would she do *that*—which is kind of weird in my book, talking that way about your own daughter, even if you're supposedly looking out for her—"

"And you told him she would?"

"No. Not exactly." He cast about for a place to set the empty glass, then gave up and hung on to it. "I may have given him the impression that, well, they could work that out between themselves. You know, like when the furniture store advertises leather couches on sale for three hundred bucks and you get there and there's only one at that price, and it's teal."

"I see. Simple salesmanship."

"Sure."

"So your girls *don't* have sex with clients?"

"I wouldn't know. That's up to them."

She made sure her skepticism showed on her face. "I'm sorry, but I need to know. If they do, then you're a pimp, which isn't my problem. If they aren't supposed to but do anyway, and take in money that you're not getting a cut of—"

He came closer. "I thought you said I wasn't your suspect."

"I didn't think you were." She would not step back.

"I don't do violence in this line of work. I don't need to."

Toddlers lied with more conviction. "Since you're already annoyed with me, let me point out that Sarah Taylor used to work for you."

"Yeah, your cousin was by, asking me about that too."

"How did you know Frank is my cousin?" she asked out of curiosity.

Georgie smiled in a way she really didn't like. "I know lots of things. Look, I had Sarah in my stable a long time ago, but she couldn't stay off the juice long enough to turn a profit, so I cut her loose. Haven't seen her since. In those days, I'll admit, my girls definitely slept with clients. That was the whole point."

"But not now."

"Okay, look. I'm going to give you a lesson in escorting. Business 101, right?"

"Sure."

"I charge enough that, whatever arrangement the girls might make with a client, I don't care. I've been paid, understand?"

"Ye—ess."

"So say the girls make more if they do have sex with the guy. The client is happy and might request them again. The girls are happy to have repeat customers and so am I. Everybody wins."

"What if a girl made her own arrangement and bypassed you completely?"

"Of course that can happen. No system is without problems. But I would fire that girl, and eventually the client would get tired of her. Now she's got no client and no job. Everybody loses."

"I see."

"It's a business, Ms. MacLean. Nothing worth killing nobody over."

"Okay. I get that. So Jillian's father got angry at the, um, implication that Jillian would have sex for money?"

"I'll say. Jillian came in later that night for a job, so I told her about it. By then I was laughing, but the poor kid started to cry. We had a cocktail party, like this one, and she kept having to run to the ladies' room and fix her makeup. Pain in the ass, really."

"What did her father say, as closely as you can remember? Did he threaten Jillian?"

"Hell no, he threatened *me*. Said if I touched her, if I even spoke to his baby girl again, he'd come over and bash my head in. Like I'm the one calling on the phone for her, you know? Oh, and then he'd have me thrown in jail. That was about it. I guess he thought better of it, because I never heard from him again. No visits, no cops throwing me in jail." He shook his head with sympathy rendered false by the smile on his face. "Poor Daddy."

"But he didn't say anything about Jillian?"

"Not to me. I don't know what he said to her later, because she seemed kinda depressed for a couple of weeks. But she kept working. She'd come in with this sort of grim, go-to-hell look on her face. I'd have to jolly her before the job started."

"Jolly?"

He cocked an eyebrow at her. "Tell her she looked beautiful, throw in a joke, that sort of stuff. What did you think I meant, force a little Ecstasy down her throat until her mood lightened?"

"Just checking."

"Not that she wouldn't do a tablet or two once in a while. But it was never much with her, and stopped totally when she got pregnant. She wouldn't even drink, then. Nothing but diet ginger ale. For these types of things"—he jerked his head toward the party room—"I'd have to make arrangements with the bartenders in advance for that damn diet ginger ale. The clients don't want teetotalers around. It makes them feel vulnerable."

"Interesting."

Apparently she didn't sound interested enough, because he straightened and pressed his empty glass into her free hand. "Speaking of clients, I need to get back to mine. If you'll excuse me, Ms.—"

"Did she say anything more about her father? Her parents?"

"Not to me, and I didn't ask. He wasn't the first irate parent I'd encountered and probably won't be the last. This isn't an easy business, you know."

"Then why don't you get into another line of work?"

He glanced toward the party again. Clouds must have gathered outside and the dimmed light softened the lines in his face. "But I meet so many interesting people."

I'll bet. She reviewed the number of expensive suits in the room. Interesting people who then owed him not just the bill but a favor, a consideration, an understanding in exchange for mutual discretion. "Did Evan Kovacic ever contact you or have any problem with Jillian's job?"

"He called looking for Jillian once or twice, but that's all. Not at all like Daddy."

"He was never a client of yours?"

"Nope, never met him." That fit with Shelly's statement, that she had introduced Jillian to Evan. "And you know, that's a good point. Why don't you just ask Jillian's *husband* all your questions?"

She tried to formulate a good answer to that, and failed.

He took his hand off the doorknob. "Oh, I get it. You think hubby killed her."

Daddy and hubby. George liked his diminutives. "I don't know yet. I'm working on it."

"How'd he do it, then? I thought she froze herself to death. Or that serial killer got her."

"I'm working on that too."

"All that hard work, and for a government salary." He pulled the door open, holding the heavy wood with one hand and cocked his head toward the party inside. "Have you ever considered a sideline? Some of the guys get tired of nothing but legs and a giggle. You could wind up with quite the following—"

"No, thanks."

"Do it for the free booze, then."

She laughed.

"Suit yourself." He passed through the door and made a beeline for the group of people, his form breaking up into a kaleidoscope of colors behind the decorated glass panels before the swinging door had time to hit him in the buttocks.

The young man reappeared from farther up the hallway, hustling along as fast as he could with a tray of empty, tinkling champagne flutes, and accepted two more from her with an unhappy sigh.

"I know what you mean, kid," she told him.

She pulled out of the parking garage onto East Eighteenth and headed south to Euclid, stopping at the corner to wait for the light and to see what currently played at the Playhouse Square theaters. She hadn't taken Rachael to a show since the Christmas *Nutcracker Suite* two years before.

So Daddy had been very angry about Jillian's work as an escort. But that had been several years ago and Jillian's body had turned up only last week. Evan had not been very angry, but three weeks after marrying him, Jillian died.

Once again, Theresa decided to keep her money on Evan. He had the more immediate motive, a window of opportunity, means . . .

Her Nextel rang. She peered at it, found the Talk button and pushed it, drifting far enough into the next lane while doing so to earn an irritated honk from a gold SUV. "Hello?"

"I see you're not at work. I'm not even going to ask why you're not at work."

"Hi, Leo. I'm—"

"I said I wasn't going to ask. Actually, it's all right that you're out and about, since you can out and about yourself right over to the old courthouse. You're wanted in court."

She groaned. Testifying in court might be the most important part of her job, the end product of all her work, but it was also a colossal pain in the neck. "I didn't have any subpoenas for today."

"You do now."

"But what case? And why the old courthouse?" Criminal cases were always heard high on top of the modern and hideously decorated Justice Center.

"It's family court. Drew Fleming is calling you as a witness in the custody case."

She nearly sideswiped the SUV again.

CHAPTER 21

"Can he do that?" she said into the phone.

"The subpoena arrived here with your name on it. Since you haven't personally received it, I suppose you *could,* technically, not show up in courtroom number three without receiving a contempt charge. But given how often we in forensics have to work with the court system, and how Mr. Kovacic has recently tarnished your reputation with same, I don't suggest it."

"You have got to be freakin' kidding me."

"I am not," he assured her, "freakin' kidding you."

"How do I get myself into these things?"

"I wonder that often myself. How you get yourself into these things, I mean, and why you've chosen to drag the lab with you on what is looking more and more like a personal vendetta. We cannot be seen to take sides, have I made that sufficiently clear?"

"Yes."

"Not, apparently, *clear enough*!" He hung up.

Theresa made two lefts to head back downtown. She wasn't even sure where to park for the historic county courthouse since she rarely went there. The parking garage eventually turned up, underground, entirely too ominous for her tastes—parking garages had to be a rapist's dream, isolated, dimly lit, with limited points of egress . . . when would the powers that be finally figure out that parking garages should be lit with lights designed to blind, like an operating room or a night baseball game? Nevertheless, she managed to get to the ground floor without any felonies inflicted upon her, to be immediately distracted by the sweeping architecture.

From the middle of the marble staircase she stopped to stare at the stained-glass depiction of Law and Justice, and noticed too late the man who paused beside her.

"Beautiful, isn't it?" Richard Springer said. The defense expert who had complained about her to the medical examiner appeared dressed for court, in a conservative blue suit and with a leather briefcase.

Theresa had had too long a day for subtlety. "You aren't here for Evan Kovacic, are you?"

"Never heard of him."

"Good." She continued up the stairs to the third floor and followed the signs.

Springer came along. "I suppose you've heard that we aren't going to have to face off on the witness stand after all."

"No one told me." Theresa stopped walking when she found courtroom number 3, but still did not look at her temporary companion. If she ignored him, he might go away.

"The charges were reduced to statutory, time served."

Now she looked at him. In fact, she stared in horror before sinking to the bench and resting her face on one upturned palm.

After a moment, she felt a vibration in the wood. He had sat down beside her.

"Look, if it's any consolation, it had nothing to do with your stupid shoe print."

What did that matter? The scumbag was still walking free.

As if uncomfortable with the silence, he went on, "It had more to do with the fact that the judge at the preliminary hearing didn't seem convinced by the girl's story. It turned out she had neglected to mention quite a few things."

She lifted her head slightly, still staring at the patterns in the marble tile. "Such as?"

"Such as, she invited him to her bedroom, and not for the first time, and that the weapon used was a rubber pirate dagger, a souvenir of the family's last trip to Disney World. Basically she had to come up with a story for her parents, and then couldn't stick to it."

This did, she admitted to herself but not to him, make her feel better. But it didn't make her any less guilty. Her work had been sloppy. "Thank you for telling me."

He grinned, with a glint in his eyes that no doubt charmed most female members of any jury. "Does this mean you no longer consider me a whore?"

She could not hedge to that extent. "No, you're still a whore. But I'm hardly perfect."

This did not seem to be the answer he had expected, but didn't appear to bother him either. He said only, "Until next time, then." To her relief he did not offer to shake hands, but set off to his next perfor—testimony.

Drew passed him, coming up the hallway. He had given up the

knit jacket for a navy blazer she suspected had last been worn for his high school graduation. "I tried to call you directly but it didn't go through, I guess. Thanks for coming."

"I didn't have a choice. You had a subpoena issued in my name. Drew, what the hell are you doing?"

"I have to try to get Cara. You know he'll kill her if I don't."

Other people bustled around them, their footsteps echoing on the cold marble, bouncing off the three-story-high ceiling. That was the hell of it —she did know. She felt absolutely certain. It was the only explanation that fit all the known facts. Evan had killed Jillian, almost perfectly so. How much easier would it be to kill Cara, a helpless, orphaned infant? "Do you have a lawyer yet?"

"No. I'll represent myself."

She put a hand to her face to stifle the groan. "Drew. You do understand that the odds of succeeding are very slim. You are no blood relation to Cara and you were not married to her mother."

"But Evan killed her mother."

"Do you have any proof of that?"

"No. But you do, right?"

"*No*, Drew, I don't, that's what—"

"Mrs. MacLean. Why am I not surprised to see you here?"

Evan Kovacic and his attorney had come up behind her. The attorney appeared as impeccably dressed and as unflappable as he had in the M.E.'s office. Evan wore a dress shirt and tie and appeared unhappy, either about her presence, the court case, or having to put on a tie.

She opened her mouth to tell him that she had received a subpoena and *had* to be there, realized it would not do her any good, and shut it again.

The attorney held the door open for all of them. "Shall we go in?"

Civil hearings were very different from what Theresa had become accustomed to in criminal trials. For one thing, she didn't have to twiddle her thumbs in the hall until called to the stand. For another, there were no opening arguments, no posturing to be done for the jury's benefit. Underneath a painting of the Pilgrims, and hemmed in by the darkly paneled walls, the judge asked each side why they were there and implied that their answers should be precise. No other spectators or participants appeared.

Evan's attorney began, setting forth the facts of Cara's birth, Evan's marriage to Jillian, and Jillian's death, adding that no one else had applied for guardianship except for Drew, who had no legal relationship to the infant. Then it was Drew's turn to speak. He did this horribly, stammering, stumbling, and dwelling for far too long on how much he had truly loved Jillian. The judge glanced at his watch more than once, and finally interrupted. "Mr. Fleming, I granted an expeditious hearing because I understood there to be some emergency as to the well-being of a child. Do you have any facts to present to indicate that Mr. Kovacic would be an unfit father?"

"Only that he killed Cara's mother, Your Honor."

Everyone became very still, except the judge. He seemed merely confused. "I'm sorry, *what* did you say?"

"He murdered Jillian."

Now Evan's attorney sprang up. "Your Honor, this is the purest and vilest slander—"

The judge stopped looking at his watch. "How is he supposed to have killed—"

Drew shouted over the other men. His voice changed, as Theresa knew it could, stress breaking the words into dangerous shards. The judge caught the change and stared. "That's the only reason he wants Cara, for her money. Then he'll kill her—"

"Your Honor, we intend to file charges against Mr. Fleming for these baseless allegations—"

"They were married three weeks, Your Honor." Drew sucked in a breath, obviously working hard to get his voice under control. It worked, somewhat. "Three weeks, and a perfectly healthy young mother ends up dead?"

"—a felony charge of slander and harassment—"

The judge appeared thoughtful, or at least curious. "How did she die?"

"Ask her." Drew pointed at Theresa, in the second-to-last row of seats. "She knows."

All four men in the room, plus the bailiff and court reporter, stopped and stared at her.

"And who is she?" the judge asked.

She could only hope that Drew would not introduce her as Wonder Woman.

The walk to the witness stand took forever. She passed Drew on his way back to his seat, and successfully resisted the urge to slap him on the back of the head. She had no idea what to say, and wished for Don, or at least Leo, and thought what a funny story this would make to tell Paul over dinner, if, of course, Paul were still alive to hear it.

The bailiff swore her in. She took her seat.

"Yes, Your Honor?" she replied when he said her name.

"Has Mr. Kovacic been charged with the murder of his wife?"

"Not that I know of."

"Is he a suspect in her death?"

How to answer that? "He is to me" didn't seem reasonable . . . though she *was* a death investigator and she *did* suspect him, which didn't seem quite legitimate . . . such was the self-esteem, still, of a female raised in the twentieth century. . . . With no other strategy in sight, she bunted. "The investigation by the Cleveland Police Department, to my knowledge, has not been completed."

The judge didn't care about her strategy. "So is he a suspect?"

"I couldn't say, sir. It's not my investigation." Was she throwing Frank under the bus? Would he kill her if she did?

"Then why are you here?"

Good question, she narrowly avoided answering. Then she made the mistake of looking at Drew. Skinny, runny-nosed, devastated Drew, who focused on her as if he had terminal cancer and she stood with the last vial of a known cure. Drew remained a problematic human being, but maybe the only one left on the planet with Cara's best interests in mind.

She turned to the judge. "There are many unexplained factors in Mrs. Kovacic's death." She listed the location of the body, Jillian's state of apparent contentment, and the absence of any obvious cause of death.

"So you don't know why this woman died? What does it say on the death certificate?"

"The death certificate isn't complete yet." Drew should have called Christine, Theresa thought. She'd have impressed the judge and made mincemeat of that lawyer. Christine made mincemeat of most people.

"Is there any reason to suspect foul play?"

"It's unusual for a perfectly healthy young woman to drop dead, Your Honor."

"Absence of proof is not proof of absence." The judge repeated what Frank had said, so primly that Theresa had to look down to keep from glaring at him. The worst part, of course, was that he was right.

"Mrs. Kovacic committed suicide, Your Honor." Evan's attorney molded his features into a properly empathetic mask to accompany the statement. "She walked out into the woods and let herself freeze to death. Postnatal depression could have played a part."

"To do so she'd have to walk three miles in subfreezing temperatures without frostbite," Theresa put in. "Which is highly unlikely."

"No one dragged her to that forest. No one tied her to that tree or made her stay there," the attorney persisted.

"How would you know that?" Theresa demanded.

"Why else would a perfectly healthy woman sit down in the freezing outdoors unless she intended to die? You said yourself there were no signs of foul play."

"I—she—"

The judge said her name, waited for her full attention. "Do you believe this woman was murdered?"

Her mouth became too dry to form words. But the judge had not asked what she could prove or what Leo would think was prudent to state. He had asked her opinion after placing her under oath.

"Yes, Your Honor. I do."

Evan leaped to his feet. "That's a lie! This woman's working with Fleming—"

"Your Honor! This is a clear violation of my client's—"

259

The judge spoke over both of the men. "Do you have any proof?"

She tried. "Only my training and my experience in over ten years of working with both homicides and natural deaths—"

"Any other proof? Any physical evidence that implicates Mr. Kovacic in the death of his wife?"

She thought of something. Probably nuts, but worth a try. "It would help me to complete my investigation if Mr. Kovacic would give me his consent to search Jillian's living areas."

Evan had sat, but now jumped up again. "Your Honor! I asked the police to step in when Jillian disappeared. Mrs. MacLean searched my house then! What the hell is she looking for, and why didn't she find it before?"

Theresa protested, "At that time I was investigating a disappearance with no signs of foul play, not a murder. Had I known Jillian's body would show an . . . *unclear* cause of death or signs of transport, I would have conducted the search differently."

This excuse brought her no comfort, nor did it impress the judge, who said, "Search warrants and the like are not my bailiwick. If this man needs to be investigated for murder, tell the police."

Theresa worked hard to keep an even tone of voice. "I understand perfectly, Your Honor. Everyone in this room is here because they care about little Cara's well-being. If I could complete my investigation, it would put everyone's mind at ease, and surely Mr. Kovacic's most of all. He must want to know what happened to his wife."

She thought it sounded good. Then she glanced at Evan. Then his attorney, and then the judge. Not one was buying it.

"I don't want this woman anywhere near me or my home, Your Honor," Evan said.

"Despite the neat bit of extortion on Mrs. MacLean's part—" began his attorney.

"Once more," said the judge, who had probably spent his days in family court listening to participants hurl the wildest accusations ever concocted on the face of the earth, "I don't issue search warrants and I don't allow my courtroom to be used to persuade reluctant witnesses to cooperate in same. Do you, or do you not, have any evidence in hand that implicates Mr. Kovacic as having caused the death of his wife?"

Drew watched her, his gaze so intense it sucked the air from the room into its path.

"No, Your Honor."

Evan sat back down.

Drew wilted before her, his hands gripping the antique wooden railing, his forehead sinking to his fingers.

"Then I have no choice but to grant the custody of Cara Perry to her mother's legal spouse, Evan Kovacic. This decision is permanent and binding. Next case."

CHAPTER 22

Theresa didn't know what else to do except go back to work. She could do nothing more for Jillian Perry. She had examined every fiber, tested every hair, wrung as much information as she could out of her own coworkers. She had reached a dead end, and now Evan had custody of Cara. Game over.

Several reporters had gotten wind of her testimony—no doubt through Evan's lawyer, who wanted to portray her as irrationally biased—and called to ask about it. They were, as always, referred to the M.E.'s office. None called to ask any more about serial killers, since the semen in Sarah Taylor had come back to an East Cleveland man with a history of sexual assault. If he didn't come up with an ironclad alibi or at least some good answers to questions the officers had for him, he would probably be arrested for her murder.

And he had a dog. A large Doberman pinscher.

That left the boy, Jacob Wheeler, on her slate. Not much had been turned up about him. His habits and movements remained sketchy, shrouded by the veil of secrecy teenagers maintained in the face of authority figures. When kids did talk, they didn't say much. Jacob had been a loser, poor and uninteresting, but with just good-enough grades and friends to avoid close scrutiny by a post-Columbine school administration.

Theresa had found nothing of interest on his clothing, so now she pulled out the plaster cast she had made of the shoe print behind the tree. She had not been trained as a shoe print expert, so the cast would have to be sent to the state lab, but they would not accept it until they had a suspect's shoes for comparison. It did not match Jacob Wheeler's; one did not have to be an expert to tell that much.

The treads were quite clean, as the snow had been too deep to allow dirt to penetrate and now had melted. Still, some deposits remained. She set the cast tread side up underneath her stereomicroscope, fully aware that the work served only to distract her mind from Evan's custody of Cara. The odds of finding anything significant amid all that snow were slim to none, and at any rate, she had no items from a suspect for comparison.

With the lens brought into focus over the rough, undulating plaster surface, she began to see tiny pebbles of stone, sand size when not magnified. Some were pretty, but not helpful to anyone but a forensic geologist. A piece of something yellow that crumbled into dust when touched—oops—also defied identification. Two fibers stuck to a piece of tar had evidently chosen that moment to release themselves from the bottom of the shoe, and were fixed to the plaster. Upon closer examination, they were covered in the gunk Theresa had sprayed into the print so that the plaster, which warmed as it set, would not completely melt the shoe print before the cast hardened. She cleaned that off the fibers and mounted them.

She identified one as black cotton, and the other one as an orange-colored trilobal-shaped synthetic.

Orange.

Jacob's bedroom had orange carpeting, and trilobal had always been a popular shape for flooring textiles. It hid dirt well. Perhaps the killer had been in Jacob's bedroom. That would not be surprising; they had always assumed that Jacob met someone he knew in the woods. It seemed an unlikely spot for a mugging.

She pulled her head back from the stereomicroscope to take another look at the cast. The length of it seemed rather small. A girlfriend? His mother?

He had certainly been a trial. But would his own mother fracture his skull and then leave him to freeze to death in the woods?

Maybe. It wouldn't be the first time.

She took another look at the yellow, crumbly substance and scraped some of it into a glassine fold. It could be a tortilla chip, Jacob's last meal. Suppose, during their argument, he had swept some to the floor . . .

But the shoe print seemed too big for the tiny woman, and at the scene she had worn hiking boots, which would have deeper and more complicated treads than this print.

Then there was the scrap of paper in Jacob's hand. Possibly a comic book.

She picked up the phone. "Frank? No, I'm not calling about Jillian Perry."

*　*　*

They didn't need a search warrant to enter the house Jacob Wheeler had shared with his mother. Ellen Wheeler welcomed them in. Anything to help find out what had happened to her son.

The cluttered little home hadn't changed much during the intervening days. The dust had thickened on the end tables and a sludge had formed at the bottom of the coffeepot, as if Ellen had done nothing else in the intervening time except drink caffeine and stare out the front window, as she did now, waiting for her son to return home.

"Thanks for letting us come by," Frank said.

She didn't turn from the window. "He's gone. It doesn't matter."

The boy's bedroom hadn't changed any either. It remained a testament to the untidy habits of teenage boys, where clothes, food wrappers, papers, and CDs remained where they had been dropped. Theresa pulled on latex gloves with the uncomfortable feeling that Ellen Wheeler had fallen into a catatonic depression, or else intended to preserve the place like a shrine.

Well, I don't blame her. If anything happened to Rachael I'd probably leave—

Don't think that.

There were certain thoughts that could not be permitted to enter her head if she wanted to keep working in this field, and putting herself in the shoes of victims topped the list.

Frank entered the room behind her. "Still don't know where to begin, huh?"

"Sort of." She had been looking for anything that seemed out of place, that didn't have the same amount of dust as its neighbors. That was silly, though, since Jacob had been living in the room nearly up until the minute of his murder, so not enough time would have elapsed to show a difference in dust deposited on relevant items. Like, say, a comic book.

Still, three things leaped to the eye: the wound-up cord to his video game joystick, a printed flyer at the foot of his bed, and a neatly stacked pile of comic books on the nightstand. They stood out as the only neatly stacked pile of anything in the room.

The half sheet of paper on the bed turned out to be a sort of program for Jacob's funeral, held two days previously. No doubt Ellen had left it there as an offering to the shrine, or had perused it while surrounded by her son's belongings, or whatever reasoning passed for sanity following the death of a child. The cord to the joystick stood out because, again, it was the only cord so wrapped. Perhaps she had begun to clean up before abandoning the idea, since the rest of the wires and accessories had simply been swept to the foot of the TV stand.

The comic book on top of the stack had a dramatic cover of black and blue with the figure of Batman in the foreground. Theresa picked it up and riffled the pages.

Page 15 had lost its bottom corner.

She set it on the bed carefully, as if it might explode, and then took a square of sealed plastic out of her camera bag. She needed to make sure—after all, Jacob might have been routinely hard on all his comic books.

She didn't even have to take the torn piece out of its plastic evidence bag to see where it matched the torn page. That, in forensics parlance, was known as a jigsaw match, and considered an absolute identification.

Theresa wanted to cry.

"What is it?" Frank asked.

"I need to check one other thing." She began to search the closets—Jacob's, Ellen's, and then the small one by the front door. On the floor, in a jumble of shoes and boots, she found a pair of rubber overshoes with plain tread lines crossing the sole.

Theresa glanced to her left, where Ellen Wheeler rested in an armchair, one hand holding up her head.

"Yes," she said.

Theresa waited, still crouched. Frank, with that cop's instinct, waited as well.

"Yes, those are the boots I wore when I killed Jacob."

Theresa straightened slowly, still holding the comic book. "Is this what you argued about?"

"He stole it. He insisted he didn't, but I know he didn't have any money. He stole everything. I might have been able to cope if he'd at least told me the truth, but the constant lying wore me down."

Unobtrusively, Frank pulled out a notebook and a pencil.

Ellen lifted her head from her hand, as if finding just enough strength to tell her story. She nodded at the boots. "My husband left those rubber boots behind when he left us. I can pull them right over my shoes."

That explained why the size of the shoe print seemed too big for Ellen Wheeler, the depth of the print too shallow for the size of the shoe.

"I told Jake it had to stop. The same thing I've told him every day for the past four years, more or less. So finally he said it was my fault, that he wouldn't have to steal things if I'd only give him more money, if I'd only be a decent enough mother to provide for him. I moved toward him. I would have tried to kill him with my bare hands right then if he'd given me the chance. I still want to, sometimes. But when I think about him before his teens, when we would spend the summers thinking up new things to do—"

"What happened then?" Frank prompted.

"He snatched the comic off the counter and started to leave. I pulled it out of his hands."

Theresa said, "A piece ripped off. He had it in his fist."

"Did it? I didn't notice. He stalked out of the house. I put on my rubber boots and followed him, not difficult in the snow. I was screaming at him. I'm surprised the neighbors didn't notice—but then it wasn't anything new. He kept walking away, ignoring me." Her chin sank to her hand again. Frank scribbled a note, obviously not concerned with Miranda rights. Technically, since Ellen Wheeler had not been placed under arrest, they did not apply. But Theresa knew anyway that she would not recant her confession. Unlike Evan, Jacob's mother had not tried to destroy the evidence of her guilt. She had brought it home and kept it safe.

"He always ignored me, as if I only existed on this planet to serve him. I gave him *life*. And then I gave him the best life I could provide. Why the hell did I deserve so much contempt?" She didn't look to them for an answer. Theresa guessed she had given up expecting one.

"So you circled around the back of the tree to get in front of him."

"Yes."

"And picked something up?"

Ellen took a while to answer that one, a sob brewing underneath the skin of her face. "A piece of wood. A branch, I suppose, but it was fairly big. I don't know why. I didn't even know it was in my hand until I hit him with it."

The sob began to leak out, in tiny but steady teardrops.

"What happened then?" Theresa prompted.

"He stood there and glared. I saw blood start to ooze from under his hair, but he didn't seem hurt. Furious enough to kill me, though he didn't raise a hand. I was so angry"—she looked to Theresa for understanding, one mother to another—"and at the same time I was *horrified*. I'd never struck him before in his life, never. I couldn't believe it."

Theresa had been there, so angry with her child that she had felt sickened at herself for such rage. But never, thank God, to the point of violence.

"I walked past him. He didn't say a word. I threw the branch away somewhere, I don't remember where, I just didn't want to touch it anymore. I turned and looked back, but he didn't follow me, didn't want to come home. He had sat down next to the tree."

Now she turned her face up to Frank. "That's what happened, isn't it? My baby sat down by that tree and just died. I came back here and drank coffee and let him freeze to death."

His mouth worked once or twice before he found a gentle way to ask, "You didn't go back to check on him?"

She wiped the moisture from her face with a quick, cat's-paw-like gesture. "I wasn't going to go chasing after him this time. He was going to have to face the fact that he needed me, or he could . . . freeze to death. The one time I decided to be firm with him and stick to it, and he died. He died."

She let her head fall back against the armchair, spent. The story had ended. Theresa didn't know whether she should feel sympathy or revulsion, or what would be wrong with both.

"Ellen Wheeler," Frank began. "I'm placing you under arrest for the murder of Jacob Wheeler . . ."

"It's about time." Rachael slammed her textbook shut and had her coat on before her mother even thought about taking hers off. "They're leaving at seven and you know how cranky Dora gets if she has to wait for me."

"Huh?"

"Skiing tonight! Can I borrow twenty bucks too? In fact, can I just have it, since I kind of lost track of what I owe you so far? Forget the skis, I'll just rent some. Come in, into the garage, go go go!"

Theresa did not mention that she had just solved another teenager's murder, or how precious life could prove to be, or that Rachael should be glad she still breathed instead of fretting about a social engagement. Theresa merely slid her body back into the driver's seat, which had managed to cool to frosty in the approximately ten seconds since she had left it, and pulled out onto the road. "Skiing?"

Rachael tossed an impossibly large sack over the seat back—no doubt containing her boots, gloves, scarf, phone, makeup, and probably her iPod, so that she could add the peril of deafness to an already hazardous sport. "You never pay attention, Mom. Remember the birthday party last weekend? Dora and Jenna said I should come on this ski trip with them? Gun it, you can make this light."

Theresa hit the brakes on purpose. Since Rachael had gotten her license, it had become important to demonstrate safe driving skills. "When will you be home?"

"Probably eleven."

"More like ten."

"No, eleven."

"How about nine thirty?" The light changed, and they moved forward.

"Why ten?"

"What part of 'school night' don't you understand?"

"Okay. But it's your cousin who's going to pick us up, so if I'm home late you'll have to take it up with her." Rachael had mastered the art of the preemptive strike.

"I'll keep that in mind."

"You know, if I had my own car, this wouldn't even be an issue."

Theresa, however, had mastered the art of selective hearing. "Uh-huh. Are you dressed warm enough?"

"Warmly. It's an adjective, l-y."

"Do you want a ride or not?"

"I'm perfectly warm."

She eyed her daughter's pants. "They don't look like snow pants."

Rachael bubbled up at the interest. "Exactly! They're new. They've got this cottonlike fabric but it's practically waterproof, like good nylon."

"Nylon isn't waterproof. It's the weave and the treatment—"

"But it's thin and flat, so you don't have to look like a toddler in a snowsuit. They're great. You can tell I have a butt in them." She put her hands underneath her as if making sure.

"Actually, I was okay with not being able to tell."

"Well, of course. You're a mom. You'd have me in a burka if you could." For all her fondness for the new pants, however, she seemed to be wrestling with them, wrenching both arms behind her back until one hand emerged with a small white tag. "Man! That thing was driving me crazy."

"That's not true about the burka. I just don't get this skiing-at-night thing. It's bad enough you have to hurtle down a snow-covered hill, but you have to do it in the pitch dark as well? What keeps you from running into trees? Or each other?"

"Um, maybe the huge floodlights they have along the slopes? They're lit up like a Walmart. And I have a light stick."

They pulled onto her cousin's street. "But do the trees have light sticks?"

"There they are! I told you Dora would be ticked if I got here late."

She dropped the clothing tag into the ashtray and dragged her large bag forward from the backseat. The car had not yet come to a complete stop before the passenger door opened. "See you, Mom."

Theresa snatched her daughter's arm and held it, arresting Rachael in midflight. "Be careful."

Rachael tried to pull her arm away. Perhaps annoyance and overexcitement made her say, in the callous way children can have, "There won't be any bank robbers on the ski slopes, Mom."

"I mean it. That's a large area, it's dark, and it's very cold out."

"Okay." Rachael took the time to look into her mother's eyes and repeat the word before making her escape.

Theresa watched Rachael join her relatives, then waved to her cousin, now shepherding the girls into a minivan. She hadn't been worried about bank robbers, only broken bones and bad sprains and frostbite.

Not to mention that the last girl she had seen in a snowy woods had been very, very dead.

Arriving home for the second time that evening, she grabbed the junk from her car and dropped it on her kitchen table, fed the dog, changed into the heaviest set of pajamas she had, and poured a shot of vodka into a glass of flavored diet water. Then she sat down to open bills, grateful that none was overdue. Still, how to afford college in another year . . .

She threw the bills on the table. The square, shiny piece of fabric Rachael had ripped from her pants scooted away and Theresa caught it before it sailed off toward the floor. Years as a fiber analyst made her read it: MADE IN CHINA. NYLON/ TENCEL.

Tencel.

Evan snowboarded. Evan liked to have the latest innovation, the coolest stuff, and, Theresa would bet, pants that showed he had a butt.

Drew, of course, could also own a pair of Tencel pants, but so far he had seemed to live in knit jersey and have no interest in sports. Jogging pants were not likely to be made of Tencel, and police officers wore wool uniforms at this time of the year.

She thought of calling Frank to tell him she needed to get into Evan's pants, but doubted he would see the humor. Or the probable cause. She'd need more than a fabric tag for that. She needed the last item on her list. Means.

WEDNESDAY, MARCH 10

"I'm surprised you come in this early," Theresa said, bouncing from one foot to the other. The raw wind had cut through her coat in just the ten steps from her car to the front door.

"Just me," Vangie said, pulling a set of keys out of a slouchy gold lamé bag. "Georgie doesn't roll in until ten or so. But the phones get going right about eight."

Theresa followed her through the opened door, so grateful for the warmth inside that she spoke without thinking, "I wouldn't think your clientele got up that early. Um, I mean——"

Vangie only laughed as she divested herself of bag, coat, scarf, and gloves. "Partiers aren't morning people. Party planners, on the other hand, are definite A types. Georgie said you might be looking for me."

"I need to ask more about Jillian, any tiny detail you can tell me."

The young woman swept long curls out of her face and switched on a coffeemaker. She had obviously set it up the prior evening because it immediately began to perk. "There are two kinds of girls who work here, the kind who know exactly what they're doing and the kind who have watched too many movies."

"They think they can work a few jobs and then marry Richard Gere or Ed Harris?"

"Exactly. Jillian was in the second group."

"And did she meet a——"

Vangie watched the dark liquid drip into the pot. "She thought she did, once. He was an older guy, plenty of money, successful. Just like Daddy."

"What happened?"

"She was wrong."

Dr. Christine Johnson found her waiting by the loading dock. Theresa greeted the younger woman with, "This is it."

"This is what?"

"The moment of truth. I need a cause of death on Jillian Perry and I need it right now."

The doctor shifted a tote bag to her other shoulder as they fell into hurried steps on the way to the elevator. "Tell me about it. Stone has been pestering me for two days for a conclusion. I said I'd settle for 'unknown means,' but he hates to do that unless it's a decomp."

"Yeah, I know." The moving metal box creaked and moaned and took an inordinate amount of time to reach the second floor. "Why don't you take the stairs?"

"My thighs don't want to."

Theresa eyed the woman's slim waist. "You wait until you turn thirty, missy. Your whole metabolism suddenly turns against you. You'll be taking the stairs in skyscrapers to work off one more calorie."

"You're just a bundle of cheer this morning, aren't you?"

"There's more. Evan got custody of Cara. He is officially her next of kin. That baby's days, maybe minutes, are now numbered unless we can prove murder."

"Okay, shut up. I mean it. Not another word until I get a cup of coffee."

Theresa complied, even waiting until after settling her body onto the ammo locker in the miniature office, a steaming cup held up to her sinuses. "Even the phytoplankton refuse to help me. I collected soil samples from parking lots at the Rock and Roll Hall of Fame and at the building on Old River Road where Evan had his business meeting the day Jillian disappeared, but it didn't do me any good. I got Emily at the Natural History Museum to come in early today and take a look at it all, but the types of diatoms in each sample don't vary enough to be significant."

"Mmm," Christine said into her coffee cup.

"I guess it depends on water depth, light, whether there are rocks or sand at the water's edge . . . the ones from Old River Road show some differences, probably from the industrial influences along the river. So now Evan will probably sue me for cleaning tires without a license and it didn't even do me any good. Which leads me to you, missy. Can you go over your findings again? Maybe something will ring a bell."

"My findings were all negative. No pulmonary emboli to indicate an overdose of narcotics. According to the tox report, she had nothing more than a mild sleeping pill in her system, nothing that would depress her breathing until she died or make her sleep through a trip to the freezing woods. Plus, there was no amylase in the vitreous humor, no elevated levels of catecholamines, to indicate death by freezing. But there again, there might not be." She ran her hands through her hair, which only encouraged the waves to become unruly. "I found some cerebral edema but that could mean a lot of things."

"So her heart just stopped?" Theresa asked.

"Yes . . . well, no." Christine picked up a manila folder already placed front and center on her desk, and flipped through a few pages. "Hearts don't stop for no reason. There's no sign of infarction. She might have stopped breathing first."

"As if she were smothered?"

"No imprint of her teeth on the back of her upper lip, no petechiae. It's pretty hard to smother an adult unless she's already unconscious, and there's no reason she would have been unconscious, no knockout drugs, no blow to the head, no seizure."

Theresa had grown used to dead victims telling her who they were, what they had done, and how they died. But Jillian could not. Perhaps it was time to look at the situation from the other end. "Evan is an engineer with a degree in chemistry. He had time to plan and clean up. He has tools and equipment in the factory outbuildings. Maybe he came up with that holy grail, an undetectable poison?"

Christine rolled her eyes. "Sure. And maybe he teleported Jillian to the woods when he was done. I ran all the poison assays. Even if we couldn't identify it, there would be some sign of one. Elevated levels of amines or metals."

Theresa recalled the miles of electrical cords that had snaked across the concrete floor of the factory building. "Electric shock?"

"It would leave burns and signs in the heart. Come on, you know that as well as I do."

"I'm grasping at straws here. The only thing we're relatively sure of is that she stopped breathing."

"Yeah. Everyone stops breathing. Just before they die."

"But no one cut off her oxygen."

"Not by strangling, smothering, or putting a plastic bag over her head, no," Christine confirmed.

Behind the plastic reality ball and the electrical cords, behind the group of spectators, there had been tall metal cylinders, high and round, like small grain silos. They had been painted the same color as the walls and therefore blended into the background, obviously left over from the factory's previous owners, the carbon makers.

"What if they—he—removed the oxygen from the air?"

"Come again?"

What had the chipped paint on the side of the tank read? She closed her eyes and concentrated.

N_2. The cylinders might be empty. Then again, they might not.

"What about nitrogen? He has rows of gas tanks there. What if he filled the air with nitrogen?"

Christine frowned. "I'm not following you. Like he opens all these air valves and floods the room with nitrogen? It would have to be an awful lot, and why wouldn't it kill him and the baby?"

"They weren't there."

"It isn't like gas, you know, like putting your head in the oven. Nitrogen won't kill you in and of itself. Only if the oxygen content of the air fell too low to sustain life."

"But that would kill her?"

"Sure."

"Without leaving any signs?"

The doctor plucked a bayonet off her desk and balanced its two ends between her hands as she thought. "I'd have to check the literature, but as far as I know, yeah. Nitrogen is a natural component of the blood, so the toxicology would seem normal. But how do you get an apartment airtight enough to flood it with nitrogen? It wouldn't chase the oxygen out . . . though I suppose it would be no trick for him to rig a timer to the tank. He could take the baby and leave, come back when the gas has been turned off, and open the doors and windows. It wouldn't leave any sign in the apartment. Or the car. A car would make a handy little gas chamber, almost completely airtight."

"It works well enough with carbon monoxide," Theresa agreed, wishing she'd taken a closer look at the windows on Evan's Escalade or Jillian's car. She could have swabbed them with a little alcohol, run the swabs on the FTIR to look for adhesives. But— "The tanks I saw aren't portable. Maybe it wasn't done in the apartment. Maybe he took her out to the factory."

"Again, how does he turn her atmosphere anaerobic? Set up some kind of oxygen tent? And why is she—"

Theresa had a vision of the clear plastic frames over the assembly table. "He already has one. Big enough for a body to fit, and it already has piping outlets built into it. Damn, I can't believe I didn't think of that." She explained the factory setup to Christine.

"Great. So Jillian lies on this table while Evan attaches nitrogen at one end and a vacuum at the other and reduces her oxygen levels until she passes out."

"Right."

"Why?"

"What do you mean, why?"

"Why does Jillian go along with this? She didn't struggle. Aside from those vague bruises on her forearms, she's got no defensive wounds. She didn't break her nails clawing at the glass. She just laid there and died."

"You said she had a sleeping pill in her system."

"I can't believe it would be enough for her to sleep through being carried to another location and placed in a gas chamber."

Theresa shuddered. "How long would it take?"

"Not long at all. Once the amount of oxygen in the air gets under twenty-five percent, she'd be unconscious in seconds and dead in minutes."

"And no chance that she'd sleep through that."

"I can't see how. Once her lungs began to gasp, she'd wake up, unless she had way more narcotics in her system than we found."

Theresa stood up, dying to act on the information and no longer able to withstand the handle of the ammo locker pressing into her bottom. "But suffocation by nitrogen would produce your autopsy findings. Or lack thereof."

"I'll need to do a little research, but I believe so. What, you think your cousin's going to give you a search warrant based on an educated guess?"

"Maybe. Now that I know what to look for."

"And what would that be? A tube leading from the nitrogen tanks to this hood you were talking about?"

"No, I'm sure he could explain that, and if he couldn't he would have gotten rid of the hookups by now. No, I mean hairs, fibers, fingerprints, anything that would show Jillian Perry died while stretched out in that Plexiglas cocoon."

Frank answered on the second ring. "Where are you?"

This seemed like an odd way to open a conversation. "At the lab, of course. Look, I know you're sick of hearing about Jillian Perry—"

"You have no idea how sick. You haven't heard?"

The coffee floating around in her empty stomach began to boil. "Heard what?"

"Drew Fleming kidnapped Cara."

She nearly broke off the phone's flip top pressing it to her ear, as if proximity might make his words more sensible. "What?"

"He went to the apartment and pointed a gun at the nanny. He made her pack a diaper bag for him with stuff for Cara, bundled up the baby, and left."

She noticed the wind behind Frank's voice, whining across the surface of his phone. "Is he on his boat?"

"We're there now. He says he'll shoot anyone who steps onto the dock."

"Is he trying to get away?"

"That's going to be a little difficult with a foot of ice on top of the water. He could ice-skate a good distance, but that boat ain't going anywhere."

She sat down in a task chair; not the best choice as its wheels started to scoot away and she nearly slid off. "So he has no way out."

"Best case, he figures that out and realizes that he loved Jillian too much to kill her child. Worst case—"

"He decides to take her with him. There's not a lot of difference between those two choices, Frank, when you realize that the only reason he took Cara is because he believes Evan intends to murder her."

Silence on the other end, save for the bitter wind. "That's not good."

"I'm coming down there." She flipped the phone shut before he could protest.

CHAPTER 24

Of the knot of cars in the otherwise deserted parking lot, at least half had their engines running, patrol officers taking advantage of the tradition that their vehicles must be ever ready for action by keeping them ever warm. But Theresa had lived through the gas shortages of the late seventies and couldn't bring herself to do that. Besides, Leo would have killed her if he'd found out.

She took nothing but her ID, her cell phone, and her ChapStick, and followed the chaotic trail of the shoe prints in the snow. At the crest of the hill, she saw figures conversing in pairs or triplets, standing by the marina entrance, the gas pumps, and lined up along the pier. The fifty-foot finger of dock that led to, among others, Drew's houseboat remained clear.

As she grew closer, she noted Frank out on the pier and Evan standing with his lawyer near a group of what looked like plainclothes police officers. She meant to walk past the man without speaking, but he felt differently.

She had never been a physical girl, taking on running and scuba diving for their calorie-burning qualities only; otherwise, she never joined pickup games of baseball or touch football. But now she learned what a flying tackle was. Or at least what one felt like.

Evan struck her from the side, his momentum carrying them several feet before dropping her to the frozen ground. The snow provided very little cushion as his full weight flattened her, and her head managed to find the one narrow strip of concrete sidewalk in the area. The air left her lungs and threatened not to return. She could not comprehend his words as his face appeared above her, framed by the sky, which, she only now noticed, had turned blue.

With breath came hearing. "You bitch! You put him up to this! He's going to kill my baby and it's all your fault!"

A scuffling sound, and at least four men, including his lawyer, pulled him from her, which would have been better if he hadn't stepped on her shin at least twice while getting to his feet.

Then hands levitated her up as well, much less gently than she would have thought her age, sex, and general innocence in the matter warranted. One set belonged to Frank.

"What are you doing here?"

"I'm all right, thanks. Even the back of my head where the sidewalk put a dent in my skull."

"I can see you're all right. What are you doing here?"

She staggered toward the dock, putting some distance between herself and Evan before answering. "I can talk to Drew. He thinks I'm the only one on his side."

"Maybe not after that custody hearing yesterday, huh? I heard you didn't help him out so much. And what did you say about the back of your head?"

"Sidewalk. Concrete. It's okay, brains still inside the cranium, I think. I gave the custody hearing my best effort, and Drew would have seen that. Let me talk to him."

"SWAT's got control of the scene."

"But he'll listen to me. He knows I agree with him about Jillian."

"You agree that Evan wants to kill Cara? Yeah, that's going to make him put down the gun."

She paused with him, away from the other men, next to the snow-covered rocks and the weirdly silent sea at the edge of the land. "Maybe it will. I didn't get a chance to tell you, but Christine and I might have figured out how Jillian was killed."

"Christine?"

"The pathologist." When he continued to look blank, she added, "The pretty one."

"Oh. Her."

She gave him the scenario entitled Death by Nitrogen, in twenty-five words or less. She kept the technical parts to a minimum since his attention always returned to the motley houseboat dangling over the ice, as if it might explode any second.

"So you want to go out there and say, it's all over, I've got the goods on Evan, turn Cara over to the authorities and she'll be safe?"

"Something like that."

He walked along the water's edge toward the pier. "It's not a bad idea. Problem is, this is a hostage situation now."

"Yeah?"

"So I'm not calling the shots. They're going to have to bring in the whole team."

"Don't tell me Chris Cavanaugh—"

"—will be here in ten. I don't know why you don't want to see the guy."

The planks of the wooden dock vibrated only slightly under her feet, held stiffly in place by the frozen water. "Maybe because, fairly or unfairly, almost dying with him last year sort of put me off his company."

"Maybe. Remember how you had such a crush on that kid in my band who came over to practice one day and said hi to you, and you ran outside and made your mother drive you home because you were too scared to say hi back?"

"No," she lied.

"I can't believe you could forget that."

"I can't believe you called that a band." She flipped open her cell phone, scanning the list of incoming calls. Drew had called her to come to court, but she had been on the line with Leo and hadn't picked up. Now she highlighted his number and pressed Talk.

"What are you doing?" Frank asked.

"Everyone thinks I started this, and maybe I did. Now I'm going to finish it."

Drew picked up on the third ring. "Uh—hello?"

"Drew? This is Theresa MacLean. Are you in your houseboat with a gun to Cara's head?"

"Of course not! I would never hurt—I mean, not yet. But you understand why I had to do this, don't you? Of all people, you know."

"Yes, Drew. I know. Look, you're going to need a go-between. I'm coming out there."

"No," Frank said.

"Yes! Please!" Drew said. He gave a little huff of exertion, as if he had shifted a twenty-pound baby in his arms. "We have to do something or they'll give Cara back."

She switched ears, sliding her free hand under her arm to keep it warm. "What are you planning to do, Drew?"

"Just come out here, and we can talk. You'll have to jump onto the deck, I took the plank down."

"Absolutely not," Frank said. The group of heavily bundled-up cops farther down the pier began to show more interest in her conversation with Frank. Their faces, pinched with cold, turned toward her.

She stepped onto the dock that led to the back of the *Jillian*, covered the receiver with a gloved hand, and told her cousin, "I'm the only person he's going to trust, Frank."

Drew's voice sounded much farther away than sixty feet, coming from the tiny phone. "I can't let him take her back. He'll kill her. You know that. Besides, you had a baby, didn't you? I've never tried to take care of one before. I might need some help."

Cara chose that moment to start crying, her peeved mewls quite close to the phone.

"Absolutely not," Frank repeated.

The SWAT commander materialized next to him. "This isn't our policy—"

"Come down here," Drew demanded.

Theresa spoke to her cousin, again covering the receiver. "He's surrounded by big men with big guns and he's got a baby in his arms. I'm a lot more afraid of what you'll do to him than what he'll do to me."

"What if he bears a grudge against you for your family court appearance?"

"Come on!" Drew's voice floated up from the phone in her hand. "Get out here and help me, or I'm leaving with Cara."

She took another step along the dock.

"Wait. Take this. It's a mic with a GPS." The SWAT guy used her to block himself from Drew's line of sight and tucked a thin rod about the size of a pencil into her coat pocket. He clipped it to the flap so that the tip stuck out.

"Where's he going to go?" she demanded. "The lake is frozen solid."

"Exactly. He can get off that boat and walk across it—keep it for the mike, okay? You talk to him from the dock, right? You *do not* get on that boat."

She aimed her gaze straight into his crystal blue eyes, and lied, "Right."

Frank insisted, "She can't do this. Am I the only one who sees that here? Chris Cavanaugh will kill us."

Theresa and the SWAT commander answered in near unison: "I don't give a shit what Chris Cavanaugh thinks."

"Come out here right now!" Drew wailed, his voice beginning to crack.

Theresa mouthed an apology to her cousin and put the phone to her face. "I'm coming."

Then she walked down the icy dock toward the rear of the *Jillian*.

Frank called after her, "This is a far cry from exiting out my back door. And what am I supposed to tell your mother?"

"Tell her I went to save a baby." Then she paused, and turned slightly to throw back over her shoulder, "Never mind, I'll tell her myself. Drew Fleming is not going to hurt me."

At least she hoped not.

CHAPTER 25

Getting onto his boat, however, looked like a killer. She would have to leap from an icy dock to an icy deck, over a two- to three-foot expanse of frozen lake. In the summer, child's play. In the winter, a great way to break a hip.

It occurred to her to use one last niggling prick to her psyche to get her to make this leap: Her career had become troubled, but coming out of this situation with a healthy baby and no bloodshed would make her a hero. All the sarcastic supervisors and defense experts in the world wouldn't be able to change that.

Please, God, don't let that be my only reason.

And while we're at it, don't let Drew kill me. That would upset my mother.

"Drew! It's Theresa. I'm coming aboard."

He slid open the door just an inch, enough to say, "All right, come on. Don't slip."

"Easier said than done," she grumbled as she bent her knees. She made it with two inches to spare, though her bottom smacked the rear gunwale and the impact reverberated throughout her bones. The boat swayed in its hammock.

Drew slid the door open another inch, and Theresa pushed it farther to enter, actually grateful for the rush of warmth and the shelter from the constant icy wind. She sniffled, rubbed her hands, and let her pupils expand to take in the darkened interior.

The houseboat had not changed much since her first visit, except perhaps for a fresh dusting of clutter on the uppermost layer of the surrounding surfaces. Drew wore his standard baggy pants and the knit, zippered jacket. He bounced with an internal mania but his eyes were clear and dry. Cara, warmly bundled up in pink blankets in his arms, cried in sporadic bursts. His left arm supported her back and head. He held her legs in the crook of his right arm and a Luger in that hand.

Theresa drew in a deep breath. Now that she had arrived, she hadn't the slightest idea of what to do except to remain calm and keep Drew talking instead of acting. "Has she eaten lately?"

Drew glanced down at the baby in his arms as if unsure of how she'd gotten there. "I don't know. I forgot to ask the babysitter when I—took her. I got some stuff, though. Look."

He gestured with the gun's barrel to his kitchen counter, littered with diapers, formula, and a stuffed tiger. Theresa cleared off the stove, found a pan, filled it with water and heated up the formula, turning her back to him without hesitation. She had nothing to fear from Drew Fleming. Or so she told herself.

The activity did not slow her heart rate, but she managed to keep her voice steady when she faced him again. "I know how worried you are about Cara, Drew, but you have to know that this was not a good idea. It only makes you look unstable."

"What else was I supposed to do?"

"And by default it makes Evan look more innocent."

"The court made him her official guardian. If she dies, he gets the whole account. Why would he wait?"

"He wouldn't dare do anything to Cara now, not with all the scrutiny over Jillian's death."

"There is no scrutiny!" He gave the baby an agitated rocking, prompting another startled cry from the infant. "Your department released the body. The police aren't investigating. No one cares about Jillian except you and me."

Theresa swirled the formula in its warm water bath, wondering how much to tell him. "I've found something out, though. I think I know how he did it."

This appeared to stun him, so she made a grab for the baby in case he dropped her, thinking too late that sudden movements were not a good idea. But he handed the baby over without a pause and focused on this new information. "You do? How?"

She told it simply and slowly, with plenty of pauses for transferring the formula into a bottle and finding a comfortable seat so that the baby could drink without movement and, Theresa hoped, sleep. She emphasized the painlessness of Jillian's death, well aware that dwelling on how his loved one came to leave the earth might push him to his own personal brink.

"So she just went to sleep?" he said at last.

"Yes."

Now his eyes filled with tears. "It's not fair."

"No, it's not."

"She was too young."

Unbidden, the memory of the marble floor came, with Paul's blood spreading in a dark pool. He had not simply gone to sleep. He had to sit and wait, soaked in his own fluids, knowing what that seepage meant and able to tick off every last second of his life. Did he think of me? Did he think of his first wife, dead of cancer before her thirtieth birthday?

Who did he regret leaving more?

An unworthy question, but humans are such unworthy animals.

Cara pushed the bottle away, finished, not bothered by Theresa's inner upheaval. The baby had most likely felt nothing else from the adults around her for the past week, and had grown used to it. "Drew, we have to—"

"It's worse on us. The survivors, me, you—even your mother. Your father died when you were young, didn't he?"

"How did you know that?"

"I found a bio that *Cleveland* magazine did on you last year."

"My father died of an aneurysm. It's different."

Was it? Did it make her pain over Paul any worse than her mother's had been? And why had the similarity never—

"At least Jillian could die with hope. We have to live without it."

She could feel the tears filling her eyes, a wave that seemed to start at the back of her head—not for the dead, but for the living she'd been too wrapped up in herself to think about lately. She bit her lip to divert the tears, which never worked. "Drew—"

"We could help each other."

She shook her head as if to clear her hearing. She hadn't taken off her coat and now the cabin seemed a bit too warm. "What?"

"We understand each other, you and I. The kind of grief that will last the rest of our lives. If your fiancé had a child, you'd do anything for that child, wouldn't you?"

"Yes." The word erupted before she'd finished hearing the question.

"He didn't—right? But I have Cara. In a way Cara is even more important than Jillian, since Jillian chose Evan. But Cara is innocent. I'll give anything for her, even my life, to keep Evan from harming her. And you'll help me, won't you? You wouldn't be here now if you didn't feel that way." He sprang from his chair and neatly sidestepped the coffee table in two paces, dropping the gun on the corner and collapsing to his knees in front of her as if proposing marriage. Or begging. "You have to help me save her. You're the only one who can."

"That's what I said, Drew, I only need a little more time and I can—"

"It won't work. Even if you can prove she died from the nitrogen, you won't be able to prove he did it. He'll have thought of every detail. It's what he does for a living. It's how he fooled Jillian in the first place." He reached out and slowly took the baby bottle out of her right hand, holding her fingers in his. She fought the instinct to pull away. "I have a snowmobile. The stockbrokers who own that Grady-White two spaces up leave it under their hull with the keys in it because they come out every weekend. It's got gas—I checked. We can get over the water before the cops even know what's happening, be at Burke Lakefront Airport in ten minutes. A friend of mine loads cargo onto air express planes and there are two leaving this afternoon, for Pittsburgh and St. Louis. Depending on which one we take—"

"Drew!"

"My boss at the bookshop can get my funds to me, and I packed my most valuable editions to take along and sell. We won't be millionaires, but at least we'll be safe." His eyes danced in the hazy indoor light, and she thought that maybe she *was* afraid of Drew Fleming, just a little.

"Drew, I can't—"

Her phone rang. Drew jumped back, dropping her hand.

Breathe, she told herself. In and out. "I think I should answer that."

Drew looked around for his gun as if trying to remember where he'd left it.

"It's just a phone, Drew. And if it keeps them from approaching us—"

He reached over the table and picked up the Luger, but then moved to the window, peering out from behind faded canvas curtains. "Yes, answer it."

She pulled out the phone, which showed an unfamiliar number. "Hello?"

"We have to stop meeting like this," Chris Cavanaugh said. The Cleveland Police Department's star hostage negotiator, whose star had dimmed only slightly in the months since the bank robbery.

"I couldn't agree more."

"How is everyone in there? How's the baby?"

"Just fine."

"We're going to get through this okay, Theresa," he said with that firm, deep tone of voice that brought to mind his dimples and his utter self-possession, and which would be so terribly comforting to someone on the brink of panic. But somehow it always had the opposite effect on her.

"I know that. Unlike our last encounter, Chris, I am not in any danger here. Drew is not going to harm me or Cara. He just wants to talk." She enunciated her words carefully, turning her head so the man at the window would be sure to hear her.

"Does he want to talk to me?"

She asked. Drew shook his head. "No, he doesn't."

"But it's okay with him if you stay on the line?"

She inquired. "He says it's fine."

"What does he want?"

"He wants Cara removed from Evan Kovacic's custody."

"Yeah, your cousin filled me in on your theory. We'll have to find a compromise."

"You're good at that."

"I hope someday you can speak to me without sneering."

Tears pricked at her eyes again. Why could she not concede an inch to this man? "I'm—look, I'm—"

"Never mind. One thing, though. Don't listen to Drew about grief. He's wrong. It doesn't have to last the rest of your life."

Her brief thawing iced over again. "How would *you* know?"

She hung up.

"What's the matter?" Drew asked, leaving the window. "What did he say?"

"He wants to know what your demands are." She pondered Cavanaugh's words. The microphone pen in her pocket—she had forgotten about it. They had been listening to her conversation the whole time, which meant that they knew about Drew's snowmobile escape route. She had to keep him calm and on the boat. But for how long?

"I heard you tell him. He said no, right?"

"No, he said we'd have to work out a compromise. I'm sure we can get protective custody for Cara. Families with Dependent Children always removes children from a home if there's a chance of abuse, so it can't be that hard—"

He sat across from her, the Luger held loosely in one hand. "But they won't give her to me."

"Not immediately, of course. She would be cared for by the state until this is settled, which should be only a few days."

His eyes watched the infant in Theresa's arms as she stretched in her sleep, one tiny fist protruding from the blanket. "I saw Jillian in her from the first day, when I visited the maternity ward. She has Jillian's eyes. It's as if Jillian lives on in her."

"It always seems like that with parents and children, but it's only true to a point and sometimes isn't true at all. I know, I have a daughter. She's an individual." How to get out of this? Drew wouldn't budge unless they took custody away from Evan, but the state had no obligation to remove the child unless the stepfather became a suspect in a crime, and she could not provide probable cause to prompt same, certainly not while holed up in a houseboat over a frozen lake. Catch-22.

"And being so close to her for a few hours like this," Drew went on as if Theresa hadn't spoken, "I don't think I can let her go. I've already lost Jillian. I can't say good-bye to Cara too."

"But it's not—"

"If somehow it came about that you had to say good-bye to Paul all over again, could you do it?"

The words pierced, like an ice pick to her gut. No. No, of course not.

Pull yourself together. "Cara is not Jillian, Drew. She's a baby who needs a lot of attention and—"

The phone rang.

"I'm sorry, Theresa," Chris told her without preamble. "I never manage to say the right thing to you."

"One person out of a city of four hundred and fifty thousand isn't bad, Chris." *Going to be bitchy to the last, aren't we?*

"I need to keep Cara," Drew said to her, a touch too loudly, as if he wanted Chris Cavanaugh to hear him. "Yes or no?"

"Drew—" she tried.

Chris asked, "What does he mean, keep? Permanently? Another hour? I thought he just wanted her away from Evan."

"Yes or no!"

"Drew, it isn't that simple, you know that. You're not a blood relative—"

"It's going to be that simple." He stood up and crossed to an old-fashioned black plastic telephone. "You and I and Cara are leaving. I have to carry this pack with the books, so you'll have to hang on to her. They won't shoot at us, not with you and Cara along."

"Drew, you have to think of what's best for Cara, and I'm sure that flying over partially frozen ice is not it." She did not think about the open line in her hand, with Cavanaugh listening at the other end, and apparently Drew didn't either.

"It's solid." He put his hand on the phone.

Theresa thought of the freezing water churning below the stiff surface. Lake Erie was the shallowest of the Great Lakes . . . it froze fast but thawed fast too. Plunging into the frigid green—"I won't go. I can't, Drew, I'm scared. And I won't let you take the baby over it either."

"It's the only way. Cara is all I have now." He picked up his phone. "And you."

"Theresa," Chris said in her ear.

Drew held the receiver to his ear but made no move to dial a number. The expression on his face smoothed to bland shock, an unblinking surprise. "It's dead."

They had heard his plan over the microphone and taken the simplest of precautions. They had cut his phone service. He could not contact the friend at the airport.

She allowed herself the tiniest sigh of relief. Drew remained more stunned than angry; he had no way to determine the presence of the microphone, probably assumed that cutting his communication would be standard procedure for the situation, which, of course, it was. "Drew, all you want to do is keep Cara safe. So do we."

"There is no we, Theresa. They'll take her away from us and give her back to Evan. They did it once and you can't give them a reason not to do it again."

"But—" Words came with difficulty, mostly because she agreed with him.

He picked up the small nylon backpack and strapped it on. "Let's go."

All right, she thought. Screw the hostage-negotiation manual. Chris might not be allowed to lie to him, but I can. I can lie through my teeth. "I can get them to put Cara in protective custody and give me a search warrant to examine the factory's nitrogen tanks. I'll find the hoses and things he used to pump the gas from the tanks to the plastic hood. He won't have any way to explain that—"

"Circuit boards," Drew said, reaching over his head to add a box of 9-millimeter ammunition to the backpack.

"What?"

"The nitrogen hoods are for soldering the circuit boards for the game hardware. Here's another blanket for Cara. We don't want her to catch cold."

Theresa blinked at him.

He zipped the pack shut, and carefully, chillingly, clicked off the safety on the gun. "Soldering in an oxygen atmosphere will allow metal oxides to form on the contacts of integrated circuits and capacitors. Then they don't conduct as well and you'll have problems with the board. They have to be soldered in a nitrogen atmosphere. Everyone knows that."

"Not everyone," she corrected, absently wrapping the sleeping Cara in a small wool blanket. So Evan had, again, a perfectly reasonable explanation for the nitrogen hood, though perhaps not for the solder on Jillian's shirt. "But if I can find any trace of Jillian inside the hood—hairs, pink fibers, a fingerprint—he can't explain that away as the standard manufacturing process."

"He won't let you in."

"I'll get a warrant."

"If you could have, you would have already." Drew was not stupid. Obsessed, perhaps, but not stupid.

Lie. "My cousin is the detective in charge of the investigation, Drew. I will *get* a warrant."

"Come on. Let's go." He motioned at her with the gun.

Her patience with him began to wear thin. "That gun is older than you and me put together. Are you sure it even shoots?"

He pointed it at a window and fired. The deafening boom blasted the thin houseboat walls and glass and tufts of canvas spattered everywhere. She turned her face away, shielding the baby.

He had fired out a porthole window facing north, toward the dock where the police had massed. *Frank is out there,* she thought. *Chris!*

Cara screamed.

"Drew! What did you do that for? They'll think you fired at—"

But he was already in motion, as if he heard gunshots every day, moving toward the front cabin, Luger in his right hand, grabbing

Theresa with the left. The coffee table bit into both her shins and then her feet got into gear, and she found herself in Drew's bedroom. A wooden set of thin steps led to the upper deck. Cara still screamed.

Theresa had only a moment to see past the bright hole in the ceiling, glowing with the hazy afternoon light, to notice how Drew had decorated his bedroom. The walls, the mirror, even the ceiling had been covered with cards and Post-it notes and photographs, but mostly photographs. Of Jillian. Jillian smiling, Jillian washing her car, Jillian with Cara, Jillian on the boat. Close-ups, midrange, some so far away that Jillian herself had probably been unaware of the camera's presence.

And one of her. Theresa. A snap of her leaving the medical examiner's office, her face slightly obscured by a blanket of falling snow. It lay on the coverlet, on top of a newspaper and yet more pictures of Jillian.

"Go up," Drew shouted, thrusting her elbow forward with such force she had no choice but to comply. She braced herself with one hand, holding the baby with the other. She had no desire to poke her head out into the open when surely the SWAT forces were now flowing down the wooden planks, ready to neutralize the threat.

Don't shoot me, she prayed. Don't shoot me.

The pocket mic. Say it aloud, idiot.

She pulled herself up, advancing step-by-step on the steep ladder. "Don't shoot me. Don't shoot me."

"Don't worry, they won't." Drew came directly behind her, his head bumping her bottom.

She exploded onto the empty front deck of the houseboat. The wind made her eyes tear but felt sweet and refreshing after the stuffy indoor cabin. The front of Drew's boat fell off into open space, like a catamaran, without the protection of side gunwales. She did not feel secure enough to stand on the snow-covered and trembling deck. No shots rang out, though the cops had advanced. Over the tops of the storage lockers cluttering the deck, she saw the dark forms only three boat slips away. They stopped when Drew emerged.

"Don't shoot us," she shouted.

"Get down on the ice, Theresa," Drew instructed, and pulled Cara from her arms.

"What? But—"

With his back against the lockers, he pushed her with his feet, so quickly that she slid across the snow-covered deck before she even had time to think about grabbing for a hook or a railing. Then suddenly she was falling free, loose for a very short moment before the frozen ice met her, hard enough to break bones.

CHAPTER 26

Her left hip, leg, and arm hit first, but her neck managed to keep her skull from striking the surface. The breath left her lungs for the second time that hour.

"Catch," Drew shouted from above her.

"Wha——?" She had barely managed to struggle to a sitting position before a cloth bundle hit her face, then tumbled into her arms—Cara, her wailing renewed. The gunshot had been bad enough, but falling through open space had really upset the infant. Her face glowed bright red in anger and fear. Theresa hoped her nose hadn't been broken by the falling child.

Drew managed to land on his feet, with only one foot skidding a bit. The bulky houseboat now hid them both from the SWAT team.

"Come on." He pulled her to her feet, with some difficulty. She had put off getting new shoes and the tread on these had worn nearly smooth. The snow gave some traction, but the driving wind kept the coating of it to a thin sheen.

"Are you crazy? You just shoved me off a boat, and Cara too. What if I had dropped her?"

He pulled her arm. If she wanted to stay on her feet, she would have to move as well, planting her soles as flatly and solidly as she could.

She was on the lake. On the ice. On the treacherous Lake Erie ice, from which they pulled two or three dead sportsmen every winter. It had to be a certain thickness to support weight, but how could you know what that thickness was? Surely it must vary according to water flow and depth and sunlight—

Drew held the gun pointed at her, either to convince her to cooperate or because the natural position for a right-handed person in cold weather would be to keep the arm crossed on the chest, the barrel pointing to the left. He had his left hand wrapped around Theresa's upper arm like a vise.

"Point that gun away from me."

He didn't. Perhaps that required too much coordination in a stressful situation. Perhaps he meant to keep the gun right where it was.

They dodged through the vacant slip next to them, the SWAT team's thunderous approach making the wooden dock quiver.

"Point that gun away from Cara, Drew." She put every bit of authority she could muster into her tone.

"They're not going to separate us," he told her.

"I won't let you hurt her."

"They won't separate us. Here's the snowmobile."

Theresa ducked her head to avoid the sharp V of the Grady-White's hull. "I'm not getting on this, Drew, not with Cara. The ice will collapse and we'll drown."

He turned the key. The motor, damn its well-tuned mechanical soul, roared to life without a flutter.

"It's been right at thirty-two for two days now—"

"It will take a lot longer than that to thaw this lake, Theresa."

"How do you *know* that? The depth varies so much and there's got to be warmer water coming up the river—"

Abruptly he pushed, and she fell back on the seat, one hand clutching at the controls to keep from falling over backward. Cara's screams had subsided into mere crying, but this movement startled her anew.

She could hear Frank's voice above it all: "Theresa!"

Drew straddled the seat behind her, reached around her, and twisted the handle. The snowmobile shot forward, over the ice.

Don't crack, she mentally begged the ice.

Don't shoot, she mentally begged the cops.

The rear of the snowmobile fishtailed as Drew turned the corner at the end of the line of docks. Then they were in the main marina area, the snowmobile's belt churning away at the snow and ice. Her feet on the running board and Drew's arms on either side of her were all that kept her from falling off.

Drew sped up as they approached the opening to the larger area within the break wall. Jumping would not be an option.

Okay, she thought. The ice is not opening up and the snowmobile is not sinking into the frigid depths, pulling you down like an anchor. Frank and the others must have heard the plan about Burke Lakefront Airport. They will be waiting for you there. Stay calm and keep Cara warm and you can get away from Drew then. As soon as you get off this bloody ice.

He kept the gun pressed into her left side, driving with one hand. She elbowed the barrel away from her, so that if his hand clenched, the bullet would not shatter her abdomen. With careful concentration, she pulled one leg up and over the seat so she could clench it between her knees and hold herself in place.

The wind drove into her face like straight pins. She would have spoken, tried to keep the listening cops—were they still listening?—apprised of their position, but her jaw had frozen shut.

She looked down at Cara, her tiny face barely visible through the petals of blanket. The baby had quieted, apparently fascinated by the gray clouds passing overhead.

They passed completely out of the marina. Through eyes closed to slits she scanned the shoreline; they raced past a set of red and blue flashing lights along Lake Road, but the lights fell behind when they rounded Whiskey Island. Then Drew turned the snowmobile a bit too sharply and they spun in a 360-degree circle. Three times.

When her stomach returned to its original orientation, she nestled her face as far into the collar of her coat as she could and thawed her jaw out enough to protest: "Drew! What are you doing?"

"Sorry."

"Slow down!"

"It'll be okay. I rode this thing before, once."

Once?

Then the mouth of the Cuyahoga River came into view and she forgot all about pursuing cop cars and Drew's lack of experience with wintertime vehicles and returned to the pressing need to get off this ice *now*.

The ice ahead became roughened, rocky. Then it stopped altogether.

The river had been opened for the cargo ships. The Coast Guard had cut up the ice, churned it out so that the water had become a pool of slush instead of a solid surface.

"Drew! The river! *Stop!*"

Her hysterical plea prompted both Drew and Cara to action.

The baby burst out with a startled yell, and Drew cut back on the throttle.

Theresa took one arm from the child and put her fingers over Drew's, trying to twist the handle toward them and lower the speed even further. "The river is broken up! We're going to go into the water! Turn!"

Slowing or even stopping would not be enough, she knew. Several winters previously she had helped piece a man back together after he had not left himself sufficient clearance to stop before the shoreline. A snowmobile on ice was not the same as a car on asphalt. It had no brakes.

She pulled at the left handle to turn them toward the break wall. That direction took them farther from land, but better that than crashing into the rocky edge of Whiskey Island.

With both hands on the handlebars, Drew corrected their course, heading straight for the river opening to the north of the abandoned Coast Guard station. Only two hundred feet remained between them and the cold water.

"Stop! We'll drown!"

"It's frozen!"

Forty feet.

"The Coast Guard broke it up!" She found herself stretching out her foot, as if she could somehow create some resistance to their forward motion, anything to slow that inexorable headlong rush to death. "Stopstop*stop*!"

"We'll make it!"

The river drew closer.

Twenty feet.

Theresa yanked the key from its slot and dropped the curled, brightly colored cord on the ice. Then she balled up her right fist and knocked Drew's arm away from the throttle, cutting it back and changing their direction at the same time. The engine died, and silence roared in her ears, with only the swishing sound of the snowmobile against the ice as it spun out of control.

But it kept spinning toward the river.

"Theresa! No! We have to go!" Drew protested.

She could see it now, a deceptively white expanse, lumpy underneath the latest dusting of snow. It could not have refrozen in only one day. Not solid.

"It's water, Drew. It can't hold us." Now she did put her foot down on the sliding surface, checking for traction, something to support her leap from the snowmobile.

"It's frozen, look at it."

"They broke it up the other day." The snowmobile continued to spin, albeit more slowly. Stop, she begged it. Just *stop*.

He continued to protest. "It was ten degrees last night."

Cara screamed. Theresa felt like joining her.

"We can make it."

She could not wait for the snowmobile to come to rest. As soon as it straightened out, Drew might propel them across the lumpy area at the edge of the river. She braced her right foot on the running board, knocked Drew's arm away from the throttle, and pitched herself and the baby into space.

She landed on her feet, for a brief instant; then her slick shoes slid out from beneath her and the spinning vehicle smacked into her right hip. This threw her to her knees. Shock reverberated through all her bones as her kneecaps smashed into concrete-hard ice. She clutched Cara tighter as her body continued in motion, falling forward until she had to use her elbows to keep the infant from slam-ming onto the hard surface beneath them. She heard a loud snap and hoped it wasn't one of her bones, but it must have been her forehead striking the ice.

Drew had finally come to a stop, at the edge of the river, still straddling the snowmobile. "Come on," he shouted, as if she had fallen off accidentally instead of run for her life.

She struggled to her feet, pulling the blanket closed over Cara's delicate face. Whiskey Island sat at least six hundred feet away, but the old Coast Guard station protruded from it like a lollipop on a stick of seawall. Only two hundred feet of ice separated her from the historic buildings. "Drew—"

Another crack split the air. Were the cops shooting at them? She looked toward the Coast Guard station but saw no one, though of course snipers wouldn't stand out in the open—

Another, softer sound. At her feet.

She looked down. A dark line had formed in the ice, running in a jagged sweep from the river back toward the land.

The world, it seemed, grew very still.

"Come on," Drew repeated.

She looked at him. "The ice is cracking."

"What?"

Another split branched off from the first, making a snapping sound. "Listen to me. The ice is cracking. Get off that thing and come with me. Quickly."

"But we can make it," he insisted. His hands moved in a sort of end-over-end fashion, and feeling a new chill she saw why. The key she had ripped out of the ignition had a tether; he must have attached the other end of it to his coat or the vehicle and had now reeled it back in.

She stepped backward and turned, gingerly placing each foot flat on the surface to distribute the weight. The snapping continued, all around her.

"Theresa!"

She tried once more, pausing to look back at him. "Get to the Coast Guard station. *Now!*"

"At least give me Cara."

She didn't answer, just took another step. Perhaps this would force him to follow her. Though if he were very fast he might be able to intercept her, cut off her escape route, and she'd have to run all the way to Whiskey Island instead, and at the rate the ice was cracking—

The baby's cries had subsided to whimpers. They had covered half the distance. She heard a click as Drew tried to start the snowmobile, but did not waste time by glancing back. Her worn shoes worked against her, sliding against the ice. She fell and waited for the sickening break to crackle in the air, but the ice seemed not to notice her weight. It cracked for reasons of its own.

After falling a second time, she decided to work with the ice instead of against it, and slid her feet along the surface as if skating. Forty feet. She could hear the sirens wending their way toward her.

Another crack, louder than the others.

"Theresa!"

She fell again. Pushing herself up with one hand while holding the baby with the other, she saw Drew, still at the edge of the river, snowmobile tilted down slightly by the uneven, disturbed ice. He had finally given up on the ignition and dismounted, but froze two feet from the vehicle, gazing in horror at his feet.

The front of the snowmobile began to sink. Then a crack rent the air, louder than any she had heard so far.

She met his gaze across the expanse; Drew looked at her with one last, forlorn hope.

As she formed her lips to call his name, the river opened up and swallowed him, the snowmobile, and the ice, churning it up to a stew of seething white chunks.

"Drew!"

Her voice echoed in the sudden silence.

As a sort of denouement, a second section of the ice collapsed. She turned and rushed for the land in an awkward, scrambling gait, clutching the baby so hard that Cara wailed.

Red and blue lights penetrated her snow blindness. She heard other voices but did not stop to look up. The ice continued to crack in whispering lines, calling her name.

"Theresa!"

Ten feet. Then the snow turned sharply upward at the seawall of the old station, devolving into a smooth drift that surely masked the jagged rocks underneath. That would not be fun to navigate, not in her shoes—

Then Frank had stumbled down the barrier and was on the ice in front of her. Her cousin's face seemed whiter than the winter months could warrant.

"Drew," she told him.

"Give me the baby."

"Drew." She made it to him, though she could feel the tremors through the surface beneath her as the ice collapsed, its collapse coming closer to them with every moment. "Drew."

"I know. A rescue unit is on the way."

"It took him."

Frank gently removed Cara from her arms, then turned and handed her off to one of the several other officers making their way down the slope to the ice. Then he put one hand on her wrist and one arm around her waist and turned her away from the river with iron determination.

It frustrated her and she screamed, *"Drew!"*

"Rescue is on its way, Tess. Now get off this damned ice."

The rocks proved just as difficult to traverse as she had expected, particularly while looking behind her for any sign of Drew. He could get to the surface, surely? And swim to the edge? He had been, as always, underdressed, so it would not be as if he had a thick, wet parka dragging him down. But that backpack, full of books—

Another man dropped to the rocks in front of her and began to help Frank move her strangely reluctant body to safety. "Are you all right, Tess?"

"Cavanaugh." She felt herself looking at him oddly, but couldn't help it. What was *he* doing here?

Then she craned her neck to look behind her. "Frank, listen, it's not even cracking close to shore. He'll come up in the open area and then someone needs to get out there and grab him because he won't be able to swim very—"

"Push," Chris said. From on top of the seawall, he pulled both her arms. Frank lifted her by her waist, and in this extremely ungraceful manner she returned to solid ground. Good. From the new height she could see the river, a deep green mass of slowly moving liquid, the ripples from the swallowed ice already fading to nothing.

She did not see Drew. "Where is he?"

"They're looking for him," Frank told her, and indeed the river's edge had become dotted with men watching for any sign of the pursued.

All right, she thought. With that many eyes, surely someone

would see him when he surfaced and then they could pull him out. If they only had some Coast Guard members in this Coast Guard station, members with those big orange life vests, well trained in water rescues, even freezing water rescues; if only the station hadn't moved to the East Ninth pier years before and left this shell as only a historical landmark . . . "Where's Cara?"

"She's safe. We've got her." Chris still had his arm around her, which felt good. It *was* freezing out. She also suspected she'd fall down without the support.

"I know that. Where—" Then she caught sight of the bundle of blankets, now being passed from a uniformed officer to the baby's stepfather, Evan. He smiled his thanks and gratitude with that boyish grin that charmed everyone at first. The officer smiled back, happy to be the hero, happy to have avoided a tragic situation. All's well that ends well.

Cara continued to cry—she had never stopped—but Evan didn't take a moment to comfort the infant. Instead he looked around, not at the water but the people. She waited until his gaze got to her and stopped. Only then did he allow the boyish, relieved smile to slide into something else, something more personal and ominous.

If she harbored any doubt of his crime or his intentions, any at all, they disappeared. She knew every thought in his mind as if he spoke them aloud.

He had won. Drew had, very decidedly, lost.

So had she.

Chris was speaking, saying, "Come on, Theresa. We've got to get you out of this cold."

Frank spoke with the bluntness of a close relative. "Your ears are turning red."

She slipped her arm out of Chris's grasp and patted her pockets. The microphone pen had disappeared, had probably fallen from her coat during the trip. She hoped the SWAT team didn't plan on billing her for it. "Frank. When you were listening to our conversation on the boat, was Evan there? Was he standing within earshot?"

"You mean when Drew outlined his getaway plan?"

"Before that. About Evan using the nitrogen to kill Jillian."

"I don't know."

The man in question finally got tired of the stare-off and turned away, watching his step and jiggling the baby in his arms as he left the scene. "It's *important*, Frank!"

Chris told her, "He was standing about two feet behind Frank when I got there, and I came in just as Drew said that Jillian had died too young, et cetera. You should have waited for me. I could have given you a camera."

"So he heard me."

"Come on," Frank complained. "Let's get out of this wind. Did he hear you detailing how he murdered his wife? Yes. Which is another reason you're going to avoid the guy like a hantavirus, right?"

"He's going to go straight home and destroy it all." She wrapped her arms around her torso, but she didn't feel cold. Rage warmed her from the inside.

"Come again?"

"If there is any evidence left, if he didn't clean Jillian's fingerprints from the inside of that hood or throw out the sleeping pills he slipped her, he's going to go do that right now."

"He could have done that long before now anyway," Frank pointed out.

"Inside the apartment, yes. But he had no reason to think we'd ever look at the nitrogen hood. He might have missed that. Frank, I need a search warrant."

"Why do you keep saying that to me—"

"We've got to keep him from getting to that outbuilding and—"

"—when you know I can't do it. You still have no probable cause. Certainly nothing that happened today implicates Evan, only the extremely unstable Drew Fleming. And personally, I'm not convinced that a guy that obsessed wouldn't eventually get fed up and strike out at the object of his obsession."

"It wasn't Drew! It was Evan!" She watched Evan walk away, his back firmly turned on the entire incident, the prize in his arms. A prize worth a million and a half, enough to keep his empire afloat until the income from the new game began to roll in. She started after him. "We have to get that baby away from him *right now*."

Frank moved forward with her, but held her elbow to keep her from outpacing him. "Don't be ridiculous. Kovacic doesn't need the baby dead to get at her money, and any judge would want more than a theory to have her removed."

Chris, always the diplomat, added, "Besides, he'd be crazy to do anything to the kid now, and from what you've been saying, he's anything but crazy."

"That's exactly the argument he would make if it came to trial, that he would never do anything so stupid. Maybe he'll even say it's his fault, that he put her to sleep on her stomach or he put her in his own bed and rolled onto her, but he's had so much trauma lately that he couldn't sleep and—add in crocodile tears for the media, and it will be a performance worthy of the red carpet. All he has to do is pop her into his easy-bake nitrogen oven and he's all set. Instant crib death."

"What do you want me to do?"

"Can you keep him busy for a few hours while I look at the factory?"

Frank stopped trying to walk, spun her in a one-quarter turn and grabbed both her arms. "Evan did not kill Paul. Do you understand me? *Evan did not kill Paul.*"

The world seemed to pause. Even the biting wind off the lake seemed to quell itself. "What did you say?"

"I'm saying maybe a vendetta is easier to deal with than grief. I don't know if you're right or wrong—maybe Evan is some kind of master criminal—but I know that some fights you win and some you lose, Tess. We lost this one."

She felt her face begin to crumple, but he would not relent, saying only, "Come on, let's get in my car. Your ears have turned white."

Both men tugged at her arms, and her worn shoes slid along the snowy ground. "But—what about Drew?"

"They're doing all they can," Chris reminded her, and indeed she heard the distant *wuffwuffwuff* sound of an approaching helicopter.

Evan had almost reached the end of the seawall, ready to step onto the solid ground of Whiskey Island. He turned there, and glanced back. Even at that distance she could feel the slap of his gaze as it found her.

For the first time that day, she began to shiver.

Theresa went home. Half a workday remained, but she didn't care. Leo could fuss all he wanted, but she couldn't imagine what she would be able to do at work if she did return. She had failed. Evan had Cara and there was nothing she could do about it.

Her mother plied her with oxtail soup.

Theresa thought, ate, and spoke with the detachment of extreme intoxication but without the corresponding euphoria. "I thought you served chicken soup for colds. Oxtail is for flesh wounds."

"You seem wounded enough to me," Agnes said.

"Mom." Theresa had to focus on the words to get them out. "When Dad died—"

She paused for so long that her mother, as always, helped her out. "I had you. You and Jackie and David. I got through it. You will too."

After her mother set off for an afternoon shift at the restaurant, Theresa took a cup of tea to her kitchen table and did nothing. Absolutely nothing.

By the time a knock sounded at her door, the tea had grown cold and her knees, drawn to her chin, had stiffened into place. It took her a minute to stand up, then another to walk with a numb bottom and a sore hip, and another to order her overprotective Lab into the basement. In the meantime, the person knocked again.

Chris Cavanaugh stood there, his face carefully composed into a mask of bad news.

She didn't ask, merely waited.

"They found his body."

"Oh." She did not move, her hand on the knob. Her mind formed the intention of telling him that while it was nice of him to tell her personally, it did not mean that he needed to stick around, but her body confounded this intention by erupting into sobs. They began in her stomach and moved up to her face, until the tears, heated by rage, seemed to burn her skin.

Chris reached for her, but she managed to avoid him by stumbling blindly around her kitchen until she reached a counter. With her back to him, she choked out, "I really need you to leave."

"I think you could use some company," he suggested, his voice disturbingly close, behind her.

She gripped the Formica. "No. Thank you."

It seemed to take forever for him to think this over, or perhaps it only seemed that way because a mental image came to mind of Drew's limp body reeled into shore like a piece of flotsam, useless detritus that no one wanted, and this time the sobs convulsed her, bending her body until her forehead knocked against the dishes in the strainer.

"The hell with that," she heard Chris say, and found her body gently turned until her face rested against his shoulder, his arms across her back, one of his hands in her hair.

It took a while for her heartbeat to slow until it nearly matched his, and her lungs to take in enough air to breathe in a more or less normal manner. But tears continued to come each time she pictured hopeless, hapless Drew, lying still on the frozen riverbank.

She made one last effort. "You can let go of me now."

"In another minute."

Always the negotiator. Well, didn't the most effective negotiations involve both give and take?

"Chris, I need a favor."

"Really?"

His fingers moved gently through her hair, and she wished he'd stop that even though it felt— "I need to borrow something."

She heard a door open and shut, and before she could ponder why that might be and whether she should open her eyes and do something about it, Chris said, "Hi. I'm—"

"The hostage guy," she heard Rachael say. "I remember."

CHAPTER 27

Theresa threaded a strap through the handle of a crime scene kit and slung it over one shoulder, leaving her hands free. Then she began to climb. The worn tennis shoes that had served her so ill on the ice were an advantage here, allowing her toes to fit into the small diamonds of space in the chain-link fence. She slipped at least every other time, but made it to the top.

She had never understood why people considered barbed-wire fences so impenetrable. She had gotten over one with ease at seventeen, simply by noticing that the wire had a break at the opening, where the gate swung freely. She hadn't been breaking into a place, of course, she'd been sneaking out of a roller rink, but . . . she wondered if Rachael knew how to get over a barbed-wire fence, and resolved not to ask.

Long before she reached the top, three things became clear to her: She had not been wearing heavy winter clothing the last time, she had not been carrying at least forty pounds of equipment in a backpack and a hard case, and she was no longer seventeen years old.

Not to mention the fact that her left hip still ached from falling off Drew's houseboat.

She got her toes settled on the top of the gatepost and used the support to lift her leg over the three remaining rows of wire. Then she very carefully worked in reverse to swing her body onto the carbon company grounds. *Very* carefully. Layers of winter clothing protected her from the barbs, but if she slipped, they would cut her face to ribbons.

Her body moved, but the crime scene kit stayed on the outside of the fence, the legal side, and it took her another few moments to untangle the strap and convince it to follow her. She wondered what the residents of Birdtown would have thought of her if she had tried this one hundred years before, or what her Bohemian great-grandmother would say. Probably *Come down from there this instant, young lady.* Until she learned of a risk to the child, then it would be more like *Get your little* dupa *in there. Just wear your babushka.*

These thoughts kept her mind off jumping the last six feet, her numb fingers no longer able to cling to the links. She scanned the property. She had entered from the far end of the factory grounds after parking on a side street called Magee. The covering of snow lay unbroken except for the triangular patterns of rabbits criss-crossing the expanse. She did not see any cameras at this end of the property and had never seen any outside cameras anyway, only inside. She trudged the seven hundred feet toward the second out-building, making little effort to keep out of sight. The brick structures hid her from the apartment building, and again, Evan would not have the manpower for surveillance. She felt certain he would be spending a quiet evening at home, free from witnesses, planning how best to announce the news of his stepdaughter's tragic demise.

Or cleaning up any last trace of his wife's murder, since a light shone inside the windows of her destination, building number two.

She pulled at one of the double doors, very gently, and watched for a while through the crack. Dim light from the ceiling lamps filtered down to the row of manufacturing equipment with the nitrogen hoods, but she did not see anyone inside.

The door opened several inches and stopped, chained from the inside. She set her burdens down to retrieve a bolt cutter from the backpack. The steel did not give easily, however, and after trying to cut the links, and then the padlock, she finally just loosened the coil of chain enough to create a gap no wider than ten inches. She managed to squeeze herself and her bags through it. Uncomfortably.

Inside, she entered the fenced area and tucked the crime scene kit behind one of the huge nitrogen tanks, then climbed to the catwalk. The windows were too high to look through, but at least she didn't have to crawl below them to keep her figure from appearing in silhouette. From the hard case she removed the piece of equipment Chris had given her, affixing it to the corner of the railing with electrical tape. It took her a while, but this span of time convinced her that her arrival had gone unnoticed. Evan did not appear. If he had the camera's monitor on, somewhere in the apartment building, he wasn't paying attention to it.

The air felt cold, but the ancient radiators kept the temperature slightly higher than that of refrigerators. Freezing couldn't be good for the equipment.

At the nitrogen tanks she took a moment to trace the path of the hoses on their way from the tanks to the manufacturing hoods, traveling beneath the grate in the floor. Then she retrieved her crime scene kit and approached the workstations.

There were manufacturing hoods in a row after the initial assembly area. They did not have gloves mounted in the sides for human hands but plenty of doodads inside to construct the circuit boards via computer. She had no idea how that would work and didn't care. All she wanted to see was the inlet for the nitrogen gas.

The Plexiglas formed, now that she could examine it more closely, a tight fit. Jillian would not have had much room to move around, assuming she moved at all. But this meant there would have been ample opportunity for Jillian's hair, skin, and the fibers of her clothes to catch on the belt and the robotic arms and the fittings. Theresa got out her camera.

This was the risky part. The flashes might show in the windows, alerting Evan to an intruder. However, the windows were awfully high, and only the rear windows in his apartment faced this building. As long as he hung out in his kitchen and living room, she should be all right. Unless Cara cried and he went to the nursery, of course. Unless he decided to leave the baby alone to come out and get some work done. Unless he retired early. After all, it had been quite a day for him. Then all he'd have to do would be to glance out his bedroom windows at the precise moment she snapped a photo.

She had to take the chance. Photographs might be her only evidence, and besides, to photograph before collecting had been too thoroughly ingrained for her to ignore.

A slight brushing sound startled her and she dropped to her knees, as if the row of equipment would hide her. Silly, since the row ran lengthwise through the building and she would be instantly visible on either side of it.

Nothing happened. Perhaps it had been the cat.

Perhaps Evan would stroll past the monitor and notice her working as the camera sent the images over the airwaves. She could have turned the cameras off or covered the lens with a glove, but had feared that a blank screen would be even more noticeable.

After some photographs of the general equipment, she got out a small halogen flashlight and opened a hood. The Plexiglas side swung silently into the air. First she examined the inside of the Plexiglas. If Jillian *had* been conscious inside the hood, surely she would have banged or pressed on the glass to get out. But no prints appeared on the inside—plenty on the outside, but the inside remained clear. She did find a pink fiber on the latch mechanism, which she plucked up with Teflon tweezers and secured in a fold of glassine paper, careful not to breathe. More than once, fibers had slipped away from her, pushed by even that slight draft.

Without any further discoveries, she repeated the process on the next hood. It proved cleaner than the first, so she returned to it. At least the first hood had a pink fiber, surely not a color that Evan wore. If it would only match Jillian's polo shirt . . .

With her head thrust into the work area, a glistening spot on the frame caught her eye. The Plexiglas hood, when closed, fit into a metal track at the edge of the work area, and this track had a spot of oil or liquid about the size of a quarter. She rubbed it with a dry swab and packaged it, then repeated the process with a second swab. This she examined quickly before packaging. Tiny flecks of pigment stained the cotton, and it gave off the telltale whiff of phenol.

Suddenly some things made sense . . . or at least she had a theory. Skiers used light sticks for night activity. Glow sticks burst into light through a reaction of hydrogen peroxide and phenol, substances used similarly in DNA analysis. Evan would have been working in the dark, not wanting to draw attention to the factory's lighted windows, with a light stick dangling around his neck, just as when snowboarding. He would have shoved Jillian into the hood and slammed it shut, catching the stick under the edge of the hood and cracking it. Then, when he pulled the unconscious Jillian from the hood, her arm brushed the liquid, leaving the stain on her sweatshirt.

Not conclusive, of course, but every little grain of circumstantial evidence could add up to a weight around Evan's neck.

Then, under the belt, she found a hair. The end of it had wound around the pulley that guided the belt through a passageway into the next hood. She tried to untangle the thin strand, but even the Teflon tweezers couldn't help her disassemble the mechanism.

The far door opened.

The hair broke.

Evan stood in the doorway, dressed in a bulky sweater and carrying a small black gym bag. He saw her instantly, and froze.

So did she.

The door swung shut behind him. The slight clap it gave as it closed seemed to her like the final beat of her heart, echoing into the empty night.

He set the bag down, slowly, without moving his head. He did not seem particularly surprised to see her, nor did he seem particularly disturbed. "Mrs. MacLean."

She said nothing.

He took a step toward her, watching carefully, as if wondering when she would run and where. "What are you doing here?"

She did not run. "You know."

"Collecting your precious trace evidence? Find anything?"

"Just the phenol from where you cracked your light stick."

"Hmm." Another step, though he didn't seem to be in a hurry. "Yeah, I forgot about that. By the way, the cops standing there also heard you propound your theory. But I don't see any of them here with a warrant."

"No, you don't."

"They didn't believe you, did they?"

"They didn't think a judge would feel strongly enough about it."

"Poor, poor Theresa. First your fiancé gets killed, your one fan drowns, and now your coworkers think you've lost your mind. You've been abandoned on all sides, haven't you? You can't prove I killed Jillian. You'll never be able to prove I killed Jillian."

"I know."

He blinked.

She didn't wait for him to catch up. "I know now that I can't prove it. Hairs and fibers don't mean a thing because you cohabitated. The plaster that settled to the bottom of your snowboard bag when you knocked it into the wall removing her from the apartment, that could have gotten into Jillian's pockets during some home-improvement project. The blackberry bush caught on your snow pants and ripped some Tencel fibers off, putting you in the woods by Jillian's body, but we have lots of skiers in this area who might own pants like those. The diatoms from your car tires can be found in any lakeside parking lot. I'm sure you threw out the sleeping pills."

He said nothing.

"But it doesn't matter in the long run. Death by nitrogen suffocation can't be physically proved, not at this point. I can't prove murder."

He watched her without expressing the slightest sign of relief at her admission of failure.

"At least not in a criminal court."

He no longer came toward Theresa, but stayed between her and the door, a tower of muscle and flesh. She didn't move anything but her mouth in case it startled him into attacking, like a cobra or a rabid dog.

His curiosity won out. "What are you doing here, then?"

"Remember O.J.?"

"Huh?"

"I said I couldn't prove murder in a criminal court. A civil court, however, is quite different. Almost everything is admissible, and even more so in family court, where the only concern is the well-being of the children. I didn't have enough to win Cara's freedom during your first round at guardianship. I will have enough for the second. I have Jillian's means of death, a death that could only have been engineered by you. I have the fibers I just collected from the hood. Most important, I have Cara's father."

Lot's wife, formed into a salt sculpture, couldn't have been any more still. She could swear Evan had stopped breathing. With his voice strangled and low, he asked, "Cara's father was some john. Jillian didn't even know which—"

"Jillian didn't have johns. She had knights in shining armor who would take her back to their castle to love and live, happily every after. At least that was what she hoped, but until you—or so she thought—it had never happened. The knight she tried out before you fathered Cara. Nicholas Cannon. Your source of capital. Attendee of numerous trade shows and meet-and-greet cocktail parties, keeping an eye on his investments, scouting out new ones."

Evan seemed to absorb this in the blink of an eye, without it angering or even annoying him. "Interesting. But he doesn't know, right?"

"According to Vangie, his armor was tarnished when Jillian realized he did not have marriage in mind. He didn't consider her a queen or a princess or anything but a reasonably priced consort to help him get over the death of his wife. Jillian gave up. One month later she told Georgie about her pregnancy. Let's put two and two together here. You're the engineer, you should be able to do that."

"So can a financier. Jillian pushed out a kid who might be his and he doesn't even ask about it? Obviously he doesn't care."

"But did he know? I'm guessing you don't talk about your— family—much in the work setting. Too busy showing off, a wunderkind, a bad boy playa of the digital world. Cannon might know about Cara. Then again, he might not."

Her chattiness on the topic finally caught his attention. "You haven't told him."

"I plan to, tomorrow morning—"

"What makes you think I'm going to let you walk out of here?"

"—unless we can come to an arrangement."

Finally, surprise. "You want to make a *deal*?"

"I'll apply for guardianship myself. Let me take Cara, and you keep the money. As her guardian I will invest it in your company on her behalf. You'll be able to pay Griffin Investments what you owe them for financing the factory. By the time she's twenty-one, that account will be ancient history and Cara will never know it existed. Once that is taken care of, we can see if a paternity test proves my theory, and if Cannon wants to be a father to his daughter. Even if he doesn't, Cara will still be alive and you won't have a baby on your hands."

He considered this. For about ten seconds. "You want to make a *deal*."

"You want the money. I want Cara and myself to live past this evening. Everyone wins."

Another long pause as he thought. Examining all the angles. Probing for booby traps. Then he said, "That's like asking Alastair to make a deal with the vampires. There can only be one winner."

"This isn't a stupid game, Evan!"

The gym bag on the floor trembled and let out a soft coo.

"You're right," Evan said. "It isn't."

Theresa felt the blood drain from her face so quickly the skin seemed to burn. She had been right. She hadn't even known how right she was. "You brought her out here to kill her."

"First things first," he said, and lunged.

CHAPTER 28

She had time to turn back and start to run toward the opposite door, remembering too late that she hadn't gotten the chain off and it would take her too long to negotiate the gap. He would be on her long before that. That left the catwalk, or the cage around the nitrogen tanks. Over the sound of her frenzied breathing she could hear his pounding steps behind her, and knew she'd never make it up the steps ahead of him.

With one outstretched hand she pulled the wire-mesh gate closed behind her. It slammed shut with enough force to shake the wall of fencing and the catwalk it was attached to overhead. It shook again as Evan slammed into it from the other side.

Nose to nose through the loose chain link, he said, "You've got nowhere to go."

"Maybe this castle has a secret passageway," she hissed.

If only that were true, but this was not the castle in Evan's video game. Behind the tanks lay only a solid brick wall. Added to that, she had no way to secure the gate. It had retained its hasp, but not its padlock, and even if it had, it would be positioned on the other side. Evan's side. Only her fingers through the mesh and her too-worn shoes pushed against the floor held it closed.

And Evan pulled.

She held it, bracing one foot against the bottom of the fence.

Evan pulled harder. He was much larger than she was, and stronger. The gate began to open.

The latex gloves did little to keep the thin mesh wire from biting into her fingers. She needed to grab the piping, the frame of the door, where she could get a better grip and more leverage, but she didn't dare let go of the mesh long enough to do so.

The gap widened by another inch. Her fingers began to slip.

With one thrust Evan jerked open the door, his body flying into the fencing as he got behind it. Pulling it shut no longer remained an option. She turned to run without knowing where to go.

Theresa hadn't taken half a step when she felt his hand grab her jacket, yanking her backward. His arms closed around her from behind, pinning her elbows to her hips.

She shouldn't have turned. Straight on, she could have gone for his groin or his eyes, something, anything. This way she had nothing but her legs, trying to hit a target behind her.

He dragged her from the cage. She kicked her feet around wildly, forcing him to struggle to keep his balance. He staggered, with her, toward the row of machinery.

The far door opened. Evan halted, and Theresa stopped struggling, stunned by this unexpected event.

Jerry Graham stepped in from the cold. His jaw fell open, and for a moment no one moved. "Evan! What are you doing?"

"Help me!" Theresa shouted. She had not counted on Graham showing up, not at all. But perhaps neither had Evan.

"Grab her legs," Evan instructed his partner.

"Evan—what? What are you doing?"

"She broke in here to get more evidence. She's going to take Cara away."

Theresa repeated, "Help me. He's going to kill me, the same way he killed Jillian."

Graham stared at his friend. "You killed Jillian?"

"This is our chance. Cara's bank account will get us through the backstretch. We're going to make it."

"He's going to kill Cara too, by smothering her in the nitrogen hood. She's there in that bag."

Jerry Graham's gaze dropped to the small duffel at his feet, which rocked a bit. A faint wail did not convince him and he pulled the opening wide to see inside.

Then he straightened. Slowly.

"Evan," he said, as if begging his partner to program all this code in a way that would make the picture clear. "Evan, come on."

"Help us," Theresa said again.

Evan's grip on her had not loosened, not by a nanometer. "We need the money, Jerry. If Cannon had agreed to finance the factory as well as the game, we would have been okay. But there isn't any other way to make the payments on this place *and* start up production on the sphere, and the game isn't going to be done for two months, at best. You know that."

Graham stared at him.

"This is our chance, Jerry. We'll be on top. Your products, my code. Leading the world."

Graham gave no sign of agreeing, disagreeing, or even comprehending.

"Help us," Theresa said, despair gathering in the pit of her stomach, weighing her down.

"Now *get her legs*."

Theresa hoped, as the man left Cara in the gym bag and came toward them, that he would help her. She continued to hope even as he paused to unlatch the nitrogen hood and raise its Plexiglas lid, and up until he came closer and bent down to grab her ankles.

Jerry Graham was not going to come to Cara's rescue. He had made his decision.

She drew her legs in and used Evan as an anchor to punch Jerry with both feet. His breath came out in a whoosh and Evan stumbled backward, letting go of her arms to steady himself.

Remaining on her feet gave her a few seconds of lead time. She sped past the nitrogen hood and toward the open door. Leave Cara? Pick up Cara? She had to—but then they'd—

Evan tackled her, much as he had that morning. But this time she wouldn't land on snow.

She fell forward with Evan on top of her, her line of sight reduced to a jumbled array of wall, door, and floor. Evan's arms around her at least protected her elbows, but her already-sore left hip smashed into the concrete with a shattering jar and the last bit of momentum rolled up from her body and into her head. Helpless to stop the flow, her skull hit the floor with a smack of finality.

Her eyes closed.

She heard voices, oddly muffled. The light, through eyelids barely cracked, hurt her pupils. The moving blobs of color that initially greeted her sorted out into Evan and Jerry.

There was nothing wrong with her vision. Their images had that bit of distortion because she was looking up at them through Plexiglas.

Her knees were drawn up and pressed against the top of the hood, immobilizing her legs. The conveyor belt and its gears and pulleys bit into her spine from neck to hip. Her left temple throbbed, sending jolts of searing pain through her brain at random intervals. Surely she had fractured her skull. Perhaps it would help if she didn't try to think.

Jerry ducked out of sight for a moment, but she heard his voice. "Have you thought this through?"

"Of course I haven't thought it through. I didn't expect her to be here!"

A draft started up next to Theresa's head, ruffling her bangs ever so slightly. Moving her neck hurt too much, so she relied on her peripheral vision to see a round hole through the glass wall of the hood. The air swept over her face and disappeared into that hole. A vacuum. They were sucking the air from the hood. Next step would be flooding it with nitrogen gas.

Evan continued to grumble, "I thought that cousin of hers would sit on her, at least for tonight."

Jerry came back into view on the other side of the hood. "They're not going to believe another suicide. What are you going to do with her?"

Theresa's throat began to feel dry, or perhaps it only felt that way because she knew her oxygen supply now slipped out of that small hole.

"*We*, partner. What are *we* going to do?"

"Fine, what are we—?"

"I'm thinking a car accident. We'll go down to the Metroparks, drive her car into a ditch. The roads are slick and she was pissed off. She bashed her head on the steering wheel. Any bruises and other stuff will be attributed to the crash."

"The pathology won't match."

"Yeah, but in the absence of any specific cause of death, they'll eventually write it off as a fluke. Just like Jillian. All their tests will be negative, and you can't prove a negative."

She placed one weak hand against the Plexiglas, pushed. Evan's gaze turned downward, to her, but he made no move to interfere.

She pressed. The glass didn't move. The latch didn't even rattle.

"Throw the valve," he told his partner.

Jerry hesitated one last time. "Isn't there any way—"

"Turn it!"

Jerry's hands moved toward the regulator mounted on the side of the hood, and she heard the sibilant hissing sound of air rushing in. Or rather, not air, but the gas that snaked through the series of hoses that ran up the trench in the floor, secure underneath their gratings, and over to the huge storage tanks in the corner. The nitrogen tanks.

She pressed again, squirming. The hood did not move.

Evan watched her, looking into her eyes—to watch the life fade from them, or merely to ensure the completion of the next logical step in this process.

"What was that?" she heard Jerry ask.

Evan looked away from her. "What?"

"That flash."

She closed her eyes.

CHAPTER 29

She heard their steps move away from the hood, toward the nitrogen tanks. Her right hand reached underneath her, pushed aside the rubber conveyor belt, and pulled out two items she had stored there. One was a flathead screwdriver, which she used to pop the hood latch loose from its hook while she pushed upward on the Plexiglas with her legs. With her left hand she continued to depress the shutter-release button on a tiny remote.

She rolled out of the hood, her worn tennis shoes making only the faintest slap against the concrete floor. Evan and Jerry were disappearing into the group of nitrogen tanks, their backs to her. She probably should have waited until they were completely out of sight, but she would not have that much time. Everything depended on the next three seconds.

Nestled in a dark corner behind the nitrogen tanks, her camera took a flash photograph every time she triggered the shutter via the remote. She kept her finger pressed down now, without release, hoping to slow their progress by blinding them.

They found this exasperating, to judge from their annoyed shouts; the noise evidently covered the sound of her feet as she reached the mesh gate, swung it shut, closed the hasp, and locked it with a padlock—which had been the second item hidden beneath the conveyor belt.

"Hey!" she heard Jerry say, but not because he realized her treachery. More likely he had found the end of the rubber hose that ran from the second nitrogen tank to the manufacturing hood. She had sliced through it upon her arrival.

"It's a camera," Evan said, and she heard a crashing sound that made her wince. Leo would make her pay for that Canon, and they didn't come cheap.

Then she turned and walked to the entrance. Cara had begun to fuss, but quieted when Theresa removed her from the gym bag and warmed the infant against her shoulder. Behind her, the chain link rattled with fury.

She turned. Evan pulled at the fence as if he could rip it down with his bare hands. He couldn't, of course; it had stood thus since before he was born. She watched for a moment to see if they might find some way out she hadn't anticipated, but they didn't. The fencing extended thirty feet upward, to the catwalk, and ended in a ceiling of more mesh.

Theresa pulled her cell phone out of her sock and called Frank. He asked rather more questions than she considered necessary but eventually assured her that both the Lakewood and Cleveland police would be there in five.

Her two prisoners were surprisingly quiet. Evan stared at her as if still blinded by the camera's flash. She moved to the center of the floor so she would not have to shout, but stayed far enough away to have a head start. Just in case.

"The cops will arrive in a few minutes," she told them.

"How——? How did you——?"

She patted the baby's back. "It's like this—you remember how on the second level of the castle you find out you have to have the silver ax and so you go all the way through the first level again looking for it before you finally ask the dwarf and find out the silver ax is in the second-level dining room all along, behind the queen's portrait?"

He stared.

"I decided to plant my weapons in advance."

"And take out the nitrogen," Jerry muttered.

"Yeah, that too. What's ironic, Evan, is that you might have killed me anyway by turning on the vacuum and sucking out the oxygen. But once Jerry opened the regulator to what should have been your murder weapon, I became supplied with all the clean air I needed." She didn't add that she had not counted on Jerry being there, and if one of them had stayed with her while the other investigated the camera flashes, she might now be dead. Of course, if Jerry had not proved as murderous as his partner, the camera diversion would not have been necessary.

"Lucky for me I can fake dazed and helpless. Jillian really was helpless when you put sleeping pills in, what, her dinner? Did she pass out or just get sleepy enough to go to bed? Then you redressed her, neglecting to tuck her polo shirt into her jeans, underneath the sweatshirt—which, by the way, is how most women dress themselves in cold weather. Then you brought her out here. What did you do, lower the oxygen levels until she couldn't have regained consciousness if she wanted to, then left her alive long enough for the pills to metabolize and indicate a lower dose? I think that's what the jury will find most heinous, how you let her lie in there for hours, allowing her blood chemistry to destroy the evidence. Hours during which you could have changed your mind. What did you do? Watch TV? Play Minesweeper?"

"Jillian was a whore! Nobody cared about her! Not even you—I saw it on your face when you first came to the apartment. You were there, what, five minutes?"

Theresa nodded, accepting her culpability in the previous events.

"I hadn't gotten rid of anything yet. I hadn't washed the snowboard bag or thrown out the towels I used to wrap her arms—"

She interrupted. "Why? So that the rubber bands wouldn't leave bruises?"

"Or the sleeping pills. I left them right in the medicine cabinet, hiding in plain sight. But you never looked."

What she had said before remained true, that none of these things would have seemed suspicious even if she had noticed them, not without the additional information from Jillian's body. But, as before, this did not comfort her. "No, I didn't."

"Evan—" Jerry Graham said.

"Shut up. She still can't prove it. Let the cops show up. This woman's deranged and traumatized, and it's our word against hers—and there are two of us. Just *shut up*."

Theresa shifted Cara to her other shoulder, catching the distant wail of a police car siren. "No, there's the video too."

This did not cow Evan, it merely confused him. "What?"

"Your surveillance tape. You have two cameras mounted in the corners of this building. Your assault on me has been caught by electric eye. Your own electric eye."

"Good luck. Those files are password protected."

"They're also transmitted by remote. Running wires in this ancient building would have been too difficult, wouldn't it? Do you know—well, I'm sure you do, given what you do for a living—that wireless video can be intercepted by another router? I borrowed one from a friend who uses it for hostage situations. Of course I told him I needed it to tape my daughter's school talent show tonight without paying forty dollars to the PTA. I also had to promise to have dinner with him, but that's another story."

"What are you *talking* about?" Graham complained. He had his hands on his knees, slightly bent over from the waist, as if he were about to throw up.

"Ever sit in your backyard with your laptop and use your neighbor's expensive wireless DSL? I did something similar, I have to confess. Your surveillance video is showing up on the laptop in my car, and being recorded by same."

"Really," Evan said, displaying a ghost of his trademark smirk. "Are you sure about that?"

"I saw this interior plain as day before I scaled your fence."

He nodded. "Not bad. Unfortunately for you I turned the cameras off before I came out here. You have no video. You have no proof."

Theresa nodded and patted the baby's bottom. "That was probably wise of you, given what you had in mind. I had a bad feeling you might. After all, Captain Alastair shoots a spear into the raven guarding the east hallway to keep him from squawking while he plants the dynamite in the rain barrel. Same concept."

Evan's smirk began, reluctantly, to recede. "So—"

"So I installed a backup. It's up there." She swung one arm wide, pointing to the corner of the building behind her. If they looked closely, they would see the small camera taped to the catwalk railing. The police car siren sounded close enough to be in the parking lot. In fact, it sounded close enough for the car to come through the wall any moment now. "I had to borrow that from my friend too. I hope that doesn't add a lunch or something."

"Another camera," Evan said quietly, as if to himself.

"Plus, mine is better. It has sound as well as video."

Jerry's legs gave out and he sank in slow motion to the floor. Evan, on the other hand, straightened up.

"I learned from you, Evan. Think of every possibility and plan for it. Take risks when they're necessary"—Theresa shifted the baby to her arms, feeling her own face crack in a smile at seeing the tiny girl's wide eyes and rosebud lips—"and they're worth it. You do that in your game. You did that in your murder. You really made only one mistake."

As the door burst open behind her, letting in the frozen air and the sound of running feet, Evan asked, "And what was that?"

She told him, "You pissed me off."

She slipped into the thinly cushioned seat next to her mother just as the lights in the auditorium dimmed after the intermission.

"You didn't miss her. There are four acts before her and her friends."

"Good."

Agnes turned, studied her daughter's face in the illumination of the stage floodlights. "You look flushed."

"I ran from the parking lot."

"Uh-huh. But you're okay?" The curtain opened, revealing two boys with acoustic guitars.

"I'm great," she assured her mother.

The woman in front of them turned around, but not to admonish the chatting. "Hi, Theresa. Haven't seen you since—geesh, I think it was the science fair."

"I've been around."

The boys burst into a scratchy rendition of a country-western classic. One of their parents, several rows over, did not want to wait for the final chord and began to clap. Theresa settled back into her seat and listened to the boys sing about regret. She would have liked to close her eyes and tune out for a while, but who knew, Rachael might date one of these kids in the next year or two, so she'd better pay attention.

Thank you, Jillian, for teaching me that the price of carelessness might be too high.

And that every woman is a princess in someone's eyes.

CHAPTER 30

Chris Cavanaugh straightened up from the railing outside the Pier W restaurant and glanced a bit nervously at the fishy, slushy water thirty feet below. A biting wind sent his hair awry, but of course this slight imperfection only increased his charm. "Can we go in now? It's freezing out here."

"No, it's not. It's breaking up," Theresa told him.

"The water?"

"The winter."

"How do you figure that? My ears are about to snap off and it's snowing even as we speak."

Straining her eyes to the east she could see the barest tip of the Edgewater Marina, where she and Drew had skimmed along the ice, and resisted the urge to shiver from more than the cold. She brushed off the flakes now littering her nose, both literally and figuratively. "Yeah, but your nostrils don't stick together when you breathe in anymore. Come on, you're a Cleveland boy. You can't feel that?"

"I'm past the point of feeling much of anything."

"You're kind of wimpy for a special response team guy, you know that?"

"Hey!"

"You got cool gadgets, though, I'll give you that."

"Glad the camera and the router could help you out."

She nodded, still facing the wind. "I might not have needed them if I had been a little more thorough at the start. By the time I finally got suspicious, Evan had already begun destroying the evidence. He left the duffel bag in a Dumpster downtown, Jerry told us. When we searched the apartment the second time, he had flushed the sleeping pills and melted the bottle in the microwave. I should have kept my mouth shut in Stone's office. I kept tipping him off."

"Well, you got him. But hey"—Chris turned her to face him—"don't do that again. Not like that. I would never have lent you that equipment if I had thought you were going to—it could so easily have—"

"Ended badly."

He tilted her chin up to face him, thought better of it, and settled for grasping her shoulders. "Some risks aren't worth taking."

"Come inside. Then see if you still feel the same way."

"Finally!"

"I hope you don't mind," she told him as they bustled into the warm restaurant. "I invited someone else to join us."

He saw them instantly. "Let me guess."

Nicholas Cannon sat at a corner table, holding Cara in his arms. The baby's fists pumped through the air above her, encircling and wrinkling what appeared to be an expensive silk tie, but the man didn't seem to care. A younger couple sat with him, leaning in from each side, apparently egging the infant on.

Theresa explained before they made their way to the table.

"Cannon had no idea Cara was his daughter. Jillian had broken off their affair before she knew she was pregnant, and when he saw her again, she had married. He never saw the baby, never asked her age, and just assumed she belonged to Evan."

"Who's that with him?"

"His son and daughter-in-law. As it turns out, they've been trying to conceive for years and have been on a waiting list for an adoption for the past two. Since Nicholas is Cara's next of kin, he can allow them to legally adopt her. No waiting, no fostering."

Chris stepped aside to let a waitress by and watched the family for a moment. "He doesn't seem to be in any hurry to give her up. Well, shall we?"

He held out an elbow, and she slipped her arm through it. "Sure. Oh, by the way—"

"What?"

"You're buying, right?"

NOTES AND ACKNOWLEDGMENTS

First of all, I have to thank Medical Examiner's Investigator Brett Harding, who gave me the method of murder while chatting over an autopsy one day.

Dr. Andrew Wolfe, who helped me, as before, to get the exact chemistry right. My nephew, Brian, who gave me some hints about the murky world of venture capital. Another nephew, Alex, who is my resident reference on video games. Sharon Wildwind, who is both a critique partner and one of my medical references. Leslie Budewitz, for legal information. And my husband, Russ, a walking reference library of all things mechanical and historical.

And, of course, I'd like to thank my personal miracle worker, Elaine Koster, and Stephanie of the Elaine Koster Literary Agency.

BIBLIOGRAPHY

American Institute of Physics. "The New Virtual Reality: Human-Interface Engineers Create Virtual-Reality Experience by Letting Users Walk in Rotating Sphere." *Science Daily*, April 1, 2006, www.sciencedaily.com.

Harding, Brett E., MBA, and Barbara C. Wolf, M.D. "Case Report of Suicide by Inhalation of Nitrogen Gas." *American Journal of Forensic Medicine and Pathology* 29 (2008): 235–37.

Herz, J. C. *Joystick Nation*. Boston: Little, Brown & Co., 1997.

King, Brad, and John Borland. *Dungeons and Dreamers*. New York: McGraw-Hill/Osborne, 2003.

Spitz, Werner U., MD. *Medicolegal Investigation of Death*, 3d ed. Springfield, IL: Charles C. Thomas, 1993.